SON OF
ANGER

DONOVAN COOK

First paperback edition November 2020

Cover design by Limelight Publishing
limelightpublishing.com

ISBN 978-1-8383008-1-4 (paperback)
ISBN 978-1-8383008-0-7 (ebook)

www.donovancook.net

To my amazing wife, Anna.
You are the wind in my sails,
the Northern Star which sets my course.
Without you, this novel would never have happened.

CONTENTS

Chapter 1 1

Chapter 2 11

Chapter 3 23

Chapter 4 37

Chapter 5 44

Chapter 6 58

Chapter 7 76

Chapter 8 86

Chapter 9 100

Chapter 10 116

Chapter 11 125

Chapter 12 140

Chapter 13 150

Chapter 14 165

Chapter 15 174

Chapter 16 182

Chapter 17 191

Chapter 18 208

Chapter 19 216

Chapter 20 229

Chapter 21 242

Chapter 22 255

Chapter 23 272

Chapter 24 286

Chapter 25 301

Chapter 26 312

Chapter 27 325

Glossary of Terms 337

The Gods 339

CHAPTER 1

Olaf held his axe to his side, his shield in front of him. His knees bent as he constantly shifted weight from one foot to the next, ready to move at any moment.

The man before him wore only a faded tunic and loose-fitting trousers, armed with a spear and shield. From the way he held his spear, it was easy to see he was not an experienced warrior. The young man stood rooted to the spot, his legs stiff like the roots of a tree, while he looked for a weakness in Olaf's defence. Even though Olaf was a farmer, he had been a warrior once. He had felt the crush of the shield wall and the hot spray of blood as his enemies died around him.

"Come on, boy! You going to attack or wait for me to die of old age?" Olaf provoked the young man. "You scared of an old farmer?"

The young man screamed as he attacked, aiming high with a lightning fast spear thrust. Olaf ducked low behind his shield, not having enough time to lift it. At the same moment, he lunged forward into his oncoming attacker, punching out with his shield as soon as they collided. The reverberating sound startled the cows as they grazed in the nearby field. Birds scattered from the barley they had been feeding on, screaming their discontent at being interrupted. The young man grunted as the air was knocked out of his lungs and was sent sprawling backwards. Olaf smiled as he watched his nephew lying on the ground, gasping for air like a fish out of water. The boy lacked skill, but he was fast. He could be a fine warrior, as his father had been. Bjørn had been a great warrior, the champion of Jarl Thorgils. The jarl Olaf had once served and who ruled these lands. His nephew Ulf, Bjørn's son, looked a lot like his father, but he was not as tall or as wide. He was still young though, only sixteen or seventeen winters; he would grow some more.

"Thor's balls boy! Enough!" Olaf roared as Ulf attacked again. He deftly stepped aside, using his shield to deflect Ulf's spear jab. Olaf kicked Ulf in his exposed side, sending him sprawling to the ground again. Before Ulf could get up Olaf planted his foot in his back, pressing him to the ground. Ulf tried to twist and turn, hoping to free himself, but was not strong enough. The more he tried; the harder Olaf pressed. Eventually, Ulf gave up and just lay there panting like a dog in the summer's heat, his anger and energy burnt out. Although Olaf knew it would return. It always did.

"Good boy." Olaf removed his foot. "Let's get cleaned up for dinner before your aunt flays us both." *At least he kept hold of his spear this time*, Olaf thought as he watched Ulf pick himself up from the ground and walk to the stream which ran close to their farm.

"Almost skewered you there." Olaf turned to the worried voice of his wife Brynhild who'd been watching from the doorway of the longhouse.

"Never even close," he lied, examining the edge of his axe instead of looking at his wife.

"Don't like you using real weapons."

"Makes it more realistic," Olaf replied.

"And if you don't manage to get out of the way in time?" She crossed her arms as she stared at her husband.

Olaf only shrugged, not wanting to have this argument again.

"He won't mean to hurt you, but accidents happen," she said, softening her voice. "Maybe it's time we let him go on his own path, I don't think being here is doing him any good. We've played our part since he lost his father," Brynhild said, walking over to comfort her husband. He was a good man, but he was blinded by his devotion to his brother.

Still, Olaf said nothing, preferring to watch their daughters chase butterflies in the tall grass than face his wife.

"He's old enough to go raiding. Perhaps the jarl will take him on," Brynhild said as she got to her husband. She didn't want the boy to go, but she knew he was unhappy on the farm. She also worried about his temper. He was as unpredictable as the weather, calm one moment and then a raging thunderstorm the next. Brynhild didn't want their girls to have to grow up tiptoeing around him, never quite sure how he might react to things.

"Aye, I was of his age when my brother took me raiding for the first time." Olaf stroked at his beard, while his eyes glazed over. "But he's not ready yet, his anger still controls him."

"His anger will kill you one day. It's best he takes it out on someone else," Brynhild said, exasperated.

Olaf knew she was right; she was always right. He turned and looked at their small farm, which consisted of a few cows, a goat and a small field where they grew vegetables and barley. Olaf sighed. "Perhaps, but I'll not take him to Jarl Thorgils. The boy won't be safe there."

Brynhild smiled at her husband, even if she didn't understand his bitterness towards the jarl he once served. "Will you let him take his father's weapon? You know he loves that sword; he drools over it like the ogre king drooled over Freya."

"Ormstunga?" Olaf pictured the double-edged sword with its name engraved on the blade. On its golden half-circle pommel, Jörmungandr encircled the Valknut. The grip, made of dark-red wood, had a gold ring in the middle. The guard, also made of gold, had two intertwining fire breathing serpents. Written on them in runes was a reminder not to be careless with the sharp blade. It had been in the family since the day it had been forged and had been given to Bjørn by their father. Bjørn had sent many warriors to Valhalla with it. Olaf had managed to retrieve the sword in Bjørn's last battle before it could be taken by another. He hoped to one day give it to Ulf.

"No, he's not ready for Ormstunga. He'll need to prove himself in battle and to Odin first. She needs a warrior who understands himself, not a child who cannot control his temper." Olaf did not like saying this, but he knew it was true. Ulf had to prove himself worthy of Ormstunga's trust.

"He'll not like that. Ever since he was a boy, all he could talk about was using that sword to kill his enemies."

"Aye, well you don't always get what you want." Brynhild saw the pain in Olaf's eyes. She knew he wanted Ulf to be like his brother was, but they could never quell his anger. Maybe Olaf was accepting that Ulf was no Bjørn.

"When you plannin' on telling him?"

"Tonight maybe, after–" he paused as he looked into the distance. "Now who in Thor's name is that?" Brynhild turned and saw a large man slowly approaching their farm from the north.

"Doesn't look very friendly," Brynhild said as she took in the giant man. He was larger than anyone she had ever known, with huge boulder-like shoulders and trunk-like arms. His face was almost troll-like, with a round misshapen nose in the centre.

"Get the girls and go inside," Olaf whispered to her, as his old warrior instinct kicked in. "Good day, stranger. What brings you out here?" he asked.

"Was passing through the valley when I saw your farm. Thought I might slake my thirst and perhaps get some food," the ogre said, his voice sounding like two rocks grinding against each other. "Might be I can get more than I bargained for." His eyes lingered on Brynhild as she called her daughters to her.

Brynhild froze on the spot. She could see the wolf grin which parted his moustache from his beard.

"We are poor farmers with not much to share, stranger. But if you carry on east over them hills, you'll soon come across the hall of Jarl Thorgils. He can provide you with better hospitality." Olaf was feeling uneasy about the way this stranger was looking at his wife.

"That's a beautiful woman you have there. Must be nice having her warm your bed at night." The stranger's eyes were fixed on Brynhild as she gathered her girls around her. He licked his lips and stared at her rounded hips.

"Better watch that tongue of yours, stranger." Olaf glanced over his shoulder, willing Brynhild to go inside with their daughters, but she was rooted to the spot in fear. His daughters clutched their mother's legs. At least the hound was with them, a growl escaping its throat as it eyed the stranger. Olaf stepped to the side, blocking the stranger's view of his wife and children.

"You ever kill a man, farmer?" the stranger asked, scratching the side of his thick neck.

"When it's been needed."

The stranger smiled his ugly smile again. "Aye, I can see that, but it's been a while since I'd wager."

"My axe still remembers how it's done, don't you worry."

The stranger was almost beginning to like Olaf; not many men had the courage to stand up to him. It'd be a pity to kill him, but a woman always felt better when she was taken from another man. "Name's Griml. I tell you this so when you find the other men I have killed in Valhalla, you can share a drink with them," he said, seeing the confusion on Olaf's face.

Olaf was unnerved by Griml's confidence. But he kept his face set as he crouched behind his shield, keeping his axe ready by his side. He just needed to give his family enough time to get inside and bar the doors.

"Come on then farmer, let's see what you got."

With a roar that sounded across the valley, Olaf ran at Griml who twisted out of the way.

"Not bad, almost had me there." Griml smiled.

Olaf stood still, watching Griml. Their positions had now changed, with Olaf facing his hall. He saw Ulf poking his head around the corner of their house to see what was happening. He willed Ulf to grab his family and take them into the house.

"My turn, I guess," Griml said before running at Olaf. Olaf swung his axe at him, but Griml caught his hand in a crushing grip, lifting Olaf up as if he were a doll, before punching him in the face with his giant fist. With a crunching noise, Olaf's head snapped back. Blood ran down his lip. Dazed, Olaf tried to hit Griml with the rim of his shield, but Griml caught it and ripped it away from Olaf. Helplessly Olaf hung there.

Griml was about to punch the hanging Olaf in the stomach when he heard the scream behind him. He turned in time to see Ulf jabbing his spear at his face but could not get his head out of the way quick enough. Griml felt the tip of the spear slicing through his cheek.

"That wasn't very smart, boy," Griml said, still holding onto Olaf as a trickle of blood ran down his cheek into his beard.

"Don't know, I think it made you prettier," Ulf said, holding his spear in both hands in front of him.

Griml let go of Olaf, who just dropped to the ground, too disorientated to stand, and turned to face Ulf. "No one has ever cut my face before." He stamped down on Olaf's arm, breaking it as easily as if he stood on a twig, his eyes fixed on Ulf. Olaf screamed in agony.

"Don't worry uncle, this troll will die for what he has done to you!" Ulf held his spear in front of him with both hands, the tip pointed at Griml.

"Troll, hey. The last person to call me that died a very painful death," Griml growled as he bent to take Olaf's axe from his now-useless hand. The axe looked tiny in his huge hands.

"Not my fault you look like one, you sure your mother wasn't fucked by a troll in the mountains one night?"

With an angry roar, Griml shot forward with great speed. Ulf thrust his spear in Griml's direction, hoping the giant man would run onto it. But Griml wasn't a mindless boar. He grabbed hold of the spear shaft and chopped it in two with Olaf's axe, before he spun around and drove the spear point into Ulf's ribs. Ulf felt the blinding hot pain screaming through his body as he heard Brynhild scream. He looked down and saw the broken spear shaft sticking out of his side, his tunic already darkened by his blood as it flowed freely from the wound. Ulf fell to his knees and looked over at his uncle, who stared back in anguish.

"Uncle...." was all he managed before everything went black and he collapsed to the floor.

"Well, uncle," Griml said as he walked back to where Olaf lay staring at the body of his brother's son. "Your axe is good for chopping wood, I'll give you that."

Before he got to Olaf, Griml heard a loud growl behind him. He turned around and saw the big hound standing in front of Brynhild and her daughters, its front legs spread out wide and its shoulders hunched as it made itself look even bigger than it already was. "That's a pretty dog you have there, but you really think it can protect you when your husband couldn't?"

"Get him," was all Brynhild said.

The hound launched itself at Griml and leapt for his throat. Griml stepped aside and with a swift movement decapitated the hound with Olaf's axe.

"This is a good axe, uncle," Griml said as he studied its edge for the first time, unfazed by the fresh splatter of blood covering his face. He glanced at Brynhild and saw her standing there, frozen in fear and shock, but keeping her daughters behind her skirt as if she could somehow protect them. "Don't you worry, pretty, it's not your daughters I'm after. But before we can have our fun, I need to make sure there won't be any more interruptions."

Olaf had to do something; he could not let this monster get to his family. He took one last look at Ulf, lying there with the broken spear shaft sticking out his side, no sign of life coming from him. *I'm sorry, brother, I have failed you.* The pain in his arm was excruciating, but he had to save his wife and daughters. He was their last hope. Clutching his broken arm to his chest, Olaf took his knife from its scabbard and waited for Griml.

Griml turned back towards Olaf after killing the hound. He was surprised to see a knife in Olaf's left hand. It must have been on the back of his belt. But Griml didn't care. That knife would not save Olaf. Griml attacked with a vicious axe swing, which Olaf just managed to dodge. Olaf struck back with a cut of his own, just catching Griml's arm, but not cutting deep enough to do anything. Griml feinted with an axe chop and when Olaf twisted his body to dodge it, Griml punched his broken arm with his free hand. Olaf screamed as the pain shot through his arm and into his chest like a burning fire. The distraction was all Griml needed as he buried the axe in Olaf's chest, cutting through the collarbone and severing the fingers on the hand of the broken arm. Griml let go of the axe and took a step back, as Olaf just stood there looking at his wife and daughters.

"I'm sorry," he said to them before spitting out a mouthful of blood and dropping to the floor, still holding onto his knife.

Brynhild screamed as she saw her husband die. She urged her daughters to run, if only to spare them from what would come next, but they refused to let go off her as the bloody Griml started walking towards them.

"Now, let us have some fun," he said with a big monstrous grin on his blood-covered face.

CHAPTER 2

Where am I? Ulf looked around, but it was too dark to see anything. It was so cold he thought the blood would freeze in his veins. *This must be Niflheim*, he thought, remembering the stories his aunt used to tell him about the frozen lands where the giant Ymir had been born. *Am I dead? But why am I in Niflheim? I held on to my spear. I made sure I did. I should be in Valhalla.* But Ulf saw no hall, no fallen warriors fighting. He didn't see the wolves who were supposed to guard the gates or the eagles that flew high in the air above its golden roof. He didn't really see anything in this dark. *I must be in Niflheim. Is it possible I dropped my spear?* Ulf heard a whisper, like leaves rustling on their branches. He walked towards the sound, trying to make out what it was saying. With a squelch, his boot sank ankle-deep in mud. If his feet weren't already numb from the cold, he would have felt the icy water pouring into his boots. Screaming, he fell into the icy water, the air taken from his lungs by a frozen hand. He tried to get up but struggled to find firm ground, all the while spluttering and spitting out the strangely metallic tasting water. Niflheim was supposed to be a land of ice, not mud and water. *If this isn't Niflheim, then where am I?* He heard the whisper again.

"Who's there? Show yourself!" he shouted into the void.

There was no response, only an eerie silence which made him shiver. *Damn this!* He groped around, looking for something to help him out of this marsh. His hand landed on something. It wasn't hard nor soft. *An old tree branch maybe*, he thought as he pulled it towards himself. Something came off in his hands. It felt fleshy and cold, but Ulf could not see what it was.

"Bjørnson." He heard the whisper floating through the air. Ulf forgot about the stuff in his hands. *I must have misheard*, he thought, feeling a worm of fear crawling up his spine.

"Bjørnson." It came again. Something about that made him afraid. He couldn't understand why. Why was the voice calling him that?

"Who's there?" he asked again, shivering from the cold and fear.

"Bjørnson, come."

"What?"

"Come, Bjørnson, you must see."

See? See what? How can I see anything? It's too damn dark to see. A light appeared behind a hill, like a sunrise answering his thoughts. Ulf wished it hadn't as he saw a marsh of death and decay all around him. A nightmare you would never want to find yourself in. He was surrounded by skeletons and decayed bodies of men and women, floating in blood. Next to him was a body, its arm missing. He panicked and screamed.

"Bjørnson." The voice came again. "Come and see."

Even through his fear, Ulf did not like being called that. He had once adored his father, but not anymore. His father had abandoned him. But the voice didn't care.

"Come, son of Bjørn, come and see."

"My name is Ulf!" Ulf's anger poked through his fear.

"No, that is not important. You are the son of Bjørn, that is important."

Ulf was shocked by those words. How could his name not be important? It was his name; it was who he was. He looked up and saw a cloaked figure standing there, silhouetted by the light coming from behind, holding a long, gnarled staff.

"Who are you?" Ulf asked, unable to hide the fear in his voice.

"Come, Bjørnson."

Ulf didn't want to, but he did not want to stay here either. He wondered if the figure was there to take him to Hel.

"This is not Hel, Bjørnson," the figure said, reading Ulf's thoughts.

"Then where am I?"

"That is not important, Bjørnson"

"My name is Ulf!" he screamed at the figure.

"Come and see, Bjørnson."

Ulf started climbing up the hill, towards the figure.

"Who are you? Where am I?" Ulf asked again, struggling to form the words. He had never felt this afraid before.

"Come, Bjørnson"

"Please, tell me! What is this?"

The figure said nothing. To Ulf's surprise, it turned and walked away.

"Wait!" Ulf urged the figure. He forced himself to follow, fighting the fear paralyzing his limbs.

Ulf got to the top of the hill but couldn't see the cloaked figure. What he did see, though, shook him to his core – a familiar giant mountain troll surrounded by warriors trying in vain to kill it.

"This is what you want." A voice came from beside him.

Startled, Ulf turned and saw the cloaked figure standing there. He couldn't see the man's face, only a long grey beard protruding from the dark hood. The hand holding the staff looked ancient, mottled skin stretched thin over the bones beneath.

"What I want?" Ulf heard the fear in his own voice.

The cloaked figure did not respond and pointed towards the troll. Ulf turned and saw the troll glaring at him, ignoring the warriors trying to kill it. With a thunderous roar, it charged, knocking all the warriors aside. Ulf froze. He did not want to fight that.

"How? I have no weapons, no armour!" he protested. All he was wearing was his trousers and tunic. Still covered in the blood from the marsh, he fell in. He looked up as he felt the ground trembling beneath his feet. The troll was getting closer.

"You cannot run, Bjørnson," the figure said beside him. "You must kill it."

"Kill it! How?!" Ulf screamed, his bulging eyes fixed on the troll.

"Trust in your blood, Bjørnson. Embrace it."

Ulf opened his eyes. At first, he saw nothing, just a blurry vagueness of his surroundings. Then as his vision began to clear, he saw a thatched roof above him. The air he breathed was a strange mixture of decay and fresh herbs, combined with the musty smell of wet dog. *Where am I?* The last thing he remembered was the troll in the bloody marsh. The old cloaked figure. *Embrace your blood.* Ulf looked at his side and was surprised to find he had been injured. The troll couldn't have done it, he was sure of it. Somebody had recently dressed the wound, judging by the dark stain on the dressing. He lifted the dressing to look at the wound. It had been cauterized like they would do on the farm when one of the cows cut itself – the smell of his wound reached his nose causing him to lurch and vomit on the ground.

With a groan, he looked up and saw a young boy sat there, a big grin on his face. He had a soft feminine face with bright blue eyes – Ulf guessed he was a few winters younger than him. He took in his short slim body that was almost frail-looking. But his hands were very large with short fat fingers. Ulf thought the size of his hands was strange, considering how small the rest of him was. The boy was wearing trousers that only went to his knees and no shoes, his feet dirty and dry. He had an old, worn tunic which had been patched many times.

"Who are you?" Ulf asked.

The boy just stared back, not responding, but still grinning his idiotic grin.

Ulf tried again, thinking he had not spoken clearly, but got the same result. He felt the anger bubbling inside his stomach, or at least he hoped it was anger.

Ulf growled in frustration. "If you don't answer me, I'll…" He didn't know how to finish. He was in no condition to do anything. "Fuck it." He looked at the roof again, taking a deep breath to calm himself down. After a few moments, he turned his head to the boy again. Ulf began to wonder if the boy was real.

"You did this?" he asked the boy. The boy shook his head. "You don't say, much do you?" Ulf said, happy to get at least some response.

"Boy's a mute. You have a better chance of getting the trees to talk."

Ulf heard an old voice from somewhere. At first, he thought it was the cloaked figure but then realized this voice was different, less commanding. An old man limped into the hut, a large shaggy dog behind him -- a cross between a wolf and a bear. Ulf tried to get up again but couldn't. The pain was too much. The old man was reed-thin with a stooped back that made it difficult to guess his height. Definitely not the cloaked figure from the marsh. The cloaked figure was tall and stood straight.

"Though, I wish the trees would stop talking. Like naggin' wives, they are," the old man said, cackling to himself. The large hound licked the boy's face and sat down next to him. It looked at Ulf with the same expression as the boy. *Great, another one.*

"Where am I?" Ulf asked, still looking at the boy and the dog.

"In my hut," the old man said, unhelpfully. He walked over to Ulf and lifted the dressing off the wound. He prodded it with fingers which were bent with age and had large bony knuckles. The old man sniffed the wound, his eyes directed at the roof of his hut and then nodded, satisfied with what he saw. "The Norns are kind to you, you will not die from this."

"What happened?" Ulf asked the old man. He looked familiar to Ulf, but Ulf could not remember from where.

"You don't remember?" the old man asked with no concern in his voice.

"I remember the bloody marsh. And a figure, an old man wearing a cloak. And the–" Ulf stopped when he saw the confused look on the old man's face. "What?"

"Young Ulf, there was no bloody marsh. Although there was a lot of blood. And the old man?" The old man went silent for a while, stroking his scraggly beard as he thought.

"No bloody marsh?" Ulf's head was starting to hurt. What did the old man mean there was no bloody marsh?

"We found you on the farm," the old man said before Ulf could say anything else. "Thought you were dead."

"The farm?" The headache was getting worse, but new memories came through the pain. He studied the old man again. "I know you." Ulf could see the old man clearer now. He saw his long thin face with his long scraggly beard and patchy hair, his big bushy eyebrows above his mismatched eyes, his right eye blue and his left green. The taut skin of his face crisscrossed with deep lines, a testament to his age. "You're the old man who comes to the farm. You trade with my uncle."

"Aye, that's me."

"My uncle?" He now remembered training with his uncle like they normally did after they finished their work for the day. Other memories started forcing their way into his mind, like needy children desperate for attention. But Ulf still could not make sense of any of it. "My uncle, and Brynhild? Are they...?" Ulf couldn't finish the question. The look on the old man's face stopped the words in his throat.

"I'm sorry, young Ulf. You were the only one we found alive."

"In the marsh?" he asked, still confused by everything.

"The marsh must be a dream, boy," the old man answered with a shake of his head. Hearing those words cleared the fog in Ulf's head. He now understood the wound in his side.

"What...What about my cousins?" Ulf asked. He hoped they had somehow escaped, or at least not suffered a cruel fate. Everybody had still been alive the last time he had seen them.

The old man regarded him and shook his head. He had seen many things in his long life but did not want to bring those images back to his mind.

Ulf looked at the roof of the hut again and tried to control the sudden rush of emotion. They were dead. All of them. Olaf, Brynhild, Ingrid and Unnr. His only family, dead because he could not protect them. Because he had been dumb enough to think he could defeat the giant man. He struggled to breathe; he had failed his family. Ulf clutched his sides as he screamed, his tears unable to take the pain away. The hound howled while Ulf cried as if sharing his pain.

The old man took the young boy by the shoulder and led him away. "Come on, boy. I think it best we go outside."

"Where are we exactly?" Ulf asked the old man. It was the first time he had spoken in days.

The old man was startled, like he had forgotten Ulf was there. "We're in the forest of the Vanir," he said after a while, before returning to his task.

"The Vanir?"

"Yes, you know; Njörd, Frey and his sister Freya–"

"I know who the Vanir are," Ulf cut the old man off. "But what do you mean the forest of the Vanir? I thought all these lands belonged to Odin and the Æsir." Ulf heard a crash of thunder in the distance followed by the heavy patter of rain. The gods were listening to this conversation.

"Mmmm." The old man looked up, thinking the same. "No, not these forests. They are old, these trees. Been around since before the Æsir came. No, they belong to the Vanir, especially Frey and Freya." He walked to a small cauldron over a fire in the middle of the hut. After adding the contents of his hands into the cauldron, he picked up a ladle and stirred, sniffing the rising steam. The hut filled with the aroma of wild onion and herbs. With a squint of his eyes, the old man turned around, looking for some missing ingredient while muttering to himself.

"How does the forest being old make them belong to the Vanir?"

"Simple, these lands belonged to the Vanir long before the Æsir came from the east." The old man found what he had been looking for. He chopped a handful of mushrooms and added them to the cauldron.

"How do you know this?"

"The trees told me."

"The trees?" Ulf was beginning to understand why this old man lived in the forest.

"Yes, young Ulf, the trees. Nature speaks to you if you have the will to listen to her. She has told me many of her secrets. Too many, I fear." He stopped again and listened to the rain falling on the roof of his hut.

DONOVAN COOK

Ulf sensed he was afraid of something. "What you mean by too many?"

"Do you believe in the gods, young Ulf? You do not wear any symbol of the gods on you." There was an intensity in his eyes which made Ulf shiver.

"The gods took everything I loved away from me."

"Aye, the gods are cruel, but that doesn't answer my question. Do you believe?"

"I don't want to, not anymore." Ulf looked away from the old man's stare.

"The gods don't always care about what you want. They can be very selfish." He went quiet as he turned around. "Did you know Odin often disguised himself as an old man wearing a cloak when he went wandering?" the old man added over his shoulder.

Ulf watched him as he prepared the broth for tonight's dinner, trying to make sense of what he had just said. *Did Odin send him the dream? But why?* Ulf didn't understand and decided to look for the boy to distract himself, but as usual, he was not there.

"He's hunting again?" Ulf asked, wondering why the boy was out hunting while it was raining.

"He likes to hunt." The old man flinched at every crack of the thunder; perhaps he believed the thunder god Thor was after him. Ulf remembered something his uncle had told him about the old man.

Beware of that old fool, Ulf. He is more dangerous than he looks.

His danger lies not in his arms. Some people say he is touched by the gods, others say he is just simple.

If Ulf had been stronger, he would have beaten it out of the old man, but he was still too weak. At most he could sit up and maybe take a few steps, but then the pain became too much. The boy was a curiosity too. He was always watching the old man. Ulf could see there was something in the boy's eyes, some hidden shame mixed with anger. The only normal thing in this hut was the dog. He was the only thing not hiding something.

"Why doesn't the boy have a name?" he asked.

"Because he doesn't." The old man froze as loud thunder ripped through the air. He stood as still as a rock, waiting, listening. Then as if realizing there was no danger, he went about his business.

"You don't know the name of your grandson?" Ulf ventured, hoping this would help him get more information.

The old man barked a laugh. "He is of no relation to me. I thank Frey every day for that." The old man glanced at him and Ulf saw something in his eyes. A little shine that made Ulf feel uncomfortable.

"How did he come to be living with you then?" Ulf suspected he knew, with the boy being mute. Some people saw it as a curse to have a child like that.

"Found him wandering in the forest a few years back."

Ulf tried to picture being abandoned like that. He was lucky, Olaf and Brynhild had looked after him. Thinking of them threatened to release the emotions he had been struggling to deal with for days, so he asked another question. "Then why keep him?"

"He has his uses." That shine again. "Besides, I'm too old to hunt now and the dog is too dumb."

"How old are you?" Ulf had never really thought about the old man's age, but now that he mentioned it, Ulf was curious.

"Old enough to have fucked your grandmother," he responded with a cackle.

CHAPTER 3

The large raven landed on a branch overlooking the small clearing. Twisting its head to one side, it stared at the small hut with its beady eye. The hut looked like it had been there almost as long as the forest had existed, as it leaned against the large oak tree. Its roof was covered with old branches, the few leaves on them browned and dried by age a long time ago. Smoke slowly leaked out of the small hole in the roof. The aged timber holding the hut together had turned grey and was covered by moss and lichen, adding some green and brown to the otherwise sad-looking colour. The raven came here every day and watched the routines of the old man and the boy. It would see the boy leaving the hut soon after sunrise and go into the forest to hunt, sometimes accompanied by the large dog. It would watch as the old man sauntered out of the hut, some days looking more satisfied than others. The old man would sit and talk to the trees like they were old friends. There was another person in the hut, a new arrival who the raven rarely saw, but could always smell. He would occasionally limp out of the hut, sometimes helped by the boy, and relieve himself against the tree. The raven had a deep interest in the tall skinny youth. It would try to talk to him, calling his name and asking after him. But the young man only ever glared at it. The raven looked to the sky through the trees. It was turning a soft blue, which meant the sun was slowly climbing into the sky.

Looking back at the hut, it realized the boy had not left yet, and neither had the old man come out to talk to the trees. Something had happened, something not good. The raven screamed at the hut as it hopped from one branch to the next in its excitement. It had begun.

Inside the hut, Ulf woke to the sounds of the raven croaking outside the hut. He'd been having the same dream again. The one in the bloody marsh with the troll trying to kill him. At least now he understood it had only been a dream. He took a deep breath to clear the smell of blood from his memory, but that only made it stronger. *Kraa-Kraa*, the raven outside screamed again. Ulf sat up, glad he could move around freely again. He struggled to understand why the smells from his dream were so strong and why, with every breath he took, they only got stronger. In the corner of his eye, he saw the boy sitting on the ground beside the sleeping old man and his dog. *Strange*, he thought, *the boy normally tried to avoid the old man.* And the old man was usually awake by now. He looked at the boy and with a shock realized the smells were not from his dream, but from the hut. The boy had a bloody knife in his large hand and his face was contorted. Ulf struggled to understand the scene before him. The old man and his dog had been massacred, the ground around them covered in blood and gore, mixed with the contents of their bowels. Death had come for them in the night and it came in the form of the young boy, covered in the blood of his master. For a moment, Ulf thought the boy was going to kill him too. Ulf didn't know if he had the strength to defend himself. But the boy's face relaxed and he smiled at Ulf.

"You killed him, huh?" The question seemed pointless, but Ulf didn't know what else to say. He was surprised he hadn't heard anything. Perhaps he had and just thought the sounds were part of his dream.

The boy nodded. Ulf had seen the way the old man leered at the boy and had blocked out the grunting and the whimpering noises he heard some nights. He had also seen the way the boy moved the mornings after. The boy had had enough. He stood up and stared at the knife in his hand, like he had only just realized it was there. He looked back at the large dog and Ulf saw the sadness in his eyes. Perhaps he had not meant to kill the dog but had no choice.

"Now what?" Ulf asked, looking at the blood-covered knife in the boy's hand.

The boy dropped the knife and walked to a pile of furs in the corner of the hut. He threw the furs to the ground to reveal a large chest. Ulf had never seen the chest before, but then it had been covered up the whole time he had been here. The boy stood by the oak chest and turned to Ulf, who sensed the boy wanted him to look inside. Gritting his teeth against the pain in his side, Ulf got to his feet and walked over to the chest. Its lid was cracked, it smelled damp, and the metal hinges were browned by rust. There were some holes in it which looked like worms had gotten to it and feasted themselves fat. Opening the lid with a loud creaking noise, Ulf could not believe what was inside. He struggled to breathe as his mind tried to understand what he was looking at.

He lifted out his uncle's axe, recognisable by the pattern on the blade which resembled the waves on the sea, and the worn leather strap wrapped around the bottom of the handle. Ulf took deep breaths to control his anger while he struggled to understand why the old man had been hiding these things from him. Putting the axe down, Ulf noticed the other items in the chest. He found his uncle's Mjöllnir pendant, which he always wore around his neck. It was beautifully made of carved ivory from a walrus tusk and decorated with delicate patterns and swirls. Ulf didn't wear one, he had never wanted to, not after the gods took his parents away from him. He also found the necklace made of colourful glass beads his aunt loved to wear. Olaf had brought it back from a land far to the west when he was younger and had given it to her.

Among the other items were clothing, knives and other trinkets which had belonged to his aunt and cousins. Ulf was struggling to control his rage. He closed his eyes and took a step away from the chest. Was the old man ever going to tell him about these things? He picked up his uncle's axe again, gripping the handle so tightly his hand started hurting. If the boy hadn't killed the old man, then Ulf would have. The raven outside started screaming again, its cry sounded like a word, being repeated over and over.

Revenge, Revenge.

Revenge, Revenge.

Ulf nodded as he understood. Griml. Ulf had no idea where to find him, or how to kill him. He needed help but did not know where to find it. Ulf realized there was one thing missing from the chest. His heart wanted to rip out of his body as he tore through the layers of clothing, animal skulls, and old weapons, but he could not find it. He could not find his father's old sword. Ormstunga.

"Was there a sword at the farm when you found me?" he asked the boy. "It has a gold hilt. It's very easy to see." The boy shook his head and indicated at the chest. Everything they had found was in there. Griml had taken the sword. Ulf screamed in anger as he flipped the old chest over, spilling its contents over the floor. With closed eyes, he stood there panting as he clenched his fist by his side. He had to find that sword. His whole life he had wanted nothing but to use that sword to prove he was better than his father.

Ulf walked to the fireplace in the centre of the hut, being drawn there by the flames and added more wood. As the flames got bigger, he sat and placed his uncle's axe and Mjöllnir pendant in front of him, along with other things that had belonged to his family. He had no idea what he was doing, so he just did what felt natural. Ulf picked up the axe and using the same knife the boy had used to kill the old man and his dog, he carved the names of his family into the handle.

"Odin!" he started, "Odin, I swear to you and all the gods of Asgard, that I will not stop until I have found the man responsible for the deaths of my family. And when I find this man, I will kill him and avenge those he has taken from me. The son must avenge the father, like Vidar will avenge you in Ragnarök. Brother must avenge brother, like Vali avenged the death of his brother Baldr. And with the death of Griml, I will retrieve my father's sword. But until then I shall not touch another. I swear nothing will stop me, not even death itself, from feeding Griml to the ravens and sending his soul to Niflheim! I shall have my vengeance. This I swear to you, Odin Hrafnagud, the raven god!" He cut his hand with the blade of the axe and smeared his blood over their names, painting the haft red. Ulf looked up and was surprised by the intensity he saw in the boy's eyes. But that intensity gave him an idea. The son must avenge the father, that was the custom of their ways. But Olaf had no son, only a nephew. So now the nephew had to do what the son could not, unlike Vidar, who was the son of Odin. He looked at the boy again and smiled. Vidar.

"You need a name," he said. The boy nodded and from the look in his eyes, Ulf felt the boy already knew what he had in mind. "What about Vidar? The son of Odin who avenged his death. You've had your vengeance, and now together we can find mine." Ulf smiled and was happy to see the boy, now Vidar, nodding his approval. Ulf needed to make an offering; the gods would not help him otherwise. But he had nothing to offer except for the hut and the things inside. *Fuck it, it's worth a try,* he thought.

"Accept this offering I make to you, All-Father!" Ulf said as he added more wood to the fire. He would burn the whole hut down and everything inside. He hoped Odin would accept this. The gods usually wanted more substantial offerings, but this was all he had to give.

"It's time to go," he said to Vidar. To his surprise, Vidar was ready. He had collected his meager possessions and had found some food for them. With that they left the hut and stood outside, watching as the flames took hold of the small building. To Ulf, the flames were like his rage, ready to destroy anything in its path. He had to be cautious from now on. He could not afford to give in to his anger and pride like he did when he had attacked Griml. Ulf had to stay alive long enough to kill Griml and regain the sword that belonged to him. When most of the hut was aflame the two companions turned and walked away, not yet sure of where their journey would take them. Or how long it would take. Vengeance could be a long road.

The sun was sitting high in the sky when they reached a small clearing in the forest. After a few weeks of living in the stuffy hut, the air in the forest felt fresher than before. Ulf breathed in the rich forest aroma of damp ground and green leaves, feeling his anger being calmed, as if Freya had placed a soothing hand on his head. *Even the sounds seem louder*, he thought as he heard the birds singing in the trees. There were twigs snapping in the distance, a constant reminder they were not alone in this old forest.

"Let's rest here," Ulf said. He was tired and the pain in his side was making it difficult to carry on. His mood was in contrast to the sunny weather as he sat down and tried to figure out what to do. He didn't have much of a plan, didn't even know where to go. There was Thorgilsstad, but his uncle had always told him to stay away from there. But Ulf didn't know of any other jarls.

Vidar, on the other hand, was smiling. Ulf guessed Vidar felt free, but he didn't understand why Vidar had waited so long to kill the old man.

"Why now?" he asked Vidar.

Vidar looked at him, confused at first, but then he understood the question. His replied by pointing at Ulf.

"You waited for me?" This made no sense. How did Vidar know that he would be there?

Vidar shrugged and then nodded. A yes and no answer.

"How did you know that I would not kill you instead? Thralls who kill their owners must be killed themselves. Those are the rules of our land."

Vidar only smiled and shrugged.

Somehow, he knew. Ulf felt a bit uneasy and it was not because of the pain. It felt like there was more to this silent boy with his large hands. Before Ulf could say anything else, he saw Vidar scanning the trees at the other side of the clearing. The smile disappeared from Vidar's face, replaced by a snarl that reminded Ulf of a dog.

"What is it?" Ulf asked, realizing the birds had gone quiet. He got back to his feet and took Olaf's axe from his belt.

In response to his question, a man jumped out of the undergrowth. Ulf pushed Vidar behind him and held the axe ready, though he wasn't sure what he was going to do. The man had a long hunting spear, which he now pointed at Ulf and Vidar. He looked as surprised to see them as they were to see him.

"Who are you?" he asked. He had a strong voice which spoke of confidence.

"Nobody important," Ulf replied. "Who are you?"

The man smiled at the response. He was the same height as Ulf, but sturdier. He had a round face with light hair, braided and tied at the back. His beard, the same colour as his hair, also had a thick braid and went to the top of his chest. Ulf could tell by the many arm-rings he wore and his bunched-up shoulder muscles that the man was an experienced warrior.

"My name is Snorri Thorgilsson," he said with a broad smile as he stood up straight and stopped pointing the spear at them. He must have decided they were no threat.

"Thorgilsson? As in Jarl Thorgils?" Ulf should have guessed he was someone important by the quality of the clothes he was wearing.

"Yes, I am the son of the jarl. You mean to kill me." He was smiling at the thought. Even Ulf doubted he could kill the warrior, especially with his side still hurting.

Vidar started pulling at Ulf's sleeve, but Ulf ignored him. He didn't want to take his eyes off the man facing them. Again, Vidar tugged at Ulf's sleeve, more persistently this time. "What?" Ulf turned to look at Vidar but kept an eye on the warrior in front of them.

Vidar pointed to the trees as a large brown bear walked into the clearing, behind the man who called himself Snorri. But Snorri hadn't noticed the bear and must have thought Vidar was pointing at him.

"What does he want?" Snorri asked Ulf as the bear crept closer. Ulf had never seen a bear as large as this one.

"Behind you," Ulf answered and was shocked to see Snorri laugh.

"Those are my men, nothing to worry about."

"There are no men behind you."

The bear was almost on top of Snorri when he turned to see what Ulf had meant. "Odin's balls!" he exclaimed as he tried to bring his spear around. But the bear was faster and hit Snorri with the back of its paw, breaking the spear in half and sending Snorri flying through the air. Ulf reacted and charged at the beast, the pain in his side forgotten. It turned to Ulf and roared at him as if challenging Ulf to a duel. As Ulf reached the bear, it stood on its back legs, towering over him. Ulf swung his axe at it, but the bear swatted it away. It then came crashing down on its front legs, clawing at Ulf at the same time. Ulf jumped back, avoiding the sharp claws, but before he could do anything else, the bear ran at him. It roared in frustration as Ulf rolled out of the way, feeling his side protesting at the movement. But Ulf couldn't think about that now. This bear seemed intent on killing him. Looking past the animal, Ulf saw Vidar still standing there. He was surprised to see Vidar not looking worried or afraid. Instead, he stood there smiling, like he was watching a horse race. Still focused on Vidar, Ulf didn't see the bear coming back at him until it was too late. He sensed the giant paw before he saw it and tried to twist out of the way but was not fast enough. Sharp pain spread across his face as the bear's claws sliced through his skin, the force of the blow sending him spiralling to the ground. Ulf landed hard and struggled to get up. The right side of his face was burning and already his right eye was starting to lose vision because of the swelling. He waited for the bear to finish him off, but instead it stood there watching him. Ulf put his hand to the side of his face and was not surprised to see the blood on it. He felt angry at himself. This was not the way he was supposed to die. He struggled back to his feet, ignoring the dizziness in his head and the pain in his side.

"I will not be killed by you," he growled at the bear. He had lost the axe, but he wasn't going to let that stop him. The bear seemed to smile at him before charging again. Ulf roared at the bear and charged as well. He jumped to the side as they met in the middle, avoiding its paws, but having no way to attack himself. He had to find a weapon. He couldn't see the axe, so that left only the spear which Snorri had. But he didn't want to ask Snorri for help. The bear came at him again. This time Ulf threw a punch, catching the bear in the side of its head as it charged past. He realized the punch had hurt him more than the bear as it turned and swung its paw at him. Ulf ducked underneath and ran past the beast. *Fuck it*, he thought as he held out his hand towards Snorri. "Spear!"

"No," was the response he got. Shocked, Ulf turned back towards Snorri.

"What do you mean no?!"

"How do I know you won't try to kill me with it?" Snorri was on his knees, one hand clutching his chest, the other holding the broken spear.

"What!" Ulf couldn't believe what the idiot was saying. He was fighting for his life and Snorri felt like playing games.

"Fucking spear now!" he shouted at Snorri, keeping his eyes on the bear. He felt the warmth of the blood as it ran down his face. His right eye was swollen shut now. He had to finish this fight, or the bear would finish him.

"No, I'm not giving you a weapon to kill me with."

"Why would I want to kill you?" He turned to Snorri, who was looking rather amused. "There's a fucking bear if you haven't noticed!"

"And you are doing a great job keeping it busy," Snorri responded with a smile. "My hirdmen will be here soon and then we can kill it after you tired it out."

Ulf was stunned by this. He almost forgot about the bear as he turned to look at Snorri. "Are you fucking serious!" The bear came at him again, and Ulf had to roll under another paw swipe and ran to the other side of the clearing, trying to increase the distance between him and the bear.

Snorri knew he should help the young man, but he was surprised at how fast he moved. The bear was like no other bear he had ever seen. It was bigger and faster and seemed intent on killing

Ulf. But somehow Ulf had stayed ahead of the bear the whole time. Snorri had never seen anyone move like that. But the cut to Ulf's face looked bad and Snorri could see that Ulf was losing too much blood. It was time to help.

"Catch!" Ulf turned and Snorri threw the spear towards him. The throw had been awkward and poorly aimed and landed between Ulf and the bear. Ulf ran for the spear at the same time as the bear charged towards him. But the bear was faster and looked like it would reach the spear first. Ulf had no choice, so he dived for the spear. His hand grabbed hold of the shaft as he rolled underneath the bear. Without looking, he stabbed up, feeling the spear sliding past ribs and into the bear's heart. It roared in agony as its momentum ripped the spear from Ulf's hands. The bear came to a stop and shuddered for a moment as its heart finally gave out and it dropped to the ground, dead. Ulf's vision was starting to blur as he struggled to his knees, unable to stand from dizziness. He was breathing heavily, not yet believing he had killed the bear. The edges of his vision were going dark. He watched the bear, expecting it to get up, but it didn't. Ulf then heard a noise he did not understand at first but then recognised the flap of a wing and the cry of a raven.

"Which one are you? Huginn or Muninn?" He was struggling to get the words out; his mouth did not seem to want to obey him. "It doesn't matter, go back to your master. Tell Odin I will not die until I've had my revenge! You hear me! I will have my revenge!" Ulf heard the flap of wings as everything went black and he fell to the ground.

Snorri got to his feet, still not sure what he had just witnessed. He was still staring at the unconscious Ulf when his companions came into the clearing.

"What happened?" one of them asked, looking at the dead bear and Ulf lying next to each other.

"You wouldn't believe me if I told you," Snorri said, looking in the direction the raven had flown.

"Where's your spear?"

"Half of it is over there," he said pointing to the broken shaft, "and the other half is inside the bear."

"You put it there?"

"No, he did," Snorri replied, pointing at Ulf.

"Really? He looks a bit skinny to be killing bears."

"Aye but kill it he did. Fought like Thor himself."

"Still, a bit rude to be using your spear. What if you needed it?" the man asked Snorri. He looked to his companions who all seemed to agree with him.

"Who's the boy?" another of the group asked after spotting Vidar at the other side of the clearing.

"He's with him," Snorri said, pointing to where Ulf and the bear were lying. He had forgotten about the boy.

"The bear?" one of them asked, looking confused. He got cuffed over his head as a response.

"It's OK, friend, we won't hurt you." Snorri tried to look as friendly as possible. Which was not difficult for him.

Vidar stared at the men. They looked dangerous, but the one they met before the bear attacked did give his spear to Ulf. Vidar knew he could trust Snorri, so he walked towards them.

"What's your name?" Snorri asked. Vidar shook his head and pointed to his mouth. "Can't speak, huh?" This day was just getting more and more interesting.

"Now what?" one of the group asked.

"Now we take these two to my father, he'd be very interested to meet them."

"Why not just kill them and claim the bear?"

"No, there's something about that one," he said, looking at Ulf's prone body. "And besides, he saved my life." He guessed that was true. He wasn't sure if he could have killed that bear on his own.

"And the bear?"

"Bring it too."

CHAPTER 4

Ulf opened his eyes and stared at the ceiling. He saw the crossbeams of darkened wood and the blackened underside of the thatch. For a moment he thought he was back in the old man's hut, but the room he was in was bigger and there were no plants or skulls hanging from the beams. Even the air smelt different, fresher than he remembered and with no hint of the herbs mixed with decay. Instead, there was the sweet smell of honey, stronger than he would expect it to be. Ulf decided he wasn't in the old man's hut. He was somewhere different, yet familiar.

Turning his head to get a better look at the room, he saw something that was familiar, yet different. Vidar. The boy sat there, cross-legged on the floor beside his bed, just like he had done when Ulf had woken up in the old man's hut. He had the same happy grin on his face. But he wasn't wearing the old ragged tunic from that day. Instead, he had a new clean tunic, with matching trousers and leather shoes. Vidar's face had been cleaned as well. Seeing Vidar brought a memory to Ulf. The old man, he was dead. Killed by Vidar. The dog too. An image flashed in Ulf's mind of Vidar sitting next to the bodies, covered in their blood and looking like some monster from the sagas of old. The two of them leaving the burning hut. Ulf remembered fighting the bear. He realized he couldn't see out of his right eye. As he moved his hand to his face, he saw it had been bandaged. He wondered about that as he felt the right side of his face and to his shock, he found it was covered with something sticky. Ulf prayed to the gods he hadn't lost his eye. He started to panic and wanted to rip the covering from his face when he heard a voice that sounded oddly familiar to him.

"Do not do that, Ulf!" came the commanding voice of a woman.

Ulf froze. He turned to the sound of the voice and saw a woman watching him from the partitioning which separated the sleeping chambers from the rest of the house. She had a long slender face with pronounced cheekbones and a pointed chin. Her blonde hair was braided into a thick braid which came over her shoulder. Even in the dim light, Ulf could see she was quite beautiful, in spite of the stern look on her face.

"How do you know my name?" Ulf asked after taking a few breaths to calm himself. He glanced at Vidar, thinking he had told her but remembered Vidar couldn't speak. He looked back at the woman as she came closer to inspect his face. He saw her more clearly now; she looked a few winters older than Brynhild. Ulf noticed her wise green eyes, bright like a new blade of grass.

"I would know the son of Bjørn anywhere. Even if I hadn't seen him or his father for more winters than I care to count," she said as she gently pulled the covering off Ulf's face. Ulf felt a sharp stinging pain as it snagged on something, but she managed to pull it off without hurting him.

"My eye?" he asked as he saw dried blood on the covering. Three neat red lines. He realized now why he could smell honey so strongly. It had been used on the wounds on his face to help them heal.

"Your eye is fine," she reassured him. "The bear missed it by a finger's width. You should thank the gods for that." She wiped his face with a damp cloth, cleaning away the dried blood. "Luckily, the cuts aren't too deep. You'll be left with scars, but they shouldn't affect you otherwise."

"Thank you," he said, although he was not sure why. He felt uncomfortable around this woman. She seemed familiar to him, but he still couldn't place her. He saw her glance at his hand and saw the curiosity in her eyes. "Where are we?" he asked before she could say anything about it.

"We?" She had a confused expression on her face.

"Me and Vidar," he said pointing to the boy, still sitting in the same spot. For a moment Ulf was worried he was the only person who could see him.

The woman looked at Vidar with a warm smile. The way Vidar beamed back at her, told Ulf the two of them were already acquainted. "Vidar," she repeated with a warmth he didn't expect from her. "That's a fitting name," she said in a knowing voice. "You don't remember me, Ulf?"

Ulf studied her face again, taking in as much detail as he could in the dim light, but could not. Ulf felt a headache starting in the back of his head. "No, I'm sorry."

She smiled at him. "Don't be. It's been a long time since you were here, and I can see you have been through a lot recently." She regarded the scar at his side. He had been so distracted by his face and the new surroundings he had forgotten about that. But something she said caught his attention. He had only ever been in two places his whole life. And in the clearing, the warrior, he said something as well, but Ulf could not recall what it was.

"There was a man." Ulf was struggling to remember what he looked like. The harder he tried, the more his head started to hurt.

"My son."

"Your son?" Ulf was starting to remember now. *Snorri, son of Thorgils. Jarl Thorgils.* "Thorgilsstad," he groaned.

"Yes," she confirmed. "Welcome back, Ulf Bjørnson."

Ulf did not like to be reminded of his father. It was one of the reasons why he'd never been back here since they moved to the farm. "Don't call–"

"Ah, he is awake! See, Mother, I told you he wouldn't die." Ulf was interrupted by a loud voice. He turned and saw the man he had seen in the clearing.

"You." Ulf looked at the man. He had taken the braids out of his hair and wore it tied up on top of his head. He had no weapons with him but still looked dangerous.

"No, my friend. You," he said with a big grin that took the edge off his appearance and made him look surprisingly friendly. "I have never seen anyone fight a bear like that." He stopped when he saw the confused expression on Ulf's face. Ulf could not remember much of his fight with the bear. Most of it was a blur.

"I don't think your friend remembers what happened. Maybe you should fill him in, you've been happily telling the story to everyone else since yesterday," the woman said to her son.

Since yesterday? Ulf was even more confused now. "How long have I been here?"

"You've been here for two days," the woman responded, but she didn't look worried. "You had lost a lot of blood by the time my son got you here, so you'll be feeling a bit weak for a few more days. All you need to do is rest." She turned to her son and gave him a look that would frighten the frost giants. "So, no dragging him out of the bed until I say you can."

"Yes, Mother," Snorri responded with a mischievous grin. He grabbed a stool and sat down next to the bed.

"Come Vidar, let's get you something to eat." The woman took Vidar and led him out of the room. Vidar seemed happy to go with her, which made Ulf feel a little jealous.

"Girl, some ale for me and my new friend here," he said to a thrall who Ulf hadn't noticed. The thrall left and Snorri turned to face Ulf, the big grin back on his face again.

"You wouldn't give me your spear!" Ulf remembered, although he wasn't sure how. He tried to grab hold of Snorri. But Snorri was too fast, and Ulf just fell out of the bed.

"Well, I had my reasons." Snorri laughed as he helped Ulf to his feet.

"That I would kill you after I somehow survived the fight the bear?" Ulf retorted. As he got to his feet, the whole room started spinning so violently, Ulf thought a giant had picked up the house and thrown it. In his left eye he only saw sparks and, realizing his mistake, he collapsed to the ground.

"But you did survive the fight with the bear." Snorri smiled as he supported Ulf, but before he could help Ulf back onto the bed, his mother walked in.

"I told you he needed to rest!" she scolded Snorri and rushed over to check on Ulf. "By Frigg, you never listen." She was relieved that he had not re-opened the cuts on his face, but still he looked very pale.

"He lunged at me. What was I supposed to do?" Snorri protested, the smile still on his face.

"He wouldn't give me his spear," Ulf groaned. He wanted to explain himself to the woman. He wasn't sure why he cared.

"What does he mean by that?" She raised an eyebrow at Snorri.

"Well…" Snorri hesitated. He'd kept that part out of the story he'd been telling, knowing it made him look bad.

"Well?" the woman asked. She folded her arms across her chest, waiting for Snorri to explain.

"When he was fighting the bear, he asked me for my spear."

"And you didn't give it to him?"

"Not straight away."

"Why not, Snorri? The bear could have killed him."

"He acted strange when I told him who I was. I thought he might have been somebody who I had wronged in the past." Snorri's explanation was weak, but it was all he could come up with. His mother was not a woman to cross. "Besides, the bear didn't kill him," he added as if it could justify his actions.

"He got lucky. The gods must have helped him."

"No, Mother. The gods were there, but not to help." His voice had gone serious now. His mother regarded him and nodded. She understood. She also knew there was something else Snorri wasn't telling her.

The thrall walked in with two cups of ale, and after a look from the woman, she turned around and walked out again, taking the ale with her. Snorri was about to protest but decided not to.

"You know him?" Snorri asked. His mother had always been kind to strangers and believed in helping those in need, but never had he seen her be so compassionate before. Even letting him stay in their house. He remembered seeing the shock on her face when they brought him from the forest.

"You don't recognise him?" she asked her son. Snorri studied Ulf, who had fallen asleep again. He saw the square face, with the strong cheekbones. The straight nose and its round tip. His eyes, grey like the blade of his sword and filled with an intense anger. From his short beard, Snorri guessed Ulf was a few winters younger than him, but it looked like he had lived a difficult life. Snorri shook his head. He didn't know who this person was.

"This, my son, is the son of Bjørn. Your father's former champion," the woman said, without taking her eyes off Ulf.

Bjørn, Snorri thought. That was a name he had not heard in a long time. He remembered the large warrior from when he had been a child. Bjørn had always been very kind to him, but not to many others. Snorri also remembered the angry son and how he would fight anyone who mentioned his father; it didn't matter who it was. In the end, they had to leave as it was causing too many problems.

And Snorri had brought him back.

CHAPTER 5

Unfamiliar sounds woke Ulf up the next day. For a while he lay there on the soft feather mattress, feeling like he was floating on the clouds as he listened to the noises. He realized the sounds were women talking somewhere in the house. They were too far for him to hear what they were saying. It was strange to hear people talking. After weeks of living in the old man's hut, he had gotten used to the silence. Ulf decided he preferred the silence. The sounds of the women talking and laughing were starting to irritate him. That and the thought that he was back in Thorgilsstad. He had never wanted to come back to this place. Not after what it had taken from him. Even on the farm, they had barely spoken of Thorgilsstad. Olaf and Brynhild had decided to pretend it didn't exist until Olaf needed new tools for the farm which he could not make himself. Ulf had never gone with Olaf, always preferring to stay on the farm. But Ulf needed their help, so he had to keep his hatred of this place to himself.

His face started itching, which in his current mood did not help. He was about to scratch it when he remembered the scars. Gently he touched the right side of his face, feeling the three scabby lines which ran down his cheek. The woman had been right, the bear had come close to taking his eye. *Lucky me*, he thought as he gently stroked the scars on his face, feeling the itch from them slowly disappearing. He realized he could fit his thumb between the lines. Most of the right side of his face was now scarred. He wondered what Brynhild would say if she saw him now. He tried to push those thoughts from his mind, but it was like pushing the waves back with your hands. They always found a way through. Ulf heard a noise beside him. Turning his head, he saw Vidar sitting there with his over-sized hands resting on his lap.

"You been there the whole time?" Ulf was surprised he hadn't noticed him before. Vidar smiled and nodded, pointing at the dirty bowls on the floor which showed he hadn't even left his side to eat. "Help me up." Ulf was tired of lying in bed. It felt like all he'd been doing recently was lying in bed, recovering from some wound or another. He expected to feel dizzy again as he had the day before, but when Vidar helped him up, he was happy to find it did not come. But even sitting on the bed, he felt weak. Ulf remembered Snorri's mother telling him he would for a few days but he was still surprised by how weak he felt. He stood up on shaky legs, and were it not for Vidar supporting him, he would have fallen. The scar on his side felt tight, but he was glad it had now healed. Ulf smiled to himself, imagining what he must look like. Covered in scars, yet he had never even been in a battle. He was also shocked at how loose his trousers felt. He must have lost weight over the last few weeks. Ulf had never been a big man. Tall, but not big. It was hard to grow big when you lived on a small farm, with not a lot of food.

"You are up, I see." Ulf looked up at the sound of the woman's voice. It was the same commanding voice as the day before, but there was a hint of softness in it. Standing next to the partitioning was Snorri's mother. Her hair was the same as the day before, but the different coloured dress told Ulf he had slept another day away. "How do you feel today?" she asked him.

"Where's my tunic?" was all he could think to say, still leaning on Vidar for support.

"Your tunic was ruined by all the blood. And dirty."

"What am I supposed to wear then?" Ulf knew he shouldn't be difficult, but the thought of wasting another day irritated him.

Snorri's mother crossed her arms and stared at him, a hint of a smile in her eyes. "Just like your father."

"I'm nothing like my father."

"Do you even remember him?"

"I remember he abandoned me." Ulf clenched his fist. He did not like talking about his father.

"Your father died in battle; he did not abandon you." Snorri's mother was dismayed to discover this was what he believed. Bjørn had doted on his son, especially after Ulf's mother died. But Bjørn had been a warrior and the jarl's champion. He would never sit out of a battle, no matter the risks.

"Same thing. Olaf was more of a father to me than he was." Ulf let go of Vidar and straightened himself up. Clenching his fists, he glared at the woman. But she was not afraid. Instead of backing down, she stared at him with an intensity that almost quelled his own anger. Brynhild had always been a strong woman, but Ulf got the feeling this woman could make Brynhild seem meek.

"I'll get you one of Snorri's tunics. It might be too big for you, but it's better than nothing." With that, she turned and left. Ulf looked at Vidar who shook his head, not really understanding what that was about, while also silently reproaching Ulf for his behaviour.

"I know. I shouldn't have done that." Vidar gave him a questioning look. "I don't want to talk about it." Vidar shook his head again and went after Snorri's mother. "Great," Ulf muttered. He walked back to the bed and pressed down on it with his hand. He was not used to sleeping on something this soft. On the farm, he only had a bench to sleep on.

A thrall walked in with a folded tunic in her hands. "Lady Ingibjorg has asked me to bring you this," she said, handing the tunic to Ulf.

He turned to her and took the tunic, feeling the softness on the fabric. But he could not take his eyes off the girl. She wasn't tall, but not short either and had a slim body. She wore a simple shift which hid most of her body, but her breasts still managed to draw his eyes. The girl shifted on her feet, feeling uncomfortable with him staring at her body. She cleared her throat. Ulf looked up at the sound, paying attention to her face for the first time. She had an underrated beauty about her. Her delicate face had a small nose and mouth, which made her eyes seem bigger than what they were. Her brown hair was kept short, a style which was expected for thralls. But to Ulf, it seemed to suit her. He realized she was waiting for him to say something.

"Um…." he stammered, not knowing what to say. Even though she was just a thrall, he found it difficult to speak to her. The girl lost patience and left, rolling her eyes at him. As she walked away, Ulf could not help but look at her behind and only saw Snorri leaning against the partitioning with his arms folded and a big grin on his face when she walked past him.

"A real lady's man you are." Ulf found his friendly tone confusing. He still did not understand why Snorri treated him so warmly. "I'd be careful around her. She's Mother's favourite, many men have lost *things* for daring to touch her." He put enough emphasis on the word for Ulf to understand what he meant.

"We didn't have any thralls on my uncle's farm. Brynhild was the only woman there." Ulf felt he needed to explain.

"Aye, your aunt's not the same as a beautiful young thrall."

Ulf nodded. "Thank you for the tunic." He put it on, feeling the soft fabric almost stroking his skin. This tunic was softer than the ones he was used to wearing. Compared to this it felt like his old tunics scratched his skin. He caught himself wondering how he had managed to wear them all his life.

"Come on, let's go meet the others," Snorri said leading Ulf out. They walked past the partitioning and Ulf saw the longhouse he had been staying in for the past two days. It was bigger than Olaf's, much bigger. Even the central hearth was bigger. In the near corner, he saw a loom where the thrall who had given him the tunic was busy weaving something. It reminded him of Brynhild. She used to spend a lot of time weaving, constantly having to make new clothes for him and Olaf. Farming wasn't exactly kind to clothing. He also saw a red-headed boy, a winter or two younger than Vidar he guessed, sat on a bench near the entrance to the house. The boy glared at them with a hostility Ulf didn't expect or understand.

Snorri saw where Ulf was looking and shrugged. "Don't mind him, that's just my little brother." He glanced at the boy. "Would have been better off with a sister, she'd have bigger balls than him." He laughed at his own joke. The boy looked angry at the insult, which Snorri didn't bother to hide from him. Ulf got the feeling this happened a lot.

As they left the longhouse, Ulf was blinded by the bright sunlight, causing him to pause until his eyes adjusted. The sun still sat high, even though it was almost early evening, meaning Ulf had to shield his eyes from the glare. When Ulf managed to see again, he saw Snorri standing in the middle of a square. Children were running around, playing with wooden swords, laughing and screaming at each other. They were being chased by a few well-fed dogs, which were barking in excitement as they tried to take part in the game without understanding what it was. Thralls were also running around, but not with wooden swords and not laughing and screaming. Instead, they were silently carrying baskets or other things they needed to complete their tasks. In the distance, Ulf could hear the sound of metal striking metal. A smith's workshop, some distant memory told him. Above all of this was the sound of birds flying around and singing their songs. All this noise assaulted Ulf's ears, which were more used to the silence on the farm where he had spent most of his life.

"Welcome to Thorgilsstad!" Snorri exclaimed, his arms wide as he officially welcomed Ulf to his home.

Looking around the square, Ulf could not help but be impressed. The square was large enough to fit enough men to fill five ships. Turning, he faced the hall of Jarl Thorgils. It might not have been the biggest hall in Norway, but it was the biggest hall Ulf had ever seen. It was also the only hall he had ever seen. The walls were made of dark timber beams and were five times as long as they were wide. It was taller than the other houses around it, at least the height of three men in the centre, which meant even the biggest of men could stand comfortably inside. Not that there was a lot of standing in the hall. Men don't drink standing. This all supported the bowed roof, made of thatch, which gave the hall the appearance of an upside-down ship. At each end of the roof was a carving of a dragon's head, protecting the occupants from the evil spirits who come out at night to steal a man's soul. To enter the hall, you had to go through two large wooden doors decorated with carvings of the beasts of the forest. Supporting these doors were two doorposts with the images of elves carved onto them, as was the custom of the north men. Ulf vaguely remembered the hall from his childhood, before Olaf and Brynhild moved to their farm. But he did not remember it looking this impressive.

On either side of the hall were two longhouses. The one he had spent the last two days in, which he guessed belonged to the jarl and his wife – Ulf wondered where they had been sleeping – and another.

"That's my house," Snorri said, seeing him look at it. But Snorri said no more about it. There were more longhouses, smaller than the ones on either side of the hall, built around the square. Ulf guessed these were for the warriors who lived here with their families. He wondered whether his father had lived in one these with him, but then dismissed the thought. He didn't want to think of his father. Behind the houses, in the distance, Ulf could see more houses that looked like farms, with fields and animals around them. There was a forest in the distance where they could hunt for food and entertainment. In the centre of the square was something that caught Ulf's eye. There were three standing stones, the middle one taller than the other two. Walking towards them, Ulf saw they were statues dedicated to the gods. The middle stone had a carving of Odin, recognisable with the one eye and the two ravens on his shoulders. On his right was Thor, with his hammer, Mjöllnir, and on Odin's left, was Tyr. Ulf could tell because of the missing right hand, which had been bitten off by the giant wolf, Fenrir. All three gods were represented in war gear, wearing helmets and what could have been brynjas. Ulf was so transfixed by these he didn't hear Snorri walk up to him.

"These are the gods we worship. Odin as the father of all gods, Thor as our protector and Tyr, because we are all warriors here and he is the god of battle," Snorri explained. Ulf guessed he understood. There were so many gods it was hard to worship them all. Most people chose one or a few gods based on their needs. On the farm, Olaf and Brynhild always sacrificed to Frey. As the god of fertility, he was needed to ensure the crops would grow and the cows and goats reproduced. At the end of the square was a path that led to two wharves in the bay, which was surrounded by small forest-covered hills. Ulf remembered a time when a traveller from the north had visited Olaf's farm. He had told them of the huge mountains and the many waterfalls from the lands he was from. The traveller claimed the mountains were giants who had been caught by the sun and turned to stone. Ulf wasn't sure if he believed the story about the giants, but how else would you explain mountains as huge as the traveller described? He noticed a ship attached to one of the wharves, its mast removed.

"That's my ship," Snorri said proudly when he saw Ulf looking at her. "She is called Sae-Ulfr." Sea-Wolf. Ulf didn't know much about ships, but this one looked beautiful, even from this distance. She appeared sleek and fast with her long slender shape. Ulf pictured her slicing effortlessly through the waves. Behind the ship, on the other side of the bay, Ulf saw another hall, with a few buildings around it.

"Who lives there?" he asked Snorri, who was looking at a pretty thrall walking past.

"That's the hall of Jarl Amund, my father's kinsman." Snorri led Ulf to his father's hall.

"Your father isn't here?" Ulf asked. There were two wharves, but only one ship.

"No, my father's out raiding." Snorri looked towards the bay with a melancholic expression. "Come, there are people I want you to meet." He turned and led Ulf back to the hall and through the doors.

It took Ulf's eyes a few moments to adjust to the darkness inside. But once he could see, he realized the inside was just as impressive as what he'd seen outside. There were two rows of carved timber posts, which ran the length of the hall. A stone hearth, with a blazing fire, was in its centre. With no windows, the smoke had to go up and escape through a hole in the centre of the roof. The floor was nothing but pounded earth, adding an earthy aroma to the already smoky air. The walls were decorated with different coloured shields and different weapons, souvenirs of past battles. Benches and long tables lined the inside of the walls, where people could sit and drink, or sleep when they've had too much. At the far end of the hall, were two high seats made of darkened oak, one slightly higher than the other, where the jarl would sit beside his wife. Both seats were decorated with carvings, but from where Ulf stood, he couldn't see what they were. He assumed it would be of animals, maybe to match the doors. From there, the jarl could be seen by everyone during a feast. There were some people in the hall, some of them looked like thralls who were cleaning and stoking the fire to make sure it doesn't die down. There were also groups of men sat together, talking while they shared cups of what Ulf guessed was ale. The low murmur stopped when Snorri and Ulf walked through the doors as everyone stared at Ulf. Snorri ignored this and led Ulf to one of the groups. He guessed they were companions of Snorri.

"Now this bunch of goat-fuckers are my hirdmen." The men looked up and judging by their bleary-eyed expressions, they had been drinking for a while. But even through their drunken eyes, Ulf could still see the violence in their souls and realized with a shiver these men were killers. They were the type of man he needed to become if he wanted to avenge his family.

"Ahoy, is this the one who slew the spear with a broken bear?" one of them yelled in drunken greeting. Even sitting down, Ulf saw this one was shorter than the rest, but he had a squat frame with a thick neck wider than his head. He wore his long brown hair tied up, the sides of his head shaved and covered in tattoos of snarling beasts, a bear on one side and a wolf on the other. Violent eyes sat on top of a large round nose, which despite the few scars he had on his face, had not been broken. His short bushy beard was decorated with silver and gold rings, which Ulf guessed once belonged to other men.

"No, Thorbjorn. He killed the bear with a broken spear. Although it's a bit rude to use another man's spear. It's like using his wife," another one said. He was almost the opposite of Thorbjorn. Tall and slim, though you could see he had muscular limbs. His hair was the same reddish-blonde Ulf had seen on Snorri's brother in the longhouse. He had a flat face with thin lips and thick eyebrows. The other men in the group laughed at this, and after clinking their cups together got back to drinking. Ulf clenched his fists at this, feeling an insult in there somewhere.

"Don't mind these idiots," Snorri said. "They were almost there to help with the bear." Snorri looked Ulf in the eyes and Ulf was surprised to see the excitement in them. "The courage you showed in attacking that bear, Thor himself would be jealous." Snorri picked up two cups filled with ale and handed one to Ulf. "To the Bear-Slayer." He raised his cup. "SKAL!" he toasted and drained it, rivulets of ale running down his beard and dripping onto his tunic.

"SKAL!" everyone echoed before draining theirs. Ulf wasn't sure how to respond; he had never been the centre of attention before and wasn't sure if he liked it. Instead, he looked at the golden liquid in his cup which he did not feel like drinking.

"Did you really think I would try to kill you?" he asked Snorri who was getting a thrall to re-fill his cup.

"Huh, no. But if I gave you my spear and the bear decided to attack me, then how would I have protected myself?" he responded with an innocent expression on his face.

"You could always use that giant cock you are always bragging about," Thorbjorn put in, making everyone laugh again.

"Considering how his wife doesn't want him in her bed anymore, I bet that's the last thing the bear would've wanted," the tall one said, looking quite serious. This made the group laugh even more, with one of them falling off the bench.

"The bear was prettier than my wife," Snorri mused, scratching his stomach.

"Speaking of the bear. My axe, what happened to it?" Ulf asked. He had already lost his father's sword; he did not want to lose his uncle's axe. Especially not as he had sworn his vengeance on it.

"Your axe?" Snorri thought with a frown which made Ulf feel anxious. But then Snorri smiled and turned to one of the thralls,

"Go get the bundle I was keeping for our guest." As the thrall ran off, he introduced Ulf to the men. "Well, Thorbjorn you have now met, the tall one is Oddi, the son of Jarl Amund from across the bay and my kinsman."

"Oddi Viss they call me," he interjected, Viss meaning Wise.

"No, they bloody don't," one of the group said, which caused more laughter as Oddi's face went red.

"These two are the brothers, Brak and Brak. And the one on the floor in the dog piss is Asbjorn." They raised their cups as Snorri said their names. Asbjorn picked himself up from the floor and sat on the bench, smelling the wet patch on his tunic. Satisfied, he shrugged and took a drink from his jug. Ulf nodded in acknowledgement.

"The brothers have the same name?" Ulf asked, looking at them. They were easy enough to tell apart because one was fatter than the other.

"Aye, our father, who is also Brak, wasn't very inventive with names," the smaller brother replied.

"And it's also a family tradition that all men in our family have the name Brak. At least that's what our father tells us," the other one put in, "but you can call me Brak Drumbr. It means thick, as in thick-muscled," he added with a smile. The others laughed and this time Ulf could understand why. Drumbr did mean thick, but not thick-muscled. More like thick as in fat. The name fit him well.

The thrall returned carrying a large bundle in her arms. She placed it on the table and got back to her chores. The bundle was wrapped in a thick fur pelt and Ulf wondered if that was from the bear. Snorri unwrapped the bundle and Ulf saw his uncle's axe. Ulf picked up the axe, relieved he hadn't lost it. He ran his fingers over the names, feeling a strange comfort from them.

"Whose names are those on the handle of your axe?" Oddi asked, staring at the axe's handle with great interest.

"They're the names of my family." Ulf saw the glances between the men but wasn't sure what they meant. "They were killed by a man named Griml. He almost killed me too, but I survived thanks to Vidar." He decided not to mention the old man.

"That explains the scar on your side?" Snorri said. They had all seen it.

"It does," Ulf responded looking at the bear pelt. He didn't want to tell them the story, so he changed the subject. "What's this?"

"This is your reward for killing the bear," Snorri said as he picked up the pelt, after realizing Ulf wasn't going to explain. "It gets cold in the winter and the Bear-Slayer needs a bear pelt to stay warm." He handed the pelt to Ulf who was too stunned to speak.

"Why were you there?" he finally managed to ask.

"We were hunting... wolves," Thorbjorn explained, with a quick glance at Snorri. "Some bóndi and his family had been killed." Ulf was too transfixed by the bear pelt to catch the meaning in Thorbjorn's words.

"Aye. With my father out raiding, I am responsible for the safety of the village and the outlying farms. When we heard about the attack, we thought it could be a fun hunting trip. Got a bit more than we bargained for." He gave Ulf a slap on the shoulder.

Ulf didn't understand what was going on. Too much was happening too fast and he was struggling to keep up with it all. "Thank you," he finally said after he realized the others were staring at him.

Snorri smiled at him and lifted his jug. "To Ulf!" he exclaimed again.

"To Ulf!" they all echoed and drank deep.

CHAPTER 6

The next day, Ulf felt like he was dying. It felt like the dwarves of Svartalfheim were trying to tunnel out of his head. And that was before he had even gotten up. For a while he lay there with his eyes closed, because opening them was too painful. From the dry sourness in his mouth, he had a good idea about the cause of his suffering. He couldn't remember much about the night before but remembered drinking a lot. More than he thought was possible.

After being introduced to Snorri's hirdmen, he sat down with them as they carried on drinking. They still seemed wary of him, especially Thorbjorn, who kept looking at him with a guarded expression. But after a few hours of drinking, they warmed up to him. He had also been introduced to the rest of Snorri's crew, but couldn't remember their names. They had all wanted to hear the tale of how he fought and defeated the bear, but Ulf didn't want to tell it. He preferred just to sit and listen. Snorri, on the other hand, was happy to tell them. But with every re-telling, the story changed. By the end Ulf had been so drunk, he didn't even care anymore how the story was told. And now he was being punished. Ulf wondered if the gods ever felt like this after their legendary feasts.

Ulf felt somebody kicking his foot. At first, he ignored it, thinking it was a thrall who was cleaning. But the kick came again, harder this time. Reluctantly he opened his eyes and groaned at the pain this caused him. Even the dull light in the hall was too bright for him.

"Well, if it isn't the great Bear-Slayer," Ingibjorg said, a strong hint of sarcasm in her voice. She was standing over him with Vidar by her side, a big grin on his face.

"Do the gods get hangovers?" Ulf asked, covering his eyes with his hand.

"I wouldn't know. Besides, that's not important." She turned and walked away without explaining any further. Vidar stayed behind and sat on the bench.

"What's her problem?" Ulf asked, more to himself than to Vidar. But Vidar shrugged anyway. With the help of Vidar, Ulf got to his feet, but he felt unsteady. The hall seemed to be spinning a little, but Ulf guessed he was the only one who felt it, as no one else seemed aware of it. Ulf saw the thrall from yesterday approaching him with a cup in her hand.

"Lady Ingibjorg asked that I give you this. She said it will make you feel better." She handed Ulf the cup. As soon as he saw the ale inside, he felt his stomach clench and it took all his self-control not to vomit. Vidar noticed his discomfort and laughed a silent laugh.

"You seem to enjoy my suffering." Ulf glared at him. Vidar shook his head but couldn't keep the smile off his face. "It's because of that stuff that I feel like this," he said to the thrall. "How will it make me feel better?"

"I don't know," she responded.

Ulf took the cup and after a moment's hesitation drank from it. His stomach reluctantly accepted the ale and to his surprise, he managed to keep it down. He felt the fog clearing from his head and the spinning seemed to stop. *Maybe that's why the gods were always drinking mead and ale.* Ulf realized the thrall was still standing there, watching him with an expression he did not understand. "What is your name?" he asked, not knowing what else to say. He still felt uncomfortable around her.

"Hulda," she responded with a small smile.

"Hulda," he repeated. It meant hiding or secrecy. Ulf wondered if that implied something. He handed the cup back to her. "You were right, I do feel a bit better." From the corner of his eye, he saw Vidar looking past him. Following his gaze, he saw Lady Ingibjorg sitting in the jarl's high seat, watching them.

"I better go, I have a lot to do," Hulda said, seeing Ingibjorg as well, her voice soft but somehow strong.

"Do you know where I can find Snorri?" Ulf asked before she had a chance to leave. He saw some men sleeping on the floor and benches, but it didn't look like Snorri was amongst them.

"I think he is outside," she said before walking away. Ulf looked at Lady Ingibjorg again. She was still looking at him with her guarded expression. For some reason his face started to itch. He fought the urge to scratch but lost in the end and scratched around the scars, trying not to pull the scabs off.

"Let's go, I need some fresh air," he said to Vidar who was standing by his side now. As they left the hall, Vidar waved to Ingibjorg, who smiled in return. Ulf felt a tinge of jealousy. Somehow the two of them had formed a bond which he did not understand.

The sunlight blinded him as he left the hall. Like the day before, Ulf was met with the sounds of children laughing and screaming. Women were shouting at them and the dogs were barking after them. Even the smith's shop in the distance could be heard. Today, all these sounds were even more excruciating. He squeezed his eyes shut and rubbed his temples. "Remind me not to drink so much next time." Vidar had that grin on his face again, which Ulf was beginning to dislike. After adjusting to the light, he saw Snorri and his hirdmen by his longhouse next to the hall, checking their spears. None of the men were wearing any armour, but all had their swords or axes. Snorri saw Ulf and Vidar and waved them over.

"Here he is, our new hero and his pet!" Thorbjorn shouted when he saw them. Ulf could only grunt in response.

"Looks like you had a rough night." Snorri looked amused by the sight of Ulf. Ulf looked down and saw why. His tunic was covered in stains which he hoped was food but was pretty sure it wasn't. Ulf rinsed his face in a bucket of clean water, feeling the cool liquid soothe his itching scars, before walking towards Snorri and his men.

"Going hunting?" Ulf asked, suddenly feeling uncomfortable being surrounded by Snorri and his men now he had no ale in his veins. He sensed Vidar feeling the same next to him. The men looked even more dangerous in the bright sunlight and Ulf had to fight the urge to put his hand on Olaf's axe, as he now called it, which was tucked into his belt.

"Aye, hoping to catch some boar. There's a large male in the forest we've been unable to catch. He gave us the slip last time." Snorri didn't seem to sense their uncomfortableness.

"As I remember, it was Thorbjorn who slipped, or so he says," Asbjorn said. His hair was braided, like most of the men's. Only Oddi's hair was tied up with a leather thong.

"Looked more like he jumped out of the way," Brak Drumbr added to the annoyance of Thorbjorn.

"I fucking slipped. Why would I jump out of the way?" Thorbjorn said, defending himself.

"Maybe because the boar was bigger than you," Drumbr responded, laughing so hard he dropped his spear. Thorbjorn didn't seem that short. True, he was shorter than everyone here and only just taller than Vidar, but Ulf couldn't imagine a boar bigger than him.

"It was not!" Thorbjorn's face was turning red. This only made everyone laugh more. Snorri left the men to their bickering and led Ulf to one side.

"You don't have to join us if you don't want to," he said, something in his voice making Ulf feel even more uncomfortable. He looked to Vidar, who stood watching the other men argue. Ulf noticed the way people glanced at him as they walked past the group of men. They were suspicious of him, but Ulf could not understand why.

"SNORRI!" the shrill voice came before Ulf had a chance to say anything. All eyes turned to the woman standing in the door of the longhouse with a screaming baby in her arms. "How many times have I told you not to let those idiots near here?" She pointed at the men who were stunned into silence. A small boy appeared behind the woman, giving Snorri a gap-tooth grin.

"I don't think you have met my wife," Snorri said to Ulf, with not a hint of warmth in his voice. Her flaming red hair was tied on top of her head, and she had a small pig-like nose that seemed out of place on her face. "This is the *lovely* Gunnhildr," he said sneeringly.

"Lovely my arse," Thorbjorn whispered. Gunnhildr glared at him.

"And this little warrior," Snorri said as he picked up the boy who had ran to him while his mother was distracted, "is Thorgils." The boy had Snorri's face, but his mother's nose. It looked better on his face than hers. Young Thorgils smiled at Ulf until Ulf smiled back. "Look at that, you made the Bear-Slayer smile," Snorri laughed.

"Did you really kill a bear with only an axe?" the boy asked, his eyes as wide as the full moon.

Ulf looked to Snorri, who smiled, before answering, "Is that what your father told you?" The boy nodded his response. "Well, I guess that's what happened."

"Thorgils Snorrison! Come here!" Gunnhildr shouted. "And you lot, fuck off!" she added before turning back into the house.

"Love you too," Snorri responded, putting his son down and turning to Ulf. "It was an arranged marriage with another jarl. My father needed the alliance, so I got stuck with pig-face."

"She seems nice." Ulf was still staring at the door of the longhouse. Snorri gave him a dubious glance.

"Anyway, like I was saying. You don't need to join us on this hunt. From the looks of you, you need to rest, eat, get some meat back on your bones."

"I'd like to come, and besides, I think Vidar here could be quite useful in tracking down the boar. He grew up in the forest after all," Ulf said, pointing to Vidar. Vidar nodded enthusiastically.

Snorri looked like he was about to object before Thorbjorn interrupted them. "Are we going or not? Ulf can use my spare spear." He handed the spear to Ulf. Ulf took the spear, feeling the weight of it. He still felt weak, so he gripped the spear tightly in order not to drop it in front of Snorri and his men.

"Can I come too?" Everyone turned and saw Thorvald standing there. He was holding a spear, and on his back, Ulf saw a small bow with some arrows. There weren't many similarities between him and his older brother. Where Snorri was tall and thick-muscled, Thorvald was short and slim. He had narrow shoulders, instead of the broad shoulders of Snorri. Even their faces were different. "Mother said I could," he said before Snorri could reject him. Ulf heard the others silently cursing behind him. Snorri turned with a grunt and walked towards his men.

"Great. This'll be as fun as being fucked in the eye by a giant," Asbjorn grumbled as he took his spear and walked towards the forest.

A rolling thunder echoed around the men as they walked through the forest in search of their prey, causing them all to stop and look at the source. But they didn't look up to the sky at the grey clouds forming over their heads. Ulf patted his stomach.

"No wonder we haven't found anything to kill yet. Your stomach's like Heimdall's horn, Gjallarhorn," Thorbjorn complained. Somewhere in the forest, a raven cried, adding its voice to Thorbjorn's.

"That's not what Gjallarhorn sounds like," Oddi put in, stroking his bearded chin.

"What in Odin's name are you talking about?" Thorbjorn said, twisting his head to the side to look at Oddi.

"I think the Gjallarhorn would have a more mournful sound. Less growling and more moaning, like a sad sorrowful noise. Ulf's stomach sounds more like a wolf growling a threat."

"Is this another of your wise observations, Oddi Viss?" the smaller Brak brother asked, pronouncing Viss in a mocking tone.

"Well, I can't help it. These thoughts just come to me. Like they are sent to me by Kvasir, the wisest of the gods," responded Oddi, either not noticing Brak's tone or choosing to ignore it.

"Well, next time keep these thoughts to yourself, Oddi Óviss," Thorbjorn growled and then sped up to walk beside Ulf and Snorri. Óviss meant the opposite of wise.

Ulf noticed Snorri had been quiet for most of the day, only saying a few words when he needed to. He thought it might have been because of the confrontation Snorri had with his wife, or because his younger brother, Thorvald – who was walking at the back, had joined them. But now he wondered if it was something else.

"You going to tell us how this Griml killed your family?" Thorbjorn asked while pushing a low hanging branch out of the way with his spear.

"No," Ulf said, not liking Thorbjorn's attitude. All morning he had been goading Ulf.

"I find that a bit odd, I do." Thorbjorn glanced at Ulf, his eyes full of suspicion.

"That's your problem." He wondered why Snorri didn't say anything. It felt out of character, but then Ulf didn't really know Snorri that well. They were interrupted by a yell from behind. Ulf was surprised at how fast everyone turned and presented their spears to the threat as birds shot to the sky, screaming. The threat turned out to be Thorvald.

"I... I ..." he stammered while looking down at his feet.

"Spit it out!" Snorri snapped.

"I saw a... squirrel." Thorvald held his spear behind him.

"And a squirrel made you scream like a girl?" Brak Drumbr asked, the amusement obvious in his voice.

"It caught me by surprise!" Thorvald looked up for the first time, his embarrassment being replaced by anger. His hands went to his side, his knuckles white as they gripped his spear tight. This show of defiance only made Snorri's hirdmen laugh.

"By Loki, Thorvald Ragi thinks he can scare us," Brak Drumbr put in while laughing with the others. Ragi meant craven, an insult that stung the young Thorvald. His eyes started to water up, but he was determined not to cry in front of his brother and his warriors. Ulf didn't laugh with the others. He didn't know the boy well but thought they were harsh on him. He also noticed Snorri not laughing but staring at his younger brother with a hard look in his eyes.

"I am no craven," Thorvald whispered, his voice barely audible over the humming insects.

"Enough of this," Snorri said. The men stopped laughing but kept the smiles on their faces. "Let's keep going, we have a boar to kill." He gave one last contemptuous look at Thorvald before he turned and followed the trail Vidar had left for them. As the others followed, Thorbjorn fell in next to Ulf again.

"Why did you kill your uncle and aunt?" Thorbjorn asked after a while. Ulf stopped in his tracks, stunned by the question. "Did your uncle not let you fuck your aunt? Was that it? So, you killed him and had your way with her?"

Ulf glared at Thorbjorn. "I did not kill them," he said through gritted teeth. He looked to Snorri, but Snorri looked away.

"So you say. But Odin knows, I saw their bodies," Thorbjorn said as if that explained everything. "And I find it strange they all were killed, but you were not." The others moved into a large circle around the two of them.

"Snorri, what is this?" he asked, hoping Snorri would put an end to it. But Snorri said nothing.

"I think they made you angry and then you killed them. Slaughtered them like animals."

"Stop it." Ulf felt his anger rising. He felt the familiar heat in his chest as the flames were being stoked.

"You raped your aunt and killed her daughters."

"No!" He gripped his spear with both hands, trying not to lose control of himself.

"Did you rape them too? Or maybe you just made them watch?

"Enough!" Ulf charged at Thorbjorn. He didn't care that Thorbjorn was a warrior and a killer. Ulf swung his spear at Thorbjorn, who easily jumped aside. The spear struck the ground where he had been standing. Thorbjorn punched Ulf in his side, hitting him in the stab wound. Ulf felt the blinding pain as the air was knocked out of him and he collapsed on the ground. He lay there clutching his side, gasping for breath as Thorbjorn circled him, still holding his spear in one hand.

"You got balls, kid. But now you are dealing with a real warrior, not an old farmer." Thorbjorn looked at Snorri. "You still think he didn't do it?" Snorri didn't respond. He only looked past Thorbjorn at Ulf, who was slowly getting back to his feet, still clutching his side.

"I did not kill them," Ulf struggled to say as he tried to get air back into his lungs.

"I don't believe you." Thorbjorn turned to Ulf. He dropped his spear and drew his sword, Bloodthirst.

Ulf glared at him. He gripped his spear tightly, holding it in front of him. "I don't give a fuck what you believe, you ugly goat-fucking dwarf! The gods know the truth."

Thorbjorn smiled at the insult. He shrugged his shoulders before taking two quick steps forward and raising his sword. Ulf lifted his spear to block, but it was only a feint. Instead of bringing the sword down, Thorbjorn punched Ulf in the chest. Not hard enough to knock the air out of him again, but it still hurt. Ulf struggled to stand straight as he tried to breathe through the pain. Thorbjorn came at him again, jabbing and swinging his sword in a measured and deliberate attack, allowing Ulf to block with his spear or move out of the way but constantly pushing him back. To Ulf, it was like Thorbjorn was teaching a child the basics of swordplay. The grin on Thorbjorn's face showed Ulf this lesson could get him killed. Ulf wasn't sure why they blamed him for the deaths of his family, and why Snorri didn't stop this. He glanced at Snorri who still stood there, his arms folded and his face expressionless. The rest of the men were just as quiet; even the birds were. They were all watching and to Ulf, it seemed like they were waiting for Thorbjorn to get tired and kill him.

"Snorri, stop this!" he begged. He knew he could not defeat Thorbjorn. But Snorri only looked on. Ulf saw the sword swing almost too late and managed to deflect it using his spear. He saw a chance as Thorbjorn's strike left him exposed and brought the butt of his spear up to hit Thorbjorn in his head. But Thorbjorn expected the move and caught the spear with his free hand. He smiled at Ulf before punching him in the face with his sword hand. Ulf staggered back but managed to stay on his feet. He could feel his eye swelling up, but did not feel any pain, not yet. His biggest problem now was that he had lost his spear, which Thorbjorn was still holding onto.

"You really should keep hold of your weapon," Thorbjorn said, looking at the spear in his hand. "Tyr only knows how you managed to defeat your uncle." He had an arrogant sneer on his face as he dropped the spear. Before Ulf could respond, Thorbjorn attacked again. A flurry of sword swings that Ulf always just managed to avoid.

Again, Ulf felt Thorbjorn was toying with him. That he could kill Ulf whenever he felt like it but decided not to. His left eye was starting to blur, and he felt the dull pain on that side of his face. Ulf's side was also hurting from where Thorbjorn had hit him. The pain made twisting out of the way difficult, but he had no choice. Thorbjorn came at him again, swinging his sword in a wide arc. Fed by his anger, Ulf jumped aside, mirroring the move Thorbjorn got him with and punched Thorbjorn in the face. It was not a hard punch, Ulf didn't have the strength for a hard punch, but it was enough to make Thorbjorn stumble backwards. Instinctively, Ulf followed up and kicked Thorbjorn in the chest, sending him flying onto his back. Ulf picked up the spear and pointed the tip at Thorbjorn's neck, placing his boot on his chest so he couldn't get up. He sensed the others reacting without having to look at them. But he didn't care about them as he fought to control the anger racing through his veins.

"I did not kill them!" he shouted at Thorbjorn, spit flying from his mouth. Thorbjorn only smiled back.

"Enough!" Snorri ordered, stopping his men from making the situation worse. He took a step forward. "Ulf, step away from Thorbjorn."

Ulf looked around him while he caught his breath. He saw the others creeping closer, their spears pointing at him. With a look at Snorri, he dropped the spear and took a step back. Vidar came through the undergrowth and ran to Ulf's side, baring his teeth at everyone like a young wolf.

"It's ok, Vidar," Ulf said. He placed a hand on Vidar's shoulder to keep it from going to his aching side. His face was hurting now, and he realized he couldn't see much out of his left eye. "If they wanted me dead then I'd be dead already." Ulf watched Thorbjorn, who was getting to his feet. He had a satisfied smile on his face as he wiped the blood from a cut on his upper lip with the back of his hand.

"Well, that was fun," Thorbjorn said, sheathing his sword and picking the spear up. He walked to Ulf and presented it to him. Ulf hesitated but then took the spear. The men relaxed at that, as if it was some kind of peace agreement. "So, if you didn't kill them, then what happened?"

Ulf was too tired from the fight to do it again. He dropped his head and took a deep breath, trying to calm himself down. "Did you really see them?"

"Yes," Snorri answered. "Some traders came a few weeks ago, said they stopped by Olaf's farm as they always do. But they only found death. My father sent us to investigate." He took a step towards Ulf. "I know you didn't do it. I don't know how, but I know it. But there are others who think you did, especially those who remember you as a child."

"Like your father?"

"Perhaps, although he didn't say anything to me."

"And you, Thorbjorn, you really believe all those things you said?"

"I don't know, lad. But after fighting you, I don't think you could have done." Ulf looked confused, so he explained, "Your uncle died fighting, and Snorri said he had been a good warrior."

"So, this was a test to see if I was good enough to have killed my uncle!" Ulf grit his teeth, his pains forgotten as he took an angry step towards Thorbjorn.

Thorbjorn just looked at him with an amused expression. "Something like that. We had to be sure, lad," he explained.

"Everybody found it strange their bodies were there, but yours wasn't. And then you show up alive and well-ish." Snorri looked around him as the others agreed. "You have to admit, Ulf, that does seem a bit strange. A bit Loki-like."

"I told you. Vidar found me"

"A small boy carried you away from there and then sealed your wound," Snorri said with a raised eyebrow.

"It might be possible judging by the size of those hands," Brak Drumbr said, pointing at Vidar's large hands. But nobody was paying attention to him. They were all waiting for Ulf to respond.

Ulf looked at Vidar, who nodded, somehow understanding what Ulf wanted. Ulf briefly wondered if this might actually be Odin's son. "There was an old man."

"What old man?" Snorri asked.

"An old forest godi. He'd been living in the forest near our farm for as long as I can remember. He used to trade with my uncle for supplies. He and Vidar found me and took me away after realising I was still alive," Ulf explained. He was struggling to stand straight from the pain in his side.

"And where is this forest godi now?" Asbjorn asked, his tone unbelieving.

"Dead. Vidar killed him." Ulf eyed Vidar as he said this. Vidar puffed out his chest and could not hide the smile on his face.

"Why would Vidar kill him?" Oddi asked.

"He had his reasons." He saw the others weren't sure if they should believe him. "It's his story to tell, not mine."

"How the fuck is he going to tell us the story! The boy can't speak!" Asbjorn flung his arms in the air, scaring the birds out of the tree behind him.

"We could always use some Loki magic. That should get him talking," Oddi suggested.

"Do you know any Loki magic?"

"No, not really. That is a problem," Oddi admitted.

"You said some Griml killed them? Who is he?" Snorri asked, interrupting the other two to get back to the topic at hand. "And why haven't we heard of this Griml?"

"I don't know who he is." Ulf told them the story of what happened that day. How he had tried to kill Griml and failed. How he found out everybody was dead, and that his father's sword had been taken. It was not easy, but he didn't feel like the others were judging him for his failures. Everybody was silent when he finished.

"Well?" Oddi asked Snorri.

"I believe him." He regarded Ulf for a while before asking, "What do you plan to do?"

"What?! Just like that!" Asbjorn turned to Snorri. "He gets a lucky punch on Thorbjorn and now we all believe he didn't do it?"

"You saw for yourself, Asbjorn. The kid is not a great fighter." Thorbjorn shrugged at Ulf to show he meant no offence. "Fenrir has a better chance of breaking Gleipnir than Ulf has of killing his uncle in a fight."

"He could have killed him in his sleep," Asbjorn countered before turning to Ulf and pointing his spear at him. Ulf stood there not knowing what to do. He didn't want to fight Asbjorn. And from the look on Asbjorn's face, it looked like Asbjorn would kill him.

Snorri moved fast and stepped in between Ulf and Asbjorn so the spear was now pointing at his neck.

"Lower your spear, Asbjorn," Snorri growled at him. "Ulf did not kill his family. There is no way he could have done it. You saw the same thing we did. Olaf died fighting." The spear wavered as Asbjorn thought this through. The rest of the men were tense, unsure of how to respond.

"Fine." Asbjorn lowered his spear to the relieve of everyone. "But I'll be watching him."

Snorri nodded and turned to Ulf, "What will you do, Ulf?" he asked as if nothing had happened.

"I want to find Griml and kill him. I want to avenge their deaths," Ulf said with conviction. He took Olaf's axe from his belt and showed them the names he had carved on the handle. "I have sworn an oath to Odin that I will avenge my family."

Snorri smiled. "That day, in the clearing when you fought the bear. I saw something I did not understand," his eyes intensified, "until now. I will help you."

"What?" Ulf was stunned. He saw from the expressions on the others' faces they didn't expect this either.

Snorri held up his hand to silence him. "I feel our lives are tied somehow. I don't know what the Norns have planned for you, but I'll be there to help you." Ulf didn't know what to say.

"Help him how?" Thorbjorn asked with a sideways glance at the other men. "Run around and look for Griml?"

"Midgard's a big place, a lot of hiding places. It'll be even harder than when Thor hunted Loki for plotting the death of Baldr," Oddi added.

"You think this Griml changed himself into a salmon like Loki did?" Brak Drumbr asked, scratching his head as if he thought it was possible.

"I never said I'd go hunting for Griml," Snorri said before anyone could respond to Brak Drumbr, and when he saw the disappointment on Ulf's face, he added, "I have a duty to my father. But we can teach you how to fight like a real warrior, not a farmer. After that, it's up to the Norns; they control our fate."

Ulf thought about this. He knew he couldn't ask for more from them, but if he could learn to fight like they did, then he'd be able to get his revenge. "Fine by me." He held his hand out which Snorri took and the two men shook on their deal.

"I need a drink, all this made me thirsty," Thorbjorn said, happy this was done.

"Aye, good idea," Brak agreed.

"Where's Thorvald?" Snorri looked around and realized his brother was not there anymore.

"Must have run off when the fight started," Oddi ventured.

"Coward," Thorbjorn put in.

"Vidar, did you see him?" Snorri asked. Vidar shook his head. He'd been watching the fight, not paying attention to Thorvald. "Thor's balls! Come on, let's just hope he went back to the village. Tonight, my brothers, we celebrate!" He turned and walked back to his father's hall, knowing the way without needing to orientate himself. The others followed, cheering in anticipation of another night's drinking.

CHAPTER 7

They found Thorvald waiting for them in the square. He stood straight-backed and arms crossed, looking like a conqueror who was watching his fallen foes grovel for mercy. And he had a good reason to. Standing beside him, also straight-backed and arms crossed, was Lady Ingibjorg. But unlike Thorvald, there was no smug look on her face. Instead, she wore the look of a disappointed mother as she watched her son and his men approach.

"What were you thinking?" she demanded by way of greeting.

"I don't know what you are talking about, Mother," Snorri responded as innocently as possible.

"Don't play dumb with me. Thorvald told me what you did."

"What did we do? We went looking for that large boar we've been trying to catch."

"Thorbjorn attacked Ulf!" She glared at Thorbjorn as she said this. She knew exactly what he had done. Thorbjorn tried to make himself even smaller than he was.

"Relax, Mother. It was a misunderstanding." Snorri spread his arms in a conciliatory pose.

"A misunderstanding?" she repeated in a condescending tone. "What kind of misunderstanding leaves Ulf with a swollen eye and Thorbjorn with a bloodied lip?" She turned her gaze to Thorbjorn, seeing how his moustache had absorbed the blood.

"I'm fine, Lady Ingibjorg. Really, it was as Snorri said. A misunderstanding." Ulf felt he had to say something.

"Do not Lady Ingibjorg me!" she snapped at him. "You are our guest. You should be treated with respect. On top of that, you are injured."

"What did Thorvald tell you, Mother?" Snorri looked at Thorvald, his smug expression disappearing as he realized where Snorri was going with this. "He ran away before anything happened."

Ingibjorg shifted her glare from Ulf to Snorri. "He might not have seen everything, Snorri. But do not take me for a fool. I know how much you and your men like to fight." She passed her green eyes over everyone as she said this, making all of them drop their heads a little. Even Ulf felt cowed by her. Around them, people were pretending not to be paying attention, but Ulf could see the constant glances aimed their way as the villagers were trying to eavesdrop.

"I apologise, Mother. But we had to find the truth about what happened to Olaf and his family," Snorri explained, hoping this would calm his mother's ire.

"And how does a fight in the forest do that?" she scolded him. "Thorbjorn could have killed Ulf."

Thorbjorn opened his mouth to speak, but the look Ingibjorg gave him made him realize it was best to keep quiet.

"I..." Snorri started and then realized he didn't know how to answer her. He took a deep breath, trying to calm his nerves. He would rather face an enemy shield wall, intent on ripping him to pieces, than face his mother when she was in this mood.

Lady Ingibjorg only shook her head. "Did your misunderstanding help you discover the truth?" she asked when she saw Snorri wasn't going to answer.

"It did," Snorri responded, looking relieved when he understood his mother was ending this conversation. "Ulf couldn't have killed Olaf."

"You all agree with this?" she asked them. They all nodded – apart from Asbjorn, she noticed. Ingibjorg watched the group, seeing them shuffle from foot to foot. Part of her enjoyed making experienced warriors squirm like children. "Good, but do not let this happen again." With that, she turned to leave.

"That's all!" Thorvald complained. "You aren't–"

"Enough, Thorvald!" she said, silencing him. He looked back at his brother and his men and decided it was best to take his mother's advice.

The next day they were in the hall, digging through some old chests to find armour for Ulf. "Here, you can use this." Snorri gave Ulf an old leather jerkin.

"Can't I get a brynja, like your men have?" Ulf studied the vest made of thickened leather, worn smooth over the years.

"You need to prove you are good enough to wear a brynja," Snorri responded, before handing him a bowl helmet. Ulf wanted to argue, but realized it was pointless.

"Brynjas are expensive and much sought-after," Brak explained. "Wearing one in battle shows you are a great warrior, but it also makes you a target. Warriors will be flocking your way, desperate to prove themselves and take that brynja from you."

The first day of training did not go well for Ulf. They were using blunted swords and axes covered with thick leather, instead of the sharpened weapons that Olaf liked to use. This meant Snorri and his men did not hold back, as Ulf found out after a few heartbeats as he lay on the ground, nursing a sore arm.

"Your uncle might have taught you how to fight, but we will teach you how to kill and survive," Snorri said to Ulf, his expression showing they weren't playing games. Ulf got back to his feet and picked up the axe he was using. The leather jerkin was uncomfortable. Ulf was not used to wearing things like this and felt restricted. The thick woollen tunic he wore underneath, although necessary, only made things worse in the hot summer sun. Ulf was hot, uncomfortable and hurting, but he was determined not to give up. He had to avenge his family, and he understood to do that, he had to learn everything he could from these trained killers.

"You think too much," Snorri said a week later after Ulf found himself on the ground again. He had been sparring against Brak, but as with the others, Ulf was no match for him. "It makes you slow and predictable," he continued after seeing the confused expression on Ulf's face, as he got back to his feet.

"Are you not supposed to think when you fight?" Ulf asked.

"Only if you want to die," Thorbjorn said, as bluntly as always.

"How do you think you killed the bear?" Snorri asked before Ulf could respond to Thorbjorn.

"With a spear?"

Snorri laughed. "Yes, and with instinct. You did not have time to think, the bear would have killed you otherwise. Every time you dodged it and moved out of the way, that was instinct." He turned serious. "I know you don't like talking about your father, but my father had always said fighting was in his blood. My father told me your father had boasted his family were descended from Tyr, and war flowed through their veins."

His uncle had told him something similar once. "That didn't help me or my uncle when Griml came to our farm." His face darkened as he remembered that day; one he'd thought about every day since.

"Perhaps, but you weren't properly trained. Next time the two of you meet, it'll be a different story," Snorri smiled. "Now, let's go again, but this time don't think about it, just do it. Again." He nodded to Brak.

Brak attacked before Ulf had time to set himself, aiming high in an attack that would have sliced Ulf's head off, if Ulf hadn't ducked below the swing. He felt the air move on the back of his neck, before straightening up. Brak reversed the swing, not giving Ulf enough time to bring his shield up. Ulf jumped back to avoid the backhanded cut. He saw his opening and attacked with a chop that would have broken Brak's collarbone if he hadn't gotten his shield up in time. The men parted briefly, before Brak attacked again, not allowing Ulf to think about what was happening. He defended instinctively as he deflected a stab from Brak with his shield but did not see the shield punch which pushed him back a few steps. Brak followed up with another lunge, which Ulf took on the shield, before twisting out of the way. He did not want to be caught out again. But Brak did not punch with his shield. Instead, he stood his ground and followed Ulf's movement. He saw Ulf bring his axe around for a counterattack and ducked under Ulf's arm. As Ulf's axe went over his head, he shoved Ulf hard in the chest. Ulf felt the shove and knew there was nothing he could do as he fell to the ground again.

"Better," Snorri said as he watched Ulf lying on the ground, breathing heavily from the short fight. "But you still think too much."

They were interrupted by a shepherd boy running down the hill, screaming as if he was trying to wake the gods. "Ships! Ships!"

"Think that could be your father?" Oddi asked, looking out to the bay where they could see three ships in the distance.

"Aye, I think it might be." He covered his eyes to block out the sun and stared at the approaching ships. "They're not travelling very fast, so it's not an attack."

Ulf was surprised they were so calm. "How can you be sure it's not an attack?"

"They're travelling too slow," Snorri responded, his eyes still on the ships. "When you attack a settlement on the beach, you come in as fast as you can, so they don't have time to prepare a defence. And besides, only those who know these waters can navigate past the islands in the mouth of the bay. And all the people who know these waters are sworn to my father."

"Aye, the speed these are coming at, you could have a few jugs of ale and sober up again before they arrive," Thorbjorn said, scratching his neck.

The shepherd boy was still running around telling everybody about the ships; a few dogs were following him now, barking in excitement and adding to the noise. Ulf saw Ingibjorg walking out of her longhouse with Vidar in tow.

"Looks like your dog has a new master," Asbjorn sneered, seeing where Ulf was looking.

"He's not a dog," Ulf responded defensively, but it did seem like Vidar preferred spending time with Ingibjorg these days. He shook his head to dispel the thought and focused on the ships.

"Let's go and greet our arrivals," Snorri said. He walked to the hall and dropped his shield. After giving his helmet to a waiting thrall, he went to the wharf, his hirdmen a step behind him. Asbjorn waved for Ulf to join them. Ulf did not like the look in Asbjorn's eyes but decided to follow.

"Looks like your father," Ingibjorg said as they reached the wharf. She was wearing a long-sleeved blue dress decorated with two beautifully carved brooches. Her blonde hair was braided and tied into two separated knots on the back of her head. Her lips had been reddened, but Ulf didn't understand how she had done that. It wasn't something he had ever seen Brynhild do. She also had a colourful glass bead necklace around her neck, the likes of which Ulf had never seen before. He guessed Thorgils had brought it back from a raid. It must have taken her a long time to get ready and Ulf wondered how she knew her husband would return today. The area around the wharf was now crowded with the wives and children of the returning warriors. The air was a strange mix of excitement and nervousness as the families waited to see if their men had returned safely.

"Aye, that does look like it could be Thorgils' Pride and next to her, War-Bear and Sea-Eagle," Snorri smiled. He glanced back at Ulf and could not hide the nervous look on his face.

"You'll finally get to meet the jarl," Asbjorn added in an amused tone.

"Yes, that will be very interesting to see," Ingibjorg smiled. Ulf turned his attention back to the bay – awed by the sight of the three sleek Snekkjas as they glided through the water with menacing grace. All three ships sat low in the water, so low you could reach over the side and get your hand wet. He watched as the pairs of oars rose and dipped in unison, hearing the sound as they hit the water. Even with their sails tied up, they were still a frightening sight as they approached. Vidar had the same awed expression on his face; he gave Ulf a big smile, unable to hide his excitement. Turning back to the ships, Ulf noticed they didn't have the beast heads mounted on the front. His uncle's words entered his mind.

They only mount the beasts when they approach the foreign shore. When the raiders return home, they remove them so as not to scare the spirits of their homeland. Ulf wasn't sure if that was true, but he guessed he would find out one day. As the ships got closer, he saw one was bigger than the others. That had to be Snorri's father's ship, Thorgils' Pride. Ulf wondered how many men she could take.

"Thorgils' Pride has a crew of fifty men, fifty-two if you include my husband and his steersman," Ingibjorg said. She always seemed to know what people were thinking. Ulf touched the Mjöllnir around his neck and saw Ingibjorg smile at the gesture. Thorvald appeared by his mother's side. He was wearing one of his fine tunics and trousers and simple leather shoes with barely a mark on them. His hair was neatly brushed back, and Ulf guessed if he had been old enough to have a beard, that would have been combed as well. Snorri by comparison looked dirty and unkempt.

The ships finally reached the wharves, one docking on each side. An older version of Thorvald was the first to climb off the ship. Jarl Thorgils had a face which had once been oval-shaped but was now more rounded. He wore a scowl which looked like a permanent feature, accompanied by many deep wrinkles. His long red hair, tied behind his head, was speckled with grey, and matched his beard and long moustache with rings tied to their ends. Thorgils smiled when he saw Ingibjorg walking towards him, the scowl still firmly in place. He looked like a man who spent a lot of his time worrying about things. Even though his body was slightly rounded with age, he still had the bearing of a warrior. Thorgils wore a sword and an axe on each side and a small sax-knife on the front. On his arms, Ulf could make out a few arm-rings, in silver and gold. This was a jarl who made his fortune in war.

Next to get off was a huge man. Taller than Ulf, he had broad shoulders and a narrow waist. He had thick muscly arms and a massive barrel-like chest. In one hand he carried a large two-handed axe, which Ulf guessed was his main weapon, but he also had a silver-hilted sword on his waist. The warrior moved with the fluidity of a man who had spent his life fighting, and despite his size, seemed very light on his feet. He was not a person you wanted to face in a shield wall, Ulf decided.

"Who is the big guy?" Ulf asked to no one in particular.

"That is Ragnar Nine-Finger," Brak answered, his respect for the warrior evident in his voice. "The jarl's champion and the best warrior people here have seen since your father, they say."

"Nine-Finger?" Ulf asked, looking at Ragnar's hands.

"Aye. They say he lost his finger in a bet."

"A bet?" Ulf turned to Brak, with a raised eyebrow.

"I swear on Freya's tits. He was gambling, they say, and ran out of gold. He felt his luck was about to change so he bet his little finger on his left hand. But Loki was watching this, and he made sure Ragnar lost. Ragnar cut his own finger off and gave it to his opponent, who many believe was Loki in disguise."

Ulf was trying to work out if Brak was making fun of him, but he looked sincere. "What were they betting on?"

Brak scratched his beard, trying to remember. "I think it was over two sea eagles fighting over a fish."

"And Ragnar's eagle lost?"

"No, he bet on the fish," Brak said, like it was a natural thing to bet on. Ulf could only shake his head as he tried to understand the story.

"Father, welcome home!" Snorri clasped his father's arm and patted him on the shoulder. Thorgils did the same; he looked pleased to see his eldest son. "The raid was successful, I take it."

"Thanks to the mighty Odin, it was." He looked towards Ulf as he said this. There was an instant change in his face. The smile was replaced by scowl more serious than the one he appeared to naturally wear, and his face turned red.

"What in Odin's name is he doing here?"

CHAPTER 8

"Father, this is—"

"I know exactly who he is," Thorgils interrupted his son, his icy glare still focused on Ulf. Thorgils' face creased as he bared his teeth, making his wrinkles even deeper. He turned to Snorri, yelling in his face, "I want to know why he is here. In my home!" Snorri took a step back, trying to avoid the spit flying towards him.

"He's my guest," Snorri said in a firm voice. His eyes flicked towards Thorvald who had a big smile on his face.

"Your guest!" Thorgils took a step towards Snorri. Everyone had gone quiet, even the birds flying above. To Ulf, it seemed as if the whole bay had stopped to watch the confrontation, everyone and everything holding their breath. "After what he has done!"

"I know what he has done, Father." Snorri squared his shoulders and faced his father. He respected his father but knew he could not appear weak. "And what he hasn't."

The only person not nervous about this confrontation was Thorvald. "I told him not to, Father." He took a step away from his mother and towards his father. "But he wouldn't listen to me." He was now standing by his father's side, looking as smug as a dog who had managed to steal his master's food.

Snorri growled at Thorvald, like an older wolf growls at a young pup for straying too close to its meal. Thorvald flinched as he took a step back. Vidar looked nervous as he hid behind Ingibjorg. He was about to go towards Ulf when Ulf signalled for him to stay where he was.

"Ragnar!" Thorgils shouted for his champion without taking his eyes off Snorri. "Seize this man. And kill my son if he gets in your way." A collective gasp rose from the crowd. Ulf watched the jarl's champion drop the chest he had been carrying in one hand and gently put the axe down from the other, before rolling his shoulders to loosen them. The thud of the chest hitting the wharf made a child cry in shock. His mother tried to calm him, but never took her eyes off Ragnar. Snorri tensed as Ragnar started walking towards them with the confidence of a man who knew he could not lose.

"It's ok." Ulf put a hand on Snorri's shoulder and took a step forward, putting himself between Snorri and Ragnar. He had not killed his family and was fed up being accused of it. Ulf clenched his fist as he watched Ragnar getting bigger and bigger with every step. But as Ulf watched the champion, he realized he wasn't seeing Ragnar anymore. Instead, he saw the troll from his dreams. His heart started beating faster, spreading the flames of his anger until Ulf could not take it anymore. With a roar of defiance, he ran at Ragnar who was briefly stunned by this unexpected move. But Ragnar was a warrior of reputation, so he recovered quickly and threw a straight jab. Ulf ducked below the jab and ran past Ragnar. Once past his shoulder, Ulf turned and launched himself into the air. Using this momentum, Ulf threw a hard punch, catching Ragnar on the side of his face as he turned to follow Ulf's run. The punch was enough to drop Ragnar to one knee. Shocked whispers came from the crowd;

no one had ever done that to Ragnar Nine-Finger before. Ulf took a step back while shaking his right hand, but Ragnar just got back to his feet with a smile in the corner of his mouth.

"Now you die, pup," Ragnar said before storming at Ulf. Ulf braced himself, trying to remember what Snorri and his men had taught him. But all his mind could do was see the troll charging at him, his mouth open in an angry snarl that would give children nightmares. Ragnar threw a hook, which Ulf avoided, but the follow up punch caught Ulf in the chest. He landed on the wharf with a thud. Ulf had never felt anything hit him that hard. It was like Thor had struck him with Mjöllnir. He struggled to breathe as he saw Ragnar standing over him, a satisfied grin on his face. Ulf tried to move, but it felt like Thor had left his mighty hammer on his chest, the legendary weight of it too heavy for Ulf to lift. It reminded Ulf of his uncle and their last sparring session. His uncle who was now dead; dead because of him. Ulf grit his teeth as the memories added more wood to the fire in his veins, giving him the strength to get back on his feet. Ragnar was surprised – not many had managed to get up from a punch like that. Ulf stood rigid as he breathed in deeply, trying to douse the fire coursing through him.

"Your funeral, pup," Ragnar said and threw another jab at Ulf's already-bruised face. Ulf twisted out of the way, surprising Ragnar and punched him in the stomach. Ragnar smiled at Ulf, amused the young man thought he could hurt him. Before Ulf could do anything, Ragnar grabbed hold of him. He lifted Ulf up and threw him down onto the wharf. The wharf shook from the impact, making Ragnar worry he might have broken it. But when he didn't fall into the water, he smiled. Ulf, on the other hand, did not worry about the wharf as he lay on it. His pain-filled mind was trying to work out how he ended up on his back again. He tried to get up, but his arms felt weak.

"Stay down, Ulf!" He heard Snorri shout. *Never,* Ulf thought as he struggled to get back on his feet again. He stared at Ragnar, seeing the amused smile on the warrior's face. Ulf set himself again, gritting his teeth against the pain from his chest. Being thrown on the ground did not help his hurting body. Ulf attacked again with a swinging punch, but Ragnar simply took a step back, batting the punch away like he was swatting a fly. He grabbed Ulf by the throat, squeezing hard as he watched Ulf's eyes bulge.

"I'm bored with this now," Ragnar pulled back his arm for what would be the fight-ending punch.

"Enough!" Ingibjorg's voice stopped Ragnar's arm as effectively as a shield. He turned to her with a look of confusion as he still held Ulf by the throat.

"What is the meaning of this!" Thorgils demanded of his wife.

She turned to face Thorgils. "You have not been here for many weeks, my husband." She walked towards him and took his hands in hers. "The boy has an interesting story to tell. I think you should hear it," she said calmly, knowing her power over her husband. Thorgils was silent for a while, looking from his wife to Ulf. The crowd watched anxiously, some of them not wanting the fight to end but not willing to speak against the wife of their jarl.

"Father, listen to Mother," Snorri implored.

"I will hear his story if he is willing to tell it. But that does not mean that I will spare his life," Thorgils growled, his blue eyes fixed on Ulf who raised his hand in agreement while still being held by Ragnar. With that, the jarl turned and walked to his hall. He needed a drink. Ragnar grunted and with one last look of contempt at Ulf, he let go of him.

"This isn't finished," he said as Ulf dropped to the ground.

Ingibjorg looked at her son, Snorri. "Go see to your friend and keep him out of sight until I can calm your father," she said before following her husband. "You too," she said to Vidar, seeing how eager he was to get to Ulf.

Ulf thought he heard a hawk as he lay on his back. He looked up and saw the bird flying circles above him. It felt as if the bird was watching him. *Olgr.* The word came to him. It was one of Odin's many names. It meant hawk – and protector. He lifted his head and saw Ingibjorg standing by the entrance of the hall, watching him. Ulf felt a shiver run down his spine. He looked for the hawk again but could not find it.

"That wasn't a clever thing to do," Snorri said as he got to Ulf. He helped him to his feet. "Ragnar is not a person you want to upset. Getting on Loki's bad side would be a better idea."

"Aye, you are as brave as Tyr but as smart at Thor," Thorbjorn put in. He picked up Ulf's helmet which had fallen off at the beginning of the fight.

"I didn't kill my family," Ulf said, like that explained everything.

"And this was your way of proving that?" Snorri asked. He tried but failed to keep the amusement from his voice.

"Well, that certainly showed them," Thorbjorn said after Ulf nodded. "I need a drink after watching that."

"Me too. At least it looks like Ulf's been paying attention in the training. There were some good moves in that fight," Snorri laughed.

"Did anyone see the hawk?" Ulf asked, wanting to make sure that he was not seeing things.

"What hawk?" Snorri asked, looking at Thorbjorn who only shook his head. Ulf glanced at Vidar, who had a knowing smile on his face as he nodded. He mouthed the word Olgr to Ulf. Again, Ulf felt that there was more to the boy than he thought.

Later that evening Ulf sat alone with Vidar in Snorri's house. Everyone else was at the feast in the hall held in honour of Thorgils' return. The feast had been going for a while and Ulf had not been summoned. Perhaps the jarl was waiting until the next day to speak to him.

"Finally, we get a chance to speak." Ulf groaned when he heard the voice. It was not the one he wanted to hear.

"What do we need to speak about, Lady Ingibjorg?" He turned to her. He was surprised he had not heard her enter the hall. Even Vidar looked surprised. Ingibjorg said nothing, just walked to them and sat on the bench beside Ulf. To Ulf, she was a picture of nobility as she sat there with her back straight and her head up. He saw she was wearing a different dress from before, this time a red strap dress, with a matching underskirt. He touched the scars on his face as they sat in silence. They had stopped itching a while ago. Now they were just three ragged lines that ran along his face. Hulda, Ingibjorg's thrall, liked them. She and Ulf had started talking when she was helping in the main hall. He wasn't sure how he felt about her, but he enjoyed her company. "I never thanked you for my face," he finally said.

"You don't need to thank me; you saved my son's life."

"Not sure about that," Ulf admitted. Ingibjorg said nothing at that, but Ulf saw her smile. They sat in silence for a while longer. Ulf saw Vidar looking at Ingibjorg and the warm smiles they gave each other. "You two seem to get along," Ulf said, trying to keep the jealousy out of his voice.

"Why do you think so?" Ulf heard the smile in her voice.

"You spend a lot of time together and–" he hesitated.

"And?" Ingibjorg prompted him.

"You seem to understand him. Better than I do."

"Because I listen to him." Ulf looked at her, not sure what she meant. She looked back and smiled. "Vidar would rather spend more time with you, he trusts you more than anyone else." Ulf wondered if she knew what had happened in the old man's hut.

"Then why doesn't he?" Ulf asked looking at Vidar. Vidar just stared back, almost as if he was talking through Ingibjorg.

"He is afraid of the men you spend your time with, even my son."

"He has no reason to be afraid of them," Ulf said, but then he looked back to Ingibjorg. "Does he?"

"They say my son is a great warrior, just like his father." She smiled at that. "If only they knew the truth in that." She continued before Ulf had a chance to ask what she meant. "But he is reckless, arrogant, too wild-spirited."

"So, he shouldn't be trusted?" Ulf did not understand what she was trying to tell him. He scratched his short beard while waiting for Ingibjorg to respond.

"My son believes that there is a special bond between the two of you. Like your fates are connected."

"What do you think?"

"I agree with him. The two of you are connected. There is a reason you were brought back here Ulf; you just need to find it." She stood up and walked to the door, pausing as she got to it. "Embrace your blood, young Ulf. It is the only way you can win." With that, she left, leaving Ulf stunned at her last words. He turned to Vidar, who had a strange smile on his face.

"Did you tell her?" He wasn't sure why he was asking. Vidar just shook his head and looked to the door as Snorri entered.

"My father wants to see you." The words came out blurred. Ulf had to steady himself against the wall as he stood up with Ingibjorg's words still ringing in his head. "You ok?" Snorri asked.

"Fine," Ulf lied. He turned to Vidar. "Come on, let's get this over and done with." They followed Snorri to the hall, stopping in front of the open doors. Ulf took in the carved animals, thinking that they almost seemed alive as they moved in the dancing flames of the torches. He saw the wolf with its pack following close behind him as they chased the carving of a deer in a never-ending scene.

"You should leave your axe here." Snorri's voice snapped him out of his dream. "Ragnar is still looking for a reason to kill you, best not give him one." Ulf agreed and left his axe with the guard at the door, seeing the suspicious look in the man's eyes before following Snorri, with Vidar close on his heels.

The hall was filled with the smell of roasted meat as thralls were busy turning a spitted boar over the fire in the hearth. The fat dripped off the carcass into the sizzling flames, as the slobber dripped from one's mouth in anticipation of the meal. All the benches were filled by drunken warriors boasting of past exploits, both in bed and on the battlefield. And by bændr and traders, talking about their business deals and lands with the same zeal. Thralls were running around filling up cups and drinking horns, or otherwise staying out the way. Ulf saw Hulda standing behind Ingibjorg, who was back in her seat by her husband's side. She was watching Ulf, but he couldn't read her expression. The jarl was deep in conversation with what looked to be a wealthy bóndi, who kept rubbing at his nose like he was trying to reassure himself it was still on his face. Ulf wasn't prepared for the smoky air which caught in his throat and coughed. There was instant silence as everybody, including the thralls roasting the boar, stopped what they were doing and looked at Ulf and Vidar. Snorri decided now was a good time to introduce them.

"Father," he said, indicating to Ulf and Vidar. "Ulf and Vidar, as you requested." He stepped to one side, allowing Ulf and Vidar to pass, but followed as they walked through the hall towards his father. Ulf's stomach growled as they passed the roasting boar. He had not eaten since morning. Everyone was looking at them, but Ulf kept his gaze fixed on the jarl. Vidar felt no such constraint and was gawking at all the food and drink on the tables.

"Ulf Bjørnson," the jarl said when they stopped in front of his seat. Ragnar had stood up and walked to stand next to his jarl, if only to remind Ulf of his presence.

Ulf set his jaw and looked Thorgils in the eyes. "Do not call me that."

"Call you what?" Thorgils asked, perplexed.

"Bjørnson. I don't like it," Ulf responded, sensing the shock from the people around them. The bloodline and one's family's past deeds are as much part of you as your present exploits. It was a great honour to acknowledge them and an insult not to.

"What do you mean, you don't like it?" Thorgils leaned forward in his seat, both hands on the armrests, as if he was about to launch himself from it. "Do you know what your father has done for this village?"

Ulf took a step forward, his hands clenched tightly by his sides. He lowered his head, but kept his eyes fixed on Thorgils. "I know exactly what my father had done. And what he hadn't." He saw Ragnar take a step over, a snarl on his lips, but Thorgils raised his hand to stop him. "I know how my father proudly went to battle to fight for his jarl. I know how he stood by his jarl's side in the shield wall. How he fought like a god and slew many who came before him." Ulf paused for a second, taking a deep breath through his nose. He raised his head so that Thorgils could see his whole face; so that he could be reminded of Bjørn. "I know how his jarl tripped on the entrails of a slain man. How he fell on to his back and could do nothing but watch as his enemy was about to send him to Valhalla."

He saw Thorgils face go red, but he did not care. Not anymore, not with the anger running through him and feeding his arrogance.

"I know how my father used his shield to block the blow meant for his jarl, even though he was facing two opponents himself. I know how his opponents used this moment to bury their swords in him."

The hall was completely silent, not even the mice in the roof were making a noise.

"I know how his brother, my uncle, could not get there in time to save him. How my uncle had taken my father's famed sword and brought it to me. How he had to tell a young boy that his father, who he adored, who was the only parent he had left, had sacrificed himself to save his jarl. How he had died bravely in battle and how he was at this very moment drinking with his ancestors in Valhalla."

Ulf's fists were shaking with the rage that was coursing through him. He felt the tears running down his face but did not care.

"I know how my father chose his jarl over his son," he almost growled those last words out.

"Your father performed his duty as a jarl's champion," Thorgils growled in return, his face still red, his knuckles white from gripping the armrests of his seat.

"What about his duty to his son?" Ulf shouted. Thorgils was taken aback by this outburst. "What about his duty to return to his son? You claim I killed my uncle! Olaf was more of a father to me than Bjørn was. Brynhild was the only mother I had known." The silence continued; no one knew what to say or do. Thorgils looked like he was about to erupt like a volcano at being spoken to like this, but Ingibjorg placed a hand on his shoulder which seemed to calm him.

"My dear husband," she said, still looking at Ulf, "we all remember those days. A young boy angry at the loss of his father. We remember the hard choice Olaf and Brynhild had to make, choosing to leave here and find a new home somewhere where the boy could not be reminded of all he had lost." She looked around the hall, making sure that everyone was listening. "We have seen Olaf many times since and remember how he spoke in great pride of his young nephew, but also of his nephew's anger. How no matter what, it would not go away. How he would curse the gods and blame them for the deaths of his parents." She walked to Ulf and stood in front of him. Ragnar took a small step, his hand on the hilt of his sword. "I think we can forgive Ulf for tonight. It can't be easy being back here, with everyone wanting to remind him of something he would rather forget." Ingibjorg turned and faced her husband. "What do you think, my love?"

All eyes turned to Thorgils, eager to hear what he would say. The entire hall was holding its breath. "My wife has spoken wise words, as usual," Thorgils said after deliberating for a while. "We shall forget what has been said here tonight." The look he gave Ulf showed that he had no intention of doing so.

"A wise decision, my husband," Ingibjorg continued. "Our son believes Ulf innocent of the deaths of Olaf and Brynhild. I for one agree." Again, she looked around the hall, making sure she had the attention of the room. She didn't need to. The entire hall was drawn to her words like a moth drawn to the flame. "Another was responsible, and Ulf bears the injuries from trying to save them. Many have seen them."

Thorgils cleared his throat, if only to remind everyone of his presence. "My son and my wife have spoken in your favour," he said in a deep voice that carried along the hall. "I have no choice but to take them at their word." He stood up and took a few steps forward. "Ulf, if you swear to me, then I will allow you to stay in Thorgilsstad." He spread his arms as he said this. He was not convinced by his wife's clever words, but she knew more about this world than most. Everybody was watching Ulf, eager to see what he would do.

"I cannot swear an oath to you." There was an explosion of noise as men started shouting at Ulf, roaring their anger at his disrespect of their jarl.

"Silence!" Thorgils was going red again. He took another step forward, standing face to face with Ulf. "Why not?" he growled. Ulf could smell the sour ale coming from his breath and see the bits of food in his beard.

"I have already sworn an oath to the All-Father, Odin, to avenge my uncle and aunt." He lifted his right hand to show Thorgils the scar.

"Many have sworn oaths to the gods, but also to me," Thorgils responded.

"He has also sworn an oath to me, Father," Snorri lied. Asbjorn was about to object, but Thorbjorn warned him into silence. Ulf looked at Snorri in disbelief, unable to work out why he had lied to his father.

Thorgils scrutinized his son, who was still standing behind Ulf. "Is this true?"

"Yes, Father. I feel our fates are connected, so I offered him my help in return for his oath to join my crew."

Thorgils thought for a while, not moving away from Ulf. He nodded his acceptance and walked back to his seat. "Very well, I shall accept Ulf's oath to my son," he said as he sat down. "Now, let's get back to our feast," he said with a smile. The hall erupted in a cheer as everyone got back to eating and drinking.

"Come on," Snorri said, grabbing Ulf by the shoulder. "Tonight, we celebrate!" He steered Ulf to his men and handed him a cup. Ulf gave it to Vidar and took another for himself. He turned and saw Ingibjorg looking at him, a small smile on her lips. Ulf raised his cup to his lips and drank deep, enjoying the feeling of the ale as it went down his throat.

He had played with fire and walked away unscathed, but Ulf felt no joy in his small victory. Again, he almost lost everything because of his rashness and foolishness. He whispered a prayer to Odin, asking him for the wisdom and guidance he would need to seek his revenge. Though, despite all, he felt some optimism. He had found new friends, ones that would lie to protect him.

If only he knew how the gods were laughing at him.

CHAPTER 9

Ulf was dreaming. He wasn't sure what the dream was, but he was sure he was dreaming. He had drunk heavily during the feast. After his speech to Jarl Thorgils, Snorri's men had accepted him like he was one of their own. The last thing Ulf remembered was Hulda bringing him another drink. She had given him a smile he didn't understand. Thorbjorn elbowed him in the ribs and had given him a suggestive grin. But Ulf had been too drunk to know what it meant. And then, nothing. Now he was lying on the floor of the hall, thinking he was dreaming. But this felt too real. He felt his trousers being removed. Felt a hand take hold of him, caressing him until he was hard. He wasn't sure what this dream was, but it made him think of the dreams he had when he was younger. Only, this one felt more real. Like it was a real hand playing with him. Like the lips kissing his neck were real and not just part of a dream. Ulf felt something straddling him, taking him in, riding him. He felt the hands pressing against his chest, pressing harder as the movement sped up. This could not be real; he was sure of it. This was a dream. He wanted to open his eyes to prove it to himself but didn't want the dream to end. Then there was a moan, soft and sensual. At first, he thought it was him, but no, that sounded like a woman. Still, he refused to open his eyes. It was the kiss that did it. The kiss he had not expected. He felt the weight on him shift forward, the pressure on his chest increasing.

The movement slowed down and changed. He had never dreamt of that before. And then the kiss came. It was long and passionate, the tongue that entered his mouth and felt around like it was searching for something. The scent that filled his nose was a sweet musty smell. It was familiar, but there was a different scent mixed in. He knew who it was even before he opened his eyes. This was not a dream, this was real.

"Hulda." He saw her on top of him, or at least her outline. It was too dark in the hall to make anything out.

"Ssshh, you'll wake everyone up." She leaned back and continued riding him.

"But... I…"

"It's ok, Lady Ingibjorg said I could have you now," she whispered, her voice tinged with pleasure.

"You can have me?" He didn't understand what was happening. The sensation of her on top of him made it hard for him to think straight.

"Do you not want this?" she asked, teasing him with her voice.

"I do, but–"

"Then be quiet, or I leave." She stopped just to prove her point.

"No, don't stop." He put his hands on her hips trying to encourage her to continue. But she would not. She just sat there on top of him. Ulf could feel her looking at him, he could even feel the smile on her face. Just when he thought she was going to leave, she started moving again. She leaned back, taking him deeper. Her quiet moaning drove him crazy, encouraging him until he couldn't hold himself anymore. He lifted his hips in anticipation. Hulda felt this and sped up, squeezing her legs tighter against his body. They both came at the same time, an explosion of pleasure he had never experienced before. It left him feeling exhilarated and exhausted at the same time. Hulda collapsed on top of him, breathing heavily. He took in her smell and the smell of their sex. After a few moments of lying there, catching their breath, Hulda climbed off him and fixed her shift. She gave him a kiss and whispered in his ear.

"Don't tell anyone." With that she left, sneaking out as quietly as she entered, leaving Ulf confused. But he was too tired to care. He pulled his trousers up and felt it stick to him, a cold clammy feeling he did not like. He eventually fell asleep with a smile on his face, unaware of the figure in the shadows.

The figure in the shadows was seething. He had seen Hulda leave the jarl's house where she slept and was surprised when she had gone into the hall. It was too early for any errands, dawn was still a while off. He followed her inside, making sure he was far away enough for her not to notice him. It was too damn dark when he entered, so he could not see her. But he knew she was in there. And then, a noise. It was unmistakable. His eyes had followed the noise until he saw her. On top of someone, riding him, giving herself to him. The bitch! Even worse, he knew who she was fucking. Ulf the fucking Bear-Slayer. Somehow Ulf had tricked Hulda into having sex with him, the shadow figure was sure of it, and one day he'd make Ulf pay.

He couldn't even get turned on by watching them, by listening to her moan. Not like he normally did. He had learnt how to sneak around in the darkness. It didn't scare him like it scared others. No, he welcomed it. He knew he was protected by Loki. He had learnt to move as quiet as a ghost and use the shadows to hide. For this reason, he started calling himself the Skuggi, the shadow. He would sneak into people's houses and watch them, playing with himself. But tonight, even though it was the first time he had heard Hulda like that, he couldn't get aroused. He was too angry. When they finished, he watched her leave but didn't follow her out. He wanted to sneak over and kill Ulf in his sleep. But Ulf didn't deserve to die quietly in the night. He had to die in full view of everyone who thought he was so great. Just so that they could learn what he really was. So, the Skuggi did nothing. He watched as Ulf fell asleep while thinking of creative ways to kill him.

The first thing Ulf saw was the grinning face of Thorbjorn when he woke up.

"Well now. Somebody had a good night," Thorbjorn smiled.

"I think everybody had a good night. It was a good feast," Ulf responded, not sure what Thorbjorn was getting at.

"Oh aye, the feast was good. But we both know that's not what I mean." He winked at Ulf. Ulf wanted to argue, but he couldn't. Just like he couldn't keep the smile off his face.

"Into the hall she crept,

Floating over men as they slept.

A spirit of Freya's might,

She did not expect the wolf to fight.

But his sword of flesh she took,

And from her came a sound none mistook."

Thorbjorn started laughing, almost spilling the ale in his hand in the process. Ulf looked up and saw the composer, Oddi, sitting on the bench and combing his hair. Oddi saw Ulf looking at him with a confused expression and smiled.

"We know what she did, my young friend." Oddi looked around before leaning in closer. "But we don't know who she was. It's a mystery we were hoping you could help us with."

"I don't know what you are talking about," Ulf lied, unconvincingly. Thorbjorn and Oddi laughed at him. Ulf sat up and saw most of the hall was awake, or in the process of waking up.

"I'm sure you don't," Oddi said.

"What are you talking about?" They all turned and saw Thorvald standing there, giving Ulf a dark look. Ulf didn't understand why, he had never really spoken to the boy.

"None of your business, Ragi," Thorbjorn responded. They had started calling him that since he ran from the forest. Thorvald glared at them all then turned and left. "That boy is strange. Always looking at you like he thinks his stare will kill you."

"Maybe he believes he has some of his mother's powers," Oddi responded.

"His mother's powers?" Ulf asked. He rubbed the sleep from his eyes.

"Aye, you don't know. The Lady Ingibjorg is a witch, some say."

"No, she is not a witch," Oddi said, still combing his hair. Ulf had never seen anyone pay so much attention to his hair. "But there is something mysterious about her."

Ulf thought back to the night before, to the conversation he had with her. It sent a shiver down his spine, which he managed to hide before the others saw it. "Where's Vidar?" he asked, looking around for his friend. He found him still passed out on the floor not far from where he was.

"Poor lad is going to suffer when he wakes up," Thorbjorn said, also looking at Vidar. "Drinks better than you though," he said to Ulf, jumping out of the way of the kick that came his way.

Ulf decided to leave Vidar there, let him sleep it off. He stood up and stretched, hoping it would wake his body up.

"Snorri was looking for you," Oddi said, as if remembering why they were there.

"Do you know where he is?"

"Aye, by the troll cave he calls a house," Thorbjorn replied.

Ulf found a bucket of clean water and rinsed his face, feeling the cold water freshen him up. He sniffed his tunic, smelling the stale sweat from the day before. He needed to find a clean tunic, he decided. After taking a quick drink of ale to settle his head, he left the hall.

Outside the weather looked like it might rain, the heavy clouds covering much of the bay. It was still early, too early for the morning meal. There weren't many people outside, but he saw Ingibjorg and Hulda walking back to their house. Ingibjorg gave him one of those knowing smiles of hers, which he never understood. But Hulda just looked straight ahead, as if she hadn't seen him. Ulf shook his head; he didn't understand women.

"Ulf!" He heard his name being shouted. He looked around and saw Snorri sitting outside his house, sharpening his sword. Ragnar sat with him. He scrutinized Ulf and gave him a wolf grin, a warning more than a welcome. Both men were wearing their brynjas and had shields by their feet. Ulf walked towards them, trying his best not to glance back at the jarl's house.

"Morning," he greeted them.

"I heard myself a little story this morning," Snorri said, with a sly smile on his face.

"Looks like news travels fast in this place," Ulf said. He knew what Snorri was hinting at and didn't have the energy to argue.

"When you fuck somebody in the hall, people will talk about it," Ragnar said, his deep voice making it sound menacing. "But it's strange that nobody seems to know who you were fucking." Ragnar looked at Snorri who only shrugged.

"Well Ulf, care to share that with us?" Snorri asked.

"No," Ulf said. Snorri just smiled.

"Why not?" Ragnar narrowed his eyes.

"Leave him be, Ragnar. Ulf will tell us when he is ready," Snorri said. Ragnar waved him away and went back to cleaning his weapons. Ulf saw his left hand with the missing finger.

"How did you lose your finger?" he asked before he could stop himself.

Ragnar studied his hand and smiled. "You don't tell me your secrets, and I don't tell you mine." Ulf shrugged; he couldn't argue with that. "Come, we have things to do." Ragnar stood and walked off, without waiting for them.

"He's very secretive about that finger of his," Snorri said, walking up to Ulf. "I heard he lost it fighting a wolf."

"A wolf?" Ulf was surprised. This was not what Brak had told him.

"Aye, he was out hunting one day when he was younger. A wolf caught him by surprise and Ragnar lost his weapon. He had no choice but to fight the wolf with his bare hands." Snorri looked at his own hands as he said this, holding them in the air. "They say he ripped the wolf's head in two, but not before the wolf managed to bite off his finger." Snorri smiled at Ulf, always happy to tell a story.

"Is that true?"

"That's what I heard," Snorri responded. "Where is your axe? And jerkin?" he asked when he noticed Ulf was lacking both.

"In the hall, I guess." Ulf scratched at his short beard, trying to remember.

"Go get them and meet us in the training field." The smile on his face told Ulf more than the words did. Ulf decided not to think about it as he fetched his weapons from the hall.

Inside he saw Vidar awake, but the look on his face told of his pain. Ulf laughed, thinking back to the morning he had his first proper hangover. "How are you feeling, Vidar?"

Vidar looked at him with his green face and shook his head. Ulf only laughed. Hulda arrived with a cup of something and handed it to Vidar.

"Here," she said to him, "it will make you feel better." Vidar took the cup and drank deeply from it.

"Umm, Hulda?" Ulf began, but she gave him a look that told him to be quiet. Ulf was confused by this.

"Later," she whispered as she walked past him. Vidar smiled, like he knew their secret.

"Shut up and finish your drink," Ulf said to him. Vidar smiled and drank from his cup, his face grimacing as he swallowed the contents. Ulf laughed as he pulled his jerkin over his head and fastened it. "I'll be out training again," he said when Vidar gave him a questioning look. "It seems that when they're not drinking, they're

training. Besides, I need to get better if I want to avenge my family."
He picked up his axe and left Vidar nursing his hangover in the hall.

"Ah, here he is. The hero of Thorgilsstad," Ragnar said
when Ulf arrived at the training field. Everyone stopped what they
were doing and watched him like they were expecting something to
happen. Snorri's hirdmen walked up to him, all of them in their war
gear.

"A word of advice," Brak said to Ulf, "when the jarl is here,
always wear your jerkin and have your weapon at hand. He doesn't
like seeing men not prepared for battle."

"Unless you are a bóndi or trader," his brother added. "By
the way, we heard somebody was visited by a mysterious creature
last night." He winked at his brother.

"Don't wink at me, it wasn't me who visited him."

Ulf wondered when this would go away; the men here
seemed to gossip more than the women.

"Staying quiet then," Brak said, looking disappointed when
he saw that Ulf wasn't going to respond.

"Why are there so many people here?" Ulf asked instead.

"The jarl's back, and he likes to keep his men fit."

"How many men does he have?" Ulf tried to count them but
could not.

"Around a hundred and sixty, including Snorri's thirty. And
he got some new recruits, so Ragnar is going to teach them how to
fight in a skjaldborg, a shield wall," Brak Drumbr said, strapping on
his helmet. He had the same bowl helmet as Ulf.

"A skjaldborg?" Ulf looked around. "That seems dumb,
why waste time on that?"

"Don't let Ragnar hear you."

"A waste of time, the hero of Thorgilsstad says." Ragnar's voice echoed across the field. He was closer than Ulf realized.

"Too late," Brak Drumbr said, taking a step away from Ulf.

"Have you ever been in a skjaldborg?" Ragnar asked, giving Ulf a menacing glare. "Didn't think so," he said when Ulf shook his head. "Take your shield and prepare for an attack."

Ulf picked up a shield and stood ready, holding it in front of him so it covered his chest and lower half of his face. Ulf braced himself with his back leg, determined to withstand anything Ragnar threw at him. Ragnar smiled when he saw Ulf was ready and ran at him. He threw all his weight into a stomping kick in the centre of Ulf's shield. The blow sent Ulf flying backwards and he landed heavily on his back, to the cheer of the men around him. *I must stop ending up on my back like this*, he thought as he got back up. He glared at Ragnar who smiled back.

"Two more men," Ragnar said, walking back to his starting point. The Brak brothers joined Ulf, one standing on either side and interlocking their shields with his. They had done this before. The three of them braced as Ragnar came again, aiming another kick at the centre of Ulf's shield. The weight of the kick sent them back a few steps, but they stayed on their feet. Ulf understood the point Ragnar was making. "Seven more!" Ragnar ordered.

Seven more men joined the wall. Ulf recognised them as part of Snorri's crew. Ragnar came again, throwing all his weight behind the kick. This time the wall did not move. Ragnar took a deep breath and smiled.

"Do you understand now, hero?" he asked Ulf. Ulf nodded. "A skjaldborg is our most effective defence in battle. It doesn't matter how good you are as a fighter. If the men on either side of you don't know what they are doing, you die. You see, hero. You help defend the man on your right, just as the man on your left helps to defend you." He turned and faced everyone as he said this, making sure that all the new recruits understood his words. "Think of it as a chain. The skjaldborg is only as strong as the weakest link. Are you going to be the weakest link, hero?" he stepped in close to Ulf, their noses almost touching. Ulf could smell the staleness of his breath.

"Never," Ulf said with determination, trying to stop the anger rising in him.

Ragnar smiled and walked away. "That is why we train. To make sure there are no weak links. Give me two skjaldborgs, now!" The men split into two even-sized groups and formed their skjaldborgs, two-man deep. "Good." Ragnar smiled and took his place in the wall opposite Ulf. "Now, attack!" he roared and the two skjaldborgs came together with the sound of a large wave crashing onto the rocks. Birds scattered from nearby trees. The men strained and swore as they tried to push the opposing skjaldborg back. Ulf felt the burn in his legs as he tried not to give ground. But Ragnar was bigger and stronger. Ragnar smiled as he saw Ulf struggling. "Not bad, Bear-Slayer." Ulf couldn't respond through his gritted teeth but glared back. "Here's another lesson for you," Ragnar said as he kicked Ulf's leg. Ulf managed not to scream, but lifted his leg before he could stop himself. At that moment, Ragnar gave a hard shove which sent the unbalanced Ulf into the man behind him. The man swore as they fell back and created a gap in their skjaldborg. Ragnar took advantage and rushed through the gap before it could be closed. He smiled at Ulf, who was glaring at him while rubbing his leg. "So much for not being the weak link."

Snorri appeared from somewhere and helped Ulf up. "He did the same thing to me in my first training session." He smiled at the memory. But Ulf didn't respond. Instead, he picked up his shield and re-joined the skjaldborg.

They spent the rest of the day practising, Ragnar not letting anyone eat or rest until he was happy. This took all day and the next few days, and still he wasn't happy. Ulf didn't see much of Hulda during those days, but at least she had stopped ignoring him. Some nights they would meet up, one of her favourite places being under the large tree in the field behind the hall. The tree Thorgils liked to hang people from.

"Why do we have to meet here?" Ulf complained one night after they had just had sex.

"Because it turns me on." She took hold of him and caressed him to prove her point.

Despite his misgivings, Ulf's body could not help reacting to her hands. "How?"

Hulda stopped what she was doing, again showing her authority even though she was a thrall. "If you keep complaining, then we'll stop doing it."

"Here?"

"Everywhere." The intensity in her eyes, with the stars reflected in them, stopped Ulf from saying anything more. With a sigh he leaned back as she climbed on him, taking him inside her once again. But he still felt uncomfortable having sex under the hanging tree.

"Maybe if he taught them how to do it, instead of screaming at them, they would do better," Ulf said a week later when a recruit dropped his spear and Ragnar was threatening to skin him alive. Ragnar stopped screaming at the recruit and turned towards Ulf.

"You're fucked," Thorbjorn said, before taking a step away from Ulf.

"Ok, hero." Ragnar walked towards Ulf. "I think it's time we finish what we started on the wharf a few days ago." His face turned red as he clenched his fists. "Snorri, get the blunted swords."

"I can't fight with a sword," Ulf said. "I swore to Odin that I would never touch another until I get my father's sword back."

Those who heard this nodded and said it was an honourable thing to do. One said it was dumb and got a smack from Thorbjorn.

"Well, these are blunted, so they are not full swords," Oddi said, "I don't think you'll be breaking any oaths to Odin if you use them." Ulf took one of the blunt swords, hoping that Oddi was right. It felt unfamiliar in his hand; he was more used to holding an axe than a sword.

Both men stood facing each other, shields up and swords ready to strike. Ragnar moved first, attacking at speed. Ulf brought his shield to block the blow, but it was much harder than he expected. He felt the force of it run down his arm, jolting his shoulder and forcing him to take a few steps backwards. His arm felt numb. He tried to lift it but failed. Ragnar didn't give Ulf time to recover as he attacked again, slicing at Ulf's stomach. Ulf dodged it easily, jumping backwards and deciding against using his shield. Ragnar reversed the swing and came back with a backhand aimed high, which Ulf only just managed to duck under. Ulf saw his chance and aimed a jab at Ragnar's chest, but Ragnar got his shield there in time to block it. Ulf's arm had regained feeling and he managed to raise his shield over his head to block another blow, this one driving him to his knees. Everybody was cheering, some for Ragnar, while Snorri and his men were shouting for Ulf. Ragnar kept raining blows down on Ulf's raised shield, not giving Ulf a chance to get up again. Ulf knew he wouldn't last long; the shield was getting heavier with each blow. He waited for the next time Ragnar raised his sword to strike. Using the brief respite, Ulf kicked out, catching Ragnar's legs and tripping him up. Stunned silence was followed by cheers from Snorri's men as Ulf used the moment to catch his breath. Ragnar got back to his feet, his eyes hardened as he spat to the side.

"You're going to regret that," he growled before attacking again, swinging his sword like he was intent on killing Ulf. Ulf for his part did everything he could to block or dodge the blows, only occasionally striking himself, but all his blows were blocked. After a while, Ragnar backed off, taking deep breaths. Ulf was also gasping for air. He knew he couldn't survive another attack like that. He decided not to give Ragnar another chance to get him, so he attacked instead. He swung his sword high, making Ragnar raise his shield to block the blow. As soon as his sword hit Ragnar's shield, Ulf punched with his own, aiming for Ragnar's exposed leg. Ragnar jumped out of the way and retaliated with his own strike. Again, the blows came so fast that Ulf had no time to think, only to react. But he always managed to get out of the way or get his shield up in time. His arms were getting tired though, and he wasn't sure how long he could go on. He jabbed his sword at Ragnar's waist, but Ragnar twisted out of the way and brought his sword up in a vicious swing which stopped very close to Ulf's neck. Both men stood there, stuck in that pose, as they breathed heavily, sucking in as much air as they could. There was silence all around as everybody was waiting to see what would happen.

Ragnar smiled and lowered his sword. "Not bad, but you're dead." Ulf was breathing heavily. He dropped his sword and shield, unable to hold them in his shaking hands. He had never been pushed so far, but he still came short. Ragnar would have killed him if this had been a real fight. He saw people from the village had come to see the fight, including the jarl who stood there with his arms crossed. From this distance, Ulf couldn't see his face clearly.

"That was a good fight." Snorri grabbed his shoulder after Ragnar walked away and called an end to the training session. Snorri was impressed with how much Ulf had improved. "No one has ever lasted that long against him."

"Not even you?" Ulf asked.

"I'm not dumb enough to fight him," Snorri laughed. Others came to pat him on the back, but Ulf wasn't paying attention to them.

Thorgils had watched the fight with a grim expression on his face.

"You are not happy, my husband." Ingibjorg appeared by his side, her ever-present thrall there too. Thorgils looked at Hulda. He didn't find her attractive, but like most men in the village, he was drawn to her because he couldn't have her. But unlike some men, he was smart enough to heed his wife's warnings. She was not a woman to anger.

"I have too many concerns to be happy, and now you and my son have given me another one," he half-growled.

"You still think he did it." It was a statement rather than a question.

"Yes." He saw no point in lying to her, she already knew. "But I don't understand why you think he didn't." He faced his wife, "You remember him as a child, when he tried to stab me with a knife?"

"It doesn't matter what he did or did not do." She watched her son and his friends talk to Ulf. "I believe Ulf is here for a reason."

"A reason?" Thorgils regarded Ulf. "What reason?"

"Chaos," she said with a smile. "Danger is coming, a danger that could ruin everything you have built, my husband." She looked into his eyes as if she was searching his soul. "And Ulf will be the chaos that brings it here."

Thorgils did not understand what she meant. But then, he rarely understood what she meant.

"Trust my words, my husband," she said, seeing the confusion in his face. "Odin brought Ulf back to us and," she looked up, noticing the eagle soaring high in the sky, "he is watching to see the chaos unfold."

CHAPTER 10

Ulf stood outside Snorri's house, combing his beard as he watched the approaching bændr. Spring had finally arrived, and Ulf was glad of it. He didn't like winters. He didn't like the cold that found its way into your bones and made you shiver no matter what you wore or how close you sat to the fire. The snow that was slippery and wet, and made tasks harder to complete. Growing up on Olaf's farm, the short winter days were spent helping Olaf mending broken fences or leaky roofs. It had always been a miserable time, having to work outside when he could barely feel his fingers, the woollen mittens he wore only helping so much. Other times they would go to the forest and cut down trees. The trees were easier to transport during the winter thanks to the snow. It was the only time Ulf appreciated it. All you had to do was tie the felled tree to an ox or two and then slide it back to the farm. As a young boy, Ulf would often sit on the tree and imagine he was riding a dragon or a giant wolf. The worst part of the winter, though, wasn't the weather. It was having to keep all the animals in the longhouse. It was too cold to keep them outside during the winter months, and there was always the risk of hungry wolves lurking around for an easy meal. So, the cows and goats that weren't killed had to be kept indoors. Olaf and Brynhild had never seemed to mind, but Ulf couldn't stand the smell. You'd think that over the years you'd get used to it, but Ulf never did.

In Thorgilsstad, though, it was different. There was no work to be done, no fences to be mended or wood to be collected. That's what the thralls were for. The other good thing was that Ulf didn't have to share his living space with the livestock. Thorgils had a special hall for the few cows and oxen he kept, as well as a space for his stallion. And there was no shortage of food here. Thorgils controlled a large area around the bay and at the end of the summer, all the bændr in Thorgils' land had to pay a land tax, or landskyld, to their jarl. This was paid with wool, milk, cheese and salted meat, anything they could afford to give and still provide for themselves. Thorgils was a strict jarl, but he seemed fair and the bændr appreciated that.

All that was left for Ulf to do was to train with the warriors who didn't go to their families for the winter, as the brothers had done. But as the winter progressed, the days got shorter and soon there wasn't enough light to train, and so they just ended up sitting around. A warrior's life, Thorbjorn had told him when he complained about it. For Ulf, it had been a frustrating time. He did not like sitting around. This meant he had time to think, and thinking was not good for him. He had spent those cold winter days wrapped up in his bear pelt and brooding over the lack of progress he was making in seeking his vengeance, his mood as dark as the night sky outside. The others had tried to cheer him up, challenging him to wrestling matches and drinking competitions, but soon they decided it was best just to leave him alone. Only Vidar had remained his constant companion through the winter months. Ulf found comfort in his silence, and he felt that Vidar understood this.

Jól, the mid-winter celebration which lasted for twelve days, was another low point for Ulf during the winter. This was the

first time he had spent the celebration without his family. He missed
them, although he wouldn't admit this to anyone. But at Jól, he had
felt their absence more keenly. He missed going into the forest with
Olaf to select the Jól tree, which Brynhild and his cousins decorated
with colourful ribbons. Or preparing the Jól log which they burnt on
the last day of the festivities to welcome the new year. Thoughts of
all the activities he would never get to share with his family
anymore, even small things like drinking the mead his aunt made
specially for Jól, tormented him. Olaf had told Ulf that he could kill
the boar they would sacrifice to the gods this year. Another thing that
would never happen. So, while everyone else was celebrating and
feasting, Ulf kept to himself.

Vidar was starting to feel more comfortable around Snorri
and his men, having spent a lot of time with them during the winter.
He had realized they meant him no harm, although he was still wary
of Thorbjorn, with his scarred face and stern expression. Even the
men had warmed up to Vidar. Only Asbjorn had remained
unchanged. To Ulf, it felt like he was unhappy with Ulf joining
Snorri's crew and there had been a few moments when Asbjorn had
drunk too much and started fighting with everyone about it. That was
until Snorri told him he could leave if he wasn't happy with it.
Asbjorn had apologised then and had been quiet about it since, but
Ulf still got the feeling Asbjorn didn't agree with Snorri.

The only interesting thing that happened during the Jól
celebration was meeting Oddi's family. Ulf had recognised them as
such even before being introduced to them. They all had the same
tall body frames and facial features. Oddi's brother, Magni, was
taller and strutted around like an arrogant cockerel. He had arrived as
if prepared for battle in his brynja and sword, even wearing his

helmet. He looked like a fine warrior and Ulf had said as much to Snorri. But Snorri only laughed.

"He'd never seen a battle, that one. I don't even think he's killed a fish with that fine sword of his."

"Then why does he dress like a war god?" Ulf had asked, taking in the helmet, lined with gold and the golden hilt of his sword.

"Likes to think he is Tyr himself."

"He is a coward then?"

"Can't say, he has never been tried or tested. The only fighting he has ever done was against untrained thralls forced to spar with him." Both Snorri and Ulf looked on as Oddi greeted his family. Everyone got a warm welcome apart from his brother. Ulf saw the icy glare Oddi gave to his brother and the brief hug that had seemed more formal than would be expected between two siblings.

"What happened between them?" he asked. Oddi was always friendly and quick to forgive any slights and insults, so Ulf couldn't understand the animosity between the brothers.

Snorri smiled at the question. "Oddi beat him in a fight. One day Magni the Cockerel," which was the byname for Oddi's brother because he usually wore brightly coloured tunics, "was busy thrashing some poor thrall bloody, claiming to be a great warrior when Oddi had enough. He took up a stick and challenged his brother to fight. Magni felt confident, he had his sword, so thought this would be an easy victory for him." Snorri laughed at the memory. "After a few heartbeats he was lying on the ground, face blue and bloody and Oddi didn't have a single scratch on him."

"That explains why Magni doesn't like Oddi, but not the other way around?"

Jarl Thorgils had greeted his guests warmly at this point, giving them all affectionate hugs before they made their way to their seats.

Snorri had stayed quiet for a bit before saying, "That's a story for Oddi to tell."

The rest of the celebration had been uneventful. Oddi had avoided his brother and spent much time with Thorbjorn and Asbjorn.

Another reason Ulf had not enjoyed this winter was the dreams he'd endured, the ones with the troll king. They came more frequently now and always followed the same path. Ulf had no axe, or any other weapon, in them now and he usually found himself running from the troll with every dream ending the same way: Ulf on the ground and the troll standing above him, its axe held in the air above its head. Then the axe would come down and Ulf would wake up, cold and sweaty. The cloaked figure didn't come to his dreams anymore, but Ulf could always hear his voice in the wind. He had tried to find comfort with Hulda most nights so he didn't have to sleep, but she only came to him when she wanted to, which wasn't often as she didn't want to go outside in the cold winter nights.

"This should be interesting," Snorri said about the bændr as he appeared next to Ulf, bringing him back to the present. He had been play-fighting with his son, using sticks as swords, an activity his wife, Gunnhildr, had prohibited. But as always, Snorri never paid any attention to her.

"What do you think it's about?" Ulf asked. The expressions on their faces were very different to the bright sunny day as they marched to the jarl's hall in grim silence. There were about six of them, all different shapes and sizes, but they all had the same long moustaches which was the fashion. Unlike the jarl's long moustache, theirs did not have finger rings attached to the ends.

"Let's go find out." Snorri walked to the hall. As always, he was wearing his brynja and had his sword, Tyr's Fury, on his belt. Inside the bændr stood in a group in front of Thorgils, who was sat on his high seat, with Lady Ingibjorg sitting next to him. Ulf noticed her attention wasn't on the bændr, but instead on him and Snorri as they entered. As always, he could not read her expression. He was starting to get used to it by now, but still at times felt unnerved by her. He and Snorri joined Snorri's hirdmen, who had already been in the hall before the bændr arrived. They were all wearing their brynjas, and as usual, Ulf felt out of place as he stood with them wearing a leather jerkin. Ragnar, as always, stood by his jarl's side, with his great axe, Head-splitter, at hand, for no other reason than to send a message to the bændr. It seemed that everyone in Thorgilsstad had come to the hall to hear what the bændr wanted, filling the hall with the constant twittering you would expect from a flock of birds feasting on a berry tree. Ulf noticed the glances that some had directed his way, the looks of disgust and suspicion. Not everyone had accepted him, but he didn't care. He was not there to be accepted.

"Took my daughter," one of the bændr was complaining. He was short and rotund and from his features and gruff voice, Ulf guessed he was a relative of Thorbjorn. "When they finished plowin' her, they ransomed her back. I had no choice but to pay and they sent her back, carrying some bastard's child." The other bændr nodded at this. Some of the women present shook their heads; they all felt for the girl. "Worst is," the bóndi continued, "they slaughtered my prize ox. Black Thunder's been with me for many years and now he is gone." There was more sadness in his voice at the loss of his ox than at what happened to his daughter.

"Father always loved his cows more than his children," Thorbjorn growled quietly to those around him.

"They stole my sheep and killed my shepherd," another bóndi added.

"I lost half my sheep and two cows!"

"And what about crops? They burnt my fields for no reason other than to amuse themselves." The bændr started shouting over each other, each wanting their grievance to be heard.

"Enough!" Thorgils shouted. He stood up from his seat. The light from the torches made him look more imposing than usual by casting shadows in the deep lines on his face. "Where are these pirates now?"

"We don't know," one of the bændr said.

"They took a ship to the islands, but which one, I cannot say," Thorbjorn's father said. "I had one of my thralls follow them."

"Jarl Thorgils, we pay you landskyld every summer for your protection. We beg you, in the name of the mighty Odin, to do something about this," one of the bændr pleaded. Thorgils was silent for a while as he stared at the bændr, looking each of them in the eyes. He sat in his chair again and rested his chin on his fist as he contemplated what they had just told him. The hall had fallen silent as he looked to his wife, wanting to know her opinion before he made a decision.

Ingibjorg had not been paying attention to the bændr. It was the same every time. The smallest problem and they came running to Thorgils, instead of trying to solve it themselves. Her attention was on Ulf and her son Snorri. Ulf had grown over the winter. His shoulders were bigger and his limbs thicker. The training and food were doing him good. Ulf wasn't as broad as Snorri, but they were the same height. She was struck by how similar in the face they were. Ulf's face was more square than Snorri's round face, and their eyes were different colours. But if you looked hard enough you saw they had the same shape, as had their noses and mouths. Ingibjorg was grateful for the scars Ulf had on his face. They had healed well and were now only three white lines that ran down his face, like the lines a farmer makes in his field, but they did enough to distract people from his features.

"Ingibjorg?" She turned to her husband at the sound of his voice.

"I am thinking of the best solution, husband," she covered for herself. "The pirates will have to be dealt with, that is obvious. What do we know about these men?" She addressed this question to the bændr.

"They are led by Kettil the Red," came the response.

"He was outlawed at last summer's Thing, was he not?" she asked to no one in particular. The Thing was a regional gathering where free men would discuss the laws of the land and settle disputes. Ulf had never been to one, but his uncle would sometimes attend them.

"He was," answered Thorgils, seeing where his wife was going with this.

"Then the solution is clear, I think." She looked to her husband, making sure that the final decision came from him.

Thorgils nodded. "My wife is right. Kettil the Red is an outlaw and therefore his life is forfeit. As are those who travel with him for the crimes which they have committed. Do not worry, my friends, you will be compensated for your losses." He turned to his son, "Snorri, ready your ship and take as many men as you need. Take some of the new recruits, this will be a chance to blood them before we take them raiding. Find this Kettil and his crew and show him our famous hospitality to outlaws in our land."

CHAPTER 11

Ulf stood on the wharf, taking in her long slender shape and graceful curves. He had never seen anything as beautiful and with a feeling of guilt, wished she was his. But she belonged to Snorri and her name was the Sae-Ulfr. *Snorri's ship was magnificent*, he thought as he studied her keel, decorated with intertwining carvings. They reminded Ulf of a mass of serpents slithering in the same direction. Snorri's crew were busy loading his ship and preparing her for the journey to find the pirates. It had taken a few days to get her ready, much to the annoyance of the bændr who had wanted Snorri to leave immediately, but Snorri would not be rushed. Snorri had wanted to make sure his ship was ready. She had to be scrubbed clean first and then be made watertight. This was done by taking moss from the shore and after mixing it with tallow, squeezing it into the gaps between the planking.

"Beautiful, is she not?" Oddi said. Ulf had been so entranced by the ship he hadn't heard Oddi approach. Ulf looked up, taking in his friend's enviable armour. Oddi was wearing his brynja, his sword, Death's Breath, strapped to his side and had his helmet in his hands. Ulf was wearing his leather jerkin over a thick woollen tunic. Olaf's axe was tucked into his belt and he was holding his spear in his right hand, his shield in the left.

"She is," he replied, bringing his attention back to the ship if only to forget about Oddi's brynja.

"Ever sailed before?"

"No," Ulf replied. "But how hard can it be?" He saw the smile on Oddi's face but decided not to ask.

Both men watched as the crew started to board the Sae-Ulfr.

Snorri was taking thirty-one men with him for this hunt, but only thirty would be doing any fighting. The extra person was Rolf Treefoot, Snorri's steersman. Rolf was an old greybeard with one foot missing. It had been replaced by a wooden peg, hence the name Treefoot. He had an intimate understanding of the seas and the waves, or so Ulf had been told. Oddi had told him Rolf had had an affair with Ran, the mother of the waves, once and that was why he knew the waters so well. Ran still loved him, Oddi had claimed, so whatever ship he sailed would never sink. Ulf wasn't so sure about that, but he hoped it was true.

"Ready?" Snorri asked appearing behind Ulf and Oddi. Like Oddi, he was wearing his brynja over a thick leather tunic. On his belt, he had Tyr's Fury and a small sax-knife, while his shield was slung over his shoulder. Snorri had a relaxed smile on his face and took a deep breath as he stood there with a spear in hand, watching the men board his ship. He frowned when he saw the recruits standing to one side, glancing at each other and avoiding eye contact with the more experienced men. It was like they were at their first spring equinox, too shy to approach any of the girls. "Rolf! Get these boys a place on the ship," Snorri said, pointing to the recruits. Rolf nodded and got busy yelling at them, his voice surprisingly strong for a man his age. "Come on, your sea chest is already on board,"

Snorri said as he climbed on board and walked with the ease of a man who had sailed many times.

"What sea chest?" Ulf frowned.

"The one I have just given you. What else you going to sit on while you row?" Snorri shouted from his ship.

Ulf rushed after Snorri, moving awkwardly as he followed him. He wasn't used to the gentle sway of the Sae-Ulfr. Snorri laughed as he saw Ulf struggle. "Don't worry, you will get the hang of it."

Ulf nodded and put his spear in the spear rack on the side of the ship, near the prow. As he sat down, he saw he was opposite Oddi and behind Thorbjorn. The brothers were behind him, and Asbjorn behind Oddi. Ulf wanted to know where Snorri would be sitting, but decided not to ask; he would find out soon enough. Instead, he tied his shield over the side, as the others had done. So far, so good.

Vidar stood next to the ship, with an angry scowl on his face and his arms crossed. He wanted to go with, but Ulf had refused. He didn't know what to expect and didn't want to be worried about Vidar as well, so told him to stay with Lady Ingibjorg instead. Vidar had nodded but he didn't look happy about it.

When everybody was on board and ready, Snorri pushed his warship away from the wharf. Dozens of people waved them off from the shore, including the jarl and his wife, grim-faced and straight-backed, with the bændr behind them. Ulf caught the nod the jarl gave to Snorri as the Sae-Ulfr drifted away.

"Here," Thorbjorn said, handing Ulf his oar. He helped Ulf put it through the oar hole on the side of the ship. After fixing his own oar into place he turned to Ulf. "Your first-time sailing? Or rowing rather."

Ulf nodded as he felt the oar in his hands, the grooves worn in by the other men making it feel comfortable.

"You got some gold in your pocket?"

"Why?" Ulf asked, unsure of what Thorbjorn meant.

"You should always carry some gold with you. If, Njörd forbid, the ship went under, then you will need some gold to pay for your way into Ran's hall. Otherwise, you'd be lost forever. Here, take this." He gave Ulf some gold coins when Ulf shook his head. Ulf nodded his thanks and put the coins in the pouch attached to his belt. He looked around the ship while he waited for the order to row. Snorri had explained that they'd be rowing as the islands weren't far, so even though the mast was set, there was no sail attached. Ulf saw that the Sae-Ulfr had sixteen rowing benches on each side – the benches being the war or sea chests of the men – and was wide enough for five men to stand shoulder to shoulder in the centre. The Sae-Ulfr could fit up to thirty-five men on board and still have some space left, but now there were only thirty-two.

"Right, you sea-whores, ready! Row!" Snorri shouted from the prow when they had drifted far away enough. Ulf followed the movements of Thorbjorn in front of him and leaned forward before dipping his oar into the water. He felt the water fighting back as he pulled on the oar, his back muscles straining at the effort. After some teething problems with the recruits, as it took them a few attempts and curses from the rest of the crew to row in time, the ship lurched forward, effortlessly gliding through the water. Ulf concentrated hard on Thorbjorn's movements, determined not to make any mistakes.

Snorri howled like a wolf, announcing the presence of his warship in the bay.

"There's nothing better than being at sea," Snorri said, patting Ulf on the shoulder as he made his way to the stern. His grin was even bigger now. "Row you fuckers!" he shouted and joined Rolf Treefoot by the stern. *This isn't so bad*, Ulf thought as he settled into the rhythm and didn't have to focus so much on Thorbjorn's movements anymore. *Slap...slap... slap.* The oars dipped into the water and pulled the ship along. The sounds of the sea birds calling in the air added to the calmness of the moment and Ulf was beginning to understand why men enjoyed being at sea. Ran, it seemed, was in a good mood today as the Sae-Ulfr glided over her domain. Ulf felt himself smiling. Rowing calmed him. It made him forget about the fire burning deep inside of him.

Men started talking and joking as Thorgilsstad shrunk in the distance. Some were talking about the anticipated fight with Kettil the Red, while others were talking about their weapons or the thrall that warmed their bed last night. Ulf stayed quiet, preferring to listen to the sounds of the water, mixed in with the voices of the men on board. His back was starting to tire, but he didn't think much of it. He was young and strong; he could deal with it. A large raven flew over the ship, crowing at the men on board. Some took it as a sign that Odin was watching. Ulf saw Snorri fingering his Mjöllnir amulet. He tried to follow the path of the raven as it flew towards the biggest of the islands in the mouth of the bay. It was called Stórr Vördr, which meant big warden. The smaller islands around it were called Smár Vördr, small warden, and Mindri Vördr, smaller warden, but Ulf wasn't sure which one was which. That's where they thought the pirates were hiding. It gave them access to the fjord and to the bay, Rolf had said. He wondered what it meant that the raven was heading that way. Maybe Rolf's suspicion was correct.

After a while, Ulf's back and arm muscles were starting to hurt, not used to this exertion. Fighting and chopping trees worked different muscles. Looking at the other recruits, he saw them tiring as well. He was beginning to think this might not be as easy as he initially had thought. Ulf looked at Oddi who was still rowing effortlessly, almost as if mocking Ulf.

"Starting to tire?" Oddi asked when he saw Ulf looking at him.

"What's the story with Kettil the Red?" Ulf asked instead of responding.

"Kettil?" Oddi scratched the side of his face, his one arm still rowing. "He's from the north. Was outlawed for killing a bóndi in a dispute over grazing land."

"Grazing land?" Ulf didn't understand killing someone for such a reason. There was plenty of grazing land to go around.

"In the north, there's not as much land as there is here," Oddi explained. "It's mainly mountains with little flat land available for farming, so there are more disputes. He was told to leave Norway at the Thing last summer, but he has decided not to. Like salmon dumbly fighting against the river," he said, his voice taking on that intonation he liked to use when he was trying to be clever. Even though it made no sense.

"Salmon do swim up the river," Thorbjorn quipped in front of Ulf, not bothering to turn his head. Oddi either didn't hear or decided not to hear because he didn't respond. Ulf smiled. His breathing was starting to get heavier now and the muscles in his back felt like they were on fire. Looking over his shoulder, he saw the island getting closer, but they still had some rowing to do. He wished they could have sailed, but knew that wasn't going to happen as he looked at the naked mast.

After rowing for some time, they finally got close enough to the island for Snorri to give the order to stop rowing. Ulf leaned forward, breathing heavily. Even at the slow pace they had been going, it had been difficult for him. His back muscles felt like they were being stabbed by hundreds of knives, and even his arms were trembling.

"Nothing like a nice little morning row to get you ready for a fight," Thorbjorn said, rolling his shoulders to loosen them.

"I don't think Ulf agrees with you," Brak said with a light voice. "He's gasping like a stag after rutting season."

"I'm fine," Ulf lied while trying to ignore the laughter around him. He wasn't sure how he was going to fight after this. He doubted he'd be able to lift his shield, but he couldn't show any weakness in front of Snorri's men. Ulf stood and stretched his back, feeling the relief of the burning pain disappearing. Meanwhile Snorri had walked to the prow and was studying the island.

"They're here alright, or else I'm being buggered by Loki." He pointed to the ship beached on a small cove on the island. They could see some men moving around on the stony beach. These men didn't seem to see the Sae-Ulfr as a threat. Ulf guessed that was another reason Snorri wanted them to row at a slow pace, and not hoist the sail. "We'll go in fast, hit them before they have a chance to realize what's happening. Odin willing, we can be back home in time for the evening meal." He looked back at the men. They nodded at him. In a quiet voice, he told them to prepare for battle. Ulf took his helmet from his new sea chest. As he put it on, he watched Snorri and his hirdmen standing by the prow and looking like gods of war in their brynjas and helmets. Snorri especially looked like he came out of a saga with a helmet more beautiful than any Ulf had ever seen. It had an eye-guard that looked like it was made from golden fish scales and matching cheek guards. The helmet covered most of Snorri's face. Brak Drumbr and Thorbjorn were the only ones whose helmets did not have eye-guards, but Thorbjorn's had a nose guard embossed with many intertwined serpents. They all had their weapons at hand. Thorbjorn with his sword, Bloodthirst, Drumbr with his large two-handed axe, Shield-breaker, his brother had his sword, Bear-Claw and Oddi had Death's Breath. Asbjorn had his sword as well, but Ulf didn't know its name. Ulf couldn't help feeling envious of them and the other members of Snorri's crew who also had brynjas.

"We'll row in fast and as soon the Sae-Ulfr hits the beach we jump over and attack hard. Make them think that Fenrir has slipped his bonds and was coming for them." Snorri wore his wolf grin again as he made sure that Tyr's Fury was in place. He took his spear from the spear rack and stood by the prow.

Ulf was about to sit down to row again when Asbjorn shook his head. "Bring your oar in, you'll not be rowing now," he said, with the same wolf grin as Snorri on his face.

"We'll be waiting at the front with Snorri so that we can jump over with him. Need to protect the jarl's son," Thorbjorn explained as he handed Ulf his spear. Ulf nodded and did what he was told, feeling the nerves of the impending fight gnaw at his stomach.

"You know what to do," Snorri said to Rolf Treefoot when he felt they were ready. He looked to Ulf and clapped him on the back. "Ready, Bear-Slayer?" Ulf nodded. "Good, I want you on my right when we stand." Ulf felt his hands shaking so he gripped his spear tightly hoping that the others wouldn't see. Snorri had picked ten men, his hirdmen and a few of the more experienced warriors in his crew to stand in the prow with him. Rolf gave the order to the rest of the crew and turned the ship in towards the island as she started moving. Ulf felt the rush of the wind and the spray of the salty water on his face as the Sae-Ulfr sped up. This would have been exhilarating if death wasn't so close.

The pirates had now realized what was happening and were rushing to get their weapons. Ulf felt his stomach clench and his bladder suddenly full. It's only nerves, he tried to tell himself. He remembered Olaf telling him about his first battle, how he was so nervous he almost pissed himself.

The Sae-Ulfr hit the beach before Ulf could think any more about it, the ripping sound of the beach parting before the Sae-Ulfr's keel bringing Ulf back to the moment. With a roar, Snorri and his men jumped over. Ulf followed, roaring his own battle cry to still his nerves. The rest of the men on the ship pulled their oars in and jumped after their leader. The pirates who had managed to get their weapons ran at Snorri and his men. They were dead before the last of Snorri's men managed to disembark the Sae-Ulfr, skewered by spears and hacked to pieces by sword and axe.

"One of them ran that way," Snorri said pointing with his spear, its tip bloody, at the trees beyond the beach. "Must have gone to warn the others." He looked around to make sure everybody was ready. Then seeing the small ship used by the pirates, he smiled. "Hrut," he called to one of the men, "grab nine men and guard the ships. Don't use the recruits." Hrut called nine men to him, all of them looking disappointed at missing the fight. Snorri looked at the rest of his men, his wolf grin ever-present, as they collected their shields from the Sae-Ulfr. "Let's go hunting," he said after Thorbjorn handed him his shield. Keeping it in front of him, he walked into the trees. Ulf made sure to be on his right-hand side and saw that Thorbjorn walked on Snorri's left. The path was not wide enough for more than three men, forcing the others to follow. They kept their shields up, not sure of who might be hiding amongst the trees. The bændr had said nothing about the pirates having archers, but that didn't mean that there weren't any.

After a short while, they came to a small clearing where the pirates had set up their camp. Small tents were erected in a circle around a fire, with a large pot hanging on a hook stand. In front of the camp stood a line of about twenty men. Like the ones on the beach, they wore no armour and were armed with only axes and spears. A few of them, who looked too young to have started growing beards, only had knives. The only man amongst them who had any armour or a sword was Kettil the Red. Ulf saw now where he got the name from. His hair and beard were flame red. Kettil wore a thickened leather jerkin, like Ulf. He had a simple sword in his hand and shield in the other. Kettil was not a big man, but his eyes were like empty pits, dark and soulless. He stood in the middle of the line of men facing Snorri's crew.

"Looks like a welcoming party," Thorbjorn said, eyeing up the pirates.

"Aye, let's hope they're as friendly as they look," Snorri responded before taking a step forward. Ulf was about to follow but then saw Thorbjorn staying where he was. He decided to do the same.

"Stop there, if you want to live!" Kettil said. He appeared confident despite facing men in better armour than his ragged crew. "Who are you and what do you want?"

"Is that how you greet your guests, Kettil?" Snorri responded, his voice light.

Kettil seemed confused by Snorri's friendly manner. "I'll not ask again. Who are you and what do you want?"

"I am Snorri, son of Jarl Thorgils." He smiled at Kettil. "Whom you have insulted."

"How?"

Snorri stood there relaxed, as if he was talking to a fisherman about the weather. He showed no concern for the armed men facing him. Ulf saw the effect this was having on some of the younger men amongst Kettil's crew. "You attacked some bændr who are under the protection of Jarl Thorgils. Now," he continued before Kettil had a chance to say anything, "you may not know who Jarl Thorgils is. But I can tell you this; he is not a man you want to anger."

"Then why is the jarl not here himself? Instead, he sends his whelp to deal with me. He must not like you very much if he is willing to send you to your death." Kettil sounded confident when he said this, and Ulf could see some of his men smiling, but most of them still looked nervous.

"The jarl is too busy to deal with a worthless prick like you."

"A worthless prick!" Kettil's face went as red as his hair. "I am the famous Kettil the Red, known throughout Norway as a ruthless and mighty warrior." He took a step forward as he said this and spread his arms wide to emphasize his point.

"You're as famous as a lice's cock, Kettil," Snorri retorted.

"Lice have cocks?" Oddi asked from where he was standing beside Thorbjorn.

"You're supposed to be the wise one, Oddi, so you tell me," Thorbjorn responded. Ulf smiled, taking comfort in their confidence to joke in front of armed men who might attack them at any moment.

Kettil didn't like this. He turned to his men. "Don't worry men, we are protected by Odin. They cannot defeat us!" He turned back to Snorri. "Kill them all!" he screamed and ran at them.

Snorri took a step back. "Skjaldborg!" he shouted. Ulf was glad of the months of training as he effortlessly linked his shield with Snorri's to form the shield wall. The brothers were on his right, with Thorbjorn, Oddi and Asbjorn standing on Snorri's left. The rest of the men slotted into place forming a wall ten men wide and two men deep. The pirates ran at the wall, screaming like they were trying to wake the gods. Ulf saw that Kettil was not running at Snorri, but rather towards the lesser-armed men in the wall. But Ulf didn't have much time to follow Kettil's movement as one of the pirates ran at him, his axe held high, ready to chop down on Ulf's head. Instinctively, Ulf skewered the man with his spear. The pirate's momentum kept him going until he got to Ulf's shield. Ulf could smell the man's fetid breath and see the dirt trapped in his pores, the hairs sticking out of his nose and the lice crawling around in his beard. He took all of this in as the pirate stood there; axe still held high, a pained and confused expression on his face. The weight of the man on Ulf's spear almost dragged him out of the shield wall, forcing Ulf to let go of it. As he reached down to grab Olaf's axe from his belt, another pirate attacked him with a spear. Ulf just lifted his shield in time, pushing the spear up and over his head. Time seemed to slow as Ulf heard the blood pumping in his ears, almost sounding like whispering voices. Ulf shook his head, trying to dispel them while struggling to free his axe from his belt. Snorri stabbed the man in the chest before Ulf could manage. The pirate spat blood on Ulf's face as he breathed his last. Snorri freed his sword before the falling body could rip it from his grip. He had a crazed smile on his face.

The fight was over not long after that. Five of the pirates were alive, including Kettil, although one lying on the ground and clutching his stomach as a dark stain spread through his tunic. Ulf stood breathing heavily and watching them. His body was shaking from the adrenaline that coursed through him, making Ulf more aware of everything around him. The wind rustled through the green leaves on the trees and cooled Ulf's hot skin. The pain in his back was a distant memory and his arms felt as strong as ever.

"You still live, Kettil. I am glad," Snorri said. Ulf realized he was breathing normally, like this had been nothing but a little stroll.

"Why do you care?" Kettil asked, "You are here to kill me."

"True, but I will give you a choice."

"What choice?"

Snorri smiled, but this wasn't a friendly smile. "Die like a man or die like a coward."

"And what of us?" one of the surviving pirates asked.

Snorri thought for a while. "You chose to follow an outlawed man," Snorri responded, leaving the survivors pondering over his words. They did not like the implication.

"I tell you what, Kettil," Snorri said, studying the blade of his sword. "I'm getting a bit bored with this and I'd like to get home before nightfall so let's make a deal."

"What deal?" Kettil asked suspiciously.

"You and me fight, man on man. If you kill me, you can live."

"And if you kill me?"

"Then your men will die quickly."

Kettil thought for a short while and smiled. He must have thought he could beat Snorri in a fight. Without looking at his remaining men he agreed and took a few steps forward. Three of the remaining pirates looked shocked. The one with the stomach injury was in too much pain to know what was happening.

Snorri's men formed a half-circle as he stepped forward, preparing himself to face Kettil. Ulf watched them, unsure about this as Snorri's men cheered him on. The two men stood facing each other. Snorri was bigger, both in height and width than Kettil, but Kettil thought himself a great warrior. Kettil stood with his shield in front of him, his sword ready to strike, whereas Snorri had his shield and Tyr's Fury low by his side. An insult to Kettil. Kettil saw this and attacked. He swung his sword at Snorri, who easily blocked the strike with his shield and took a step back, deciding not to counterattack. Kettil attacked again, this time with a backhand slice, but again Snorri blocked it easily with his shield. Kettil followed with a jab, but Snorri jumped out of the way, moving comfortably and quickly despite the weight of his brynja. Ulf was impressed. He had seen Snorri fight many times in training, even had a few sparring sessions against him. But this was different. Snorri moved like one who knew his own skill, who was confident in his sword arm. Snorri believed he could not die. The smile he wore on his face said it all.

"Are you going to attack or just keep running away from me?" Kettil asked, wanting it to look like Snorri was afraid of him.

Snorri smiled in response and feinted an attack at Kettil's head. Kettil raised his shield to block. But at the last moment, Snorri dropped to his knee and sliced his sword deep into Kettil's leg. Kettil screamed and dropped to his knees as Snorri got to his feet and smiled at him.

"Is that what you wanted?" he asked as he walked around Kettil, stopping behind him. Kettil didn't respond as Snorri plunged his sword into his back, his eyes bulging at the pain before falling face down onto the ground. Snorri cleaned his sword on Kettil's tunic, not caring about the armed pirates behind him.

"What about them?" Ulf asked.

"Kill them," Snorri said without looking at them. One of the pirates tried to run, but he was quickly killed by a thrown spear. The remaining men begged for their lives as the new recruits ran them through with their spears. The one with the stomach injury had died during the fight.

Snorri walked up to Ulf, sheathing his sword. "You fought well today." Ulf said nothing. He was surprised by Snorri's ruthlessness. Somehow, he never expected the man who was always laughing and joking to be able to condemn another to death as easily as putting on his tunic. For the first time, Ulf really understood Snorri and was glad the Norns had seen fit to put them on the same side.

CHAPTER 12

The Skuggi saw Vidar approaching the ship as Snorri's crew got ready to leave. Another new arrival that he hated. Vidar should have been killed as a baby, not worshipped. The Skuggi ground his teeth together as he watched the boy walk up the wharf. In his head, it sounded like two boulders being rubbed together, but it was barely inaudible to those around him. Everybody seemed excited by the hunt for the pirates. It was ridiculous – they were merely scum, no need to make such a big deal out of it. But then, these people were simple. It didn't matter how smart they thought they were. He decided to go to the ship; people would notice if he wasn't there. The town's people were smiling, but they were not cheering as they would when the ship went raiding. They knew it would be back before nightfall. As Snorri called the order for the men to row, the Skuggi sent a silent prayer to Loki. *If you are listening Loki, make sure that Ulf and Snorri don't return from this hunt. If you do, I will sacrifice this whole village in your name.* He looked to the sky but saw no sign Loki had heard him. That didn't stop the smile coming to his lips. Loki was a mysterious god so maybe he shouldn't have expected any signs.

Ulf took a deep gulp of his ale as he sat in Thorgils' hall, his muscles stiff and sore. The ale tasted even better after today's events. The jarl had decided to throw a small feast to celebrate the success of their hunt. The full hall was filled with a noise that sounded like bees buzzing around their hive, the only difference being the occasional roaring laughter. Ulf saw that Thorbjorn's father was still here. He was sat near the jarl, so he could be part of the conversation that went on around them. Occasionally he would look their way and lift his cup to his son, the proud smile easily spotted on his face. Thorbjorn always returned the gesture. Everyone was in a good mood. It might not have been a large raid, with the warriors returning in a ship loaded with treasures and thralls, but it had sent a message. You do not attack those under the protection of Jarl Thorgils.

After killing the remaining pirates, Snorri had allowed the men to loot the bodies of the dead. Not that there was much to take. Snorri had offered Ulf Kettil's sword. It had a simple design, but it was beautiful. Ulf had declined. Instead, Snorri had given the sword to one of the recruits who had fought well. The boy's name was Geir, although Ulf didn't know why he thought of him as a boy – Geir was almost the same age as Ulf himself. Because Ulf wouldn't take the sword, Snorri had given him one of his arm-rings instead. It was a simple bronze ring, no thicker than his little finger, with a snarling wolf head on the ends and nothing compared to the other rings Snorri had, but Ulf was strangely proud of it. It marked him as a warrior who had stood in a fight and survived. The only thing Ulf had taken for himself was a beautifully carved ivory comb he had found on one of the pirates.

"You still think too much." Ulf heard the voice from beside him, while he was looking at Vidar chewing on some boar meat. He looked at Snorri, sitting to his right. The smile had returned to his lips now. Despite the easy victory over the pirates, Snorri was subdued on the way home. They had lost two men to the pirates, one of the recruits and another who had been part of Snorri's crew for a few years now. Snorri had brought their bodies back and given them to their families. He also gave the families some gold to make sure that they would not want for anything. Ulf had seen very different sides of Snorri today: the famed warrior forever trying to fulfil his bloodlust and the compassionate leader who grieved for the men he lost.

"It was an eventful day." There was a roar of laughter as one of the men fell off the bench and spilt his ale over himself.

"That's not what I meant." Snorri took a sip of his ale, also watching the commotion at the other end of their table.

"Then what do you mean?"

"When you fight, you still think too much." Snorri looked at Ulf. There was a smile on his lips, but his eyes were serious. Ulf felt slightly unsettled by this side of Snorri. "Why do you think I threw you my spear during your fight with the bear?" Ulf shrugged, not knowing what to say. "Because I saw the natural warrior in you. That's also why a good fighter like Geir," he pointed with his cup to where Geir was sitting with Snorri's crew, on the other side of the table, "is not part of my hirdmen." Ulf wasn't sure where Snorri was going with this. "Geir is a good warrior, and maybe one day he will join my hirdmen."

"Your point being?"

"You are a better warrior than he is." Snorri took a bite of meat, chewing for a while before continuing. "You can also be part of my hirdmen." Snorri seemed to be studying him with his bleary eyes. "If I help you avenge your family, will you join my hirdmen?"

"Why?" Ulf asked with a raised eyebrow.

"I think you can be a great warrior, but you need to learn to trust your instincts."

Ulf thought back to the fight with the pirates. He remembered the calmness that came over him once he had freed Olaf's axe from his belt. The next pirate had attacked him with a spear thrust. Ulf had ducked behind his shield, feeling the spear strike against it. He opened his shield and chopped down on the pirate's exposed neck. He still remembered the hot spray of blood that had covered his face when he pulled the axe free. But he also remembered the spear thrust before that had almost killed him. The thought darkened his mood. He stared at the cup of ale in his hand and realized he didn't want to drink anymore.

"I almost died today," he said to Snorri, who seemed surprised by the comment.

"But you didn't. You live to fight another day and get your vengeance." Snorri gripped him by the shoulder.

"And when will that be?" Ulf knew he sounded like a petulant child as he asked this, but he did not want to fail his family again because of some petty fight against nobodies.

Snorri didn't respond straight away, instead, he seemed to think about the question, which annoyed Ulf even more.

"We spent all winter training every day we could and now we have to run around and chase after some thieves. I should be looking for Griml, not risking my life killing pirates," Ulf complained, feeling his body begin to shake as the flames inside him threatened to take over.

Snorri laughed at that, shaking his head in disbelief. "And where is this Griml, Ulf?" He still had a smile on his face, but Ulf could see he was being serious. "Do you know where to find him?" Ulf could only shake his head. "Look around you." Snorri pointed to the rest of the hall. "There are still people in this very hall who think that Griml is not real. They still believe you killed your family." Ulf knew this was true. He had seen the way some people looked at him when he walked past them, and how some of the mothers pulled their children away from him.

"So why are you helping me then?" That was the one thing Ulf could never understand. Snorri risked a lot by siding with Ulf and going against his father by doing so.

"I don't know," Snorri answered honestly. "There is something familiar about you that I don't understand. And it is not because you were here as a child."

Ulf gripped his cup so hard, he was worried it might break. Snorri, though, leaned back and closed his eyes. Ulf looked away from Snorri and saw Lady Ingibjorg was watching them, like she was following their conversation. But they were too far away from her and there was too much noise for her to overhear them.

"You will get your vengeance," Snorri said.

"When?"

"When the Norns decide it's time."

Ulf growled at the answer. He didn't like the idea of someone else controlling his fate. Especially not when that fate had taken everything away from him. "I don't want to wait on the fucking Norns!" He slammed his cup on the table as he said this. All those around him stopped what they were doing and stared at him, confused by his sudden outburst.

"Then tell me where Griml is and we'll go kill him. We can sail this very night if you want," Snorri responded, still managing to stay calm.

Ulf saw that those around them were still staring, including Vidar who was silently reprimanding him. "I…" Ulf started but did not know what to say.

"You will have your vengeance, brother, but you must be patient. Vengeance is a long road. But there is no point in fighting over things you cannot control. The Norns will decide when it is time for you to get your revenge. Until then we train, we fight, and we drink. Those are the things we can control," Snorri said confidently. "Today was a good day and you fought well, almost like your father." He raised his cup to Ulf.

Reluctantly, Ulf lifted his cup and took a sip of his ale. He thought back to the smiles he saw on the faces of Snorri and the brothers during the fight with the pirates. He remembered something else as well, something he wasn't sure how to explain. Something that scared him. The voices whispering in his ear, telling him to slaughter all those in his way. Ulf did not want to listen to them. To listen to the voices would mean becoming like his father.

And Ulf did not want to be like his father.

Ulf got restless as the night wore on. His conversation with Snorri had left him in a dark mood. He tried to distract himself by listening to the conversations around him, but his mind kept going back to his family. He fingered the Mjöllnir hanging around his neck, hoping Snorri was right, hoping that the Norns would give him his revenge. He took another sip of his ale, trying to dispel the thoughts from his head once again. The feast was still going strong, even though Thorgils and Ingibjorg had retired long ago. Snorri and Oddi were, as always, entertaining everyone with one of their poetry competitions. Vidar had fallen asleep beside Ulf on the bench.

"Are you ever going to tell us his story?" Thorbjorn said, finishing his sentence with a loud burp. He thumped his chest with a look of pride on his face.

Ulf smiled. "Like I said, it's not my story to tell." He thought back to the old man's hut in the forest. The way the old man used to look at Vidar. He looked at the sleeping Vidar again. It was not a story for anyone to tell. Loud laughter drew his attention to the other side of the hall where Ragnar was sat, drinking and laughing with some of the men from the jarl's crew. His relationship with Ragnar was still strained after their first encounter on the wharf before the winter. A thought came to his mind then.

"Do you know how Ragnar lost his finger?"

Thorbjorn thought for a short while, before laughing to himself. "Oh aye, I know the story." He scratched his nose before continuing. "There was a woman he was fucking, many years ago. This was before I came here. Anyway, one day she catches him with another lass. A younger, prettier one, you see. So, she grabs a knife and starts swinging it around like she's a Valkyrie with a mighty sword." He laughed at the picture in his own head. "Well, Ragnar, having none of this, reached out to grab the knife but before he could get hold of it, she chopped off his finger." He was laughing as loud as the people across the hall now. "By the gods, I would have loved to see that. What?" He stopped laughing when he saw the confused expression on Ulf's face.

"That's the story you heard?" Ulf asked, thinking of the other two stories he'd been told.

"Aye."

"And who told you this story?"

Thorbjorn thought for a while, scratching the top of his neck now, under his beard. "You know, I don't remember."

Ulf shook his head. He was too tired to care. Just then Hulda appeared behind him. Placing one of her small hands on his shoulder, she whispered into his ear. "Meet me outside, by our usual spot." And with that, she disappeared.

"Someone is in for a good time." Thorbjorn elbowed him in the side while winking at him.

Ulf rolled his eyes as he finished his ale and stood up. "Keep an eye on Vidar, will you," he said and left. Once outside, he stood for a moment and took a deep breath, savouring the coolness of the fresh air after having to breathe the stale hot air of the hall for most of the night. The sun had finally gone down, but the village was illuminated by the half-moon in the sky, casting just enough light to be able to see by it. Ulf felt more awake, the cool night air reinvigorating him. Or it could just be the thought of what was to come. A smile came to his lips then; it seemed there was another part of him that felt more awake. Deciding not to waste a moment longer, he walked around the hall to the large tree Hulda liked so much. Ulf still didn't like it but knew there was no point in complaining. Hulda wasn't there when he got to the tree. Not a big deal, he could wait. Maybe she got caught up with her tasks. She was still a thrall after all.

He found his thoughts drifting as he waited for Hulda. Again, they went back to that day on the farm. He tried to take his mind off it and focus on something more pleasant, like Hulda. But he couldn't, his mind would not let him. Just like it would never let him forget. It would have been easier trying to change the direction of the wind. But every time he revisited the fight, it was never Griml he saw. He felt his hands starting to hurt and realized he'd been clenching his fists. Taking deep breaths, he calmed himself down before Hulda could see him angry again.

He looked up at the moon and realized that it had moved quite a bit while he had been waiting. "Where is she?" he quietly asked himself. A faint breeze blew through the leaves of the tree as if answering his question. Suppressing a shiver, he decided she wasn't coming. Maybe Lady Ingibjorg wouldn't allow her to leave, it had happened before. Ulf left the tree and walked to the wharf. He liked sitting there and listening to the sounds of the water. The village was a different place at night. There was nobody outside. People did not go out at night unless they really had to. And tonight, there were better things to do than wander around outside. He felt a shiver run down his back as he got to the square, which he did not understand at first, but then saw why. The gods were watching him. It felt like they turned their heads to follow him as he walked past them. Ulf breathed a sigh of relief when he reached the wharf. He still didn't understand why but hearing the water lapping on the stony shore soothed his anger, like Freya or Frigg were whispering calming words into his ears. He stroked Sae-Ulfr's prow as he walked past her, telling her of his presence so she would not get upset. Rolf had told him that ships had their own spirits, that they were living beings and needed to be respected. Ulf sat down beside her and rested his head on her hull, trying to keep his eyes open as he stared at the sky.

But the ale in his blood and the soft sounds of the water made that impossible, and soon Ulf was asleep.

CHAPTER 13

The sounds of women screaming and men shouting woke Ulf up in the morning. His hand went for Olaf's axe which he usually wore on his belt, only to find it was not there. He had left it in his sea chest with the rest of his stuff when they got back yesterday, as no weapons were allowed in the hall during a feast. The sound of running feet on the wharf made him look over his shoulder. It was Vidar running towards him, his eyes wide and face pale. That look meant trouble. Ulf got to his feet and looked around the village but could see no sign of the attack. Vidar reached him and began pulling him along the wharf and pointing towards the hanging tree. Ulf followed, not sure what was happening, but somehow knowing it would not be good for him.

Thorbjorn came out of the hall as they rushed past it and called out after them. "What's all this noise about?!" He looked like he had just woken up himself, his usually tidy hair and neat beard a mess. He was rubbing his eyes as they struggled to adjust to the bright morning sun.

"Don't know. Was about to find out myself," Ulf responded.

"How was your night with Hulda?" Thorbjorn asked, a grin parting his brown moustache from his beard. Ulf didn't answer. Thorbjorn didn't need to know Hulda never showed. He would just spend the rest of the day teasing Ulf. Thorbjorn laughed at his silence. He took his comb out of his pouch and started brushing his beard as they neared the crowd of people by the tree, struggling to pull it through the tangles and the knots of his thick hair.

"There he is!" someone from the crowd shouted as they walked through. The three of them looked at each other, not understanding what was happening. Everybody was crowded around the base of the tree. The jarl and his wife were there, so was Snorri and Ragnar. Ulf did not like the frown on Snorri's face. It wasn't his usual calm expression Ulf was used to. The brothers and Oddi appeared by his side, like they were shielding him from something. Ulf couldn't understand what from, but when he saw the fear on Vidar's face, he knew whatever it was, was not going to be good for him.

"What in Odin's name is going on?" Thorbjorn asked.

"It's best you see for yourself," Oddi answered, his grave tone only confirming Ulf's fear.

"I knew he was no good. The jarl should have had him killed the moment he arrived!" an old man from the crowd shouted. Ulf rounded on him but was pulled back by Brak Drumbr. The man had recoiled at Ulf's expression, the three scars on his face only making him look more fearsome. But Ulf's confidence soon left him as he got to the tree and saw what all the commotion was about.

It was Hulda. She was sitting at the base of the tree where Ulf had been waiting for her the previous night. But that alone wasn't what had brought the people out, or what was causing all the glares and whispers aimed at Ulf. She was stripped of all her clothing, her pale body exposed to everyone. In her right hand, she held a knife. The blade was covered in dried blood. Dried blood from the long gash across her neck, like a sickening smile. Her breasts were dark from the blood which had gushed out and dried during the night. Ulf stood there frozen to the spot as he took all this in. He saw no brutality in the way she had been killed. It just looked like any other sacrifice, whether it was man or beast. What shocked the people and took Ulf's breath away was the name of the god carved onto her forehead. *Loki.* Ulf's hand instinctively went to the empty sheath on his belt as he recognised the knife in Hulda's hand.

"Odin's arse, lad. Now you are fucked," Thorbjorn whispered beside him. If he had recognised the knife as Ulf's, then everybody else would have as well. That explained the looks the people were giving him. And the look of fear on Vidar's face. He had never seen Vidar look afraid, not even when they were attacked by the bear in the forest. Ulf took his eyes from Hulda's body and looked at the jarl and his companions. Jarl Thorgils' face was as hard as the winters were cold, and his eyes bored deep into Ulf's. Ulf saw the anger in them, and in the way he stood, straight-backed and arms crossed. Whatever he had decided, Ulf could tell it would not be changed, just like one could not change the shape of a mountain. Lady Ingibjorg was staring at Hulda, unaware of his presence. The look on her face was one that Ulf had not seen in his short time here. Fear, uncertainty and a deep sadness. More than you would expect for a thrall. Snorri's eyes were not on Ulf or on Hulda. Instead, they were constantly darting around, looking at the men who had surrounded Ulf. His right hand was close to Tyr's Fury, but Ulf doubted he would draw his blade if it came to it. Thorvald just looked pale, like he wanted to spew his guts all over the floor, while at the same time leering at Hulda's breasts. Ragnar was the only one smiling, although it was not a happy smile. It was a smile that could mean death for Ulf. He opened his mouth to say something but realized he had nothing to say. The people behind Ulf were whispering to each other, some of them shouting obscenities at Ulf or urging the jarl to punish him. Thorbjorn shouted back, telling the people to be quiet, or else. Ulf was slightly comforted in knowing that Thorbjorn and the others were still on his side.

"When I got back near the end of last summer and saw you here, I knew no good could come from it," the jarl began. He took a step forward and placed his hand on the hilt of his sword. Ulf wondered if he was planning on using it. "But my wife and Snorri convinced me you should stay, that you did not kill your uncle and aunt." Ulf clenched his fists at the mention of Olaf and Brynhild. "You, yourself gave me such a fine speech about how much they meant to you. Them and their daughters." Ulf felt his heartbeat rising and took deep breaths as he tried to stay calm. "I decided to give you a chance, Ulf. My wife thought I should do that at least. And Odin knows she is always full of wise counsel. Just as Frigg is to the All-Father. I even let you join my son's crew at his request." The jarl paused to let the words sink in. "And now we find ourselves here. Hulda, my wife's thrall, slaughtered like a pig with your knife in her hand. Or do you deny that that is your knife?" Ulf only shook his head. There was no need to say anything.

"Father, Ulf didn't do this!" Snorri interjected.

"And how do you know this?" Jarl Thorgils glared at his son. "Were you with him all night long? I didn't think so," he said when he saw Snorri wasn't going to answer.

"I always said he was no good, Snorri!" his wife, Gunnhildr, said. She stood next to Lady Ingibjorg, clutching their youngest son to her. Ulf couldn't see Snorri's eldest, Thorgils, anywhere. They must have left him in their house with the thralls.

"Be quiet, woman!" Snorri shouted without looking at her. Her face went red, but she stayed quiet.

"Ragnar, did you not say you saw them last night?" the jarl asked his champion. Ragnar nodded.

"Aye. She said something to him and then walked away. He followed not soon after." There were whispers from the crowd of people. Some were shaking their heads at Ulf.

"Thorbjorn. You were sat next to Ulf. Do you deny this?"

Thorbjorn looked conflicted. He wanted to protect his sword brother, but not at the expense of lying to his jarl. After taking a deep breath he responded. "No, I do not deny this." Ulf knew he shouldn't be mad at Thorbjorn. He understood the man's position, but he couldn't help but be irritated by Thorbjorn's answer.

"Do you know what she said to him?" the jarl asked. Thorbjorn shook his head. She had spoken too quietly for him to hear anything, although he was sure he had an idea. But that wasn't worth mentioning. "I see," the jarl said. He looked at Ulf again. Ulf was surprised to see a sadness in his face. "Do you have anything to say, Ulf? Anything to prove you did not do this?"

Again, Ulf only shook his head. He did not trust himself to speak, not with the fire coursing through his veins.

The jarl sighed his frustration at Ulf's lack of answers. He turned to a group of men standing to one side. "Seize him."

The men of Snorri's crew went for their weapons but was instantly stopped by a shout from Jarl Thorgils. "Do not dare! I swear by Odin if any of you defend Ulf then you will all be killed!" The men looked uncertain until Ulf told them to listen to their jarl.

He did not want more deaths because of him. He watched as the men approached him. There were five of them, and they had not unsheathed their weapons. Seeing the wolf grins on their faces, Ulf remembered a time when he and his uncle went hunting. From their hiding place, they had seen a young stag being cornered by a pack of wolves. Ulf had thought the stag was done for, but his uncle had told him to watch. Before the wolves could attack, the young stag lowered its antlers and charged at the wolves. The wolves could not react fast enough, and the leader of the pack had been thrown through the air as the stag tried to break free. Ulf felt like the young stag about to be attacked by a pack of wolves. So, he decided to follow the stag's example. He moved as soon as the first man got near enough and punched him in the face, feeling his nose break as his head snapped back. Before the others could respond, Ulf kicked the second man in the stomach. The man doubled over as he collapsed. There was a scream from some of the women, shocked by the sudden violence. The third man tried to grab hold of Ulf, but Ulf ducked under the man's swinging arms and went past him, swinging a hook at the fourth man. The fourth man, an experienced fighter by the looks of him, managed to block the blow and grab hold of Ulf's arm. The third man tried to take advantage of this but did not move fast enough. Ulf kicked the man holding him in the leg, causing him to drop to the floor. The two remaining men hesitated as they saw this, unsure of how to approach him.

"For Odin's sake!" the jarl shouted, angry that his experienced warriors could not deal with Ulf. "Ragnar, get him."

"Enough!" Lady Ingibjorg's voice tore through the air like thunder. "There will be no more violence!" She looked at Ulf. He saw the sadness in her eyes. "For the sake of Hulda, Ulf, do not fight." Everybody went quiet as they waited to see how Ulf would respond. Ragnar braced himself. But after a short while, Ulf decided to listen to Lady Ingibjorg and nodded. The two men grabbed him immediately, one of them punching him in the stomach for good measure. Ulf dropped to the floor, coughing and gasping for air as they tied his hands behind his back. He remembered something else about the young stag. In the end, there had been too many wolves. When Ulf managed to get his breath back, he looked to the jarl.

"What will happen to me?"

The jarl looked deep into his eyes, like he was examining Ulf's soul before looking at the tree behind him, as if realizing where they were for the first time.

"Hang him."

Ulf felt like laughing. He couldn't think of anything else to do as he stood there, his hands tied behind his back and two men on either side of him. But he didn't laugh. Instead, he watched the faces of the people around him. More people had come to join them in the field. Ulf guessed the whole village was there to watch him hang. To see the death of the great Bear-Slayer. Again, he felt the smile on his lips. The great Bear-Slayer. That name felt like a joke. He was a fool for thinking Odin would grant him his revenge. He had thought killing the bear in the forest was a sign he would kill Griml. Maybe killing the bear was a fluke. Perhaps Ulf was meant to die that day on the farm and Odin had sent the bear to kill him. But where Griml and the bear had failed, the noose would not. It felt like the Norns were fixing their mistake, like a woman replacing a fraying thread in the tunic she is weaving. The only thing that upset him was that he wouldn't go to Valhalla and feast with his uncle in Odin's great hall. Instead, he would go to the domain of Hel, the goddess of the dead. Perhaps that was a good thing. Ulf didn't want to face his uncle and have to tell him he had failed. That he hadn't been able to avenge their deaths. But neither did he want to go to Hel, especially not after his dream. He wondered if that was where his aunt and cousins had gone. Perhaps he would find out soon enough.

He started scanning the crowd again to distract himself from his thoughts. All around him he saw either shock or eagerness on the faces of the villagers. His eyes fell on the face of the jarl. He saw a face as hard as the stone in the mountains. Snorri, on the other hand, was angry. His face had gone red and he was standing as rigid as the tree behind Ulf. Snorri wasn't looking at Ulf, instead, he was glaring at his father. He had protested, urging his father to banish Ulf instead. But the jarl had made his mind up. Ulf had become a problem he did not want. He had to die. Maybe the jarl thought if Ulf was hanged and sacrificed to Odin, then there would be no more problems. He wouldn't be around to find out, so he didn't really think about it.

Thorbjorn and the others were standing around Snorri, their attention more on Snorri than on the events unfolding around them. Ragnar looked conflicted, like part of him was happy to see Ulf hang, but another part wanted it to be him who got to kill Ulf. He had never gotten over Ulf humiliating him at the end of the summer. The only person Ulf could not understand was Vidar. He stood there, next to Lady Ingibjorg looking at Ulf. Ulf had expected him to be upset, or angry. But instead, he was smiling. Not a malicious smile, but a comforting one. It almost felt as if Vidar was trying to reassure him, but Ulf could not understand why. He was about to be hanged, there was nothing reassuring about that. Next to him, Lady Ingibjorg had an equally confusing expression on her face. She did not look upset anymore, like she had done when she was looking at the body of Hulda. Her mask was back on, preventing anyone from seeing her emotions and giving her that mystical look. But as she stared at Ulf, he felt like she knew something, something important and was just waiting for Ulf to figure it out. Ulf felt a shiver run down his spine as he looked at the two of them, standing next to each other, Lady Ingibjorg's arm around Vidar's shoulders. Then his eyes fell on the body of Hulda. Somebody had covered her body with a cloak but left her face open like they thought she would be able to see them hang the person responsible for her death. He realized he had not really thought about her since they had found her body. He had liked Hulda, but it was never more than that. She had used him, and he had let her. But he never understood why. Perhaps he would see her in Hel and ask her.

He didn't have any more time to think about it as the man who went for the rope returned. Ulf took a deep breath to calm his nerves as the rope was placed around his neck and the other end thrown over the branch of the tree. He heard the flap of wings as a large raven landed on the branch, a few fingers away from the rope. It started croaking as people pointed and whispered. Some thought it was one of Odin's ravens, come to watch Ulf hang. Odin was the god of the hanged, after all. To Ulf, the croaking of the raven sounded like laughter. He could almost see Odin sitting in his seat in Asgard laughing at him. He felt his anger rising at the thought, but then let it go. It did not matter anymore. The rope began to tighten around his neck as two men started pulling.

"Father, please I beg you. Spare his life, send him to exile instead," Snorri pleaded one more time. But the jarl did not answer him, instead, his eyes were fixed on the large raven.

Ulf looked at Vidar and Lady Ingibjorg again. They still had the same expressions on their faces, both knowing something he did not. His body tensed as he felt himself being lifted off the ground. The pull of the rope under his chin forced his mouth open, despite his efforts to keep it closed. Finally, his feet left the ground, the weight of his body now supported by his neck. The pain was worse than he ever thought it would be. A strange gurgling noise escaped his throat as it was being crushed by his weight. His heart started beating faster, so fast he thought it might rip out of his chest. Time seemed to slow, as if it wanted to drag out his agony for as long as possible. He started fighting against his restraints, desperately trying to free his hands. But it was useless. Ulf felt his strength fading. His lungs were burning, desperate for the air that would keep him alive. His body started violently jerking as it fought to get air through his constricted throat. He tried to focus on Vidar, on Snorri. On people he had started thinking of as friends, but he could not. The edge of his vision had started to blur, making it hard for him to see. The pain around his neck was unbearable now, so much so that he was beginning to wish he would just die, anything to escape this agony. With every jerk of his body, the pain just got worse. His lungs were on fire now, his tongue felt swollen, further blocking his airways. It felt like his eyes were about to pop out of his head. Slowly his world was blacking out. After what felt like an age, but was no longer than a dozen heartbeats, he thought he was finally going to die. Through all this he heard the raven, still sitting on the branch, mocking him as he hung there at the end of the rope, desperately fighting for his life.

Then there was another noise. At first, his delirious mind thought it was the gods laughing at him. Laughing at his arrogance. That he really thought he could avenge his family and retrieve Ormstunga. The loud ripping crack of their laughter rang through his ears as he suddenly felt like he was falling. Before Ulf could understand this, he landed on something hard. He heard screaming and crying, surely the sounds of Hel, the anguish of the spirits who occupy this domain. The crush around his neck was gone, but his throat was still in pain as cool air started entering his lungs. He had always thought it would be warm and fetid. He expected to taste the dead as it passed over his tongue. Instead, this air was cool, it was fresh. He didn't understand why there was cool refreshing air in Hel, but he started sucking it in as fast as possible, ignoring the pain in his throat as it protested. Slowly his vision began to clear and to his surprise, he found he was not in Hel. His oxygen-deprived brain was struggling to understand the vision in front of him as he lay there, staring at the tree. Just a broken stump where the hanging branch had been.

The crowd fell silent as everyone was trying to understand what they had just seen. Snorri's eyes shifted from Ulf to the raven flying away. A smile appeared on his lips.

"See! Odin does not want Ulf to die. Not until he has had his revenge!" he proclaimed before anyone had a chance to say anything. Thorbjorn and the brothers quickly shouted in support.

"Or maybe," said Lady Ingibjorg, walking to where Ulf was lying on the ground, still recovering from his ordeal, "Ulf did not kill

Hulda. This could be Odin's way of telling us we were hanging the wrong person."

The jarl did not look like he believed his wife. He had to admit the branch breaking was clearly the work of the gods, but he did not want to believe it was Odin's work. "Maybe it was Loki protecting his follower," he countered. Lady Ingibjorg didn't respond, she only smiled at her husband. Everyone had seen the raven; everyone had heard it. At once, everyone started shouting their own opinions.

"I didn't kill her," Ulf said, but his throat was still hurting from the rope, so it came out as barely a whisper and could not be heard over the noise of the crowd. "I didn't kill her!" he tried again; this time louder. He coughed as his voice grated through his injured throat.

The crowd fell silent, everyone looking at Ulf as he lay on his back, not being able to get up.

"And why should we believe you?" a woman from the crowd shouted. Some told her to be quiet while others agreed with her.

"My knife," Ulf responded.

"What?" Thorgils wasn't sure if he heard correctly. It was difficult to make out what Ulf was saying.

"My knife in her hand." Ulf rolled onto his knees and sat up, looking the jarl in the eyes. There was no anger in Ulf's eyes, no confusion. Instead, there was a clarity, a realization he had not been forsaken by the gods.

"You admit that is your knife then?" the jarl asked.

"Everyone knows that is my knife." Ulf coughed again, his voice still struggling to come out of his throat. "But why would I leave my knife in her hand?" He looked at the people around him and saw a sea of confused faces.

"Maybe you wanted us to know that you killed her," Gunnhildr said, sounding very confident in her theory.

"Then why would he still be here?" Oddi asked, understanding what Ulf was saying. Gunnhildr was about to respond, then realized she didn't have an answer.

"That's right," Snorri said, glaring at his wife. He walked up to Hulda, who had almost been forgotten about and indicated to her face. "And why would Ulf write Loki on her head?" He turned to Ulf, who was still sitting on his knees.

"Maybe he worships Loki?" Thorvald put in. It was the first words he had spoken since this whole thing had started. At once people started shouting at each other, Snorri's crew defending Ulf while others agreed with Thorvald. Ulf wasn't really listening, he didn't care what they were saying, or what they thought. He only cared that he was alive. Somehow, he had survived. He studied the broken branch lying on the ground beside him. It was a thick branch and looked healthy enough, so there was no reason for it to break. Or at least not any reason that Ulf could see. Ulf's head was starting to hurt. He didn't know if it was because of the hanging, or because of trying to understand the gods. Instead, he looked to Vidar who knelt down beside him and removed the noose still attached to Ulf's neck, the smile on his face bigger than before.

"Why do I get the feeling you knew this was going to happen?" Ulf couldn't help but ask. Vidar tilted his head and furrowed his brow. Ulf decided not to press any further. And besides, it hurt too much to speak.

"Enough!" Snorri bellowed. He waited until everyone had gone quiet. "Ulf would never worship Loki. Loki is a deceiver and cannot be trusted." He looked at his father. "Father, surely you must understand this as well."

All faces turned to Jarl Thorgils, who after a moment's thought nodded. He took a deep breath as he understood what he must now do. Almost as if in confirmation, his wife appeared next to him and took hold of his hand. He looked to her and she gave him that knowing smile of hers.

"My son is correct," he finally said.

"Which son?" someone asked from the crowd before he had a chance to continue.

"Snorri, you idiot!" Thorbjorn answered for the jarl, glaring into the crowd.

"Snorri is correct," the jarl clarified. "I might not know young Ulf as well as I knew his father, but he does not strike me as a person who would make a sacrifice to Loki." There were quiet murmurs from the crowd. Thorgils stared at Ulf, with Vidar kneeling beside him. The boy was using his freakishly big hands to untie Ulf. Then his narrowed eyes fell on the broken branch. So many had been hanged from that branch, many who might have been innocent of the crimes they had been accused of. This was one of those rare moments when Thorgils did not know what to do. Thorgils looked at the body of Hulda again. She was a loss that none of these people could ever understand. Looking to his wife for guidance, he saw her staring towards the branch. That was the answer. Everybody was silent now, waiting for him to speak, the only noise to be heard was Ulf coughing and birds chirping from the tree.

"The death of Hulda is a tragedy. Despite being a thrall, she was liked by everybody. Although we thought Ulf was the killer, my son Snorri raised a valid point. Ulf would not have left his knife in her hand to condemn himself." He took a deep breath. "But none of this matters. As we all have witnessed, the gods do not want Ulf to die. There is no other reason for what has happened here. Therefore, Ulf will be spared. But know this," he said, turning his attention to the fiery eyes of Ulf as he said this, "if you ever give me a reason to doubt your intentions again, I will kill you myself. Regardless of what the gods want from you."

There was a tense moment when the two men stared at each other until Ulf nodded his assent. He understood. The crowd had seen enough now and were heading back to their homes or chores. The morning's events were over. Ulf watched the people as they walked away. The warriors who fought for their jarl and his son. The wives and children. The thralls and bændr. One of them had killed Hulda and used his knife to do it. He watched Ragnar walk away, looking at him over his shoulder. Ulf humiliated him on the wharf. But he could not imagine Ragnar doing something like this to get his revenge. He had beaten Ulf many times in training during the winter.

Jarl Thorgils walked with his wife back to their longhouse. He was in desperate need of some ale. He could see Ingibjorg was still shaken from the loss of Hulda. She could hide it from everyone else, but not him. He knew her too well. Better than she realized.

"Was this the chaos you promised?" he asked her.

She thought about it for a few moments. "No, my husband, this is only the beginning."

CHAPTER 14

Lady Ingibjorg had insisted Hulda be burnt and the whole village turned out for her funeral. Ulf, absorbed by the beauty of the flames as they danced into the night sky, stood alone. Nobody wanted to be near him. He shifted his gaze from the dancing flames to the jarl and his wife. They were both stood side by side, their faces set like stone. Someone started playing a drum, beating the stretched cowhide with a stick. To Ulf's surprise, Lady Ingibjorg started singing a song about a lost Valkyrie who was returning to Odin's side after being tricked by a man to be his wife, in a low whispering voice. Her voice got stronger as the song continued and was soon joined by the voices of other women. The sound was strangely unnerving, especially the chorus, which was not words, but chanting at different pitches. The men joined in with guttural throat noises which added a haunting rawness to the song. Ulf felt a shiver run down his spine. The rising noise, encouraged by the increased tempo of the drum, reached a climax and ended as suddenly as it had started. The silence that followed was more deafening than the song had been, and Ulf could feel his heart beating fast in his chest.

He sensed movement by his side but was still caught up in the emotion of the song and did not respond to it. It was Geir, the recruit who Snorri had given the sword to after their fight with the pirates. It felt like such a long time ago but had only happened the day before. Geir stood next to Ulf, his eyes fixed on the body in the flames.

"Did you love her?" Geir asked. Ulf gave him a sideways glance. He thought it was a stupid question. But it still made him think. *Did he love her?* Ulf took a deep breath. He didn't want to answer, didn't want to talk. It wasn't because it hurt to talk, his throat still sore from the hanging. He had barely been able to eat or drink anything all day as swallowing hurt too much. He was too angry to talk. Not the same anger that usually burnt inside of him like the constant heat coming off the embers of an old fire. This was an impotent anger. An anger that he could do nothing about. An anger he didn't understand. But Geir had done nothing wrong, he had only asked a question.

"No, I didn't love her," he said in the end, "but she didn't love me either."

Geir seemed to consider this for a short while and then shrugged his shoulders. He didn't leave. Ulf ignored him and focused on the flames instead, watching as they leapt into the sky as if they were trying to catch the stars.

Ingibjorg was also watching the dancing flames. But unlike Ulf, she didn't see the beauty in them. She only saw destruction and violence. She saw how the flames destroyed everything in their path, just like they were now doing to the once beautiful body of Hulda. Just like Surtr's fire will destroy Midgard.

"We gave her our word we would protect her daughter," she said to Thorgils, without taking her eyes off the flames. The jarl responded with a grunt. "We failed. She will not be happy," Ingibjorg continued.

"We don't even know if she still lives." The jarl looked to the sky. It was a cloudy night, the only light being provided by the large fire in front of them. But he did not think it would rain. "Besides, we could not have known that this would happen. We live in a violent country, surrounded by violent people. Death is always waiting in the shadows."

"I should have known this would happen!" she hissed at him. She could usually tolerate his cynical view of the world. But tonight, it irritated her. Especially because he was right. Although she would never admit that to him. She looked at Ulf, standing not far from them, his hard expression made even worse in the light of the flames. He looked like the monster mothers warned their children about to get them to behave. One of Snorri's men was standing next to him trying to talk, but Ulf wasn't responding. Vidar was also there, as he always was, like a guiding spirit watching over Ulf. Everyone else seemed to be avoiding Ulf, even Snorri and the rest of his men.

"What do you see when you look at him?" Thorgils asked. She had not realized he had been looking at her. When she did not respond, he said, "I see something in you I've never seen before."

"And what may that be?" she asked, although she already knew the answer.

"Uncertainty." To Thorgils, his wife had always been resolute, always sure of everything around her. Like she knew what was going to happen and how to deal with it. This was why he had always valued her opinions. But recently she had been different, distracted almost.

"Nothing has been certain since his arrival." She indicated towards Ulf. "Every day it feels like I'm walking over a frozen river, not sure if the ice is thick enough."

Thorgils did not say anything. He just watched his wife, surprised by a side he had not seen for a long time.

"Ulf is like a storm," the words came out of her, without her realizing she was speaking, "slowly building up its power. Growing more dangerous with each passing moment. And like all storms, he will eventually break. When he does, he will destroy everything in his path."

Thorgils felt the same about him, which was why he had not wanted Ulf to remain in Thorgilsstad. But Snorri and Ingibjorg had convinced him it would be fine.

"And when will the storm break?"

Ingibjorg turned to Thorgils, and again he was struck by the uncertainty in her eyes. "I don't know." She looked back at Ulf and Vidar. "Vidar seems to be a calming influence on him, but I don't know how long that will last. Hulda, in her own way, had also managed to temper the storm. Together they were like a strong offshore wind, keeping it at bay. But now that she is gone, I don't know if Vidar will be enough."

"Is that why you sent Hulda to him?" He had always been curious about that. For her safety, they had agreed that no man could touch her. Not even him.

"I didn't send her to him. She wanted to go to him. She felt she could calm him, so he wouldn't be a danger to us."

And look how well that turned out for her, he thought. "What, Odin forbid, if something happens to Vidar?"

"Then we must make sure we are not in his way."

The following morning was still grey, but like the night before, the clouds did not promise rain. Instead, it seemed to reflect on the mood of the people. Life in Thorgilsstad went on as normal. The men were cleaning or fixing their equipment and weapons. The women and thralls were preparing the morning meals or weaving. All of them were trying to ignore the sounds coming from the forest. The sounds of an axe biting into trees.

Ulf was gasping as he tried to pull Olaf's axe out of the tree. He had risen early and left the hall, taking only his axe. He didn't want to be around people. He wanted to be alone, or as alone as he could be with Vidar always by his side. After the funeral, everybody had avoided Ulf. He could still see the suspicion in their eyes and the anger in the eyes of Thorgils' men. Ulf finally freed the axe and stared at the tree, its bark cut up as he spent the morning taking out his anger on it. The spirits of the forest would not be pleased, but then they could join the others who were disgruntled with him.

"It's not the tree's fault." He heard the voice behind him. He didn't know why he was surprised that she was here or that she seemed to know what he was thinking.

"I needed to–"

"I understand," Lady Ingibjorg said before he could finish.

Ulf didn't know what else to do, so he walked to a fallen tree and sat down on its trunk, still holding the axe in his hands. He looked at the red handle and the names of his family. "I'm sorry about Hulda." He had wanted to say something to her the day before but thought it was best to stay away from her. And his throat had hurt too much to talk, although it wasn't much better today.

"Me too," Lady Ingibjorg said as she sat down beside Ulf and smiled at Vidar, who was sitting on the ground by the fallen tree as he had been all morning. She breathed in the damp earthy smell of the forest, enjoying its freshness over the smoke-filled air in her house.

They sat in silence for a while, both listening to the sounds of the birds as they flew back to their trees now Ulf had stopped blunting his axe on them.

"You miss your family," Ingibjorg said, seeing the way Ulf stroked the names of his family carved on the hilt of his axe.

Ulf didn't answer. He didn't need to. Ingibjorg saw the tear that ran down his cheek.

"Why am I being punished by the gods?" Ulf asked, thinking about everything that had happened to him since the previous summer.

"What makes you think you are being punished?" She had a small smile on her lips, but Ulf could hear no mocking tone in her voice.

"First my family, then the bear and now Hulda. It's hard not to think Odin is punishing me." His aunt had always told him not to curse the gods, that they were vengeful beings, but he had never listened. Now it felt like they were taking everything away from him.

Ingibjorg nodded as she considered his words. "Odin is watching you, but I don't think he is punishing you."

"How do you know?" Ingibjorg didn't say anything; instead, she indicated with her eyes to a large raven sat on the branch above them. It tilted its head as if it was listening to their conversation. Ulf was surprised he hadn't heard the bird arrive as they normally liked to announce themselves. "But my family, and the bear–"

"I cannot speak for what happened to your family, Ulf. But why are you so certain the bear was Odin?"

He thought about her question for a while before saying, "Because it was bigger than any bear I have ever seen, and angrier."

Again, Ingibjorg considered his words. "There is another god we associate the bear with, Ulf. A god we worship here beside Odin and one you are said to be descended from."

It was Ulf's turn to consider her words now. He had never thought of this and he was not sure why. "Tyr? But why would Tyr want to kill me?"

"Perhaps he was testing you, seeing if you were ready for the journey which lay ahead of you. We do not know the will of the gods."

Ulf guessed he saw the sense in that, but there were many things he still did not understand. "But my family? Hulda?" he asked again.

"There are many mysteries in life, Ulf. Just because things appear to go against us, does not mean we are being punished. I believe the gods give us obstacles to test us, so we may learn who we are and what we can do. Or perhaps it is just a game for them, to entertain themselves as we might do with the pieces on a tafl board." She looked at Ulf and he felt like she was looking deep into his soul. "Only the Norns know what the gods are up to and they are good at keeping secrets."

"But–" he started but was stopped by the smile he saw on Lady Ingibjorg's face.

"You are angry, Ulf, and you have a right to be. But don't waste your anger on trees. You will need it for what is to come."

Before Ulf could ask her what she meant by that, Snorri appeared from around a tree. He saw marks left behind by Ulf and shook his head before raising his eyebrows at seeing his mother there.

"I was looking for you."

"There are three of us, my son. Be more specific."

"Ulf," Snorri said. If he was irritated by his mother speaking to him like he was a small child, he didn't show it.

Lady Ingibjorg stood up and straightened her dress. "Then I shall leave you to it." With that, she left them and walked back to her house. She had done what she needed to.

"What was that about?" Snorri asked, still not sure why his mother had been here.

"I don't really know," Ulf admitted. Lady Ingibjorg was still a mystery to him. He still wasn't sure if she could speak to the gods or was just very perceptive. "Why were you looking for me?" he asked Snorri to change the topic.

Snorri looked at Ulf, seeing the mark around his neck left by the noose. He still didn't understand what had happened. Ulf should have been dead, but somehow, he had survived. It was hard not to believe the gods were watching Ulf.

"I spoke to my father this morning."

"About?"

"About going raiding. I think it's best if we get you away from here for a while," Snorri responded. He had spent the whole night thinking about it. Thorgilsstad was his home and its people were his friends. But he knew Ulf hadn't killed Hulda and did not want to be caught in the middle of any conflict. He decided it was best to go away for a while, perhaps then people might move on and think about other things.

"And where would we go?" Ulf was intrigued. He had never been on a raid before.

"South."

"What's in the south?"

"Hopefully lots of gold, silver and something you want more than that," Snorri smiled his wolf's smile. He did not need to say more. Ulf knew what he was hinting at.

CHAPTER 15

"You can't be serious, Snorri!" Thorbjorn exclaimed, throwing his hands in the air. "The boy is a coward; he has no place on this ship."

Snorri stood on the wharf with his men, his hands on his hips and head lowered. "I know."

"Then why is he coming with us?" Brak asked, scratching his cheek and eyeing Thorvald who was standing with his bottom lip sticking out. He had a fine sword on his hip, better than most of the experienced warriors could afford. Even the short sax-knife he wore had a beautiful bone-carved handle. Being the son of a jarl had its benefits.

"Perhaps the jarl ordered this," Oddi added his opinion. Snorri nodded and curled his lip.

The sight of Ragnar Nine-Finger walking towards Snorri's ship with his sea chest and weapons ended that conversation.

"Is he coming as well?" Thorbjorn asked.

"Aye, somebody needs to babysit my brother," Snorri responded. He saw the scowl on Ragnar's face.

"What's his problem?" Asbjorn sneered at Ulf. He was asking about Vidar who stood with his arms crossed and cheeks puffed out.

"He wants to come with," Ulf responded.

"Why not let him?" Snorri asked.

Ulf stared at Snorri and his hirdmen. Apart from Asbjorn, they all seemed to have no problem with Vidar. "I don't want to have to worry about his safety, as well as mine."

Snorri smiled for the first time that morning. "He'll be fine, don't worry about it. We can help look after him."

"More babysitting then?" Asbjorn grumbled. "Thought this was a raid."

"Odin's sake, shut up, Asbjorn!" Thorbjorn said.

"He might be useful. He's good at tracking, we all know that," Oddi added, looking to Snorri for confirmation.

"Aye, let him come," Snorri said.

Ulf saw the big toothy grin on Vidar's face, knowing he had lost. "Fine."

"Good, now let's get going before Ran loses her good mood." Snorri turned and boarded his ship. Most of his crew were already on board. His hirdmen followed, with Ulf and the still-grinning Vidar behind him.

The families and friends of the men on board had come to wave them off, but Ulf was surprised not to see the jarl there. Only Ingibjorg was there, standing straight with her hands clasped in front of her. Snorri gave his customary howl as the Sae-Ulfr was pushed off the wharf, the villagers cheering them on and some of the children echoing Snorri.

"I'm not rowing!" Thorvald squealed when he was handed an oar. "I am the son of Jarl Thorgils!"

"You'll fucking row, or by Thor, I'll throw you overboard myself," Ragnar growled at him. Thorvald was about to protest, but the vicious snarl on Ragnar's face put an end to that. He took the oar and did what he was told to the delight of the rest of the crew. Ulf even saw Snorri smiling.

The sun sat high in the sky by the time the Sae-Ulfr rowed past the islands at the mouth of the bay and into the Vikenfjord. Ulf looked up from his oar, wiping the sweat off his face, and saw Snorri nod to Rolf.

"Sail!" Rolf ordered. The Brak brothers and few other men brought in their oars and placed them on the oar rack. Ulf was fascinated by the speed at which they moved around the ship, pulling on ropes and tying knots until the red and white sail of the Sae-Ulfr was hoisted and caught the wind. Without instructions, the rest of the crew put their oars away and relaxed, making themselves comfortable wherever they could. Some took out their weapons and sharpened the blades, others sat in little groups and talked. Snorri stayed at the stern with Rolf, the two of them working together to navigate.

"Bring out the wolf!" Snorri bellowed when they were far enough from the bay. The men cheered as the brothers fetched the prow beast from its resting place. Ulf and Vidar watched in fascination as they placed the beautifully carved wolf head, its mouth pulled back as if snarling at its foes, on the prow of the Sae-Ulfr.

"What do you think?" Snorri walked up to Ulf with his arms crossed and a satisfied smile on his face.

"It's beautiful," Ulf responded, failing to keep the awe out of his voice. He even thought he could hear it growling through its fangs. Ulf glanced at Vidar, sat next to him, and saw a slight apprehension in his face.

"What do you think, Vidar? Looks like a real wolf?" Snorri asked, showing great pride in his ship and its beast head. Vidar nodded, but could not hide the fear in his eyes.

"Odin's balls!" Ragnar shouted as the gull nearly shit on his head three days later. Those who saw it laughed, while he glared at the bird circling above them, riding the wind. Its mocking call seeming to make fun of Ragnar. Ulf didn't join in the jokes they were making at Ragnar's expense. Instead, he looked back out onto the sea and watched the waves roll by. He breathed in the salty air, feeling it soothe the fire inside of him, and listened to calling gulls and rolling waves with a smile on his face.

Ulf's neck was starting to feel better, but the bruising was still there. A reminder to all of what had happened not so long ago. He took Olaf's axe from his belt and using the whetstone from his pouch, started sharpening the blade.

"I heard your father was a great warrior." Thorvald did not have to say Ulf's name. They all knew Thorvald was talking to him. Thorvald was sitting near the stern of the ship, next to Ragnar. Ragnar never left his side. This made Thorvald confident. He started treating Snorri's crew like they were his servants. The men complained, but never openly. Not when Ragnar could hear them. Ragnar did not like this either, but he had been told to protect the jarl's son.

"They say he could slaughter an entire army and not get one scratch," Thorvald continued in his smug tone when Ulf didn't respond.

"Be quiet," Snorri warned. Everybody knew not to speak to Ulf about his father; it was safer to kick a sleeping bear.

"What? I'm just curious about the man who died protecting our father." He smiled at Ulf as he said this, hoping to provoke him.

Ulf did his best not to listen but, on the ship, there was nothing to drown him out. He had stopped sharpening the blade of the axe, but his knuckles were white as he gripped the handle. Thorvald's words were like a breath of air on the embers of a dying flame, threatening to bring it back to life. He closed his eyes and tried to focus on the sound of the waves as they splashed against the ship.

"I wonder then, if he was so great, why did he get himself killed so easily?" Thorvald continued. The rest of the men on the ship went quiet, a look of disbelief on their faces. Even the sea birds had gone quiet, or so it seemed.

"You better watch yourself," Ragnar warned him. He remembered Bjørn better than most, having been trained by him.

"I apologise," Thorvald said, but the smug smile on his face showed otherwise. "I heard it was his sword which made him so great. What was the name of it again?" Ulf felt the fire deep in his chest. Every heartbeat made it harder for him to control it as it pulsed through his veins. The sound of it in his ears sounded like the voices he had heard when they fought the pirates. They were whispering to him, but Ulf couldn't hear what they were saying. "Ormstunga, that's it." Thorvald was enjoying himself now. He saw he was getting to Ulf. "Where is his magical sword now, Ulf? I heard you

lost it, just like you let your uncle and aunt be killed. Or so you say."
The men close to Thorvald started edging away from him, casting
nervous glances at each other. No one had ever pushed Ulf this far,
and they weren't sure what to expect. Ragnar put his hand on the hilt
of his sword. He knew he should stop Thorvald, but part of him
wanted to see what Ulf would do.

Ulf was trembling, trying hard to suppress the anger in him.
He gripped the handle of the axe tighter and tighter, trying to focus
all his rage on it instead of Thorvald. Trying hard not to listen to the
voices in his head, which were getting louder, as he ground his teeth.
Vidar had woken up now and decided to move out of the way.

"You see, I agree with my father. I think you killed them. I
think you were jealous that you could never be as great as your
worthless father and decided to kill your family."

Ulf exploded before anyone even knew what was happening
as he gave in to his anger. He threw the axe at Thorvald, roaring at
the stupidity of the boy for provoking him, for pushing him to the
point where he could no longer control himself. The axe flew across
the ship, turning over and over until it buried itself into the side of
the ship, a finger's breadth from Thorvald's head. A stunned silence
followed the thud of the metal striking wood. Not one of the men
knew how to respond. Even Ragnar, his hand still on the handle of
his sheathed sword, just sat there motionless. All eyes turned to the
dark patch appearing between the legs of Thorvald as the
whimpering boy pissed himself. His stunned gaze fixed on Ulf, who
stood there still as a rock on the deck of the moving ship. Ulf was
panting through clenched teeth, his lips pulled back in a snarl. To
Thorvald, he resembled a growling wolf about to attack its weaker
prey.

Ulf hadn't yet realized what he had done as he stood there glaring at Thorvald. He saw Olaf's axe buried in the wooden side of Snorri's ship but wasn't quite sure how it got there. His rage was slowly dissipating, exiting his body with every breath. His hands started to shake by his side, and he clenched them tighter in an effort to stop them. He had forgotten about everyone else on the ship and was surprised when Vidar appeared in front of him. Vidar only smiled and nodded; the deed was done. Although Ulf wasn't sure what he had accomplished. Apart from pissing himself, the little shit was still alive.

Snorri was the first to react. Like everyone else, he was still in shock over what he had just seen, but he was the captain, the leader of these men and he had to respond. He stood up and walked to where Thorvald sat, still frozen in fear. Looking at the axe, he saw that it had bitten deep into the wood, and after a few hard pulls, he managed to free it. Thorvald finally managed to get his voice back.

"Brother, he tried to kill me!" he wailed, crossing his legs to hide his humiliation from everyone.

Snorri looked at his brother and then to Ragnar. Ragnar still seemed unsure how to respond. Everyone was. No one had ever seen a man move so fast and Snorri knew what Ragnar was thinking. If Ulf had meant to kill Thorvald, then no one here would have been able to stop him.

"You must punish him!" Thorvald continued.

"Why?" Snorri responded with a look of contempt at his brother.

"Because he tried to kill me!" He turned to Ragnar. "You saw it! Everybody did!"

"We also saw you piss yourself," Thorbjorn added, a look of disdain on his face.

Snorri walked to Ulf whose glare was on Thorvald again. There was a dangerous look behind those eyes, but Snorri didn't think Ulf would do anything now, his rage was spent. Or so Snorri hoped. "You missed," he said as he handed the axe back to Ulf. It seemed to break Ulf's trance as he looked at Olaf's axe and then to Snorri and Vidar standing in front of him.

"No, I didn't." He took the axe from Snorri and tucked it into his belt. Ulf sat down in the space between his chest and Thorbjorn's, closing his eyes so he didn't have to look at the rest of the crew. Only Vidar dared to sit next to him.

"So, you're not going to do anything!" Thorvald shouted, his voice reaching a very high pitch.

"If you yank on a wolf's balls, expect to get bit," Oddi Viss put in. This seemed to break the spell as the men started laughing and making fun of Thorvald.

CHAPTER 16

"Is Ormstunga really a magical sword?" one of the recruits whispered a while later, hoping Ulf would not hear him. The men were still stunned by what had happened earlier. Ulf kept his eyes on the seals resting on the rocks as they sailed past, pretending he didn't hear the question. He had asked Olaf the same question many times in the past, but Olaf always gave different answers.

"I heard it was," someone responded, but Ulf wasn't sure who. He didn't want to look at the men behind him, he didn't want them to see the shame in his eyes. "They say it was forged from the tongue of a serpent," the same man continued.

"I heard it was given to an ancient king by the gods. And that whoever wielded it would be undefeated," another said.

"Then how did Bjørn have it?" Thorbjorn asked, not bothering to keep his voice down. "I heard he killed the last man who owned it." There were murmurs at this. Everyone agreed it was a good question and none could think of the answer.

Rolf Treefoot gave a bark of a laugh from the stern, causing some to look at him in surprise. They thought he had been asleep. "Shows what you idiots know," he said with his hand on the tiller. "The story of Ormstunga is an old tale." He went quiet, focusing instead on the waves as the Sae-Ulfr sliced through them. The men watched, waiting for him to continue. Snorri only smiled; this was typical of the old sailor. He had probably forgotten he had spoken in the first place.

"Well?" one of the men asked.

"Well what?" Rolf looked at him, eyebrow raised in confusion.

"The story?"

"What story?" He looked to Snorri, who was sitting near him. But Snorri was enjoying this moment too much to put anyone out of their misery. Besides, it distracted them from earlier events.

"Of Ormstunga, you old fool!" Thorbjorn shouted. "You were going to tell us the tale of Ormstunga."

"Ormstunga?" He scratched his grey beard with his leathery hand. "Aye, that is a good tale. Not sure if I believe it."

Thorbjorn looked like he was about to launch himself at the old sailor before Oddi intervened.

"Would you tell us the tale? I've heard some version of it but would be curious to hear yours."

Rolf Treefoot looked at Oddi and then at the men staring at him. Like all Norse men, they enjoyed a good story and like most, he enjoyed telling one. He cleared his throat and spat over the side before saying, "It started a long time ago, in the time of the ancient kings."

"Doesn't it always," Thorbjorn muttered. He got an elbow in the ribs from Asbjorn who wanted to hear the old man.

"In the north, there lived a farmer with his wife. He wasn't old, but not young either and they had no children, not for lack of trying though. One day this farmer decided to go fishing; he was tired of only eating vegetable stew and porridge. They only had one cow, and she was needed for milk so they couldn't eat her. So, the farmer took his little boat out to sea and spent all day throwing in the net and pulling it out. By late afternoon the farmer was happy with his catch and decided to head back home. He was about to start rowing back when something hit his boat from underneath. The farmer was surprised by this. There were no rocks here and whales would not come this close to his boat. He stood up to have a better look but saw nothing. Scratching his head, he thought he must have imagined it. Just then a large shadow loomed over the farmer. The farmer turned around and saw the giant head of Jörmungandr, the Midgard serpent."

Rolf paused and surveyed his audience. He was pleased to see that everyone's attention was on him. Even Ulf was listening to his tale.

"Jörmungandr wasn't happy. The farmer had disturbed its sleep. It growled at the farmer, baring his fangs which were as tall as the highest drinking hall. The farmer dropped to his knees and apologised. He offered his entire catch to Jörmungandr, hoping this would calm the terrible beast and send it back to the depths of the sea where it belonged. But Jörmungandr didn't want the farmer's paltry catch. And besides, it was tired of eating fish. It attacked the farmer, hoping to swallow him whole, but the farmer managed to roll out of its way on that small boat of his. He had no weapon on him, only a small knife he used to gut the fish he caught. But he wasn't afraid. It's not the size of your weapon that matters, it's how you use it." This got some snickers from the men, even a few comments were directed at some of them. Rolf ignored them and continued with his story.

"The farmer knew you don't charge at something that big; you wait for it to charge at you and then at the last moment you jump out of the way and poke it in the eye. That's exactly what the farmer did. Only, he didn't poke Jörmungandr in the eye." Again, he paused. He saw eagerness in the men in front of him. They all wanted to know what happened next. Like children listening to the tales of heroes of the ages gone by. Rolf adjusted the tiller to alter the course of Sae-Ulfr.

"No, the farmer didn't poke Jörmungandr in the eye – he cut a piece off of its tongue." The men cheered, pumping their fists into the air and slapping each other on the backs. You'd think that they were watching the fight. "Jörmungandr reeled back and screeched into the darkening sky. It was an ear-piercing screech that caused the farmer's ears to bleed, but he didn't drop his knife to cover them or try to get away. He stood his ground and waited. If this vile offspring of Loki wanted to take the farmer, then he'd better be prepared to lose more body parts.

"Jörmungandr glared at the farmer, blood dripping from its mouth. The piece of its tongue was still writhing on the deck, like a giant pink worm. The serpent was more cautious now, slowly moving its head side to side, looking for the right angle. The whole time it kept its giant eyes on the small blade of the knife. The sound of thunder came from behind the farmer, but he didn't turn around. His gaze never left Jörmungandr. He knew this could be a trick by the monster to distract him and then strike when he looked behind him. So, he did not look, but the monster did. Suddenly, it jerked its head back and dove into the ocean, disappearing from sight. The waters calmed as if it had never been there. The old farmer was confused by this. He turned, expecting the serpent to appear from behind him. Instead, he saw two men standing on the deck of his boat."

"Who were they?" one of the crew asked, not able to help himself in his eagerness.

"Shut up, you fool, and let the old man tell the story," Ragnar growled. Rolf didn't like being called old, but he wasn't going to argue with Ragnar Nine-Finger.

"Both men were tall, taller than the trees which surrounded the farmer's house. One had ginger hair and carried the mighty hammer, Mjöllnir. The other was dressed for war and was missing his right hand." Rolf lifted his own hand and looked at it, almost as if he was imagining it missing as well.

"Thor and Tyr," Oddi whispered, his eyes wide.

"Aye, Thor and Tyr. They had seen the fight from Asgard and decided the farmer was too brave to die at the hands of the Midgard serpent. They rushed down and scared the monster away. The farmer was so shocked to find the two gods in his boat, that he couldn't speak. He only stood there, gaping at them like the fish flapping about in his boat. 'You are a very brave man, old farmer,' Thor said in his thunderous voice. The old man nodded, not knowing what to say. He realized he was still holding the knife in his hand and dropped it in fear of offending the gods. Tyr laughed at this and said, 'We would reward your bravery and fine fighting skill.' Still, the farmer couldn't speak. The gods waited patiently, which wasn't easy for Thor. He's not the most patient of the gods, but still, he waited for the old man to find his voice again. Finally, the farmer spoke, 'Th...thank you, but I have lost most of my catch during the fight.' Tyr saw the severed tongue of Jörmungandr, still writhing on the deck of the boat. He smiled and said, 'Wait a week, old farmer, and I shall bring a solution to all your problems.' He picked up the tongue and both he and Thor disappeared in a flash of lightning."

"What happened next? What did Tyr bring him?" Brak Drumbr asked, hopping around like a small child. Rolf scowled at him, causing him to calm down and look embarrassed.

"A week later, while the old farmer and his wife were working hard on their farm, a man wearing a cloak approached and greeted them cheerfully. The farmer's wife looked up and scowled at the stranger. 'There is nothing to be cheerful about,' she said to him. The stranger looked surprised by this and asked her why she felt this way. 'Because this poor excuse of a husband went fishing last week and came back with no fish. He told a fanciful tale of fighting Jörmungandr and of meeting Thor and Tyr. When I asked him what we will eat, he only shrugged and said that Tyr will bring us a solution.' The stranger listened to her and asked if she believed her husband. She said she didn't. The stranger asked why, and she replied, 'Look at him, he's a scrawny old goat who can barely stand straight. How can he defeat Jörmungandr? More likely the monster saw him and thought he wasn't worth eating.' The stranger laughed at this. He laughed hard and long, clutching his stomach as he did so. 'What's so funny?' the farmer's wife demanded, not pleased by the stranger's reaction. The stranger apologised and threw off his cloak. The old farmer's wife gasped in surprise and the old farmer said, 'See, I told you, woman.' Tyr stood in front of them in all his splendour and held a beautiful sword in his hand. 'The tale your husband told was true,' he said, and this was his reward.

"He showed them the sword, which he said was named Ormstunga, but didn't take the blade out of the scabbard. Tyr explained how he had taken the tongue of Jörmungandr to the dwarves of Svartalfheim and asked them to forge a sword out of it. The hilt of the sword was decorated with depictions of Jörmungandr and other serpents, a tribute to the origins of the blade. 'But,' Tyr warned the old farmer, 'as the source of the blade came out of darkness, the sword cannot be drawn in the light of the sun.' The farmer took the sword and looked at Tyr. To Tyr's surprise, the farmer didn't seem pleased. 'How am I supposed to feed us with a sword?' Tyr only smiled and answered, 'The same way many warriors have done.' The farmer protested, saying that he was no warrior and again Tyr only laughed, saying that only the best warrior in the land could have cut out Jörmungandr's tongue. The farmer thought about this for a while and agreed. His wife, suddenly beaming and smiling, agreed with Tyr, saying she always knew her husband was a mighty warrior. Before the farmer could argue with her, she invited Tyr to stay for the night. 'We may be poor, but we can still provide proper hospitality,' she said to him. Tyr looked at the farmer's wife as if he had seen her for the first time. She wasn't young, her face was worn from many years of tolling on the farm, but she was still beautiful."

"Unlike Snorri's wife," Thorbjorn interrupted, causing the men to laugh and Snorri to smile.

"Tyr stayed the night and shared food and ale with the old farmer and his wife. But when the farmer fell asleep, the wife was still awake and gave Tyr that look. You know the one I mean?" he smiled as he asked the men.

"Thorbjorn doesn't," Snorri responded. "He takes them, no matter what look they give him." The men laughed at this, but not Thorbjorn.

"When you are as small as he is, then you never get that look. How's he supposed to know it?" Brak added to more laughter and cheers.

"Fuck off, both of you," Thorbjorn said, but he couldn't hide his smile.

Rolf ignored them and continued. "The following morning Tyr said his farewells and left the farmer and his wife. The farmer's wife was glowing, like a blossoming spring flower and soon gave birth to a boy, who quickly grew up to be bigger and stronger than any in the region. But the farmer didn't want to raise crops or children. He had a magical sword and with it, he would become the greatest warrior the land had ever known, so he left them. When the farmer, now a mighty king died, the sword was passed on to his son, who he had abandoned and who some say wasn't his son, but the bastard of Tyr. They say the sword has never left the hands of that bloodline," Rolf said looking directly at Ulf, who sat there looking back at him, "until now."

"But my father gave Bjørn the sword." Snorri looked at Ragnar for confirmation, but he only shrugged. "I saw him do it." Ulf suddenly looked up, his eyebrows high. He had never heard of this before.

"No," Rolf responded, "your father never gave the sword to Bjørn. Bjørn had always owned the sword."

"Then why do we think it was given to him?" Ragnar asked, trying to remember back to the distant past to see if he already knew the answer.

Rolf sighed. He felt like he was dealing with young children and not grown men. "The jarl's sword broke when they fought in their first battle together. This was a long time ago."

"In the time of the ancient kings," Thorbjorn added to the annoyance of Rolf.

"Bjørn lent him Ormstunga, and after the battle the jarl kept it. He had heard of the tale of this sword and his greed got to him. Also, he knew that as long as he had the sword, then Bjørn would stay by his side. Bjørn was a descendant of kings and the jarl felt threatened by this."

The men watched Snorri, waiting for him to confirm this, but he only shrugged.

"And the jarl gave the sword back to Bjørn when he realized Bjørn was loyal to him and no longer a threat?" Oddi asked, stroking his beard.

"Aye," Rolf agreed. "Though, the old folk say the two men became good friends and the jarl saw no need to keep the sword anymore. So, he gave it back to Bjørn but made it look like it was a reward for Bjørn's loyalty. Some older folk say the jarl had found another reason, a more powerful reason to assure Bjørn's loyalty." His eyes flicked to Snorri and then back to the sea in front of him. No one saw this.

CHAPTER 17

There was movement in the water, something breached, but then went under again. Ulf stood alone on the dark deck of the Sae-Ulfr under a starry sky. They never sailed at night, it was too dangerous, or so Rolf Treefoot had said. There was no Snorri, Thorbjorn, Oddi, the brothers or Asbjorn. No crew, no Thorvald and no Ragnar. Not even Vidar, who never left his side on this voyage.

"Why do you think that is?" a voice asked from somewhere in the darkness. Ulf looked around but saw no one. His hand went to Olaf's axe, tucked into his belt. But it wasn't there. All he had was an old hunting knife. Something about it seemed familiar, but he could not understand what.

A terrible laugh rang through the night, chilling him to the bone. Water dripped on his shoulder, but when he looked, he realized that it was not water. It was blood. He looked behind him and saw the giant head of a serpent. It had large blue eyes, the same blue as old glacier ice, with pupils so dark and soulless it was hard to believe they were alive. The scaled head was as large as the ship Ulf was standing on, its fangs half the height of the mast. The head, as black as the night, could belong to only one serpent. Jörmungandr.

"You think you can kill me?" It seemed to laugh at him, but its lips were not moving. Blood was dripping from them, running off like water. Ulf gripped the knife hard. He felt his heartbeat increasing, his limbs shaking. But he held his ground. The monster smiled and dipped its head under the water, only to reappear on the other side of the ship.

"You are not like the old farmer. You are not as brave. In him, I saw no fear, but I see it all over your face," the serpent said to him. Or its voice did in his head.

"What are you afraid of?" said a different voice, the same one he had heard first. Ulf looked behind him and saw a cloaked figure standing there. He reminded him of the figure from his first dream, but was somehow different. Ulf wasn't sure how he knew this, but he could feel it.

"I'm not afraid," he lied. He was afraid, very afraid. But not of the giant Jörmungandr in front of him, its head moving back and forth, side to side in a strange dance.

"What are you afraid of, Bjørnson?" the cloaked figure asked again. Jörmungandr growled, forcing Ulf to look at it again. He saw something different about the monster. On top of its head stood the troll, holding his giant axe. Around his waist was something Ulf hadn't seen before. Something that looked like a large pink worm. Ulf wasn't sure what this meant, but then Jörmungandr's tongue flickered out like a viper's, and Ulf saw a bit of it was missing.

"Yes," the cloaked figure said, now standing beside him. "It is what you think it is."

Before Ulf could say anything, the troll jumped from Jörmungandr's head and landed on the deck of the Sae-Ulfr, the ship rocking so much Ulf worried he might fall overboard. It swung its mighty axe at Ulf, who just managed to duck underneath it. Ulf looked for the cloaked figure, but it was gone. It was only Ulf, the troll and Jörmungandr. But Jörmungandr wasn't interested in fighting, instead, it watched as the troll kept swinging its axe at Ulf, while Ulf did everything he could to avoid it.

"What are you afraid of?" He heard the voice again. Ulf looked up, following the sound of it and saw the cloaked figure standing on top of the mast, its handless arm hooked around it.

"I–" Ulf tried to say but had to jump back to avoid the axe. His foot got caught on something and he fell over, landing where the two sides of the ship met at the prow. The troll saw this and gave him an evil-looking sneer.

"Now you die," it said to Ulf in its gravelly voice. The troll lifted the axe high above its head, confident Ulf had nowhere to go. He was trapped in the prow of the Sae-Ulfr.

"Embrace your blood," was the last thing Ulf heard before the axe came down.

Ulf opened his eyes. He was shivering, but not from fear. He was in the tent he shared with Vidar. Ulf touched his head, expecting to find a cut where the axe would have struck him if he hadn't woken up. But he found nothing. The only evidence of the dream was the cold inside of him, which made him wonder if he'd ever be warm again. Ulf needed some air, the tent felt like it was suffocating him. He crawled out and got to his feet, feeling the warm sand between his toes. It was a warm night, but Ulf could see clouds had covered the moon, leaving the beach unusually dark. The only source of light came from the campfire, where Rolf Treefoot was sat, poking at the fire with a stick. He looked up as Ulf approached.

"Couldn't sleep?" he asked in his gruff voice.

"No," Ulf responded. "What about you?"

"When you get to my age, you find you don't need to sleep as much. Strange isn't it." Rolf stroked his beard. "When I was younger, I thought all old people do is eat, shit and sleep. Now I find there isn't a lot of any of those. Just a restlessness you can't explain."

Ulf didn't respond. He sat down by the fire, hoping it would warm him up. Rolf watched him for a bit before looking back at the fire.

"I hope my story today didn't offend you," Rolf offered.

"No." Ulf paused for a while. "My uncle never told me about Ormstunga." He looked at Rolf. The light from the fire made him look older than he really was. "Was your story true?"

Rolf watched Ulf as if judging what would be safe to say. "Which one?" he asked at last.

"The one about Ormstunga."

Again, Rolf didn't answer straight away. He seemed to be weighing up his words as he poked the fire with his stick.

"That's the story I was told by Bjørn's father. But whether the story is real or just one he made up, I cannot tell you. Only the gods will know the truth to that."

"You knew my grandfather?" Ulf asked. He had never thought of himself having a grandfather.

"Aye. He was a headstrong man. Just like Bjørn and…" he paused again and looked at Ulf, "just like you."

Ulf stared at the old sailor but decided not to respond. Even if he didn't like being told he was like his father, he knew Rolf meant nothing by it. "What about the part about securing my father's loyalty?" he asked instead.

"Jarl Thorgils has always been a very careful man. That's why he is so powerful. Most say it is because of his wife, Lady Ingibjorg and her gifts, but I think it's more to do with his understanding of people."

Ulf understood what Rolf was saying. Jarl Thorgils was a smart man, but he was a warrior and tended to see things like a warrior. Lady Ingibjorg saw everything else, even the things other people could not. He thought back to the conversations they'd had in the past and how she always left him feeling like there was more to her. They sat for a while longer, Rolf telling the tales of his youth and Ulf listening, but not listening. His attention was on the fire, watching the flames as they danced into the night. He thought of Hulda. Ulf realized he didn't miss her. His hand went to his neck, where the rope had bruised him. He hadn't seen his neck for a few days, but he imagined it was still bruised. Ulf felt guilty for what had happened to her. Even though Snorri had told him it wasn't his fault, that whoever killed her had only used his knife because it was easy to find. But Ulf wasn't sure if that was true. Despite what Lady Ingibjorg had told him in the forest, he still felt like he was being punished by the gods. Maybe they were angry at him for losing his father's sword.

"It'll be raining tomorrow." The change in Rolf's voice made Ulf pay attention to him again.

"What?" he asked.

"It'll be raining tomorrow."

"How can you tell?" Ulf looked to the sky. He saw the clouds but couldn't see any sign of rain.

"Can feel it in my bones," Rolf replied like that was all the answer Ulf needed. Ulf grunted in response. He decided it was time to go back to his tent. If he was lucky, he might be able to sleep again, and hopefully without dreaming.

It was raining when Ulf woke up again the next morning. He heard the raindrops falling on the tent, like a thousand tiny drums playing at the same time. Rolf had been right after all and Ulf was glad for the pig's fat they smeared on their tents to waterproof them. Ulf didn't know if the rain would stop them from going anywhere. Vidar wasn't there; he must have gone looking for food. Ulf put his boots on and grabbed Olaf's axe before leaving the tent. It was more than just rain, he realized, there was also a strong wind coming in from the sea. He found Snorri and Rolf by the ship. It looked like they were discussing the weather. From the look on Snorri's face, Ulf knew they weren't sailing today. He turned around and surveyed the land behind them. The beach led to tree-covered hills and Ulf didn't know what lay behind them. Oddi had told him they were in the land of the Swedes. And the Swedes did not like the Norse.

"Fucking rain," Snorri said as he walked up to Ulf. Like Ulf, he was soaked by the rain, his long hair plastered to his face.

"How long will it last, you think?" Ulf asked, still looking at the hill.

"Long enough to keep us here all day." Snorri cleared his throat and spat to the side. "Fucking rain."

"You seen Vidar?"

"He's not in your tent?" Snorri asked back. Ulf didn't respond but gave him a look which showed what he thought of that question. "Dumb question, I guess." Snorri smiled.

"I saw him go over the hill at first light," Geir said as he appeared from his tent. They had been standing close enough for him to hear the conversation. "Looked like he was going exploring or something."

Ulf thought about that and shrugged. Vidar would return when he found something or found that there was nothing to be found.

"Should we go look for him?" Geir asked, trying to show how useful he could be, as always.

"No, he'll be back," Snorri said. He also knew Vidar well enough to know there was no need to be concerned.

Vidar returned later that morning, wet but very excited. He had found a small village not far from where they were. From what Ulf understood it was not heavily guarded. And from the smile on Snorri's face, Ulf could see he liked what Vidar had found.

"Well done, Vidar. Looks like it was a good idea bringing you with after all." He turned to the men watching. "Thorbjorn, get the men ready. Arngeir," he said to one of the experienced men in his crew, "take ten men and guard the Sae-Ulfr." Arngeir's shoulders sagged as he nodded.

Ragnar arrived, with Thorvald looking wet and miserable behind him. "What's going on?"

"Vidar found a small village, not far from here. I'm taking some men to have a look. Perhaps Odin will smile on us and we might be able to get some fresh meat for the fires and some loot," Snorri responded.

"Does it look like any god feels like smiling on us?" Thorvald asked in a whiny voice, indicating at the rain. Everyone just ignored him.

But Ragnar liked the idea. "It's been a while since I killed a Swede. I almost miss the way they squeal." The men cheered at this.

"Might as well have some fun if we have to be stuck here today," Snorri responded, but then looked at his brother. "Perhaps Thorvald should stay with the ship."

"No," Ragnar said before Thorvald could respond. To Ulf it looked like Thorvald would have preferred to stay.

"Snorri's right, he'll only piss his pants again." Thorbjorn scowled at Thorvald.

"If he stays, then I have to stay. And I'm not missing the chance to gut some Swedes," Ragnar growled. The air was filled with a tense silence.

"Fine," Snorri said, shaking his head. "But he's your responsibility." He pointed his finger at Ragnar. Ragnar nodded and left for his tent, dragging the miserable-looking Thorvald behind him.

"What do you think?" Asbjorn asked. It was early afternoon by the time they arrived at the village Vidar had seen. It had stopped raining, but the sky was still grey. Snorri had about twenty men with him, including Ragnar and Thorvald. Like Snorri, Ragnar Nine-Finger looked like a war god, with his brynja and helmet. His helmet was elaborate with a gold-plated eye-guard which looked like scales.

The silver cheek guards had standing bears embossed on them. He held a shield in his left hand and Skull-Splitter, his two-handed axe which he used one-handed, in his right. Thorvald looked like he was trying to be a war god but could not quite pull it off, his thin frame not quite able to fill out his brynja.

"It looks quiet," Snorri said. The few longhouses in the village were arranged around a small circle. A small picketed fence surrounded the village, although it did not look like it offered much in the form of defence. The fields and the animals around the longhouses suggested this was a farming settlement. There were a few men who could have been warriors, but they looked too old or too young.

"Some fresh meat at least," Brak Drumbr said, licking his lips.

"Perhaps there is no jarl?" Brak suggested. There were a few murmurs as those who heard him discussed this.

"There's no sign of any ships by the beach," Oddi said, which by the tone of his voice, he found odd.

"I guess there is only one way to find out," Snorri said. He kissed Mjöllnir around his neck and sent a silent prayer to the skies. Ulf saw most men do the same, but he didn't. He wouldn't know what to say. Instead, he looked at Vidar who was sat beside him. He wore a helmet which was too big for him and had a spear, but nothing else.

"Make sure you stay close to me," Ulf told him. Vidar nodded with a fierce grin and gripped his spear. Ulf wondered if he was thinking about the old forest godi.

At Snorri's command, they charged at the village, every man screaming his own war cry. Thorvald's girl-like scream almost made Ulf laugh until he saw the few defenders there were running to intercept their charge, forming a small shield wall by the entrance to their village. Snorri ran in the middle, his shield in front of him and Tyr's Fury in his hand. Ulf was to his right, where Snorri had told him to be, and Ragnar was on his left. Thorbjorn wouldn't be happy about that, as that was always his place, but Ulf doubted they were going to stop and discuss that now. Vidar ran behind Ulf, exactly where Ulf wanted him to be.

Snorri and Ragnar hit the defenders at the same time, killing two of them instantly as they crashed through their shield wall. Ulf lifted his shield to stop a spear thrust, but before he could strike back, Oddi speared the man through the chest. Ulf ran past, feeling the spray of blood on him, and swung his axe at the next defender. The man looked too old to fight, but somehow got his shield up in time to block the blow. He swung his own sword at Ulf. Ulf ducked under the sword and punched the man in the stomach with the rim of his shield. As the man bent over, another spear streaked past Ulf and went through the defender. Ulf looked back in surprise and saw the spear belonged to Vidar. He smiled at Vidar and looked for more people to fight, but the fight was over. Half the defenders had been killed and those who could, ran away.

Snorri walked up to Ulf and saw the clean axe in his hand. "Didn't feel like killing today?" He smiled to show that he meant no offence. He had seen Ulf attack one of the defenders and saw he was covered in blood.

"Somebody kept taking my kills," Ulf responded while looking at Vidar, who was trying to free his spear from the defender's body. Snorri laughed and wiped some blood off his face.

"He's earning his food at least." Vidar smiled back at Snorri after managing to free his spear.

"Aye, that he is." Ulf looked around the village and then over the fallen defenders. "Any sign of a jarl?" he asked Snorri. None of the defenders looked like one, even a poor one.

Snorri shook his head. "Not amongst the defenders. We'll check in the hall, make sure he's not hiding in there." Snorri looked at the hall. It was small and plain. Nothing about it suggested there would be anything of value.

"Only one way to find out," Ulf agreed.

Snorri walked off, calling his hirdmen to him. "Thorbjorn, take ten men and go the back of the hall, make sure no one escapes through the back door. I'll take the rest of the men and go through the front to see if anyone is hiding in there."

"No need," Ragnar said. He was walking towards Snorri and dragging a young man behind him. The boy looked like he ran into a tree, a tree shaped like Ragnar's fist. The boy looked about fourteen winters old, Vidar's age. "Tell them what you told me," Ragnar said to the boy as he threw him to the ground in front of Snorri.

The boy looked at the bloodied men around him, men who had killed his family and friends. He looked like he might refuse but then, "The jarl has a hall, a big one. Not far from here," he said in a quivering voice.

"How far?" Snorri snarled.

The boy gulped, his face paled at Snorri's expression. "About a quarter day's walk, that way." He pointed further inland, opposite to where Snorri's crew came from.

Ragnar lifted the boy and pressed the blade of his knife against the boy's throat. "You lying, boy?" The boy shook his head so hard, Ulf thought it might fall off. Ragnar crinkled his nose and dropped the boy. A moment later they could all smell it too.

"Fucking worse than Thorvald," Brak grumbled, ignoring the glare from Snorri's brother.

"How many men does the jarl have?" Snorri asked, ignoring the stink.

"I...I don't know," the boy said, too scared to be embarrassed, "but he's gone."

"Gone where?" Snorri raised an eyebrow.

"I don't know." When he saw his answer wasn't enough, he quickly remembered something else. "F...Frankia, my father said something about Frankia."

"Your father gone with the jarl?" Oddi asked. The boy nodded.

"What are you thinking?" Ragnar asked when he saw the smile on Snorri's face.

"The jarl is gone, his hall is practically undefended." The men around smiled as he said this. Snorri turned to his men. "Hrut, take four men. Round up some animals and captives and take them to the ship. Tell Rolf we're going to visit the jarl's hall, we should be back by nightfall."

"And the women?" Hrut asked with an eager smile.

Snorri sighed, but still smiled. "Don't touch the pretty ones. They're worth more undamaged." He turned to the rest of his crew, now down to less than twenty men, as Hrut ran off with four others to carry out their orders. "Let's go see this jarl's hall."

They were greeted by a small shield wall by the time they reached the jarl's village.

"Looks like a welcoming party," Thorbjorn said as he eyed up the defenders. There were only about ten of them, but their shield wall was protected on either side by the wooden wall that surrounded the village.

Snorri scrutinized them and smiled. He turned to Brak Drumbr, "Time for your axe to earn its name." From the smiles on the faces of Snorri's crew, Ulf guessed they knew what was about to happen.

"Stay with me," Oddi said when he saw the confusion on Ulf's face. Ulf nodded and made sure that Vidar was with him.

Brak Drumbr gave his shield to one of the men and gripped his large axe with both hands. Snorri and Ragnar stood on either side, with the rest of the men falling into place. The spearhead formation gave Ulf an idea of what was about to happen. Thorvald was not so bright.

"What is he doing?" he demanded, standing to one side with his arms crossed.

"Just shut up and go to the back," Snorri responded, the frustration evident in his voice.

"No, I am the son of the jarl. I should be at the front!" The men laughed at this. His was the only armour not covered in blood.

"Do as your brother says," Ragnar growled. He wanted to fight, not explain things to a brat. But Thorvald refused to move.

"Then stay there," Snorri responded. "Men of Sae-Ulfr! Attack!" he roared before anything else could be said.

The spear formation sped towards the quivering shield wall of the defenders. Brak Drumbr lifted his two-handed axe, Shield-Breaker, over his head and roared Odin's name. Thorvald's scream was drowned out as he ran to catch up. Just before they collided with the defenders, Drumbr swung his axe, breaking shields and cleaving two defenders in half. Snorri's men crashed through the rest of the defenders, like a boulder through the early winter ice. Ulf finally got Olaf's axe dirty as he buried it in the face of one of the defenders who tried to spear Oddi in front of him. It was over in the blink of an eye as the rest of Snorri's men trampled over the defenders, leaving none alive. Women screamed and children cried as they saw the blood-covered invaders wandering through their small village.

Snorri looked at the hall, not far from where they were standing. It wasn't as big as his father's, but it was still impressive. It had a beautifully carved door post, with plain doors. It was the carved beams on the edge of the roof which looked like giant serpents climbing the roof that drew his eye.

"Brother!" Thorvald complained, having finally caught up.

Snorri turned to him, the bloody sneer on his face stopping Thorvald from saying anything else. Thorbjorn smirked at the scene.

"Search the place," Snorri said. His crew split up in small groups and got to work. Ulf realized they had done this many times before.

"Need me to do anything?" Ulf asked, wiping his axe clean.

Snorri shook his head in response as he watched Thorbjorn drag an old man out of the hall.

"Found him cowering inside," Thorbjorn said, throwing the

old man at Snorri's feet.

Snorri knelt and looked at the old man, Tyr's Fury still in his hand, and still bloody. "Where is your jarl?" he growled. The old man paled and started shaking. "I know he left. I know he has gone to Frankia." The old man nodded. "Why? What's in Frankia?"

"A man came not so long ago, a big man with a scar on his face. He spoke to the jarl and then they had a feast. The man left the next day. Just got on his ship and left. A week later the jarl took his warriors and sailed south. That's all I know; I swear on Odin's name," the old man pleaded.

"Who was the man?" Ulf asked, surprising everyone around him.

"I…I don't know. I've never seen him here before."

"Not much use this one, is he?" Thorbjorn said, understanding why Ulf was so curious about the big man. He drew his knife and knelt in front of the captive. Grabbing hold of his tunic, he held the knife to the old man's throat. "Better tell me something useful or I'll send you to Hel screaming for your mother."

The man's face paled to the point that Ulf thought he might pass out, but he somehow found his voice. "He…he arrived with a ship filled with warriors."

Could Griml have gotten an army? Ulf guessed it was possible. It'd been a year since he attacked the farm. "Did he give his name?" Ulf asked.

The man shook his head, his eyes fixed on Thorbjorn.

"What did he look like?" Snorri asked, wanting to move this along; there were other things to do and he wanted to get back to his ship.

Before the old man could answer, Ragnar stepped forward. "Why do we care about this man?"

Snorri looked at Ulf but realized he wasn't going to answer. He was still looking at the old man. Snorri doubted he had even heard the question. "I'm guessing Ulf thinks it might be the same man who killed his family."

"Why?"

"Because I cut his face," Ulf answered like that was all the explanation needed.

Ragnar shook his head at Ulf. "I have a cut on my face, you have cuts on your face. In the name of Tyr, Ulf, most warriors have cuts on their faces." Ulf glared back at Ragnar with such an intensity that Snorri stepped in between the two of them. He couldn't afford to have two of his best men kill each other right now.

"There's nothing wrong with asking," Snorri said, hoping it would calm the situation. "Answer the question, grandad."

The old man looked away from Thorbjorn to Snorri. "He ... he was big, very big and... ugly."

Snorri glanced at Ulf. "You think it might be Griml?"

Ulf thought for a while. "I don't know. Like Ragnar said, there are lots of warriors with scars on their faces." He paused for a while, trying to find the right words. "But I feel like it could be. I don't know why."

"So, what do we do?" Brak asked while picking a broken tooth from his beard.

"We should find a market town," Asbjorn suggested, surprising everyone. "If it's a big raid then someone there must have heard of it."

"And they call you the wise one," Thorbjorn said to Oddi. Oddi didn't respond, but the look on his face said enough.

"We go south to Suðrikaupstefna. Maybe we can find some

more information there." Snorri looked to Ulf, who nodded his appreciation.

"You sure that's wise?" Ragnar asked Snorri.

"I am. If we don't find any information, then we can sell the thralls and earn some coin," he said before walking away so that Ragnar couldn't ask any more questions.

Ulf watched Snorri walk away, grateful he had decided to help him. He just hoped Snorri wouldn't come to regret it.

CHAPTER 18

"A successful attack then?" Rolf asked as they returned to the ship after nightfall.

"You could say that, though not much of a reward for it," Snorri answered his steersman. They had searched the hall and found that the jarl, whose name was Gunnulf, had taken most of his treasure with him. All they had found was a small chest half-filled with some gold, silver and bronze hack pieces. Even the plundering of the defenders did not give the men much. But it wasn't a complete loss. They had taken captives to sell as thralls when they arrived at Suðrikaupstefna. There was the boy Ragnar had captured, a group of women and girls and a man about Ulf's age who had a limp. Their fear was sketched on their faces as they were dragged along by the rope around their necks. It was a cruel fate for people who had seen their jarl abandon them, but they lived in a cruel world.

"The storm blew itself out. Might be cloudy but my bones tell me there'll be no rain." Rolf tapped his leg when he saw Snorri look to the sky.

Snorri nodded and walked away. He ordered his men to get fires going and set up a watch on the captives. There was no point in losing them now. Snorri watched as his men herded the few cows they took from the farm. Some fresh meat for his crew at least. Brak

Drumbr was carrying a barrel of ale he had found in the jarl's hall. Another reason to be happy. Snorri smiled and decided to look for Ulf. He had been quiet since they heard the news about Gunnulf's visitor. He found Ulf sat around a fire with his hirdmen and decided to join them.

The moon had reached its peak by the time the meat was finished and Ulf was sat listening to the men talk about the day's fighting. Vidar had already fallen asleep; the day's events had proved a bit too much for him.

"How did you do, Ulf?" Brak asked him.

"I still live," Ulf said with a shrug. He didn't like talking about these things.

"Typical Ulf. The mysterious man with few words," Thorbjorn laughed.

"What will you do if this man turns out to be Griml?" Oddi asked. They had not spoken about it all day, so Ulf was surprised by the question.

"I don't really know," he said after a while. "Part of me is still trying to understand how he had found a ship with men. It didn't look like he had anything the last time I saw him."

"Maybe he killed for it," Thorbjorn suggested. "That's what I would have done."

"Would be easy for you," Brak Drumbr said. "Most people wouldn't even know you were there until you stabbed them in the stomach."

"Anything higher would be too high for him," his brother said, which made everyone laugh apart from Thorbjorn. He just growled some comment no one really heard. Ulf smiled. He decided he needed a piss and stood up.

"Where you running to?" Snorri asked with a mouth full of meat.

"For a piss. You want to hold it for me?" Ulf responded. He wasn't one for making jokes, but this one felt good. Snorri laughed with the rest and waved him away.

Ulf got to the water and lowered his pants. He breathed in the salty air, feeling it clear his mind of the ale he had drunk.

"Ragnar is some fighter, isn't he?" Oddi said, appearing out of the darkness. Ulf jumped and swore to himself as he nearly pissed on his trousers.

"Don't know, didn't really see him fight today," he responded. He finished his piss and pulled his trousers up, tying the string and checking he didn't piss on them. But before he could walk away, Oddi spoke again.

"I think he killed three men today. Most of our men stopped fighting to watch him do it," Oddi smiled. Ulf couldn't see it, but he heard it in his voice. "They say he made a sacrifice to Tyr for his fighting skills, so he could be the best fighter there was. Better than your father even."

"He did?" Ulf was curious now. There was something about Ragnar Ulf did not like, but he could never explain what it was. He looked over his shoulder toward the fire where Ragnar sat with Thorvald. Not surprisingly, both Ragnar and Thorvald were glaring at him.

"Aye, he cut off his little finger and burnt it in Tyr's honour. They say he woke up the next day and his hand was healed. A sign that Tyr had accepted his offer. Since that day he could not be beaten in a fight. No one could even manage to get him down on his knees. Until you sucker-punched him," Oddi laughed.

He sacrificed his finger? That was the fourth story Ulf had heard about Ragnar Nine-Finger and each story made no sense. "Do you believe that story?" Ulf asked Oddi.

"Why not? It's a believable story, I think. Everybody knows the gods appreciate personal sacrifices in their names," he said as the two of them walked back to the fire.

The Skuggi watched the two men walk back to the fire. He felt his hatred for Ulf burn inside of him. The Skuggi thought back to that night no more than a week ago. He had seen Hulda whispering something to Ulf and had known immediately what she was telling him. *Meet me by the tree.* That was his chance. He had to get Loki's attention and the only way to do that was to make an important sacrifice. He had thought long and hard about this until he understood what had to be done. The Skuggi had waited until Ulf walked out and then made sure Hulda was kept too busy to leave. When he saw people were too drunk or asleep to pay attention to him, he walked to Ulf's chest and took his sax-knife. It had been too easy. He followed Hulda out the back, without her noticing him. Or so he had thought. As soon as they got outside, she had turned to face him. He had not expected that and almost walked into her. He was confused when she gave him a knowing smile. This was not how it was supposed to be.

"It's not going to work, your plan," she had told him, her voice full of confidence. Instead of seeing the fear he had wanted in her eyes, he saw defiance and mockery. That night the Skuggi realized she was more than just a thrall. In his panic he launched at her, expecting her to move out of the way. But she didn't. She just stood there, still smiling at him when Ulf's knife went into her throat. Before he could understand what had happened, she twisted her body, forcing the knife to slice her throat open and showering him in blood.

The Skuggi shuddered at the thought of it. After that, he had waited until Ulf had given up and then dragged her body to the tree. She was heavier than he had expected. The Skuggi had carved Loki's name onto her forehead. A thought had come to him then, so clever it must have been a message from Loki. *Leave the knife in her hand.*

The following morning had been like a dream, everything had been going perfectly. Until the fucking branch broke. People had said it was because of the raven, that Odin had been watching and did not want Ulf to die. The Skuggi had been so focused on Ulf he never saw or heard the raven. He had realized something that day. They were not involved in the affairs of men anymore. Somehow, they had been caught up in a fight between the gods.

But the worst was yet to come. Snorri had decided to go raiding and now he was stuck on the ship with Ulf, with no way of avoiding him. Although he had learnt something very important about Ulf that might have made it worth his while. Ulf had a dark side, a side he couldn't control. The Skuggi smiled to himself as he thought for a way to take advantage of that.

The next morning the weather was just as Rolf predicted. There were still clouds in the sky, but the wind had changed, now blowing away from the land. The sea birds were using this wind as they glided over the grey water in search of a meal. Men hurriedly packed up their tents and loaded everything onto the ship, including the captives. There was a stream nearby which was used to fill up the barrels of drinking water for the trip, but unfortunately, there was no more ale left. They had finished that during the night. This meant some men were grumbling, but they still got on with their tasks. Everyone knew Njörd could change his mind at any moment and alter the course of the wind.

"Perhaps we should make a sacrifice to Njörd. Might help keep the weather on our side," Rolf said to Snorri as they watched the men get ready to leave.

Snorri thought for a moment, his eyes shifting between the sky and the sea. "Won't do any harm, but it needs to be quick. We need to get going." He looked at the captives. He could sacrifice one of them. It would be a powerful sacrifice, but he didn't want to waste one. Snorri then thought of the small chest they had found in Gunnulf's hall. It wasn't much, but they should get a decent amount for the captives. The gods liked shiny things. He nodded to himself, pleased with his decision, then rubbed the Mjöllnir around his neck. He just hoped Njörd would be pleased with it as well. The gods could be fickle bastards when they wanted to be.

Once everything was ready, half the crew and the captives got on board. The rest of them, including Ulf, stood by the prow of the ship, ready to push her into the sea. The tide was going out, so they had no time to waste. As soon as Snorri, who was standing in the stern, gave the order, the men on the beach pushed the ship into the water. She slid easily off the sand and the men on board used their oars to keep her in place so everyone could climb on board. When this was done, Snorri gave the order for the men to row. Rolf ordered the oars on the port side to stop and the Sae-Ulfr rotated around until she faced the right way. Another order from Rolf had half the men rowing, while Snorri, Thorbjorn and the brothers hoisted the sail, pulling on the halyards and tying the sail down when it was fully up. The Sae-Ulfr lurched forward as the wind caught in her sail, causing the men to laugh at Brak who almost fell over. Snorri took the chest they had taken from Gunnulf's hall and emptied half of it into the sea.

"Mighty Njörd, accept our offering and grant us a safe voyage across your domain," he shouted into the wind. All the men rubbed the Mjöllnir pendants hanging around their necks, with some even throwing some gold or silver over the side themselves, offering their own prayers to the god of the wind and sea. Ulf didn't touch the Mjöllnir around his neck. Instead, he stroked the shaft of Olaf's axe, feeling the names of his family carved on there. He sent a silent prayer to Odin.

"Odin, father of the gods and wisest of all. Let this man we are chasing be the one I am after," he whispered. "So that I can avenge my family and take back what is mine." Ulf heard a noise above him and saw that a large sea eagle was hovering in the air above the Sae-Ulfr. He smiled to himself, realizing Odin had heard his prayer and was watching him. Vidar nudged him and when Ulf looked at him, he saw Vidar felt the same way. The smile on his face said more than words ever could. For the first time in a long while, Ulf felt good. Like he finally knew where he was going. Other men saw the eagle as well and all thought it was a good omen.

Snorri sat down beside Ulf and watched the eagle, which appeared to be following them. "It looks like the All-Father is watching us." He had a big smile on his face.

"Looks like it," Ulf agreed, still watching the eagle. "He is guiding us, telling us we're on the right path, I think."

Snorri clasped Ulf's shoulder. "I think so too, my brother." With that he jumped up the prow, grabbing hold of the snarling wolf head and howled into the sky. One by one, the men took up the call of their leader and soon all the men, apart from Ulf, Ragnar and Thorvald, were howling. Ulf followed the eagle as it turned away; it had seen what it needed to. He turned to Vidar and the excited look on his face made Ulf laugh. *Fuck it*, he thought. Ulf took a deep breath, lifted his head into the sky and added his own howl to the chorus. The wolves of Thorgilsstad had finally sniffed their prey and Ulf was on his way to get his revenge.

CHAPTER 19

"Who do you think it is?" Snorri asked Ragnar as they watched the ship approach from the distance. They had been sailing for half a day when they spotted the other ship slicing through the water in their direction, its sail showing vertical lines of black and red.

"No idea," Ragnar said. He was the most experienced warrior on board, having been on more raids and in more battles than there were fleas on a mangy dog. But he didn't recognise those colours. "Best be prepared for the worst, I think," he said after a while.

"Aye, that's what I was thinking." Snorri looked over his shoulder and knew he didn't need to give the order. Most of his men had been with him long enough to understand his thinking and he relied on them to help the new members of his crew understand that too. He went to the stern of his ship to where he kept his sea chest. As he walked past the captives, who had been tied up to the mast, he made a note to himself to make sure they were secured and would not cause any problems. The last thing he needed if he was going to fight a sea battle was to worry about the captives freeing themselves and attacking his men from behind. Then he spotted his younger brother, sitting near the stern. He was the only one not getting his armour on. He had promised his father he would turn his brother into a warrior, but he wasn't sure how to do that. Snorri had always enjoyed fighting; even as a young child he was always getting into fights. Fighting was in his blood, but Thorvald was different. It was hard to believe they shared the same parents. There was no denying his brother was smart, but he was not a fighter. Snorri decided to leave him where he was.

"What's happening?" Ulf asked him when he got to his chest. He didn't realize Ulf had been behind him the whole time.

"We don't know who that ship belongs to," he responded, taking his brynja out of the chest and putting it on. Ulf was holding his belt for him when he finished adjusting the chain mail, so it sat better on his shoulders. He nodded to Ulf and took the belt, tightening it around his waist so it carried most of the weight of his brynja. He rotated his arms and twisted around to make sure it sat nicely and would not impede him during the potential fight.

"We're expecting a fight?" Ulf asked, his eyes back on the approaching ship.

Snorri noticed Ulf had already put his leather jerkin on, with Olaf's axe and his sax-knife secured in place. "Better to be prepared for one," he said as he pulled his Mjöllnir out of his tunic and let it hang in the open. Ulf nodded as if he understood. "Don't worry," Snorri said with his usual wolf grin. "It'll be just like fighting on land. Only more fun." Ulf smiled back, but Snorri could see there was still some concern there. He decided not to worry about it. Ulf had said he would not die until he'd had his revenge, and Snorri believed him.

Ulf watched Snorri walk back to the prow. Everybody was now armed and ready. Some of the older men were even laughing and joking, but like him, the new crew members looked nervous.

"Have you ever fought in a sea battle before?" Geir asked. He had approached Ulf after Snorri walked away. Like everyone else, he had his armour on, a leather jerkin like Ulf's, although his looked a little more cut up. He also had the sword Snorri had given him after the fight with Kettil the Red.

"No," Ulf responded. "But I'm sure there is nothing to worry about." He looked to the sky, but he wasn't sure what for.

"You think so?" Geir rubbed the back of his neck, his eyes darting to where Snorri stood.

"No, but nobody else seems to be worried, so I don't see why we should be." Ulf didn't know what else to say to calm Geir's nerves. Besides, he had Vidar to worry about. He clapped Geir on the back and walked to his place, where Vidar was sat holding two spears, his face as calm as the sea on a windless day. "You shouldn't be playing with those." Vidar only smiled as Ulf knew he would. Vidar never really listened to him.

The ships drew near each other so they could see the men on the other ship more clearly. Ulf thought it was smaller than the Sae-Ulfr, maybe only carrying twenty oars. Both captains called for the sails to be lowered so they could speak to each other. It was another example of seamanship that fascinated Ulf as he watched the ships being manoeuvred into position.

"Greetings," Snorri shouted to the other ship. "Where you headed?" He held his helmet in one hand while the other was raised in the air, like a friendly greeting.

A large man stepped forward, putting his right foot on the gunwale and resting on it. "Greetings!" he shouted back. "Why's that your business?" he asked. He looked older than the rest of the men on his ship, older even than Ragnar. He was wearing a brynja, like

Snorri, but the rest of his men either had jerkins or weren't wearing any armour. But all of them were brandishing weapons, like a wild dog baring its fangs at the wolf, hoping to put it off attacking.

"Just curious, friend."

"Do I know you?" the man shouted back. He tried to appear as if he was not concerned, but he must have been. Snorri's men outnumbered his and were better armed.

"No, I don't believe so," Snorri answered with a smile, not a friendly smile, but the smile of a predator who saw easy prey.

"Then why call me friend?"

"I thought you would rather be my friend than my enemy," Snorri answered back. One of the captives recognised the man's voice and started struggling against his bonds. Snorri turned at the commotion behind him. Before he could say anything, the captive shouted out.

"Arvid!" the youth shouted. It was the one Ragnar had captured. "Help us! Arvid!" Asbjorn smacked him with the pommel of his sword, knocking him out.

"Anyone else have something to say?" He glared at the other captives. They shook their heads, before lowering them. No one wanted to be brave now.

Arvid stood up straight and looked at the men around him. They all recognised the voice. "Where did you come from, friend?" He said the word friend with a sneer as if he already knew the answer, but needed to hear it from Snorri.

Snorri looked back at Arvid and smiled. "We found a small village, not far from here. Hospitality wasn't great though." The men around him laughed, while those on Arvid's ship bristled. "You are Jarl Gunnulf's man?"

Arvid spat over the side before saying, "Gunnulf can go fuck a goat, the treacherous bastard."

Snorri raised an eyebrow at Oddi standing next to him. If they don't follow their jarl anymore, then he might be able to avoid a fight. His men outnumbered those of Arvid, but he still didn't want to risk them. "We don't have to fight, you know."

"You afraid now?" Arvid responded. His men were brandishing their weapons and looked like dogs straining at their leashes after hearing the familiar voice on the Sae-Ulfr.

Snorri smiled at that but didn't bite. "Your village has suffered enough. And besides, many have escaped."

"Apart from the ones on your ship."

"Apart from them."

Arvid looked to the sky and then at his men. Taking a deep breath, he put his helmet on his head. "What must be done, must be done."

Snorri turned to the men behind him. "Prepare for battle!" he shouted. Arvid could be heard shouting the same on his ship.

"What are they doing?" Ulf asked as he saw men on both ships prepare the weighted ropes they used.

"We have to tie the ships together," Oddi answered. "To create a fighting platform for us to fight on."

"Aye, fighting on two moving ships is not a good idea," Thorbjorn added. "And neither is losing."

"Why?" one of the other recruits asked. They crept closer when they heard Ulf ask the question.

"Nowhere to run," Thorbjorn said. "On land, the losing army can flee, but at sea, their ship is tied up, so they can't." He looked at the recruit. "On the sea, you lose, you die."

"But what if we lose?" another recruit asked, chewing on his bottom lip.

Thorbjorn rounded on the man and grabbed hold of his jerkin. "You are a warrior of the Sae-Ulfr! We are the sea wolves; we do not lose! Ever!" His face had gone red as he screamed, spittle and all, in the young man's face.

"Relax, Thorbjorn," Snorri said as he placed a hand on his friend's shoulder, reassuring him like a guard dog who doesn't like the smell of a new visitor. "I'm sure Sigmund doesn't think we will lose."

"No, Snorri," Sigmund answered quickly, his eyes still on the red face of Thorbjorn.

"Good. Remember, trust the man on your left and protect the one on your right and you have nothing to worry about." He looked around and saw the ropes had been thrown to the other ship and the men were preparing to pull the ships together. "Skjaldborg!"

Ulf grabbed his shield from the side of the ship and looked at the snarling wolf head painted on the leather. That was the symbol for the men of the Sae-Ulfr, but Ulf's shield had three lines painted on the face of its wolf. Brak had added these to match the scars on Ulf's face.

"The Bear-Slayer needs his own design," he'd said with a laugh.

There was a loud thunk as the ships came together, causing some men to lose their balance. The sea birds circling above added their cries to the noise like they were encouraging the men to fight. Once the ships were secured together, the two armies faced each other in two neat lines of overlapping shields. Snorri stood in the centre of his line, with Ragnar on his left, both men looking like gods of war. Ulf stood on Snorri's right with Oddi and the brothers on his right, while Thorbjorn and Asbjorn were on Ragnar's left. Behind them stood a second line of men with spears, ready to stab at exposed necks over the shield wall. Ulf felt the bile rising in his stomach as he watched the warrior in front of him, his knuckles strained white as he gripped his shield. This would be his hardest fight yet and he hoped the Norns would not end his journey here.

Snorri regarded Ulf, seeing his determined stare from under his helmet. "Do you know how I know the gods are watching you?" he asked Ulf. Ulf shook his head. "Because since you arrived at Thorgilsstad, life has been very interesting," he laughed then stepped forward. "For Odin!" Snorri screamed and attacked. His men echoed his cry and moved forward as one. Arvid's men screamed their own cry and came forward, determined not to let Snorri's men board their ship. The two shield walls met on the edges of their ships, the crashing of the shields coming together almost drowned out by the birds screaming from above like a cheering crowd.

Ulf stabbed with his spear, forcing Arvid's man in front of him to lift his shield to block it. As he did this, Oddi stabbed the man in the stomach, his spear flicking out like a serpent's tongue. Arvid's man screamed as he bent over, dropping his shield as he tried to stem the blood gushing from his gut. Ulf punched the wounded man in the face with his shield and forgot about him as he fell back. The next warrior stepped into the gap with a roar as he swung a large axe at Ulf's head. Ulf got his shield up to block the blow and felt the axe biting into it. The strike rattled his arm as the noise rung in his ears. The man pulled his axe back, forcing Ulf to take half a step forward. Ulf's half scream was drowned out by the symphony of the battle raging around as he tried to stay in the safety of the shield wall, but his opponent was too strong.

"Ulf!" Snorri shouted, blocking another strike from Arvid, who despite his age was a good warrior.

As soon as Ulf was forced to step forward, another of Arvid's men stabbed at him with his sword. Ulf managed to twist his body at the last moment, and the sword cut into his jerkin. Ulf couldn't bring his spear around to do anything about this man and Oddi was pre-occupied, so he dropped it and punched the man who tried to stab him in the face. There was a crunch as his head snapped back. Vidar speared him in the neck from behind Ulf. Ulf focused on the man in front of him again and knew he had no choice. He let go of his shield just as his opponent pulled back on his axe. The warrior screamed in surprise as he fell back onto the man behind him. Before Ulf could register the breach in the shield wall, he was shoved forward from behind. Ulf froze as panic gripped him, half-expecting a sword to pierce him or an axe to chop into him. But Oddi was right behind him and as soon as he got through the breach he turned and stabbed the man facing Brak Drumbr in the back. Ulf freed his axe from his belt, his panic having released its grip on him, and used it to block the blow aimed at Oddi's head. He tackled Oddi's would-be killer and fell on top of him, hacking into his neck with his axe, roaring his defiance. Ulf felt the warm blood spray over his face and tasted the metallic sweetness of it on his lips. Gone was the fear of fighting on a rocking ship. He felt the battle rage surging through him, becoming more intense with each heartbeat. Everything seemed to slow down as he heard the whispers pumping in his ears, getting louder and louder until he could hear nothing else. The whispers became his father's voice, an old man's voice, a woman's voice. It was the voice of one but at the same time the voice of many. They demanded one thing. Chaos.

Snorri saw the breach caused by Ulf and roared in triumph. Arvid made the mistake of looking to see what happened and this distraction ended his life. Snorri stabbed Tyr's Fury over the rim of Arvid's shield and watched with delight as the sword pierced Arvid's neck just below his turned head. Arvid held on to his sword as Snorri punched his body with his shield and freed his sword at the same time. When Arvid's men saw their leader fall, they knew the fight was over, but they still fought on.

Ulf did not like the voices. That was not what he wanted to be. *Embrace your blood.* But he didn't want to. He did not want to be like his father, so blinded by his quest for battle glory that he had forgotten about his son. Or the old man in the tale told by Rolf, who gladly gave up his son in order to become a king. That was not the blood he wanted to embrace. Ulf found a shield lying on the deck and picked it up. Snorri's men were swarming onto Arvid's ship. Ulf felt the movement to the right and turned in time to see a youth swing a sword at him. He blocked it with the shield and took a step back, not wanting to kill again. The youth attacked again and again, while Ulf kept blocking with his shield. A sword suddenly erupted from the youth's chest. Both Ulf and the boy stared at it in surprise, before the boy fell. Snorri stood there, a smile on his blood-covered face.

"Stop fucking about, Ulf."

Ulf saw the fight was over by then. Those of Arvid's men who were still alive had thrown down their weapons and surrendered. Thorbjorn and Oddi were rounding them up while the brothers watched them, their weapons ready in case one of Arvid's men changed their minds. Asbjorn had grabbed a few men and was searching for any of Snorri's crew among the fallen. Ulf looked around for Vidar, feeling a fresh wave of panic when he couldn't see him. But then he spotted Vidar struggling to remove the axe still stuck in Ulf's shield, his hair and faced reddened by blood.

"Nothing like a good sea battle to get the blood pumping," Snorri said to Ulf. Ulf wasn't sure if he agreed with him. The battle rage was leaving his body now, leaving him exhausted. His hands were shaking, but he wasn't sure if that was because of his nerves or because he couldn't believe that he survived this. This short battle was more intense than any he had taken part in so far. His head started spinning and for a moment Ulf thought he might pass out. He took deep breaths, willing himself to keep standing.

"Don't worry about that," Snorri said, indicating at his shaking hands. "It usually happens after a fight, especially one like this." He turned and faced Ulf, his face becoming serious. "But, like I said many times before. You think too much." His face softened a little. "But you did well to cause that breach in their line. That turned the battle."

"Snorri." They turned to see Ragnar walking to them. Like them, he was covered in blood and had what looked like a tooth stuck in his brynja. Ulf didn't want to know how that got there. "I spoke to one of the survivors. There was a disagreement with Gunnulf, so they left him."

Snorri shook his head, grinding his teeth at the same time. He despised men who betrayed their jarl. "What kind of disagreement?" he asked.

"Wouldn't say, but I suspect it had something to do with Gunnulf's new friend."

"Why?" Ulf asked. Ragnar glared at him, the squint in his eye showed he didn't like Ulf speaking to him, but he answered anyway.

"When I asked about him, they went quiet, refused to say anything. Even after some friendly persuasion," he smiled.

"Ok, I guess that's not important now. What is, is that we now know Gunnulf's forces are smaller."

"But we don't know anything about his new friend and his forces," Ragnar countered.

Snorri just smiled at him, like this was some minor problem for them. "We'll just have to find out then, won't we." He walked past Ragnar who grabbed hold of his arm. Snorri turned sharply; his blood still hot from the battle.

"Your father did not send you out to go hunting for war, Snorri."

"My father is not in charge of the Sae-Ulfr and her men. This is my ship and my men. If I feel like hunting down some troll-fucker, then I will." The two men faced each other for a while. Those nearby had stopped what they were doing to watch this confrontation. Ulf took a step closer, Olaf's axe still in his hand. But it was not necessary. Ragnar nodded, accepting Snorri's point and walked away.

It took longer than Ulf thought it would to go through the bodies of the dead, looking for friends and plunder. Snorri had put his most trusted men in charge of collecting the plunder of the fallen. He would give it out to his men as he saw fit. Ulf sat with Thorbjorn and Vidar, drinking some water and cleaning Olaf's axe.

"That was some fight," Thorbjorn commented. Ulf nodded; he didn't feel like talking now. "That's the first time I fought beside Ragnar, and I hope it's the last bloody time."

Ulf looked up at this. He had thought Thorbjorn would have loved the experience. He was always saying you could learn a lot by watching warriors like him. "Why?"

"Because he fucking takes all the kills," Thorbjorn said, exasperated. "Didn't manage a single one today. My poor Bloodthirst is going to bed hungry tonight," he said, patting the hilt of his sword.

Ulf glanced at Vidar, who was laughing his silent laugh. He felt a bit uncomfortable sitting next to a man who was referring to his sword as if it was a baby.

"Heard you had a good time though," Thorbjorn continued. "Asbjorn said he saw you breach the wall and then jump through it without any thought." Ulf looked at him. That's not how he remembered it. Ulf peered at Vidar, wondering if he had pushed him through the gap. Vidar looked back, his innocent smile on his face.

"It was ok, I guess."

Thorbjorn scowled at him. "What do you mean it was ok? You survived where others had not. Some of our brothers will be drinking with their fathers in Valhalla tonight, and some will be drinking in Ran's hall, but you have survived to fight another day. And not just that," his face was going red now, "you held your ground and fought well. It was fucking ok, my arse."

He stood up and stormed off. Ulf watched him go, stunned by his outburst. He didn't mean to upset Thorbjorn; he just didn't feel comfortable talking about the battle. He didn't feel like he held his ground, not when he could still remember the panic he felt when he went through the breach. But Thorbjorn was right. He lived to fight another day.

CHAPTER 20

The sun was lowering in the sky when the Sae-Ulfr reached Suðrikaupstefna two days later. Ulf and Vidar had never seen so many ships in one place, the hundreds of masts pointing to the sky reminding Ulf of a forest. But this forest, its trees bare of any leaves, could provide him with a bounty richer than any mere forest. Ulf and Vidar weren't the only ones amazed by the sight. The new crew members who had never sailed to a market town before had the same raised eyebrows and open mouths as Ulf and Vidar.

"If you young un's don't close your mouths, some fish might jump in there!" Rolf shouted from the stern. They very quickly closed their mouths, but their eyebrows stayed high.

"We'll find a place on the beach over there," Snorri said, pointing to the stony beach not far from the market but also not too close. "Oddi, you stay with the ship, but keep her ready to sail at all times. I'll take the rest of my hirdmen and Geir," who beamed at being mentioned, "to the market. We'll sell the captives and see if we can learn anything useful." Rolf nodded and adjusted the tiller to send the Sae-Ulfr in the right direction.

"We're coming too." Ragnar indicated at himself and Thorvald as he walked up to Snorri.

"Fine."

"That's a lot of ships," Ragnar said, standing next to Snorri now.

"Aye," Snorri responded, "and most of them don't look like trading ships." He was talking about the Knörr ship, which was used by traders. It had a similar shape to Snekkjas like the Sae-Ulfr, but the hull was broader and deeper to carry a different cargo. Knörrs also didn't need a large crew to operate, which often made them easy pickings for pirates and other Snekkjas looking for plunder.

"What do you think that means?" Ulf asked.

"It means somebody is planning something," Oddi said.

"Could it be this new friend of Gunnulf?" Thorbjorn asked. Nobody wanted to say Griml because they were still not convinced it was him.

"We'll find out," Snorri responded, his fingers drumming on the gunwale of his ship.

"Trim the sail!" Rolf ordered as they approached the shore. They didn't want to go in too fast and damage the keel of the Sae-Ulfr. The brothers moved quickly and Ulf was amazed at how sure-footed Brak Drumbr was on the ship considering his larger size. There was a grinding noise as the Sae-Ulfr gently caressed the bottom and came to a rest. The men jumped off quickly to tie her down and to put the anchor out so she wouldn't tip over. Ulf followed them, helping where he could.

Snorri jumped over and walked up to Ulf, clapping him on the back as he got there. "You'll get used to it one day."

"I noticed you didn't help," Ulf retorted.

Snorri laughed at him and shook his head. "The joy of being the captain of a ship. Make the others do all the hard work and you can just enjoy the moment of it."

"That was some fine sailing." A voice came from behind them. Both men turned and saw a man approaching them. He was shorter than them and older. Ulf guessed he was older than Ragnar but younger than Rolf. His plaited beard was grey, and he had a slight stoop to his back.

"Thank you," Snorri responded. "But the credit goes to my steersman, Rolf Treefoot."

"You have a good steersman then, I see," the man said. "Njörd knows I wish mine was as good. He always manages to hit a rock in the open ocean." He laughed at his own joke. Snorri and Ulf glanced at each other. "Name's Ivor Runarson."

"Snorri Thorgilsson," Snorri responded and then pointed to Ulf, "and this is Ulf Bear-Slayer." Ulf nodded his greeting but didn't say anything. He did not like the way Ivor's eyes were constantly darting around.

"Bear-Slayer huh?" Ivor scrutinized Ulf, like he didn't believe Ulf was capable of killing a bear.

"Aye, killed a bear with nothing but his axe," Snorri said, the smile back on his face. He liked telling this story. Or at least, his ever-changing version of it.

"Well," Ivor said, returning Snorri's smile, "you'll have to tell me the story one day." He looked at Snorri's men disembarking from the Sae-Ulfr. "You here for the big raid then?" he asked Snorri.

Snorri shook his head. "No, to sell captives. What raid?" He glanced at Ulf again.

"Don't know much about it myself, but they say some new sea king has promised riches beyond those Fafnir is guarding, if you join forces with him to attack some city in Frankia."

"Frankia, you say." Snorri pulled at his beard and looked like he was picturing a map in his head. "A lot of gold in those lands."

"Heard the same," Ivor said.

"You joining the raid?" Snorri asked. Ulf looked over Ivor's shoulder and saw the tattered tents of his crew. The men did not look much better either as they lay around, not caring about the new ship on the beach.

"Not sure yet," Ivor said. He looked past Snorri and saw Ragnar approaching. His eyes bulged and face paled. "I'll let you get back to your business, friends," Ivor said and scurried away.

"What did that rat want with you?" Ragnar asked.

"You know him?" Snorri turned to his father's champion.

"I do. Almost killed him as well, but the bastard got lucky. He slipped at the last moment and Skull-Splitter missed."

"A lucky rat then."

"Aye, the Norns were looking after him that day."

"Looks like we were right. There is some sea king who is planning a raid in Frankia. He is promising a treasure greater than that of Fafnir, or so Ivor Rat says."

Ragnar raised his eyebrows at this. Like most warriors, he was always attracted to the promise of gold and silver. "Greater than Fafnir's," he repeated. Ragnar thought for a while. To Ulf, it always looked like he was in pain when he did so. "Did he say who this sea king is?"

"No, you scared him off before we could ask."

"Humm. Well, the captives have been unloaded. Rolf is staying on board with all our provisions. Just in case," he said to Snorri.

"In case of what?" Ulf asked.

"Let's just say Snorri is not always good at making friends."

Snorri tried to look offended, but only looked more guilty. "That was a long time ago, I've been better since."

"Aye, and Odin got his eye back," Ragnar responded.

"Best get kitted up. It always helps to look the part," Snorri said and he and Ulf walked back to the ship where their gear was.

Ulf opened his sea chest and looked at his new brynja. Snorri had given it to him as a reward for breaching Arvid's shield wall and giving them the victory. Three of Snorri's men had died, and two had serious injuries. Of Arvid's men, they counted twelve dead and five injured. After the fight, Snorri had those who surrendered stripped of what armour and weapons they had. They had been given empty barrels and told to swim back to shore. The Norns would decide who lived and died. The dead, from both crews, were placed on Arvid's ship and set alight. Ulf remembered watching the flames eat the ship and then disappear into the sea as they sailed away.

The men had cheered Ulf's name when Snorri handed him the brynja, with a gold arm-ring. It had made Ulf feel uncomfortable. He had expected to feel proud. But the events of the fight were still fresh in his mind, and so were the voices he had heard. Snorri had also given a beaming Vidar an arm-ring. Vidar had barely taken his eyes off the thing since.

Ulf took the brynja out of his chest, feeling the weight of it. He had been amazed at how heavy it was when he first took it from Snorri. Arvid had taken good care of it. There were no missing links and only a few spots of rust. Brak had shown him how to clean it using a hard brush and he had spent most of the journey here cleaning off the rust. Ulf slipped it over his head and nearly stumbled over when the full weight of the brynja fell on his shoulders. He took his belt, but then wasn't sure how to put it on.

"Let me help," Snorri said, already in his brynja.

"It's heavy," Ulf said.

Snorri nodded and took the belt from Ulf. "Arms up," he said and slipped the belt around Ulf's waist. "Take a deep breath in and hold it." When Ulf did that, he tightened the belt. "There. Feel the difference?" he asked Ulf.

Ulf did. The belt now carried most of the weight of the brynja, and it didn't feel so heavy on his shoulders.

When they were ready, they jumped off the ship and met the others on the beach. Waiting for them was Thorbjorn, the brothers and Asbjorn. Ragnar was there, which meant Thorvald would be coming with, as was Vidar. Geir was holding the rope tied to the captives.

They didn't say much on the walk to the market, which to Ulf looked like a temporary settlement, with tents everywhere. But there were signs it was turning into a more permanent place. Small wooden houses were being built here and there and Ulf also saw some which had already been finished. They were not as big as the longhouses Ulf was used to, but then he guessed these houses served a different purpose. The longhouses farmers used were built to house the animals during the cold winter months when they couldn't be kept outside. Even the houses in Thorgilsstad were longhouses, like the one Snorri lived in. The houses he saw here were shorter and not as tall. Ulf saw Vidar crinkle his face and wondered why before he smelt the odour on the breeze. It was the sour stink of a lot of people living in a small place and neither Ulf nor Vidar liked it.

"Looks like people are planning on staying here," Thorbjorn said, not bothered by the smell. Neither were the others, Ulf saw.

"Looks like it," Snorri replied without any conviction; he was keeping an eye out for anyone who might be from Gunnulf's village. It wouldn't be good if they recognised their friends or relatives being dragged along by a rope. He kept his hand on the hilt of Tyr's Fury.

"How long have they been trading here?" Ulf asked.

Thorbjorn answered him. He was always happy to talk, no matter the situation. "They've been here for as long as I can remember, but it has always been a temporary place," he said, pointing at the tents. "The traders usually arrive during the spring, set up their stalls and stay until the weather turns. Then they pack up and go back to wherever they came from."

"But now they are building houses," Asbjorn added, with the same unfriendly tone he always used when speaking to Ulf.

"Aye, maybe they think it'll be easier to just stay here," Thorbjorn suggested.

Ulf looked around at the landscape. The land was flat with a few hills. He guessed there were some farms nearby, so the people would be able to buy food. The market itself was another first for Ulf. There was a constant noise, like birds chattering in the trees, and traders could be heard shouting about their wares to anyone walking past. Olaf had told him about markets he had seen, but Ulf had never believed his stories.

"Ulf, don't embarrass us by gawking like an idiot," Ragnar said, "and tell that dog of yours as well." Ulf stared into the back of Ragnar's head, clenching his fists. Vidar touched his arm and when Ulf looked at him, just shook his head. Ulf took a deep breath and distracted himself by looking at the stalls. They seemed to sell everything here. He saw stalls selling farming equipment like hoes and axes. Some were selling wool and flax, already woven, so whoever bought it did not have to spend any time on the loom. There were stalls which sold weapons and armour. Ulf saw a variety of swords and axes laid out on the table, even a large double-headed axe which he wouldn't want to face in battle. He saw brynjas and leather jerkins, belts and a beautifully carved helmet which caught his eye. It was all silver and had an eye guard, carved to look like two open-mouthed wolves facing each other.

"I wouldn't get that here," Brak said, noticing Ulf stare at the helmet.

"Why not?"

"Not always good quality," Brak responded.

"It's true," Brak Drumbr said. "Knew a guy who bought a sword here. He was told it was made from the strongest metal there was, but in his first battle with it, the sword broke."

"Heard the same thing. You can't trust these people," Oddi said. "They would sell your mother a broken stick."

"Why would my mother want a broken stick?" Thorbjorn asked, only hearing half of the conversation.

"Suppose she could use it to make a fire?" Brak suggested. They had walked past the stall by now and moved on to one selling jewellery made from glass beads and gold and silver. Vidar walked behind Ulf, his eyes so wide, people who saw him thought they might fall out.

"What's the fucking forest for then?" Thorbjorn shouted at Brak. "Why are we talking about this anyway?"

"Ulf was looking at a helmet on old Rander's table. I only told him not to buy it there," Brak said, defending himself.

"Oh aye. Stay away from his table. Nothing but a pile of shit on there," Thorbjorn said. "The best thing to do if you see something you like is to remember what it looks like then ask Bard in Thorgilsstad to make it for you. That man is as gifted as the dwarves in Svartalfheim."

They walked past what looked to be a temporary tavern. There were benches out with tables, where you could get a drink and some of the pork being rotated on a fire not far from the benches. The benches were mostly full, but all of Snorri's men still looked longingly at the jugs of ale and the pig being spit-roasted.

"That would go down just fine," Thorbjorn said while licking his lips.

Ulf's stomach growled as he caught the smell of the pork. They had not eaten since sunrise, which made the sight of the food more painful than appetising. But the sight beyond the make-shift tavern made Ulf forget about food completely. In front of them was the thrall market. It wasn't easy to miss; the pens full of bound men, women and children made sure of that.

"Is that what I think it is?" he asked.

"Yep," said Snorri, "that's what's going to make us rich."

Ulf now understood why some of Arvid's men decided to fight to the death. He had only ever seen the thralls in Thorgilsstad, but they were treated well. *Was Hulda bought in a place like this? No, she was different.* She had not been an ordinary thrall. But still, seeing this made him feel sick. He just hoped he would never find himself in those pens. He looked at the men. Some of them had been warriors, fighting men like him and the rest of Snorri's crew, but now they stood there, dirty, beaten and worst of all – broken. He saw it in their eyes. There was no spirit left. They said Heimdall was the patron god of thralls, so Ulf sent a silent prayer to him, asking him to protect the captives they were about to sell. They had done nothing wrong. Their only fault was to be caught by Snorri's men. He looked away from the thrall pens and at Vidar. Vidar was looking at the children in the pens with a hint of sadness in his eyes. Ulf even saw a teardrop running down his cheek. It was like he felt their pain, their loneliness.

"Snorri, son of Thorgils!" a voice boomed. "I see you bring me more merchandise." A large man walked to them with his arms wide and a big grin on his face. He was a man who indulged himself too much in food and ale, his large wobbling belly proof of that. Ulf took an instant dislike to the man. Everything from his sweaty face to the bald patch on his head. His beard was thin and unkempt. But Ulf could see he was wealthy. That was evident in his fine clothing, especially the blue tunic he was wearing. Poor people could never afford to get something blue; the dye was too expensive. And the gold rings on most of his fingers added to the effect.

"Orvar," Snorri said. He was smiling, but Ulf heard no warmth in his voice. The two men shook hands and Snorri directed Orvar towards the captives held by Geir. But before he could get far, Orvar saw Ragnar standing behind Snorri.

"Well, by Odin, if it isn't Ragnar Nine-Finger. Don't you normally sail with Jarl Thorgils?" he asked Ragnar.

Ragnar sneered at the man. "I do, but not on this journey," Ragnar replied. Orvar waited for him to say more, the smile on his face showing he knew they didn't like him, but he didn't care.

"Ulf, why don't you and the others go get some food and drink," Snorri said to him. Maybe he saw the dark look in Ulf's eyes and didn't trust his friend not to split the merchant's skull with his axe.

Ulf followed the men to the tavern, where they found some empty seats and ordered food and drink.

"That man disgusts me," Thorbjorn said. "It's one thing to kill a man in battle, but another to sell a man's life away like that."

"Aye," Brak Drumbr said. "I'd much rather die drowning than live my life as a thrall." He touched his Mjöllnir to ward off the evil of his words.

"That's no way to live, I can tell you that," Asbjorn said.

"If you don't like the man, then why do you trade with him?" Ulf asked.

"He's the best at what he does."

"At selling people," Ulf said as a statement.

"We don't have to like it, but it does bring in a nice booty." Thorbjorn tried to justify it.

Their drinks arrived, which gave them an excuse not to talk about it anymore. Ulf watched Snorri and Ragnar talk to Orvar. It looked like they were haggling over the price for the captives. Ulf didn't want to see that anymore. He understood it was part of their lives, but like Thorbjorn said, he did not have to like it. Ulf turned away from it and looked in the direction they walked from, towards the stall with the helmet he had seen. Because of this, he saw the group of warriors before the rest of his companions. They looked experienced and rough, like they'd been around for a while and had never experienced anything more comfortable than sleeping on the deck of a ship. There were seven of them, all wearing brynjas and armed with swords and axes. Their shields were on their backs and they walked with the confidence of men who knew their place was on top of the food chain. And they were walking straight for the bench where Ulf and his friends were sat.

"That's our bench," one of the men said. He was of average height and squarely built. His brown hair and beard were streaked with grey and his lined face showed he led a hard life. His hand was not near his sword, nor were his companions' hands near theirs.

"Don't see your name on it," Thorbjorn said, never afraid of a fight, regardless of the odds.

"Everybody knows that's our bench."

"Oh well in that case, please forgive us then," Thorbjorn said in a voice full of innocence. "Now fuck off."

The man smiled at Thorbjorn, the way you do to indulge an amusing child. "Looks like we have a cocky one," he said to his friends. The man's friends laughed but did nothing else. "Now get lost."

"Don't think so," Thorbjorn said again. Ulf felt the area around them go quiet. Everybody seemed to stop what they were doing to watch the two groups of violent men.

"Is there a problem?" Snorri said from behind the men. Ragnar was standing next to him, looking ready for a fight.

The newcomers didn't look worried by the arrival of Snorri, Ragnar and Geir. The leader of the group looked at Ragnar like he recognised him from somewhere.

"No problem, friend," the man said, smiling an unfriendly smile. "Let's go, there's a table over there," he said to his companions. They walked to the other table and glared at the people sitting there until they left. The men sat down, not taking their eyes off Ulf and his companions.

"I leave you guys alone for a short while and you already cause trouble," Snorri smiled.

"Thorbjorn started it," Asbjorn said. "They were just asking us to give them their table back and he told them to fuck off."

"Because it's not their table," Thorbjorn said. He took a sip of his drink and asked Snorri, "How much you get for the captives?"

"Enough to make everyone happy," Snorri said, holding up a bag full of coin. The men cheered at this and ordered some more ale. But Ulf wasn't paying attention to them anymore. Instead, his attention was on a woman standing by the stall which sold jewellery. She was tall and slim, with a serious face more beautiful than he thought was possible. She was looking at a glass bead necklace, holding it into the light to see the colours more clearly. She put the necklace down and smiled at the trader, who beamed back at her. Ulf watched the sway of her hips as she walked, not noticing his ale arrive or his friends looking at him.

"I think Ulf wants to see what treasure she's got under her dress," Thorbjorn joked while the others laughed.

"That's my fucking daughter!"

CHAPTER 21

They all turned and saw the warrior they had been talking to before, on his feet and leaning forward on his hands which were spread wide on the table, straining at the neck like he was being held back by some invisible leash. His face had gone red as he glared at them with eyes that looked like they were about to pop out of his head. Jugs and cups had been scattered everywhere, the ale running down the table like waterfalls. But his friends didn't care or didn't notice as they all stared in one direction – at Ulf.

"That's my fucking daughter you are leering at!" he shouted again, smashing his fist on the table, which sent the few remaining cups to the ground.

Ulf looked back at the woman, standing there looking tall and elegant like she was Freya herself. "How could she be his daughter?" He realized he had said it out loud, without meaning to.

"That's it, now you fucking die!" The warrior stormed around the benches to get at Ulf. "First you take our bench and then you eye-fuck my daughter!" His face was getting redder, which Ulf did not think was possible. But before Ulf could react, Snorri and his hirdmen were on their feet, weapons drawn and ready to defend him. Only Ragnar and Thorvald remained sitting.

"There's no need for anyone to die today," Snorri said, blocking the warrior's path. The warrior stood in front of Snorri, but his glare was still aimed at Ulf. Snorri was half a head taller and at least a hand's width wider than the warrior, but somehow the man seemed more imposing than him.

"That's what you think, boy. I challenge your friend to an old fashioned holmgang."

"You're fucked," Thorbjorn muttered. Ulf glanced at him. He had heard the word before and knew what it meant. A holmgang was a duel between two men, usually to first blood.

Ulf looked at the warrior, taking in the man's hard eyes, the thick muscles under his brynja and tunic. Violence came off the man like a stink and Ulf could tell this was not his first holmgang. But he had no choice. "When?" he asked at last.

The warrior smiled. "Now."

"You're really fucked," Thorbjorn muttered again.

They cleared some space in the market square for the holmgang. The traders pretended to complain, but they were eager enough to pack their merchandise away. A holmgang would normally be fought on a piece of hide, laid on the ground, but none was available, so they agreed to mark the boundaries in the ground with their spears. The crowd stood on these lines and helped to form the boundary for the fight. To protect them, warriors with shields stood at the front to block any blows which might end up injuring the wrong person. Ulf stood in the centre of the square, watching his opponent stretching and limbering up. He guessed he should be doing the same, but he was too nervous. His opponent was also talking to his friends, laughing and joking. Ulf tried to distract himself by looking for the woman he had seen before, but could not find her. He felt the weight of his borrowed shield. It felt heavier than his usual shield which they had left on the Sae-Ulfr, but Ulf was sure that was just his imagination. Even his new brynja seemed to be heavier now, and he briefly wondered how he would be able to move in the fight.

"Remember, Ulf, don't think. Just fight," Snorri said as he stood next to Ulf. "The man is old, so he'll be slower than you. Use that." Ulf nodded like he understood what Snorri was saying, but he wasn't really listening. He was trying to understand why he always ended up in situations like this. Maybe Lady Ingibjorg had been wrong. Maybe he was supposed to die on the farm that day and the Norns were still trying to fix their mistake. He gripped the axe in his hand tightly. If that was the case, then he wasn't going to make it easy for them. He refused to die before he had his revenge. He had sworn an oath to Odin, and you do not break an oath to the All-Father. Ulf prayed to Tyr, his supposed ancestor, asking him for help. He looked to the sky but saw nothing that could be an answer from the one-handed god of war. *Uncle, I might see you soon in Valhalla.*

Orvar walked into the centre of the square with his arms in the air to get everyone's attention. Even through his tunic, you could see the fat on his arms wobbling, and the large sweat stains under them. The crowd fell silent and waited for the large trader to speak.

"Ladies and gentlemen. Welcome to the holmgang. Do not think this is just a meaningless case of bloodlust. No! My friends," he said, wagging his ringed finger at the crowd, "this is a fight of honour." He paused, letting the murmuring crowd think about his words. "This holmgang is about a father defending the honour of his one and only daughter."

"Bollocks it is," Thorbjorn muttered.

"To defend his daughter's honour," he continued, "against the lust of a disrespectful young boy." This elicited growls and curses from Snorri and his men. Ragnar and Thorvald kept quiet. "This will also be a fight of the generations, of young against old." Now it was the other side's turn to curse. "Both parties have agreed to the rules. But my friends, we are not barbarians, so this will not be a fight to the death. Only to first blood." There were whispers from the crowd at this. First blood could still mean death. Orvar looked at a man walking through the crowd, who nodded at him. "Now all the bets have been placed, let the fight begin," Orvar said and walked out of the square.

"Remember what I said, use your speed," Snorri said to Ulf before he left the square.

Now it was just Ulf and his opponent. Nothing else mattered. Not even his revenge. He had to survive this before he could focus on that again. Ulf thought he heard the flap of wings but didn't want to take his eyes off his opponent. Both men went into a combat stance, watching each other over the rims of their shields. The old warrior smiled, maybe sensing Ulf's fear, like wolves sensed the fear of the stag before attacking. He attacked, bringing his sword up to chop down on Ulf. Ulf lifted his shield to block the blow, but it was harder than he anticipated and sent him back a few steps. His opponent took advantage of this and kicked Ulf in the chest before he could regain his footing. Ulf landed on his back but quickly jumped to his feet. The old warrior was standing back, smiling at Ulf. He didn't need to rush this. The crowd cheered, and Snorri's men were shouting at Ulf. But Ulf heard none of it. All he heard was the rush of the blood in his ears. The beginnings of the whispers he always heard when he was in these situations. As always, he tried to block them out, refusing to listen to them. His opponent attacked again, this time stabbing with his sword. Ulf deflected the blow by turning his shield and countered, but his axe found nothing but air as his opponent jumped back.

"Not bad, boy. But not good enough," the man taunted Ulf. He attacked again, but this time faster than before. There was no stopping between strikes as he used his sword and shield to punch, jab and cut at Ulf. Somehow Ulf managed to block or get out of the way; he heard the crowd cheering and booing in the background. After a short while, his opponent stepped back, leaving Ulf gasping for breath. But the old warrior only stood there smiling at Ulf while rolling his shoulder.

"That was a nice warm-up. Now the real fight can begin." Again, the warrior attacked and again he moved faster than before. Ulf was no longer sure he could survive this fight as he just managed to get his shield in the way of a sword swing, which was followed by a punch from the warrior's shield. Ulf turned his shoulder and took the blow from the shield. He cried out as the pain jolted the joint but stayed on his feet. Somehow, he managed to keep hold of his axe. At least if he died now, he would die holding his weapon. His opponent saw this and smirked. His companions were shouting at him, telling him to kill Ulf.

"Ulf's fucked," Thorbjorn said.

"I agree, he should never have done this. The boy cannot fight," Ragnar sneered.

But Snorri only smiled. They didn't know Ulf the way he did.

"You don't seem worried," Brak said, seeing the smile on Snorri's face.

"Because I'm not," he answered. He looked at Vidar, but Vidar was not watching the fight. Instead, he was looking at the large raven that was sitting on one of the trader's tents. To Snorri, it almost seemed like Vidar was talking to the bird. There always seemed to be a raven nearby when Ulf got himself into trouble.

The old warrior attacked with one sword swing after the next. Ulf managed to avoid them by constantly taking a step back. *Move your feet, move your feet*, he kept thinking to himself. He kept going backwards until he felt the shield on his back and realized he had reached the edge of the square.

"Fucking do something. Do not embarrass us," he heard Ragnar whisper. But before Ulf could respond, his opponent saw his chance and went in fast with a stab. Ulf rolled to the side, hearing the thunk as the sword got stuck in the shield. This was Ulf's chance, but he still could not lift his arm. Instead of attacking, he moved back to the centre of the square, breathing heavily as he tried to ignore the whispering voices. The sweat was running down his face like the great waterfalls they had in the fjords in the north, stinging his eyes and being soaked up by his short beard. Some of the crowd were booing him, but he didn't care. He needed time for his arm to recover. His only other option was to drop his shield and move the axe to his left hand. But then he would lose the only thing that had kept him alive so far. The old warrior freed his sword and glared at Ulf.

"You are going to regret that," he said with a sneer. "I'm getting bored of this now; thought you would put up more of a fight." He launched another attack at Ulf, aiming high with his sword. Ulf saw this and raised his shield to block but realized his mistake straight away, as the old warrior dropped to his knee. Ulf knew he couldn't bring his shield down in time to stop the cut coming for his side, so instead, he stepped away from it. The warrior's sword struck Ulf in the side, just below his old spear wound, but because of Ulf's movement, much of the force had been taken out of it. The pain still caused Ulf to double over and he looked at his side expecting to see blood, but his new chain mail had held. He forced himself to stand straight against the pain and face the old warrior who was smiling at him before attacking again, swinging and stabbing with his sword. As before, Ulf just managed to move out of the way or get his shield up in time. Some of the crowd were cheering him on, his friends amongst them. Ulf and his opponent came together in a shoulder charge, their shields clashing with a sound of thunder rolling over everyone. Ulf was breathing heavily as he strained to push against the old warrior. But somehow he still seemed to be as fresh as when the fight first started. This had now become a competition of strength as both men tried to push the other one back. Ulf's opponent was shorter than him and had a lower sense of gravity. This gave him a slight advantage as he managed to push Ulf back half a step, but Ulf refused to give in and won that half a step back. Both men were straining and grunting until Ulf's opponent lifted his sword and brought it down hilt first. Snorri shouted a warning, but Ulf didn't hear it until after the hilt struck him on the head. The old warrior then punched out with his shield and sent Ulf sprawling on the ground. Instead of attacking, he waited for Ulf, taunting him. Ulf rolled around and got to his hands and knees, but his head was spinning too much for him to get to his feet. His skull was burning where the hilt struck him, and Ulf checked with his hand to see if there was any blood. When he saw there was none, he realized the fight was not over. He had to get back up again. He would not die on his hands and knees. He would die on his feet. He found his shield but could not see Olaf's axe. It must have fallen somewhere away from him when he landed on his back.

Using the shield, Ulf got to his feet. His vision was blurry, his ears were ringing, and everything was spinning like he was caught in a sea storm, but on land. That and the blinding pain in his skull made him want to vomit, but he fought the feeling, taking deep breaths until he could stand up straight. The crowd fell silent now, or maybe he just could not hear them through the ringing in his ears. Even the whispers had gone quiet. He turned to face his opponent, armed with only his shield. He guessed the man must have been smiling, but he couldn't tell. All he saw was a blurry figure, standing there waiting for him. Maybe that wasn't even his opponent, maybe that was some shadow creature from Hel, come to take him away. Maybe he was lying dead on the ground. No, his head was hurting too much for him to be dead. He saw the blurry figure run at him, but then some memory came to his mind. It wasn't an old memory of his childhood, or of his family. It was a memory of a sparring session with Snorri.

"You don't move your feet enough," Snorri said. "You are too inflexible." Ulf not understood what Snorri meant.

"You are like a tree refusing to move out of the way of the woodcutter," Oddi explained.

"Trees can't move, you idiot!" Thorbjorn retorted.

"No, he is right," Snorri said, the surprise clear in his voice. "Ulf is like a tree. Just waiting to be cut down. You need to move."

"Like a sparrow that turns and dodges the eagle hunting it," Oddi added, proud of himself. Thorbjorn shook his head and decided not to comment.

"Be a sparrow and not a tree," Oddi smiled

Be a sparrow and not a tree, the words circled around Ulf's head. His eyes came into focus just as the old warrior was on top of him, his sword held high, ready to slice Ulf in half.

Ulf twisted out of the way, bringing his right foot back and pivoting on his left. At the same time, he arched backwards as the sword came down and sliced through the air. Without thinking, Ulf punched the old warrior in the head with the rim of his shield. He heard a loud crack and thought he had broken his shield on his opponent's helmet, but then remembered they weren't wearing any. The old warrior just dropped to the ground, like a felled tree, and didn't move as Ulf stumbled back, struggling to regain his balance. His head was still spinning and his ears still ringing. He shook his head to clear it but regretted it instantly as the motion made him want to vomit. The crowd remained silent, rooted to the spot. Not sure what they had just seen. Only Snorri smiled. He thought something like this might happen. Snorri had seen the same thing with the bear. And his friends now understood what he knew about Ulf. He saw it in their stunned expressions.

Kraa-Kraa, Ulf heard the raven from where it sat. To Ulf, it seemed like it was telling him something. And Ulf understood what it was saying. *Until first blood.* His eyes fell on Olaf's axe, lying not far from where he was standing. He walked to it, stumbling and swaying, and picked it up, his head not liking the movement as he had to fight another urge to vomit. Axe in hand he walked toward his opponent, who had not moved. Ulf wasn't sure if the man was still alive. But rules were rules and nobody had moved to stop him. Not even the old warrior's companions. Stopping beside the warrior, he saw that there was no blood. Ulf bent down, hearing the gasp from the crowd. Ulf didn't want to kill the man. Instead, he used the axe to cut his opponent's arm, causing it to bleed. First blood.

The old warrior's companions rushed over and tried to wake him, as Ulf just stood there, ignoring Snorri and his men. He saw the man's daughter then. She stood there glaring at him, her eyes filled with hate. It was a feeling he knew well, but he didn't understand why it was directed at him. He wasn't the one who had made the challenge.

"I've never seen anything like that before," Brak said.

"Aye, I thought he was dead then. I was about to say the same to Snorri," Thorbjorn added.

They were back by the Sae-Ulfr, sitting around a fire and telling the rest of the crew about the fight. Snorri had brought a few barrels of ale and a pig carcass from the tavern so his men could celebrate Ulf's victory. But Ulf wasn't celebrating with his friends and the rest of the crew. He was lying by the fire, his eyes closed, but not sleeping. His head had stopped spinning and the ringing in his ears was gone, but he had a headache so bad that every heartbeat felt like a hammer striking an anvil in his head. And the pain in his side didn't help either. Every now and again, someone would poke him, just to make sure he was still alive. Ragnar had said it was necessary, saying that he had seen men who had seemed fine after a knock to their heads just collapse dead a while later, their spirits stolen by a Valkyrie while they were walking. So, Ulf just lay there, listening to the crew enjoy themselves.

"Another reason to celebrate," Ulf heard Snorri say, "I had placed all the earnings from the captives on Ulf and now we have more than double the coin!" The crew roared their approval. His victory had now become their victory, thanks to Snorri's belief in his friend.

"You took a big risk there," Ragnar commented.

"No," Snorri smiled at Ulf, "I did not. I knew Ulf would win."

"How? I didn't even think I was going to win," Ulf groaned, his eyes still shut against the pain.

"That's my secret," Snorri laughed.

"Fine," Ulf said as he touched a large bump on his head, wincing at the pain. Just one more for the collection.

"You're lucky the skin didn't break," Thorbjorn said when he saw Ulf probe his head. Ulf grunted in response.

"Ulf, one more thing." Snorri's voice made him open his eyes. He stood in front of Ulf, a cup in one hand and an arm-ring in the other. A gold one. "This is for you." He held the arm-ring towards Ulf, who didn't move to take it.

"I think you should give it to Oddi. I only won because of him," he said instead.

"Oddi!" some of the men said at the same time, not understanding. Oddi had been by the ship during the fight. Like the others there, he didn't even know about the fight until they came back.

"How in Odin's name did he do that?" Thorbjorn half-shouted. He was too drunk to control his volume. Even Oddi looked confused by this.

Ulf smiled and then said, "Be a sparrow and not a tree."

Everybody gaped at him, thinking he had lost his wits from the blow to the head before Oddi remembered.

"I said that to you last summer when we were training."

"You did. And before that sword came down to kill me, it was those words I heard in my head," Ulf smiled.

Snorri looked at Oddi and grinned, finally understanding. "Well then Oddi Viss, it appears that for once you lived up to your name," he laughed as he took one of the rings off his arm and threw it at Oddi. The gold one, he dropped on Ulf's chest. "That is for listening to Oddi then."

The Skuggi was also sat by the fire, smiling with the rest of the crew. But inside he was seething. It seemed to him that Ulf had been blessed with more luck than any man should be allowed to have. Every time he thought he was about to see the end of the young warrior, Ulf would somehow survive. The Skuggi had thought Loki had finally answered his prayers. He had believed Loki had accepted his offering. The boy just wouldn't die; it was almost as if he couldn't die. He took a sip of his ale, watching Ulf lie there with his eyes closed. But the ale tasted sour, like it was tainted with his hatred of Ulf. He had to be patient, he told himself. He would find a way and if what he had heard from some of the traders was true, then he might have done so already.

"Congratulations on your man's victory," Ivor said, appearing out of nowhere.

"Come and join us," Snorri said, offering him a cup of ale. "Perhaps I will tell you the story of how Ulf killed a bear with his bare hands."

"With his bare hands now. Last time I heard him tell it, it was with an eating knife," Thorbjorn said, his eyebrow raised at

Snorri's words.

"Last time I heard it, there were two bears and all I had was a stick," Ulf said, his eyes remaining closed. The golden arm-ring still lay on his chest.

"Aye, Snorri loves telling a good story," Oddi replied.

"I am not here to celebrate, friend, but to offer some advice," Ivor said, rubbing his hands together like he was nervous.

"What advice would that be?" Ragnar stood up from where he had been sitting with his ale in his hand.

"That you should get your ship ready and leave as soon as you can. Tonight, if possible."

"Why?" Snorri asked, his good mood vanishing.

"Do you know whose man that is your bear-killer almost killed?" Ivor asked, taking a step back from the drunk warriors now crowding around him.

"Whose?" Snorri asked.

"King Griml Jotun's."

CHAPTER 22

Ulf sat up so fast, his head spun as if he'd been kicked in the head by a horse. He grabbed hold of Vidar who was sat next to him, and closed his eyes as he waited for the spinning to stop.

"Is he ok?" Ivor asked, not understanding Ulf's reaction.

Snorri looked at Ulf and then back at Ivor. "He's fine, just heard something he wasn't expecting."

"He knows the king then?"

"Let's just say they're acquainted with each other." Snorri glanced at Ragnar, who had never believed Ulf's story. "But why should we leave? The man challenged Ulf and he lost. I'm sure this King Griml would accept that."

"There's more to it than that. You see, the rumour is King Griml was supposed to marry his daughter in two days' time before they set off on their raid." His eyes kept darting towards Ragnar as he said this.

"Marry?" Ulf asked. He thought again of the woman he had seen in the market. Despite the blow he took, he still remembered every detail about her. Her long brown hair, which she wore in two braids down her back. Her tall slim figure that swayed like reeds in the wind as she walked. Her deep brown eyes filled with hatred. Hatred for him.

"Aye," Ivor answered. "But they say she is very upset about her father and might cancel the wedding."

"I'm sure this King Griml can find another bride," Snorri said.

"It's not just about the woman. Her father is a powerful jarl. The alliance will give the king five ships full of men. That's what he really wants."

"Why?" Ragnar asked.

"Not sure, but some say he plans to take advantage of the infighting amongst the Danish princes."

"To capture himself some land while the sons of Godfrid are preoccupied," Oddi ventured. Ivor shrugged his shoulders, not wanting to admit to things he didn't know.

"Interesting," Snorri said after a while. "And if she cancels the wedding, he loses those ships." He scratched his beard as he thought aloud.

"How do we know this is the Griml that Ulf has told us about?" Thorbjorn asked. "There could be more than one Griml out there."

Snorri nodded at Thorbjorn, accepting his point. He looked at Ulf, who was staring back at him. There was an intensity in his eyes he had not seen in a while. Ulf was close to his prey, but first, they had to make sure this was the right one. "Tell me more about this king. What does he look like?"

"Apart from being big," Oddi added.

"To tell you the truth, I haven't seen him. We only arrived here this morning before you did." Ivor rubbed his hands together.

"Then how do you know so much?" Snorri asked, his voice full of suspicion. At the same time, Thorbjorn and Oddi took a step forward, with their hands on their weapons. The rest of the crew scanned the beach around them, looking for any signs of trouble.

Ivor seemed to shrink in size, making Ulf wonder what kind of a warrior he had been if he scared so easily. "I spoke to some of the traders. You know how they like to gossip." Ivor spread his hands in supplication, hoping this would calm Snorri and his men.

"OK, say I believe you. But why tell us?" Snorri asked.

"The traders say King Griml is a very cruel man. So, I thought to warn you." He tried his best attempt at an earnest smile but could not quite pull it off. Snorri knew if what Ivor was saying was true, then he was hoping for some reward. Word would have spread about his winnings on the fight today.

"That's very kind of you," Snorri said. "But that doesn't really help us."

Ivor thought for a short while and then raised a finger in the air like he had just remembered something useful. "The traders, they don't call him Griml Jotun – they have another name for him."

"What is this name?"

"Troll-Face. They say he is very ugly, made even uglier by a scar on his cheek."

"They're not very nice to their king," Brak Drumbr said.

"He's not their king. He is a sea king. He just showed up at the beginning of the summer with some minor jarl and has been here ever since."

"Must be Gunnulf," Oddi said to Snorri.

Snorri nodded, trying to think of anything else that might help prove this was the man they were after.

"Has he got a sword? A gold hilt, decorated with an image of Jörmungandr?" Ulf asked.

Ivor scratched his ear as he thought. "I don't know. Like I said, I haven't seen him."

Everyone was quiet for a while until Snorri spoke. "We thank you for your advice. I will think about what you have told us, that is all I can offer."

"No, I can see you are all fighting men, and if any of you can fight like your friend then I can understand why you don't take me seriously. I was a young warrior once, but I haven't survived this long by being dumb. Know when to run," Ivor offered.

"I am Snorri, son of Thorgils, this is Ragnar Nine-Finger," Snorri growled as he pointed to the men behind him. "These are the men of the Sae-Ulfr, the warriors of Thorgilsstad. My men are the bravest and fiercest fighters in all of Norway. We do not run." His men cheered at his words. "Again, I thank you for your advice. If you don't want to drink with us, then you can leave us to our celebration."

Ivor nodded and walked away. Ragnar turned to Snorri. "You had to tell him who we are."

"Relax," Snorri smiled, "he already knows who you are. Besides, I have a plan." He turned to Ulf. "You up for a late-night walk?"

"What are you planning now?" Ragnar asked.

"We need to see this King Griml. Find out if he is the one we are looking for," Snorri responded.

"And then what?"

"I don't know," Snorri answered honestly.

"I don't like it." Asbjorn stood up and walked to Snorri. "What are the chances of us coming here and just running into the man who supposedly killed Ulf's family?" If he had been expecting support from anyone, he didn't get it. Instead all around him were silent faces waiting to see how Snorri would react.

"I'll admit it is strange, but then the gods work in strange ways," Oddi answered. "Besides we came here because of what we heard in Gunnulf's village."

"And we went there because we were trapped by the rain and the wind," Brak Drumbr continued. "Seems to me the gods wanted us to find Griml." He turned to Ulf who was sat glaring at Asbjorn, unable to believe that after everything, Asbjorn still believed he had killed his family.

"Well, I still don't like it." He looked Snorri in the eyes. "I will follow you into Jötunheimr, Snorri, and you know that, but I don't know if I want to risk my life for Ulf."

Snorri nodded like he understood what Asbjorn was saying, but Thorbjorn did not. "Asbjorn, you cock! Ulf has proven himself many times over by now."

"Aye, he can fight. But that doesn't mean anything. Everyone here can fight." Ulf remained silent through all this, not trusting himself as he sat there, trying to stop the fire igniting inside of him. Vidar seemed to sense this and put his arm on Ulf's shoulder. When Ulf looked at him, he shook his head.

"Enough!" Snorri said before the men started fighting. "You don't have to come with if you don't want to, Asbjorn. My oath to help Ulf is mine alone and not for you to share."

"Asbjorn can go fuck himself," Thorbjorn said before Snorri could carry on. "Ulf is one of us now, he has stood in the shield wall and spilt blood with us. I'm coming with."

Snorri smiled. Thorbjorn was never one to avoid a fight. He looked to the rest of his hirdmen, knowing he did not have to ask them. They all nodded in return, Brak Drumbr even smiling as he did so.

"Asbjorn?" Oddi asked.

Asbjorn looked at them and then at Ulf. "Only because I'm not about to let you idiots run off and do something dumb, not because I suddenly believe Ulf." Snorri smiled and grabbed Asbjorn's shoulder.

"Ready, Ulf?" he asked.

Ulf smiled at Snorri and his hirdmen. He picked up the gold arm-ring and slipped it on. "I am," he said, getting unsteadily to his feet.

"If you vomit on me, then I'll kill you. I don't care if Odin is watching you," Thorbjorn warned.

"I would also come," Geir said, stepping forward.

"No, you stay here," Snorri said. "I need you all to be ready."

"Why?" Ragnar asked.

"Just for in case I make some new friends," Snorri smiled at him.

"I was afraid you would say that."

Snorri turned to his men. His hirdmen were ready as he knew they would be. Ulf was ready and so was Vidar.

"Let's go pay the King Griml Troll-Face a visit." His wolf-like grin was back on his face.

They found Griml's camp on the other side of the market. There was a newly built hall, surrounded by more tents then they could count. The tents closest to the hall were bigger and neatly laid out, whilst the tents further away looked like they had just been dropped randomly by some giant. There were more houses being built not far from the hall.

"Maybe this Griml is trying to make a kingdom for himself," Brak suggested as they lay on top of a hill overlooking the camp.

"It looks that way," Snorri said, "maybe he has an agreement with the king of the Swedes." They fell silent after that, not knowing what else to say. The night was clear, with only a few clouds in the sky, but with the half-moon, there wasn't enough light. Luckily the campfires made it easy to see into the camp, the only problem being that they couldn't see if there were any guards placed around the perimeter. They were also too far away to be able to distinguish any features of the people in the camp, but that didn't matter. The man they were looking for would be larger than anyone else.

"Do we go into the camp?" Ulf asked.

"Not yet," Snorri said. "Griml might be in his hall, but we can't just walk in there and introduce ourselves. If what Ivor the Rat had said was true, then Griml would want our heads."

"You don't have a plan, do you?" Thorbjorn asked.

"I do," Snorri lied.

"What is it?" Thorbjorn asked. He was looking at Snorri with a raised eyebrow, waiting for him to answer.

Vidar poked Ulf and pointed in a direction away from the hall. At first, Ulf could not see what Vidar was pointing at but then saw her. She was walking towards the hall, with two men following her. He didn't need to be able to make out her features to know it was the woman from the market. Just the way her body moved as she walked was enough. "It's her," he said, pointing in her direction.

Snorri saw what Ulf meant and a slow smile crept onto his face as a plan formed in his head. "We need to get closer." Ulf turned to him, surprised by the change of heart.

"How?" Oddi asked. "There must be hundreds of men."

"Exactly," Snorri said. He got up and walked down the hill like he was supposed to be there, his hand away from his sword, his shield strapped to his back. His hirdmen looked at each other and shrugged before getting up and following him.

"What if they recognise us?" Ulf asked when he caught up with Snorri.

"They won't," he responded. "It's too dark, and we just need to make sure we don't go near the fires."

It seemed like a good idea, but then Ulf had another thought. "What if they saw the fight? They'll recognise me."

Snorri shook his head. Ulf felt the motion more than see it. "There weren't that many warriors there. And I'm sure most of the ones who were, are probably too drunk to remember what you look like." Ulf didn't say anything after that. He didn't want Snorri to think he was afraid. He could feel the nervous energy coursing through his veins and causing his hands to shake. But it made his headache and the pain in his side feel better.

They got to the edge of the camp but found no guards in place. Walking through the camp, they made sure to avoid the light from the fires. The men they were passing were too drunk or preoccupied to even pay attention to them, or so they thought.

"Hey, you!" The group paused as a man sat by the fire they just passed called to them. Their hands slowly went for their weapons.

"You guys want a drink? Got some lovely ale here. What?" he asked his companions who were telling him to be quiet. They didn't want to share their ale, by the looks of it.

"Thank you for the offer, my friend, but we have some women waiting for us in our tents," Thorbjorn responded. Ulf felt Snorri and his men relax around him.

"Fair enough, don't let us keep you," the man said.

"Give the ladies one for us," another added with a laugh.

"Don't you worry, we will," Thorbjorn said and they walked away as the men got back to their drinking.

These men had been here a while and were used to new faces showing up at all times of the day to join in the upcoming raid. This was what Snorri had been counting on and so far, his gamble was paying off. As they got near the hall though, everything changed.

The woman they had seen at the market stormed out of the hall, her two guards rushing to keep up. A giant of a man followed them, bellowing at her.

"Woman, you come back here now. I am not done with you!"

Snorri and his hirdmen stopped instantly and stared at the large figure in the doorway of the hall. He was bigger than Ragnar. He took up most of the space in the doorway, not just with his height, but also his width. Not only that, he was ugly. He had a large head, with two small beady eyes which looked like two black pits from where they stood. His head was shaved and covered with tattoos and he had a long braided beard that went down to his chest. There was a scar that ran across his right cheek that looked like it had not healed well, and he had half of his left ear missing. If that wasn't enough for them to understand who they were looking at, then the sword on his hip was. They all could see the beautifully decorated hilt of Ormstunga, although on him the sword looked more like a knife.

Ulf was rooted to the spot, his mouth dry and eyes wide as he fought the urge to take a step back. This was the man who had taken everything away from him, and now there he stood, a king. While Ulf had been struggling to understand the new path of his life, Griml had gotten rich and powerful. Ulf was stunned, like a bull after you knock it on the head with a hammer. For the first time, Ulf was not sure if he could kill Griml. He thought of the dreams he had been having, the giant troll with the axe. Nothing Ulf did could defeat the troll. Maybe that's what the dreams had really been telling him. He had always thought they were reminding him of his oath to Odin, reminding him of what he had to do. But now standing here, with Griml somehow looking bigger than he remembered, he was wondering if the dreams had been telling him that he would never be able to defeat the giant troll. He would never be able to defeat Griml.

Snorri saw all this on his friend's face, although he did not understand it. He looked back at Griml, taking in his muscled frame and his boulder-like fists. The man was more than a warrior. He was a giant who could only be defeated by Thor and his mighty Mjöllnir.

"Who are you?" Griml asked them, his thunderous voice snapping them all out of their trances. He stood there looking at the eight men – well, seven and a boy. From their brynjas and weapons, he could tell they were warriors, but then the whole camp was filled with warriors. He wasn't sure if he had seen them before, or if they were new arrivals. All week he had to deal with newcomers, men claiming to be the best fighters, wanting to earn a place on his raid. His eyes fell on one of them, the man standing just behind the big guy who was clearly the leader of the group. He looked younger than the rest, only the boy by his side was younger still. He looked at his long hair, tied back and his short braided beard. He saw the three scars which ran along his face. It looked like he had had a run in with a wolf or something. Griml also saw the darkened skin around the young man's neck.

"Nobody, my king. We were just on the way to our tents," Snorri answered. He knew they needed to be careful. He saw how Griml's beady eyes lingered on Ulf like he was trying to remember him. Snorri looked towards the woman, worried she might expose them, but she just stared at them, as shocked to see them as they were to see Griml.

Griml, though, was still looking at Ulf, still trying to understand the nagging feeling he had. The scar on his cheek started tingling, but he paid no attention to it. "Do I know you, boy?" He pointed at Ulf.

Ulf just shook his head, not trusting himself to speak.

"Huh," Griml said.

"If we may?" Snorri gestured the way they had been walking. He had to get them out of there before something went wrong.

Griml stared at Ulf for a bit longer and then nodded. "Yes, fuck off." The woman had taken advantage of the distraction and slipped away. Griml turned to where she had been after Snorri and his men left. He saw she was gone. "Fucking women," he growled. Griml shook his head and went back into his new hall. The scar on his face was still tingling when he got to his seat and sat down. A chain, attached to his seat, snaked into one of the dark corners of his hall. "The boy who did this to me should be glad he is dead," Griml stated. The chain moved in response to his voice. "No one had ever touched my face before that boy got lucky with his fucking spear. If he was here now, I'd rip all his limbs off and make the boy watch as my dogs ate them. And when the dogs were fat on his legs and arms, I would stomp on his head." Griml sighed, "But the boy died on that farm the day I got his sword." He looked at the beautiful hilt.

"It...It's a beautiful s...sword, m...my king," came a voice from the end of the chain in the darkness of the corner.

"It is," Griml growled, "now if only this fucking scar would stop tingling."

"Ulf, are you ok?" Snorri asked as they got away from the hall. They were following the woman and her guards, making sure to stay far enough behind for them not to be spotted.

"I don't know," Ulf said. He was shaking. His chest felt like he had been kicked by a horse. He was pretty sure his heart had stopped when he saw Griml walk out of the hall.

"That was him, wasn't it?" Thorbjorn asked. "You never said he was a fucking mountain," he said after Ulf nodded.

"I didn't remember him being so big. That day, everything happened so fast, I guess I never looked at him properly." Ulf felt a new feeling now. Embarrassment. He was ashamed. This whole year he had wanted nothing but revenge. His only desire had been to find Griml and kill him. The heat of his hatred had kept him warm in winter and gave him the strength to persevere when things got difficult. But when he had come face to face with the monster of his dreams, he felt nothing but fear. Someone took his hand and Ulf saw it was Vidar. Vidar smiled at him. Ulf knew Vidar meant well, but he only made Ulf angry. He wasn't supposed to feel afraid. If he really was the son of the great Bjørn, or a descendant of Tyr, then he should not have felt fear. He felt the familiar heat in his chest from the flames that rose from deep inside him. When he looked at Vidar, he saw his friend nod.

"What now?" Oddi asked Snorri. "We know it is him and where he is. But we can't do anything about it."

"Yes, we can," Snorri answered.

"What?"

"Something Ivor said." He waited to see if the rest of them would understand, but they didn't. "He needs this marriage to happen because with it he gets five ships and the men. That would be his power. The rest of the men here, they only want the gold from the raid. After the raid, most of them will go back to where they came from. We know this because we have done the same in the past and the same has been done to us."

"So?" Thorbjorn said.

"Did you see Gunnulf?" Snorri asked instead.

"I don't know what he looks like," Thorbjorn answered, scratching the back of his head.

"But we know Gunnulf's colours. None of the shields we saw had his colours, especially near the hall. This means Griml only has the one ship we heard about, so he needs this alliance to make himself stronger."

"And how does this help us?" Asbjorn asked. He kept looking behind them to make sure that they were not being followed.

"Think about it. He needs those ships because after this raid most of the men here will leave. Some might stay if he can promise them more gold in the future. But if what he has promised them is true, then most of these men would take what they get from this raid and live the rest of their lives as rich men. Without those five ships, he has nothing."

"So, you want to stop the marriage from happening. That way he is less of a threat." Oddi saw where Snorri was going with this but wasn't sure how he was planning on doing it. "But how?"

"The woman," Ulf said, understanding Snorri's plan. "Without her, there will be no marriage." Snorri looked back and was glad to see the fire back in his friend's eyes. He nodded to confirm what Ulf had just said.

"So, we kill her?" Thorbjorn asked. Violence was always his preferred way of doing things.

"No, we take her. With any luck, Griml might follow us," Snorri answered. The men almost stopped when Snorri said this.

"I knew this was a bad idea," Asbjorn muttered, staring at Ulf.

"Are you sure?" Brak asked.

"Not really, but that's what I would do," Snorri responded.

"You want him to chase us with almost a thousand men?" Oddi asked.

"There won't be a thousand. One or two ships at the most," Snorri said. He seemed confident about this.

"How do you know?" Brak Drumbr asked.

"It'll take too long to get his whole army on the chase."

"What about the woman's father? Would he not send men?" Thorbjorn asked.

"He might not be awake yet. You all heard that crack when Ulf hit him. I wouldn't be surprised if he's already dead." Ulf looked at Snorri. He had not thought of that. Could he have killed the old warrior? He hoped not.

"You're doing this regardless of what we say," Brak said. A statement, not a question.

"Aye, and I'm guessing Ulf will join me," Snorri responded with confidence.

"You're willing to get us killed for Ulf?" Asbjorn did not like this.

"You don't have to be here, Asbjorn. You can go back to the ship."

"Of course we have to be here!" Thorbjorn almost shouted in his frustration. "Somebody needs to keep your arse alive or the jarl will have our heads. Come on Asbjorn, you know you want to." Asbjorn did not respond straight away but nodded after a short while. He might not like Ulf or believe him, but he wasn't going to abandon his sword-brothers.

"We'll need to take her soon before she gets to her camp," Oddi said after they had all agreed.

"We do," Snorri responded. "We just need to distract them long enough to catch up."

Ulf looked at Vidar and got an idea. "You ready to cause a distraction?" Vidar nodded with a smile and raced off into the night.

"Where's he going?" Snorri asked while he watched Vidar disappear amongst the tents.

"You'll see."

A short while later they heard the sounds of alarm. All of them went for their weapons until they heard a woman's voice telling her guards to back off. They could hear her speaking softly, almost maternally to somebody.

"Looks like Vidar's distraction worked," Snorri said, with a smile. He looked around to make sure that the noise had not attracted any unwanted attention, but most of the warriors around them were too drunk to care.

They crept up slowly until they saw the back of the guards. Just ahead of them, they could see Vidar on the ground like he was in pain and the woman bent over him, trying to help him. Snorri signalled to the brothers to watch their backs, and he and Thorbjorn snuck up to the guards, their swords in their hands. Oddi followed closely behind, but he didn't have a weapon in his hands. As Snorri and Thorbjorn got to the guards, they smashed them on the skulls with the hilts of their swords. Ulf's hand went to the lump on his head as he felt their pain. Oddi rushed past them and grabbed hold of the woman, careful to put his hand over her mouth so she couldn't scream. Ulf got the idea they had done this before. Oddi was struggling to control the woman as she kicked and thrashed, trying to free herself from his grip. Asbjorn ran ahead and grabbed her legs, but they were still struggling. Worried she might free her mouth and scream, Snorri walked up to her.

"Sorry," he said before hitting her on the side of her head with the flat of his sword. He hit her just hard enough to knock her out.

"Was that necessary?" Ulf asked him.

"It was." He looked around to make sure they were not spotted. Luckily for them, the men in the camp were still too busy drinking and dreaming of their future riches. "Let's get out of here."

Oddi threw the now-unconscious woman over his shoulder and the eight of them ran back to their ship as fast as they could.

"Nice job," Snorri said to Vidar as the boy caught up with them.

CHAPTER 23

"Where is she?!" Griml roared across the hall with such force it felt as if the timber posts themselves were quaking in fear of what might happen next.

"I don't know, my king," the man said, looking down at his feet. He had not wanted to tell Griml his betrothed had been kidnapped and worse, that they had somehow escaped. This was a very large camp, with almost a thousand fighting men, not to mention the countless others that roamed around, and yet none had seen anything. It was like they disappeared, as if by Loki's magic.

"Who took her?" Griml asked. The scar on his cheek was tingling even more now.

"I don't know," the man said again. The men around took a step back. Griml launched himself from his seat, moving faster than a man of his size should be able to. He grabbed the messenger by the throat and lifted him off the ground.

"What do you fucking know?" he growled at the man who was fighting for breath.

"I…" the man gasped. His face was turning blue, but Griml was in no rush to let him go. Griml's eyes glazed over as he thought of something.

"Does anyone remember those eight men outside the hall when she ran out?" he asked the rest of the group. They were all warriors but now they were cowering behind each other. Griml realized the man in his hand was dead and threw the body on the ground like a discarded doll.

"I might have seen them before, my king," one of the men said, raising his hand, his voice filled with fear.

"Where?"

"By the market, they were talking to Orvar, the thrall trader," the man responded. "It was also one of them who bashed Stigr's head in."

"You mean at the holmgang that idiot fought? Which one?" he asked after the man nodded.

"He had scars on his face and a bruised neck, that's all I remember," the man said. From the sound of his voice, it was as if he knew it would not be enough to spare his life.

Griml made him worry a bit more before shouting, "Bring me Orvar. Now!" The men ran out of the hall, almost tripping over each other to fetch the fat trader, as Griml walked back to his seat and sat down, glowering at the door.

"I need to find that bitch and marry her soon, or my plan will be ruined!" he said through clenched teeth.

The chain rattled as the voice coughed in the dark corner. "The...the plan cannot fail, my k...king."

"What do you know, you worm!" Griml glared into the shadows. He was answered by rattling chains.

They reached the ship after what felt like ages. Oddi was sweating and breathing heavily from carrying the unconscious woman on his shoulder. Snorri smiled when he saw his men were still awake, and more than that, they were ready to defend the ship if needed.

"Rolf, get the Sae-Ulfr in the water. We are leaving now!" he shouted at his steersman.

"Where are we going?" Ragnar asked, and then, "Who is that?" when he saw the body draped over Oddi's shoulder.

"We are going to Thorgilsstad," Snorri said, again loud enough that Ivor or some of his men would hear him.

"Keep your voice down. Do you want eve–" Ragnar saw the look in Snorri's eyes. "You do. What are you up to?"

"Will tell you when we are on the way." He turned to Rolf. "Now, Rolf!"

"But Snorri, it's dark."

"You afraid of the dark, old man?" Thorbjorn taunted the old steersman.

"I fucked your mother in the dark once," Rolf said before walking away. "You!" He pointed at a group of men near the ship. "Get her in the water." The men waited for Rolf to get on board and started pushing the Sae-Ulfr into the surf. While they were doing this, Snorri climbed aboard and helped Oddi with their new passenger. Other men helped push and soon the Sae-Ulfr was afloat. The rest of the crew got on board and sat on their benches, oars ready. They knew how this worked. It was dark and unfamiliar waters lay ahead, so they would be rowing for a while. Thorbjorn stood by the prow with an oar to test the water; they did not want to hit a submerged rock now.

Ulf wasn't sure if rowing was a great idea. The rush back to the ship had made his headache worse and on more than one occasion he almost fell over. But Snorri was taking this risk for him, so he sat on his sea chest still wearing his brynja, like the others, and took hold of the oar. Ignoring the pain in his side where the old warrior had hit him with his sword, he rowed in time with the men around him.

On the beach, Ivor stood by his camp and watched the ship disappear into the darkness. He wasn't sure what he had just seen, but he knew that nothing good would come of it. If he had been a smarter man, he would have boarded his own ship and followed the Sae-Ulfr into the night.

Orvar was thrown to the ground in front of Griml. He was still wearing his sleeping frock which rolled up, revealing more than the men behind him wanted to see. On his sweaty face was a mix of confusion and fear. The men had come into his tent and dragged him from his sleeping mat, one them punching the screaming girl he had been sleeping with. He looked up and locked eyes with the giant in front of him. His fat rolls seemed to wobble as he shivered in fear.

"You are Orvar, the thrall trader?" Griml asked. His voice alone made Orvar want to cry. Orvar did not think he could speak. "You spoke to some men today," Griml continued.

"I... I speak with... a lot of men," he managed.

"They sold you some thralls." He looked at the men who had just walked into his hall. They were the men of Stigr.

Orvar thought for a while, then nodded as he remembered. "Snorri Thorgilsson."

"Was he the one who fought Stigr?" Griml asked.

"No, it was one of his men." Orvar paused while he tried to remember the name Snorri had given him. "Ulf... Ulf Bear-Slayer, they called him."

"Bear-Slayer?" one of the men behind him asked.

"Bear-Slayer," came the echo from the dark corner. Orvar noticed the chain leading to it.

"Yes, they say he killed a bear with only an eating knife," Orvar said, telling them what Snorri had said about his man. He could hear those behind him muttering at this, but he was too afraid to look back.

"Where can I find this Snorri and his so-called Bear-Slayer?" Griml leaned forward as he asked this. The torches cast a shadow over his face that scared Orvar so much, he almost pissed himself.

"I believe their ship is on the beach on the other side of the market," Orvar said. He liked Snorri more than this monster, but he liked his life more than Snorri.

Griml stared at Stigr's men. They looked eager to do something. "Go to this beach and find this Snorri and your jarl's daughter." The men nodded and left without saying a word. Their honour and that of their jarl had been ruined by the events of the day and they were eager to get it back.

They had rowed past the most dangerous part, so Snorri gave the order for the men to speed up. He didn't know how fast Griml would react and did not want to get caught before he reached Thorgilsstad. He would not win this without the rest of his father's men. Snorri smiled. His father will be furious. Snorri found a spare place and an oar and started rowing with his men. He looked at his younger brother who was sleeping near the stern on the Sae-Ulfr, the contempt easy to see on his face.

"So, what did you do, Snorri?" Ragnar asked from where he was rowing.

"We saw him, Ragnar."

"Saw who?"

"Griml."

"How do you know it was him?"

"Because Ulf stopped being a sparrow and became a white tree," Thorbjorn answered before Snorri could say anything. Although he did not blame Ulf, that man was huge. Even with all his arrogance, Thorbjorn was not sure if he could beat that giant. He only knew he didn't want to find out.

"That and we saw Ormstunga," Snorri answered. He glanced at Ulf to see how he took the words from Thorbjorn, but it didn't look like he had heard them. Ulf seemed to be in a trance, like a draugr who only knew how to row.

"That doesn't mean it was him. He could have sold that sword to this man you claim to be him," Ragnar said.

They were interrupted by the woman groaning as she sat up and rubbed the side of her head where Snorri had struck her. At first, she looked confused to find herself on a ship sailing at night, but then her eyes fell on Ulf and she remembered.

"Ask her your–" Snorri started saying before their captive pulled a knife from somewhere and launched herself at Ulf, screeching like a Valkyrie. Ulf saw her at the last moment and managed to bat the knife away with his arm before she could stab him. But that did not stop her. She dropped the knife and wrapped her hands around his throat, still screaming at him. Ulf let go of the oars and grabbed her wrists, trying to get her off him, but she was stronger than he thought.

"Frigg's tits, but she's got spirit," Snorri laughed. The rest of the crew laughed at Ulf, but most were glad they weren't in his position. Thorvald, woken up by the noise, sat there with a confused look as he tried to work out what had happened.

"You bastard! You son of a whore! I hope you die! I hope you die and the ravens pick out your eyes and shit in your eyeholes! I hope a fox rips out your tongue! I hope the maggots feast on your rotten corpse as you waste away to nothing! You bastard!" The woman continued to scream at Ulf as Brak Drumbr dragged her off him. The men on board stopped laughing and grabbed hold of anything metal they had around them to ward off the evil of the curses she spouted. All but Ulf, who finally sat up, rubbing his neck.

"Be quiet or I'll hit you on the head again," Snorri said, his hand on Tyr's Fury. The woman glared at him, her eyes red and full of tears, but she calmed down. Brak Drumbr was still holding her, not wanting her to attack Ulf again.

"I did not challenge your father to a holmgang. What happened to him was his fault, not mine," Ulf said. His head was hurting even more now. He must have hit it again when he fell. Vidar tucked at his arm and Ulf saw that he was bleeding from a cut.

Aslaug got to the beach where the trader had told them the ship was. He had ten men with him. He saw one ship beached and even by the half-moon light he could tell it was in poor condition. The captain of that ship was not the man he was after. But maybe he would know where to find him. Aslaug signalled to his men and they walked to the campfire.

Ivor stood there, waiting for the men he knew would come. "Is that your ship?" the leader of the group asked. He was big and looked fierce in his brynja with his long-handled axe slung to his back.

"It is," Ivor answered. "And it is not the one you are looking for."

"How do you know we are looking for someone?" Aslaug asked.

"After what I saw and heard earlier on, I figured someone would come eventually and ask questions."

"And what did you see earlier on?" Aslaug asked, glancing at his men behind him.

"Snorri and some of his men running down the beach. One of the men, the tallest one, was carrying something on his shoulder, but I could not see what. Then they jumped on their pretty ship and rowed out into the night as if Ragnarök had come." Ivor would usually try to barter for the information, but he knew who these men were. If he didn't comply, they would just torture it out of him.

"And why did you not stop them?"

"I didn't think they would leave so quickly. Figured the something they were carrying was some food they had stolen from someone," he said, defending himself.

"That something is the daughter of my jarl and the future wife of King Griml Jotun," Aslaug growled. He took a step forward and grabbed the hilt of the knife he wore on his waist.

"I swear by Odin if I had known I would have, but I didn't. I didn't even know Snorri had left his camp." Ivor took a step backwards to keep the distance between them.

Aslaug thought for a while. They should have guessed that Snorri would leave. Griml would not be happy, and neither would Stigr if he ever woke up.

"But I can tell you where he is going to be," Ivor said, hoping that this would save him.

"And where will this be?" Aslaug asked.

"Thorgilsstad."

"How do you know?"

"He was shouting it so loud the gods in Asgard would have heard him," Ivor said, half-smiling but quickly wiping the smile off his face when he saw the glare on Aslaug's.

"Do you know where Thorgilsstad is?"

"Not exactly, but I know it is somewhere along the Vikenfjord."

Aslaug thought for a while. He looked at the men behind him, but they only shrugged. He looked back at Ivor, then had a thought. "You're coming with us."

"Why?"

"King Griml will want to speak to you."

Ivor thought for a bit and then nodded. He knew he had no choice. "Can I bring some of my crew with me?"

"No." Aslaug signalled to his men and they circled the old man. Aslaug noted how no one came to defend him. That always said a lot about a person.

"Ok, so you've taken Griml's future wife. Now what?" Ragnar asked. He stared at the woman with half a sneer as he asked the question. He didn't understand why she was worth all this trouble. She was plain-looking and a bit too slim for his taste, but Ulf could not take his eyes off her. Even after she had tried to kill him. His eyes shifted back to Snorri when he realized Snorri had not answered him. "Snorri?"

"I don't know," Snorri admitted.

The woman turned her glare to Snorri. "You mean you took me from my father and don't even know what to do with me?"

"That's our leader," Thorbjorn said with a shrug, "great at getting us into trouble, not so good at getting us out of it." She realized he was smiling as he said this.

"You never complained before," Snorri said, but he couldn't keep the smile off his face.

"Keeps things interesting," Thorbjorn responded.

"Snorri," Ragnar tried again, shaking his head. He felt like he was dealing with children. "What are we going to do with her? We can't just show up in Thorgilsstad and say to your father, 'Here's the woman of the man who supposedly killed Olaf and his family.'"

"He did kill them."

"I'm not his woman," she said, speaking over Ulf. She glared at Ulf again, who only returned her stare, while continuing to row.

"Maybe we could trade her for Ormstunga?" Oddi suggested. He had that wise look on his face again.

"Oh aye. Here Troll-Face, just give us that shiny sword and we'll give you the woman back. No hard feelings hey. Oh, by the way, Ulf wants to kill you," Thorbjorn mocked with a sneer.

"I don't see you coming up with a better suggestion," Oddi defended himself.

"That's because there isn't any! Even by your standards, Snorri, this was a fucking dumb thing to do!" Ragnar exclaimed.

Snorri only shrugged. "I don't know," he said again and then looked at Ulf. "It's in the hands of the gods now. Only they and the Norns know what will happen next."

"Well, I'm not exactly on speaking terms with them, if you haven't noticed. So, I want you to tell me," Ragnar responded. If Snorri had been anyone else, he would have killed him by now.

"Trust in the gods, Ragnar," he responded and carried on rowing.

"They're gone, but this man says he knows where they went." Aslaug said to Griml as they walked into the hall. Griml looked irritated by the interruption, but of what Aslaug couldn't say. Griml was just sitting in his chair, the same thing he did every time Aslaug came in here.

"Where?" Griml growled.

"Thorgilsstad," Ivor said, trying to keep his voice firm, but failing to do so. The hall felt darker than any he had ever been in, even though there were plenty of torches and a fire in the pit.

Griml looked at the man in front of him, taking in the stooped frame and the weaselly features. "Do you know where it is, exactly?"

Ivor shook his head. "I have never been there, my king, but they say it is a hard place to reach by ship. The bay entrance is full of islands. Only the locals know how to sail through them."

"So, you are useless to me then," Griml said. He looked at one of the men by the door. He was one of Gunnulf's, Griml remembered. "Fetch the dogs," he told the man.

"The dogs?" Ivor asked.

"They are hungry and haven't eaten yet. Maybe you'll be more useful to them than to me."

"No, wait…" Ivor was thinking hard, trying to find a way in which he could be useful. "I might not know exactly where it is, but I know which fjord you need."

"Vikenfjord," Griml said. Ivor's face paled. He tried to run, but the men behind grabbed hold of him, their grips too strong. No matter how hard he tried, he could not free himself. He saw the man enter, being dragged in by four huge ravenous hounds.

Griml gave a command and the man released the leashes. At the same time, the men holding Ivor let go of him. But before he could run the dogs were upon him. The last thing he heard through his agony was the Griml laughing. Nothing in the nine worlds could sound so evil.

"Now what?" Aslaug asked. He tried not to pay attention to the scene behind him. But he could not ignore the screams of Ivor as the dogs ripped him to pieces or the spray of hot blood that splashed on his back.

The screaming stopped at that point. One the hounds must have ripped his throat out. It was a cruel ending even for a man as low as Ivor.

Griml watched his hounds eating the dead man's body. As always, they went for the soft parts first. The stomach. However, not all the hounds could get to the stomach, so the one which was excluded started eating the cheek flesh on Ivor's face.

Griml thought about Aslaug's question.

"How do I know she didn't plan this?" Griml asked, still watching his dogs. "How do I know she didn't run off with those men?"

"She would never betray her father like that," Aslaug responded, curling his upper lip.

"You must beat her, my king," came the voice from the shadows.

Griml yanked on the chain, sending the man attached to it flying into the light. Aslaug grimaced as he saw the unrecognisable face of Gunnulf, beaten to a pulp. His tunic was torn and covered in blood. Gunnulf was grasping at the chain tied to his neck.

"Like I beat you for betraying me, worm?" Griml growled. One of the hounds looked up. A whine escaped from its throat as it anticipated another meal.

"F...forgive me, my king," Gunnulf begged.

"You can thank Odin that I did not feed you to my dogs, like the rest of your worthless crew." Griml looked at Stigr again. He needed those ships.

"We go after them."

CHAPTER 24

Ulf was tired and out of breath, but he carried on running. He didn't know why, or where to. All he knew was that he had to keep going. He could smell the death in the air and heard the splashing as he ran through the bloody water. Ulf felt something in his hand, a weight that had not been there before. Something round, which shone as bright as the northern star. He tripped and landed with a splash, swallowing some of the bloody water, but managed to keep hold of the jewel. That was when he heard the noise behind him. A low growl which soon turned into an evil roar rumbling over the marsh. Ulf felt the familiar feeling in his chest, the crippling fear which made him shiver as if he was freezing. But there was something else. Another feeling he didn't understand. Satisfaction. He looked at the jewel and smiled. The jewel belonged to the troll. And now he had it.

The troll was getting closer now, Ulf could feel it in the tremble in the ground. He jumped to his feet. He had to keep moving. In the distance, he saw the hill, so familiar to him now after all these dreams. The cloaked figure was there. The one with the long staff. He was beckoning Ulf to him. A new noise came. The thunderous roar of men. They appeared from behind the figure. Men armed with spears and shields. The cloaked figure pointed at something behind Ulf as the men formed a shield wall around him. Ulf turned and saw the troll, its face contorted with rage. On its hip,

Ulf saw the pink sliver of a serpent's tongue. Ulf pushed himself harder; he had to get to the hill. He had to get to the shield wall. If the troll got him before he reached it, then he would die. But if he could reach the shield wall, then he would survive. He didn't know how he knew that. All that mattered was that he did.

Ulf opened his eyes and saw he was still on the Sae-Ulfr. The sun was rising over the horizon, lighting up the sea in its path. All around him, men were still sleeping, but Ulf saw that Snorri, sat by the prow, was awake.

"Bad dream?" Snorri asked him. He looked like he hadn't slept at all. After a few hours of rowing last night, the wind had finally picked up. Snorri told the men to put the oars away and they hoisted the sail. As soon as the sail was up, the men made themselves comfortable and slept. Ulf had tried to stay awake but could not. As his eyes closed, he felt her glaring at him.

"Are there any good ones?" Ulf asked in return.

Snorri laughed. "Trust me, my friend. There are." He indicated to the woman. "At least she didn't try to kill you in your sleep."

"You watched her all night?" Ulf stared at her. She was sleeping by the mast with what looked to be Snorri's cloak covering her. Ulf wondered if she knew how peaceful she looked, and how beautiful with the morning sun lighting her face.

Snorri shook his head. "Didn't need to. She fell asleep soon after you did." He looked at Ulf again. Ulf saw the uncertainty on his face. Something he had never seen in Snorri before.

"What if he's not chasing us?" Snorri asked him, in a low voice so others could not hear him. "What if all of this is a waste of time and we go back to Thorgilsstad and wait for nothing?"

Ulf thought back to the dream. He remembered something Brynhild told him once.

Dreams are messages from the gods, you know. They use dreams to communicate with us.

"He is coming. We have taken something that belongs to him and he wants it back."

"How do you know?"

"Bad dream," was all Ulf said.

Snorri frowned as he nodded. He knew not to ask for more. Ulf wouldn't tell him more than that.

Rolf opened his eyes from where he had been standing, hand still on the tiller. Snorri had never seen a man sleep at the tiller like his steersman did. Last time Snorri tried it, he fell and knocked the ship off course. Unfortunately, that had been a cloudy night and they had to wait for the sun to rise to find the right course again. Thorbjorn still made fun of him for it.

"Let's hope this wind holds."

Snorri looked at the sky. It looked like it would be a clear day. The wind wasn't strong, but it was enough for them.

"Let's hope so," he said, "the men deserve a rest."

For the next few days, they carried on sailing and rowing throughout the nights. Snorri didn't want to stop. They didn't know how far behind them Griml was if he was chasing them, and Snorri didn't want to risk being trapped somewhere with Griml's ships bearing down on them. The weather had been good to them; the worst they had to deal with was a little rain, which didn't cause them any problems. They had gotten a few men to bail out the water, and apart from Thorvald, who was complaining more than the woman did, it did not bother anyone. Thorbjorn even used the rain as a chance to have a wash, not caring if there was a woman on board as he took off his clothes. He suffered the usual ridicule, but he gave it back just as good.

"The gods must be looking out for us with this weather," Oddi said one day.

"Aye, usually when you need good weather, they make sure you only have rain and thunder," Rolf agreed.

Their captive kept to herself, her eyes roaming over the men who had taken her. Her gaze fell on Ulf again as he sat, stroking the haft of his axe. She could see something carved on it but could not tell what it was. The boy next to him turned to her and smiled. He stood up and walked to her. She liked him, despite the fact that he had helped kidnap her. "Is he your brother?" she asked as Vidar sat down beside her. He shook his head. She understood by now he couldn't speak. "So, why do you follow him?" Vidar scratched his face with his large hand and shrugged. She watched Ulf again. "I feel he is caught in something a lot bigger than him. I don't think he will survive whatever the gods have planned for him." Vidar looked to the sky, his eyes intense before he shrugged again. She couldn't stop the shiver that ran down her spine. "The others seem wary of him." She had seen the looks the other men gave him. "He isn't a great warrior, I saw that from his fight with my father. Yet they seem to fear him." Vidar nodded and had a satisfied smile on his face. "How does he fit into this?" she pointed to Snorri. "He seems to respect your friend." Vidar responded by running three fingers down the side of his face. She looked at the scars on Ulf's face and wondered what Vidar meant.

They were approaching the fjord and as hard as she tried, she could not help but be interested in where they were. "I've never been this far north before." Vidar smiled in response.

"Welcome to Vikenfjord," Snorri said when he saw her stretch her neck to look over the side. She had been so quiet during the journey, that at times he had forgotten she was there. She was not bothering anyone, so Snorri made sure not to bother her. He smiled when he saw she wasn't going to respond. "I know what you are thinking."

"What?" She took the bait. Vidar just smiled beside her.

"You thought there would be more mountains. Everyone always says that when they come here from the south. 'Isn't Norway supposed to be full of mountains?' they always ask."

"Well, isn't it?" She had already asked the first question, so might as well ask another.

"To the north, yes. Nothing but mountains up there. Thor's killing ground, some call it. But here in the south of Norway, we have more hills than mountains."

"You make it sound like it's a good thing."

"Better for farming. In the north, they have very few farms. Not enough flat land. But here, we don't have that problem."

"You don't look like a farmer to me, so why care about that?"

Snorri smiled at her. "It's simple. We have a lot of land for farming, which means fewer disputes here and more time for us to go raiding other places." He signalled to the brothers to remove the prow beast and put it in its resting place. He did not want to upset the spirits of the fjord. He might need their help.

In a strange way, she saw his logic. He saw life like her father did. Along the blade of a sword and over the rim of a shield. "My father might have liked these men if things had been different," she said to Vidar. "You think he is still alive? My mother will be devastated. She never wanted this in the first place, but father insisted. He said a man that big is one you follow, but with your hand on your sword." She felt the knot in her throat and her eyes well up. Vidar took her hand and gave her a comforting smile.

Snorri took his eyes away from her and looked at the sky, feeling the wind on his face. The day was still young, so if the wind kept then they should make the islands.

"Rolf!" he called to his steersman. "Think we can get past the islands before the sun sets?" Rolf scrutinized the sky, judging the clouds and feeling the wind. He had been sailing in and out of this fjord since before anyone on the Sae-Ulfr was born, so had a good understanding of its temper.

"We might if things stay as they are." He hoped it would. The weather had been unusually good to them. But prolonged periods of good weather always made him uneasy. It usually meant a storm was coming. But this time it would not be the type of storm he usually saw.

Thorgils stood on the wharf and watched the Sae-Ulfr row into the bay. He didn't need to see the prow beast or the sail colours to know it was her. His face frowned as he played with the ring attached to his moustache. He had not expected Snorri back for at least another month. If Snorri was back so soon, it could only mean one thing. Trouble. The Sae-Ulfr was close enough now for Thorgils to see Snorri standing by the prow, his long hair dancing in the wind. Thorvald was standing next to him, so at least Thorgils knew both his sons were safe. *So why then did they come home so soon?*

"It's them?" Ingibjorg asked from behind him. He turned and saw her walk down the wharf.

"It's them," Thorgils responded.

Snorri saw his parents waiting on the wharf. Coming home after a raid would normally be a happy occasion, but Ragnar was right. His father wasn't going to be happy with what they were bringing him. He looked back at the woman and it struck him that they never asked for her name. He doubted she would have answered even if he did. He gave the order for the men to stop rowing and to bring the oars in. They were close enough for Rolf just to guide the Sae-Ulfr to the wharf under her own momentum. As they got to the wharf the brothers threw ropes to the waiting men. They pulled the Sae-Ulfr to a stop and tied her down. Snorri patted the prow like a well-behaved dog, and then jumped onto the wharf to greet his parents.

"You're back early," his father said before Snorri could say anything.

"Yes, father, but I have news that couldn't wait," he responded. Thorgils stared at his son but said nothing.

"Welcome home, my son," Ingibjorg said. "To both my sons," when Thorvald appeared beside him. Thorvald looked miserable, and she saw he had lost some weight. Thorgils had always accused her of being too soft on him, and maybe he had been right. But Thorvald had never been as hard as his brother was. Thorvald looked at her.

"Mother, Father."

Thorgils saw Ragnar disembark and noticed the troubled expression on his champion's face. Looking back at his sons he decided this was not the place to talk, so he turned and walked to his hall.

"Go get yourself cleaned up. We'll have a feast tonight to mark your return," Ingibjorg said to her sons.

"A feast?" Snorri asked. "Father doesn't look happy enough for a feast."

"Your father is never happy when you disobey him. But I feel you had a good reason," she said as she saw Ulf. The bruise on his neck was healing, but it had an ugly yellow-brown colour to it now. He seemed shaken by something, but he was trying to hide it. Whatever had happened on this raid would make for an interesting story.

"We did," Snorri responded. He saw his mother look over his shoulder and raise her eyebrow just enough for him to notice. Looking behind him, he saw why. They were helping their captive off the ship. She seemed a bit unsteady at first, but then manage to regain her balance.

"And who is our guest?" she asked her son.

"All will be explained, Mother, but if you don't mind taking her and helping her get cleaned I'd appreciate it. I'm sure she would like to be around some women after spending a week on a ship full of men."

"Your wife will kill you–"

"Relax, Mother, I did not touch her," he defended himself.

"I know, my son. But your wife doesn't." Ingibjorg looked at the woman. She was pretty enough, she thought, but then she noticed something else. The way Ulf was looking at her. That might explain a few things. "Come with me, dear, we will get you cleaned up." The woman stared at her defiantly and looked like she might refuse but then the motherly expression on Ingibjorg's face won her over.

Thorbjorn joined Snorri on the wharf. "That went better than expected."

"It hasn't even started yet," Snorri said and walked to the hall. "Ulf! Join us."

Inside the hall was as dark as ever, although the fire in the centre did its best to light things up. The open door helped as well. Thralls were busy cleaning the benches and getting the tables ready for the welcoming feast. Ulf didn't think Thorgils would want to throw a feast after he heard what Snorri had to say. There was another man in the hall who Ulf had never seen before. From the way he was dressed, he looked like someone who travelled a lot. The lyre in his hands made him out to be a skald. They were poets and musicians, some liked to stay in one place, but many liked to travel all over the land and spread stories and music. They were often the best sources of news from distant parts.

"Gudrun!" Snorri exclaimed when he saw the skald. "It's good to see you again."

"You too, Snorri. It's been a while." He had the soft voice you would expect from a skald; his hair was neatly combed and tied and so was his beard. Ulf ran a hand through his own beard. It had grown a bit, but still had the braids he had put in before they attacked Gunnulf's village. It felt messy, all tangled up and knotted. Most of the men had spent the journey on the fjord combing and cleaning their hair and beards. Even Vidar combed his hair, obviously excited to see Lady Ingibjorg again. But Ulf was too distracted to think about his appearance.

"Yes, it has. What brings you to Thorgilsstad?"

"Gudrun has spent some time in the north, spreading tales of your exploits," Thorgils said.

"What of mine?" Ragnar asked. He had just walked into the hall and heard the last part.

"No tale from the south of Norway would be complete without your name being mentioned, Ragnar Nine-Finger," Gudrun said, smiling as he greeted the warrior. "I have many interesting tales to tell from the north."

"Unfortunately, they will have to wait." Snorri turned to his father, who was sitting in his seat again. "We saw him."

"Who?"

"Griml."

Thorgils was surprised to hear this and leaned forward, resting his elbows on his knees. "Griml?"

"That's why we have returned, Father."

"And it seems our son has got quite an interesting story to tell." Lady Ingibjorg and the woman appeared from the back of the hall. The woman had told her what had happened and Ingibjorg had decided her bath would have to wait. Her husband needed to hear the woman's story.

"Who is she?" the jarl asked.

"This, my husband, is Eldrid, daughter of Jarl Stigr of the Swedes and if not for our son and his men, would now be Griml's wife."

"And she should be grateful for that," Thorbjorn interjected.

The jarl turned to his son. "Snorri, explain." Thorgils did not like surprises.

Snorri nodded and told his father of their journey, from attacking the hall of Jarl Gunnulf to kidnapping Eldrid and racing home.

Thorgils thought for a while. "How did you know that this man Gunnulf left with was Griml?" he asked.

"Ulf had a feeling," Thorbjorn answered, not caring whether the question was for him or not.

"Ulf had a feeling?" the jarl repeated with a raised eyebrow.

"Yes, Father, but he turned out to be right," Snorri responded. The jarl looked at Ulf who said nothing.

"You left out the part where Ulf killed my father," Eldrid interrupted them.

"Killed your father?" the jarl asked, perplexed by this.

"Her father challenged Ulf to a holmgang. Ulf won and when we left, he was still alive," Snorri defended his friend.

"A holmgang?" The jarl glanced at Ulf again. Maybe there was more to the boy than he realized. "That will have to be a story for another day. Where is this Griml now?" he asked his son.

"Hopefully on his way here," Snorri said with a smile. Gudrun the skald looked worried when he heard this, and Ulf wondered if he knew who Griml was.

"Here?" Thorgils rubbed his forehead with his fingers. He could see where this was going and did not like it.

"Yes, and with Ulf's sword," Snorri said again.

"How do you know he will come with the sword?" Thorgils asked, his hand now resting on his chin.

"He never goes anywhere without that sword. Although I don't know why," Eldrid answered. "I've never seen him use it."

"Too small for his hands," Snorri responded. "Probably just carries it around as a symbol of his status."

"What is so special about that sword?" Eldrid asked. She did not understand why these men would risk everything for a piece of metal. She was sure they would all die when Griml came.

"That is also a story for another day, my dear," Lady Ingibjorg said and then she looked at Ulf. "And I'm sure the next time Ulf sees Griml, he will be better prepared." Ulf gaped at her, stunned. Snorri hadn't said anything about his reaction to seeing Griml, so how could she know? Eldrid could not have said anything, as she had not seen him that night.

"Let me get this straight." Thorgils' eyes bore into Snorri's and his already-contorted face scowled even more. "You are risking a war against a self-proclaimed sea king who has an army of a size unknown to us. You are willing to destroy everything I have built in order to help Ulf, a person you barely know." His hands gripped the armrests so tightly that Ulf thought they might break.

"He'll have no more than two ships," Snorri said confidently. He hoped he was right.

"How do you know?" Thorgils struggled to contain himself. He knew Snorri could be reckless, but he never thought his son could be outright dumb. Thorgils had built everything by being careful and had slowly put himself in a position where he was one of King Halfdan's strongest jarls.

"That's what I would do."

"That's what you would do!" Thorgils burst out of his chair and charged at Snorri, who just stood there, preparing himself for what was to come. His hirdmen looked conflicted as they wanted to defend Snorri, but not attack their jarl. Even Ragnar looked unsure of what to do. Thorgils reached his son and grabbed him by the tunic, pushing him a few steps back. But Snorri did not fight back. Instead, he let his father's anger wash over him like a wave over a stone.

"Snorri is right," Eldrid said, surprising everyone. Thorgils looked at her but still held onto his son's tunic. "Without my father's men and ships, Griml only has three ships." She stared at Snorri, not wanting to help him, but seeing no choice in the matter. "By taking me, your son crippled Griml."

"This would have come our way, with or without Snorri's help, my husband," Ingibjorg added. "The gods want this. How else could they have found Griml so easily?"

Thorgils glared at Snorri, seeing the triumph behind his eyes, but also seeing that Snorri had enough respect not to show it on his face. "Assuming that Griml is coming, how far behind you is he?" Thorgils asked. He would need to start thinking about defending his people.

"I don't know, Father. A day, maybe less, maybe more. We didn't see any ships chasing us, but neither did we stop."

Thorgils let go of Snorri and went back to his seat. It felt like the entire hall let out a breath of relief.

"Oddi, send word to your father. Tell him we are expecting some uninvited guests and that they might stop at his hall first." Oddi nodded and left the hall in search of a horse. "Snorri, your men must be exhausted. Tell them to rest, they'll need to be ready if this Griml comes." Snorri nodded and was about to leave when Thorvald stormed into the hall. He had changed his clothes and his hair was all neat and tidy.

"Father! I demand that you have Ulf killed!"

Thorgils took a deep breath and looked at his wife. What had she promised him? Chaos. It was beginning to feel like it. Thorgils reached for his temple to ease the pressure building behind his eyes.

"Why?"

"He almost killed me!" the boy shrieked.

Thorgils ran his hand down his face and along his beard. "Snorri, explain."

Snorri glared at his brother with a curled lip. "He pushed Ulf too far. In fact, he had gotten a bit too cocky with Ragnar by his side and started insulting my crew. Unfortunately for him, Ulf reacted. But he never came close to killing Thorvald. He only wanted to warn him," Snorri lied.

"He threw an axe at me!" Thorvald shrieked again.

"He missed. On purpose," Snorri said.

"Ragnar?" Thorgils asked his champion who was supposed to protect his son.

"Snorri speaks the truth. If Ulf came close to killing Thorvald then he wouldn't be standing here now," Ragnar lied, more to protect himself than to defend Ulf.

Thorgils looked at Snorri and Ragnar, his scowl becoming more pronounced. Looking at Ulf, he saw the boy staring back with the same anger he always had in his eyes. But Thorgils guessed that Ulf didn't care about what Thorvald had just said.

"Perhaps Thorvald needs to learn to be more respectful of the men around him and not abuse his station," Ingibjorg said. Thorvald went red in the face. He was about to protest when he saw Thorbjorn signal between his own legs and crossed them to show he needed to piss. The message was clear. When Thorgils saw that Thorvald wasn't going to say anything more, he turned to Snorri.

"Get everyone ready. It looks like we are going to war."

CHAPTER 25

Griml had arrived. Ulf felt it in his bones, in his heart, he could even feel it in the air. After two days of anxious waiting, the mood around the village had been tense. Not knowing when it would happen, or even if it would at all. All they had to go on was Ulf's dream. Lady Ingibjorg seemed to know about it. He knew she knew because of what she had said the day before.

"You are worried," she said to him in the hall.

Ulf nodded, not knowing what else to say.

Ingibjorg smiled. "Trust your dreams, Ulf." She got up from her seat and walked out of the hall.

But Ulf didn't want to trust his dreams. In his dreams, the troll always beat him. Vidar appeared beside him and the two of them watched the smoke in the distance. Vidar didn't look anxious, like everyone else. If anything, he seemed calm, like he had accepted something important. Ulf wished he could ask Vidar about it, but it was no use. At least his young friend's calmness helped him with his nerves. The warriors had been keeping themselves busy by cleaning their equipment and sharpening their blades. Ulf did the same the day before, but there was only so many times you could sharpen an axe or clean your brynja. Others felt the same. They had to break up a fight between Thorbjorn and Oddi, who had arrived back after warning his family across the bay. Thorbjorn gave one of his usual sarcastic comments to something Oddi had said and the two were at it like starving wolves fighting over a carcass. Strangely enough though, by the evening the two of them were drinking ale together and laughing about it. Ulf wondered if he would ever experience friendships like that. He thought back over the last year and guessed that he might have already. Snorri had stood by him and supported him, even when it meant going against his father. He didn't know why Snorri did this; even the others seemed not to understand it. But Snorri had turned out to be a good friend and Ulf hoped he wouldn't die because of it.

"He's here." Ulf heard Snorri's voice behind him, as if thinking about him made him appear.

"Looks like it," Ulf responded, still watching the smoke. He could feel Snorri looking at him. "What?" he asked.

"Just wondering," Snorri responded.

"Wondering what?"

"Are you scared?"

Ulf looked at Snorri for the first time, then back at the smoke. *Was he scared?* Ulf did not know. The last time he saw Griml, he had been frozen by shock and fear. For the first time since waking up in the old man's hut, Ulf had doubted whether he could kill Griml and avenge his family.

"It's OK to be scared. I think we all are, a little. It's hard when you are facing the unknown." Snorri smiled at Vidar and saw him smiling back at him. At least Vidar seemed to understand. The boy had grown on him, he had even become part of their little band. But Ulf still didn't respond. Snorri didn't really expect him to. He wondered again at the close bond he felt with Ulf. It almost felt like the same blood flowed through their veins, but he knew that wasn't the case. "You are not alone in this, Ulf," he said and then walked away, leaving Ulf to his thoughts.

You are not alone. The words echoed in his head. Soon they were joined by other words which had been a constant for him this last year. *Embrace your blood.*

The first bændr started to arrive later that day. They all told the same story. A large army led by a giant was rampaging his way through the land, killing and torturing anyone who got in their way.

"How many men has he got?" Thorgils asked one of the bændr who had just arrived with his family.

"I don't know, jarl. But I saw at least six ships by the beach," the man responded.

"How big were the ships?" Snorri asked. That would at least give them an idea of the size of the army they would be facing.

"Some big, some small," the man responded unhelpfully.

Thorgils thought for a while, stroking his beard as he did so. This was the same answer they had gotten from everyone they asked. You can't expect bændr running for their lives to stop and count an army. But he needed to know how big Griml's force was.

"Snorri," he said to his son, "I want you to take a few men and go look at this army. We need to know how big it is."

"Yes, Father," Snorri said and turned to leave.

"There's no need for your son to go anywhere," Jarl Amund, Oddi's father, said as he walked into the hall. Thorgils greeted his kinsman with an embrace and asked him what he had seen.

"Five ships, like the bændr said. I guess about three hundred men. But it is the man leading this force that worries me. I've never seen any like him before." He looked at Snorri, "What has your son gotten us into?"

"Same mischief as always," Thorgils answered. Thorgils gave Snorri a hard stare. Five was more than two.

"Where is your other son?" Thorgils asked, noticing Magni Cockerel wasn't where he usually could be found, by his father's side.

"I have him watching them. Told him not to come until nightfall," Jarl Amund responded, proud of himself for this.

"Good move," Thorgils said. "You bring your men with you?" He did not need to ask how many men Amund had. He already knew. One didn't become the most powerful jarl in the region by not knowing things like this.

"I did, but I'm not sure what good it will do. We're still outnumbered," Jarl Amund said.

"Let me worry about that." Thorgils thought for a while longer. He could not let Griml's force get near Thorgilsstad. He had to meet him somewhere and he knew just where. "Amund, send a man to your son. Tell him to meet us by the Giant's Toe. Snorri," he turned to his son, "get everybody ready. We'll leave with the midday sun."

"Yes, Father," Snorri responded with a smile on his face. Finally, they were doing something other than waiting. He left the hall, shouting at the men to get their things ready.

"Your son always looks happy when he is about to go into a fight," Jarl Amund said.

"Aye, it's in his blood. Your son has been doing well too, you know."

"I know." He turned to face Thorgils again. "Why the Giant's Toe?"

"It's a good place. If we can get there before Griml does, then we have the high ground." Jarl Amund nodded at this.

"Get your stuff ready. We march for the Giant's Toe," Snorri said to Ulf, Thorbjorn and Oddi. They were sat on a bench outside the hall, watching the fires as they gradually got closer.

"The Giant's Toe?" Ulf asked.

"Aye, it's a small valley not too far from here. Griml will have to pass it to get here. My father is planning a welcoming party for him there," Snorri responded.

"But why is it called the Giant's Toe?" Ulf asked.

"Because of the rock that's shaped like a giant's toe and sits on one of the hills in the valley," Thorbjorn answered like it was common knowledge.

"They say that a long time ago, the valley was covered by a forest and there was a lake in the middle. One night a giant was passing through when he heard a woman singing. It was the most beautiful voice he had ever heard and so the giant followed the voice. He wanted to see who it belonged to. When he got to the lake, he saw a beautiful maiden with fair skin and flaming red hair. So transfixed was the giant by her beauty and by her voice, that he did not realize the sun was rising. The giant himself was fine, he was covered by the trees, so the sun didn't reach him, but his toe was sticking out. As soon as the sun touched it, the toe turned to stone.

The giant howled and ran away, disappearing into the forest and leaving his toe behind. The king of the land was furious when he heard the tale and ordered the forest burnt to find the giant and to punish him for spying on his daughter. They cleared the whole forest, but never found the giant or any sign of him other than his toe," Oddi explained.

"Maybe because there was no giant," Thorbjorn said, chewing on a fingernail.

"Then how do you explain the giant's toe?" Oddi asked.

Ulf only shook his head. Snorri had walked off already, shouting orders at everyone he could find.

"Tomorrow is the big day, Ulf," Thorbjorn said.

Ulf watched him but didn't say anything.

"Tomorrow you get your revenge and we all get to piss on that troll's dead body," he said with conviction. Ulf wished he could feel the same. But they hadn't seen the man fight. Before the holmgang, he had felt confident. But that holmgang had taught him something. It had shown he would never be good enough. Griml would always be better. He frowned as he thought about the dreams again.

"Let's go," Oddi said, breaking Ulf from his thoughts. "It's time to get ready." They didn't need to put their armour on as they had been living in it since they got back. They heard the war horn being blown, telling the warriors of Thorgilsstad to get ready for battle. All around them men were running around, fetching shields and weapons. Women and children came out of their houses to say farewell to husbands and fathers. For some of them, this would be the last time they would see each other, but they didn't let that stop them. Their home was in danger and they had to defend it.

Ulf could not help but feel guilty. Many of these men would be going to Valhalla only so that he could get his revenge. He looked at Olaf's axe, tucked into his belt. He wasn't sure how, but to him, it looked ready to drink blood. Maybe his uncle's spirit was in there and he could sense the battle coming. Ulf saw the men gathering in the square around the statues of the gods. The way the men stood around them made it seem as if Odin, Thor and Tyr were going to battle with them. Perhaps they were. They would need the help of the gods. Ulf patted Olaf's axe as he thought this and went to join Snorri's hirdmen.

Thorgils watched as his army gathered in front of his hall. He was dressed in his war gear, wearing his brynja which had gold links in it. It was not as strong as a normal brynja, but it made him look good. His hair was braided and so was his beard and his long moustache. As always, he had put small finger rings on the ends of his moustache. He looked at Ragnar, who looked like the war god himself, the same could be said for his son. Even Thorvald was wearing his brynja and sword. He did not quite look as fearsome as the older men, but he would grow into it. Thorgils saw Ulf approaching. Ulf had gotten hold of a brynja now, he saw. He noticed how much Ulf had changed since he had arrived here as a skinny youth. He had gotten bigger, stronger even. His hair was braided into three rows and even his beard had a thin braid down the centre. There was also an added fierceness that now shared the anger in his eyes. Ulf reminded Thorgils of Bjørn and he hoped the boy would not share the same fate as his father.

Thorgils had managed to get over two hundred men together. A lot of the bændr had volunteered, saying they wanted to defend their lands. They did not match Griml's force in number, but

Thorgils was still confident. These men were fighting for their homes and their families. Each man would be worth at least two on the battlefield. This was an army Odin would be proud of and Thorgils knew many would be joining the Einherjar soon.

"Everyone is ready," Snorri said. Thorgils studied his son. Like everyone he had braided his hair and beard so that they don't get in the way during the fight. His shield was on his back and he carried his helmet in his hand.

"Then let's get going." Thorgils climbed on his horse and faced his men. He didn't say anything to them, he didn't need to. He felt a smile on his face. Thorgils turned his horse and walked out of Thorgilsstad. He didn't need to look to know his men were following him, their footsteps behind him sounded like a drumbeat of a war song.

They arrived at the Giant's Toe with enough daylight left for Ulf to have a look at the place for tomorrow's battle. It was a low-lying field with a large hill on one side, the side closest to them. Thorgils wanted the hill, that's why he came here. Ulf did not know much about battles, but he guessed that would count for something. On top of the hill was a large boulder, which did look like a giant toe. He wondered if the story Oddi had told was true. The boulder suggested that it might have been. Vidar came to stand by his side and looked at the toe-like boulder.

"Come on, we need to get our tent ready," Ulf said. He yawned, surprising himself. On the march, he had felt fine, but with all the doubt and fear in his mind, he never had time to realize how tired he was. Even his brynja was feeling too heavy now, and he would be glad to take it off. They found a spot near their friends and set their tent up, preparing for battle.

When they were done, he went inside and took his brynja off. His tunic was soaked with sweat. He understood these things could save his life, but it was hot wearing all this in the middle of the summer. He took off the thick tunic he usually wore under his armour and replaced it with a thinner dry one. Stepping outside, he saw Thorbjorn and Asbjorn already had a fire going. Like him, they were wearing thinner tunics. Because they were not far from their home, they had managed to bring some meat and vegetables along, so at least they would be able to eat properly. Although Ulf wasn't sure if he would be able to eat. Oddi and the brothers joined shortly after, and while they were cooking the men were exchanging old war stories. Ulf guessed it was to prepare themselves for the upcoming battle.

"Where's Snorri?" Ulf asked when they started eating.

"He's eating with his father and brother," Oddi answered. "The jarl wanted them to eat together, as it may be the last time they get to do so."

"Why aren't you eating with your father and brother then?" Brak asked, while noisily chewing on some meat.

Oddi stared at his food for a while and then said, "If they wanted me to, then they would have asked." They fell silent for a bit, not knowing what to say. Some of the men understood the history between Oddi and his family and out of respect for their friend, kept quiet. Those like Ulf, who did not, thought it was better not to ask. Oddi would tell him if he wanted to.

There was no drinking that night, the jarl had forbidden it. He wanted the men to be fresh and ready for tomorrow. Thorbjorn had muttered that it would have been easier to fight when people were drunk. Gave them more courage. Ulf saw the sense in that. He wished he had some ale to numb his mind. He decided to go for a walk, maybe that would calm him down. As he stood up Brak Drumbr asked if he could join him. Ulf nodded and they walked in silence for a while past the other tents and fires. Geir appeared from his tent, still wearing his jerkin.

"Ulf, Brak," he greeted them. "Going to scout the land?"

"No, just walking off our meals," Brak Drumbr said. It almost made Ulf smile. Brak was a big solid man who loved to eat. If he was walking off his meal it was only to make space for another one.

"I see. Can I join you?" Geir asked.

Ulf and Brak looked at each other before Ulf answered, "You can."

The silence did not last long. Geir, it seemed was excited by the prospect of the battle. "I hope I get a chance to prove my worth to the jarl and Snorri," he said.

Brak looked at him. "I can't speak for the jarl, but if Snorri didn't think you were a good fighter, then you wouldn't be on his crew. And neither would you have that sword of yours."

Geir nodded as if he understood the words. "But I want to be part of his hirdmen, like you guys," he said.

"Be careful what you wish for, Geir," Brak said, looking up to the sky and fingering the Mjöllnir around his neck. "You never know which god may be listening."

Ulf saw Geir touch the Mjöllnir amulet around his neck. Brak was right. It was true that some gods wanted to help men, but there were others who liked to interfere for no other reason than their own amusement. *Like Odin had interfered in my life.*

Ulf saw a movement in the distance, on the other side of the field. "Look," he said to Brak Drumbr and Geir. The three of them watched as men started to appear, hundreds of them walking out of the forest which covered that side of the field. He heard the raven, laughing at them as it flew over their heads. And the raven had a good reason to laugh, Ulf thought.

Griml had arrived.

CHAPTER 26

Griml's army walked into the valley with the same ease as if they were on an afternoon stroll. Hundreds of men not caring about the enemy on the hill watching them.

Ulf watched them, surprised by their calmness. He thought they'd be nervous of Thorgils' men on the hill. Perhaps it was because they saw they outnumbered Thorgils' army.

"Arrogant bastards, aren't they?" Brak Drumbr echoed his thoughts. Ulf didn't answer. Instead, he looked along the hill and saw Thorgils had come out of his tent with Snorri and Thorvald by his side. Thorgils' heavily lined face was hard, whereas Snorri was smiling. Thorvald looked uncertain. Not afraid as Ulf would have expected him to be, but like he was wondering why he had to be here. After a few moments, Thorgils and Thorvald turned and went back to their tent. Snorri stayed and watched Griml's men some more before turning to Ulf. Ulf saw the fierceness in Snorri's eyes and was glad he didn't have to fight against him. Instead, he would be against the man who had been haunting him since last summer. Ulf turned back to the approaching army and realized he could not see Griml. A man that big could not be missed.

"Where's Griml?" he asked.

"Probably shitting himself in the forest somewhere," Thorbjorn said from behind him. The rest of Snorri's hirdmen had joined them without Ulf realizing. Most of Thorgils' men had stopped what they were doing to watch the approaching army. The men around them laughed, but Ulf was sure no one believed it.

"Come, let's go sleep. Nothing more to do now," Oddi said as he turned and walked away. Ulf looked at Vidar, who was at his side. Vidar nodded like he agreed with Oddi, but then turned his eyes to the trees behind Griml's men. Ulf realized he couldn't hear any birds in the air. It was like they had sensed what was about to happen and fled the area. Not even the ravens could be seen or heard.

Vidar shook Ulf awake the next morning and Ulf groaned at him to go away. But as always, Vidar never listened and kept on shaking him until his eyes opened. Ulf had not slept well. Every time he closed his eyes, he saw the troll about to chop him in half with his axe. Ulf hoped it was not a sign of what was to come. As he sat up, he saw his brynja was laid out and shone brightly in the gloomy tent. His helmet was next to it, with his belt and his sax-knife. Olaf's axe was placed on top of his brynja, making it look like an offering to the gods. Vidar had been busy. Ulf nodded his thanks and got up. He prodded the large purple-blue bruise on his side, a memento from his fight with Eldrid's father, and hoped it wouldn't affect him today as he felt the tenderness. After this he put his thick tunic on, smelling the stale sweat from yesterday's march. Over the tunic came his brynja, making him grunt as it fell on his shoulders. Ulf doubted he would ever get used to the weight of the damned thing. When the brynja had settled he fastened his belt around his waist, making sure it took most of the weight of the brynja. He twisted around to make sure he could move freely. Satisfied he could, he picked up Olaf's axe. The handle was still stained red over the names of his family. He read the names quietly to himself as he ran his finger over them. *Olaf, Brynhild, Ingrid, Unnr.* His uncle, aunt and two cousins. Killed for no other reason than one man's cruelty.

"Odin," he whispered, "give me the strength to avenge my family. Tyr, lend me your battle skill to slay the monster who took them from me. Thor, lend me your courage not to disgrace my ancestors." Ulf felt the wind pick up outside the tent and in the distance, he thought he could hear the cry of an eagle. Satisfied, he tucked the axe into his belt and, making sure his sax-knife was still in its scabbard across his stomach, left the tent. It was drizzling outside, and the skies were grey, matching the solemnness of his mood. Ulf lifted his face to the sky and let the rain wash away his grogginess and then looked for his friends. He found them not far from their tents watching Griml's camp. Both camps were a reflection of each other as men crawled out of their tents and muttered about the rain. Some washed their faces from buckets, while others lifted their faces and let the rain wash over them. Men would be checking their weapons and jerkins or brynjas before putting them on. Some prayed or made offerings to the gods, asking to survive or win great battle fame. Those who had the stomach for it would eat something, most likely porridge. And they would be doing all of this with an eye on the enemy camp.

"There's a lot of them," Oddi said as Ulf got to them.

"Aye," Snorri agreed, "means there are more of them to kill than there are of us."

"Nothing to worry about then," Thorbjorn said with a smile on his face.

"Nothing to worry about," Snorri said, returning the smile.

Ulf saw they were ready for the battle. They were all wearing their brynjas and weapons, and like Ulf, had not put their helmets on yet. Ulf was carrying his in his hand. He wanted to have it nearby if the enemy decided to attack now. The only thing he didn't have with him was his spear and shield. They were still in the tent. He stood for a while with his friends, watching the enemy camp and trying to find Griml amongst them.

"I can't see him," he said to the others.

"He's there," Snorri reassured Ulf.

"Probably still sleeping," Thorbjorn said.

"Let's get something to eat. They won't be ready for a while," Snorri said. He didn't wait for a response as he walked back towards his tent. The others followed. Ulf stayed for a short while before joining them. He didn't think he could eat but he remembered his uncle telling him a warrior should always fight on a full stomach.

You don't know how long the journey to Valhalla is.

They were halfway through their breakfast when the horn blew. The men looked up from their bowls and at each other. It was time. Snorri looked around at the seven men he thought of as friends and brothers.

"My brothers," he said with a smile, "I will see you after the battle or in Valhalla."

"After the battle or in Valhalla," they echoed. Ulf felt oddly comforted by the words, the surety behind them that they will meet again. As they went to their tents to get their spears and shields, Ulf wondered if his friends felt as nervous as he did.

"Drumbr!" Thorbjorn shouted over his shoulder. "If you get to Valhalla before me, make sure you leave me some of the mead."

"No need to worry about that. The mead in Valhalla is endless," Brak Drumbr responded.

"Not with the way you drink. You'd drink old Heidrun dry before any of us got there," his brother quipped. The men laughed as they got their spears and shields.

Ulf saw that Vidar wasn't in the tent when he went in. He thought that was strange. Maybe Vidar was already outside, but then why had Ulf not seen him? Ulf took his spear and shield and went out to meet the others. When he got to the hill, Thorgils was busy giving the orders.

"Snorri, I want you and your men on the right flank. Amund, you will be on the left flank." He looked at the two men and was satisfied with their nods. "Now, where in Odin's name is Ragnar?" Ulf realized Ragnar was not with the jarl, which was also strange.

"Ragnar?" Snorri asked, also seeing that his father's champion wasn't there. He knew the champion would want to be nowhere else right now.

"Yes, I sent him to my tent to fetch my helmet and to get Thorvald. He should be here as well."

Snorri shrugged. "I'm sure he is on his way. Maybe he had to take a piss first."

"Snorri's right," Jarl Amund answered. "I will get my men ready," he said and walked away. Ulf saw him look at his son, Oddi, and give the briefest of nods as he did so.

"Perhaps," Thorgils said. "Snorri, you do the same." The two of them clasped hands. "After the battle or in Valhalla."

"After the battle or in Valhalla, Father," Snorri responded and walked to his men.

"Ulf," the jarl said before Ulf could follow Snorri. Ulf turned and looked at the jarl. "May Tyr be with you today." Ulf was surprised by the words. The jarl had never liked him, or so it had seemed. Ulf nodded his thanks and went after Snorri.

He was surprised not to see Vidar waiting for him by Snorri's men. "Anyone seen Vidar?" he asked as he planted his spear into the ground to put his helmet on.

"No, thought he was with you," Asbjorn said. He had been less hostile towards Ulf after they had seen Griml, but Ulf still felt some distrust from him.

"He wasn't in the tent when I got there."

"He'll be here," Snorri said, smiling at him.

Ulf nodded and made sure his helmet sat firmly. The enemy line formed up opposite theirs. They were close enough so he could see the individual faces of the men who wanted to kill him. Their line was longer than Thorgils', but they had expected that. Griml had more men. A ripple ran through the line near the centre, the way wheat fields parted when walked through, and Ulf saw him. It was hard not to, he was at least two heads above the rest. He walked through his cheering men with his arms raised in the air, filled with arrogance and preening like a prized cockerel showing off its flamboyant plumage. Only, a prized cockerel wasn't so ugly, or as frightening.

Griml stood in front of his men and looked along the line of Thorgils' men like he was searching for something. Ulf did not feel the shock he had felt when he first saw Griml outside his hall, but he felt the same fear and uncertainty run through him. Griml carried on searching along the line until he found what he was looking for. Ulf. He locked eyes with him and an arrogant grin spread across his ugly face, revealing a mouth of rotten teeth. Ulf could only stare back, caught in the emptiness of the giant man's eyes. *The path to Hel, through the bloody marshes of his dreams.* Griml walked along the line of his men, his eyes still fixed on Ulf. He didn't seem to care about the two hundred other men. He didn't seem to be afraid of them. But then, fear was probably a feeling Griml had never felt before.

"What's he doing?" Snorri asked, but got no response. All around him men muttered the same question, like Snorri, not understanding what they saw.

Ulf had visions of his dreams again as Griml came closer and it took all his will not to shudder in fear. Finally, Griml stopped, directly opposite Ulf.

"Maybe he's trying to insult your father?" Oddi suggested.

"Or he wants us. We did kidnap his bride," Thorbjorn suggested.

"No, he's looking at Ulf. He wants Ulf, not us," Snorri said, frowning as he tried to understand.

Never in his long life had Thorgils seen a man like Griml. If Griml had been on his side, they could have controlled the whole of Norway. But the gods had decided that Griml had to be his enemy. Not even his. Griml would not have been here if it weren't for Ulf. But then maybe that was the gods' plan. They had wanted chaos and decided that chaos would be played out on Thorgils' doorstep. Thorgils had no illusion that this was an insult to him, regardless of how others saw it. It might even work in his favour. His men would fight harder if they believed their jarl had been insulted. Griml wanted Ulf. But Thorgils didn't understand why. From what Snorri had told him, it didn't seem like Griml knew who Ulf was. Which meant only one thing. Someone had told him. He looked around him. *Where the fuck was Ragnar?*

"Gunvald!" he shouted to one of his men. "Go and find Ragnar. Tell him I want him here now!" The man nodded and ran to the tents to look for his jarl's champion. Thorgils ran his eyes over Griml's men one more time. He saw a group of men, further back from the rest. There weren't many of them, maybe nine or ten, and they were better equipped than the rest.

"Look!" one of his men shouted. He was pointing to Griml and what the jarl saw left him speechless.

Ulf saw the movement behind Griml, but he could not look. He could not take his eyes off Griml, until Snorri said, "Is that Vidar?"

Ulf looked at the two figures who were walking through Griml's men. Vidar. Ulf couldn't breathe as he struggled to understand, his mind not comprehending what his eyes were showing him. And not just because Vidar was being led toward Griml, with his hands behind his back and a knife at his throat. But because the person who was holding the knife was Snorri's younger brother, Thorvald.

"He's what?!" Thorgils could not understand what Gunvald, who had just returned, had told him.

"Knocked out," the man answered with his eyes on the scene unfolding in front of them.

Jarl Thorgils was also watching the scene. He did not get it, he did not understand why his youngest son, his favourite son, was standing next to Griml and holding Vidar in front of him. Thorvald had betrayed him.

Ulf had never felt hatred as pure as he did watching Thorvald drag Vidar in front of Griml, forcing him to kneel in front of the giant. The smug look on Thorvald's face stoked the smouldering embers of his anger deep in the pit of his stomach. It fed the flames of his rage, the heat of his anger radiating from him as if he was a burning furnace. With every heartbeat, the whispers in his ears were getting stronger, louder. Telling him to act, telling him to forget about those around him. Telling him to run at the enemy and to save his friend. He tried to fight it; he knew it would be reckless, that he would die. But the whispers just kept on whispering their message. *Attack, attack, attack.*

Griml took a step forward and again raised his arms to the sky. His men went quiet as he looked up. "Mighty Odin! Hear me now! Hear me as I speak to you!" Griml shouted into the sky. "Accept this offering I give to you! Accept this offering and give us victory over the men who have insulted your honour!" With that, he took a step towards Vidar and pulled Ormstunga from her scabbard.

Even in Ulf's state of rage, he noticed that the clouds had parted and the sun was shining on them. He watched as Griml stood over Vidar and put the blade of Ormstunga against his neck. Vidar did not look afraid. He looked at Ulf and smiled. It was a smile that said one thing, one thing that Ulf did not want to accept. *Farewell, my friend and brother.* Griml pulled the sword back, taking satisfaction as it cut deep into Vidar's neck, almost cutting his head clean off. A shower of blood erupted as the sword moved away and the men of Griml cheered, believing they had the favour of the All-Father.

Ulf screamed. It was a scream that had been building up for more than a year. All his pain, his loss, his humiliations, his fears and most importantly, his anger came out as he screamed Vidar's name, his face as red as the flames that ate Hulda's remains. Before anyone could react, Ulf grabbed his spear and ran at Griml.

Griml saw the young warrior charging at him. He smiled in satisfaction; the boy had been right. He turned to one of his men.

"Kill him," he said before walking to the back of his shield wall. *There would be no battle today*. Griml put Ormstunga back in her scabbard without cleaning her. Thorvald followed him with a big smile on his face.

Ulf had made it halfway to the enemy line before Snorri realized what had happened.

"Ulf! No!" But he knew it was too late. Snorri had to do something. He looked to his father, hoping he had reacted faster. But all he saw was his father standing there in shock. His usually strong face was pale as he realized his son had betrayed him.

"Fuck!" Snorri shouted as he ran to his father. "Oddi, take charge of the right. Do not do anything until I say so." Oddi nodded, even though Snorri could not see him. As Snorri reached his father, Ragnar walked through the men, holding his head and looking unsteady.

"Where the fuck have you been?!" Snorri shouted. "Never mind, look." He pointed at Ulf who was storming at the enemy, still screaming Vidar's name. One of Griml's men took a step forward, getting ready to kill him.

"What in Tyr's name is he doing?" Ragnar asked. The sight of Ulf charging at the enemy like a man possessed shocked him out of his grogginess.

Snorri grabbed hold of his father. "Father!" he shouted while shaking him. It would not be good for the men to see their jarl like this.

"My son..." Thorgils started but could not get the words out.

"Fuck!" Snorri shouted, realizing what he had to do. Ulf had almost reached the enemy. If they did not attack now, then it would be too late.

"Thor's hairy fucking testicles, look!" The shocked tone in Ragnar's voice made Snorri turn and look towards Ulf.

Ulf heard nothing but his own scream as he ran at Griml's men, Olaf's axe in his right hand and the spear in his left. He had finally stopped thinking. He was not driven by his thoughts anymore. Now he was driven by his thirst for revenge, by the voices in his ears, driving him on. He didn't care whether he lived or died. All he cared about was killing Griml. Killing the man who had taken everything away from him. And anyone who got in his way.

Ulf saw the man step out of the line as Griml and Thorvald walked away. He saw the smile on the man's face, felt the confidence coming from him. To Ulf, the man moved so slowly that he knew he would be dead before he could raise his shield. Ulf changed the grip on his spear and launched it at the man, who was still smiling with confidence. Griml's man was too slow to lift his shield. The spear struck him in the chest before his shield was halfway up. It drove through the man, sending him flying back as if he was plucked away by some invisible force. Ulf moved so fast that the next man died while still trying to understand what had happened to his friend, his face still wearing a half-smile as Ulf's axe bit into his neck. At the same time, Ulf unsheathed his sax-knife and stabbed another in the neck, feeling the warmth of their blood as it sprayed over him. Three men dead in a single heartbeat. But Ulf did not stop, the voices in his head wouldn't let him. One man had just enough time to react as he swung his axe at Ulf. Ulf dropped to his knees, sliding underneath the axe and past the man on the wet grass. He hamstrung the man with his knife and jumped to his feet as the man fell to the ground screaming. Ulf sensed the spear coming from the right and without looking twisted out of the way. He chopped the spear in half with his axe and with his knife, stabbed the spear-holder through the eye, burying his knife deep in the man's skull. Ulf had never felt so alive before, never felt so free. It was like he could sense the men around him and anticipate their movements before they themselves knew what they were doing. They all moved so slowly, so ponderously that to Ulf it felt like he could kill all of them before they even knew he was there. He let go of the knife and picked the axe which had been dropped by one of the men. Ulf looked up and saw the giant back of Griml, who hadn't realized what was happening behind him. "Griml!" he shouted.

Griml turned and saw the blood-covered Ulf standing amongst his men. He just had enough time to see five of his men lying on the ground before Ulf ran at him. "Kill the bastard!" he roared at his men.

Ulf charged at Griml, determined to have his revenge. A sword came from his left, which he blocked with one axe, before punching the man in the face with the head of Olaf's axe. He heard the crunch as teeth and bone were smashed to pieces. Twisting out of the way, he dodged the spear aimed at his back and killed the man before he could realize he had just speared his own friend. Ulf ducked as another swung a two-handed axe at him and then hacked the man's skull in two. But just as he turned to where Griml was, he was sent sprawling backwards by a powerful shield punch. He looked at the smiling Griml as he lay on the ground, slightly disoriented.

"Looks like I'll have to kill you for the second time," Griml said and he drew Ormstunga from her scabbard, her blade reflecting the sunlight.

Snorri had watched in awe as his friend cut his way through Griml's men. He had never seen anyone move so fast or kill so efficiently. It was like Tyr had taken possession of Ulf's body and was fighting through him. But then he saw Griml punch Ulf with the shield. His awe turned to shock as he saw the giant standing over Ulf and unsheathe his sword, Ulf's sword. He knew he had to attack. Unsheathing Tyr's Fury and holding it in the air, he screamed at his father's men.

"Men of Thorgilsstad! Men of Amund! Charge!"

CHAPTER 27

The Skuggi, as Thorvald called himself, stood and watched with euphoria as Griml stabbed the sword down on Ulf's exposed neck. Finally, he would see the death of the man he hated so much. His plan had worked, as if Loki had aided him. It had been so easy to lure Vidar away from their camp and take him to Griml. It had been even easier to convince Griml of his plan. And now, here he was, about to watch Ulf die by his own father's famed sword.

Ulf watched the point of the sword as it came to end his life. He closed his eyes. Ormstunga was almost there, almost at his neck. In his mind, Ulf saw a warrior prepared for battle. He was wearing a brynja and a helmet. On his belt he had a sword, but not just any sword. It was Ormstunga. Ulf realized he was looking at his father, but not just his father. His ancestors as well. His entire bloodline in one form. His father's lips were moving. He was shouting at Ulf, but Ulf couldn't hear what he was saying. And then it came, as loud and clear as thunder. *Fight!*

At the last moment, Ulf's eyes snapped open and he rolled out of the way, hearing the sword bury itself into the ground. Before

Griml could react or even understand what had just happened, Ulf rolled back and with Olaf's axe chopped at Griml's arm. There wasn't enough force in the blow to cut Griml's huge arm off, but enough to break it and cause him to let go of the sword.

Griml roared in agony, sounding more beast than man while clutching his broken and bloody arm. As he looked up, he saw Thorgils' men crash into his. But instead of a wave crashing onto rocks as he had wanted, he saw a wave crash through a sand wall. Thorgils' men tore through his own, cutting them to pieces as they roared their battle cry. He looked at Ulf and saw he was getting to his feet. *Where was that boy, why was he not doing anything?* Turning around he saw Thorvald frozen in place, his face as pale as that of a draugr, his pants wet from pissing himself.

Ulf's mind was still confused. It felt like he was caught in a whirlwind and was struggling to free himself from it. All around him, he heard screams, roars and the noise of weapon against weapon. But he couldn't make sense of it. The movement around him disorientated him even more as he felt the boots pounding the ground rather than see them. And then it all stopped. The screaming, the fighting, even the moving. Nothing around him but silence. Ulf was still on his knees when he felt a hand on his shoulder. At first, he thought it was one of Griml's men, come to kill him. But when he looked up, he saw the blood-covered face of Snorri smiling down on him.

"You fucking bastard," Snorri said to him. Ulf could hear the relief in his voice and smiled back. Snorri looked down on his friend, relieved and surprised that he was still alive. It had been a desperate fight to get to him in time. Ulf's charge had distracted Griml's men, which meant Snorri's charge did not hit a strong shield wall. But still, the fight had been hard, and he had made Tyr's Fury sing as he fought his way to his friend. He could see his hirdmen had fought just as hard as they stood around Ulf, covered in as much blood as he was. All of them, even Asbjorn, were relieved to see Ulf still alive.

"What took you so long?" Ulf asked Snorri.

Snorri shrugged. "Thought there was enough time for some ale before coming to save your dumb arse." He pointed to the sword, still stuck in the ground. "Yours, I believe."

Ulf looked at the sword, for a moment struck by the beauty of it. He saw the gold pommel, with the image of Jörmungandr circling around the Valknut. It looked like the giant serpent was actually moving. He saw the thick guard, the images of more serpents engraved on it. On the serpents a warning was engraved in runes – *I am from a place of darkness. Do not draw me in the light of the sun.* Along the blade, also in runes, a single word was engraved. Ormstunga. The sword of his ancestors. The sword of his father. His sword. He wrapped his hand around the wooden handle, feeling the familiar grip though he had never held it before. Ulf stood up, pulling the sword from the ground. The sword seemed to give him more strength, reinvigorating him. He stood there, the sword of his ancestors in one hand, the axe of his uncle in another and the army his father once fought with behind him. Ulf finally understood. *Embrace your blood.* He looked at Snorri, his wolf grin on his face. Thorbjorn, Oddi, the brothers and Asbjorn were there, all smiling at him. As he looked along the shield wall, he saw Ragnar Nine-Finger and more men whose names he could not remember, all watching him. He saw Jarl Thorgils, who had come out of his trance when his men charged and had fought like Thor to get to his treacherous son.

Ulf turned to face the army of Griml and saw Griml standing behind it, still clutching his arm as he glared at Ulf.

He took a step forward. "I am Ulf! Nephew of Olaf!" *Crash*, the sound came from behind him as Snorri hit the back of his shield with the pommel of his sword. "Nephew of Brynhild." *Crash*. More men joined in. "Cousin of Ingrid and Unnr." *Crash*, louder still. "Friend of Vidar!" *Crash!* Louder. "I am Ulf! Son of Bjørn!" *CRASH!*. A thunderous sound as two hundred men struck their shields. "I am Ulf! Bastard of Tyr!" *CRASH!* "I have sworn an oath of revenge to Odin!" *CRASH!* "I have sworn to Odin that I will kill Griml Troll-Face!" *CRASH!* "I have sworn an oath to Odin that I will avenge my family!" *CRASH!* "I cannot die until my oath has been fulfilled!" *CRASH!* "Griml will die by my sword and my sword only!" *CRASH!* "Ormstunga will drink Griml's blood!" He roared this last sentence while punching Ormstunga into the air. *CRASH! CRASH! CRASH!*

"Men of Thorgilsstad! Men of Amund!" Snorri roared. "Attack!" With that, two hundred men moved forward as one. Griml's shield wall collapsed as the men in front turned to run, unnerved by what they had just witnessed.

Griml watched it all fall apart in front of him. He had thought he had gotten Odin's favour, but for some reason, Odin had rejected his sacrifice. For the first time in his life, Griml felt something other than anger and bloodlust. For the first time in his life, Griml felt afraid. A feeling so unfamiliar to him, like breathing underwater, that he did not know what to do as he watched Ulf and his friends cut their way through his men. Most of them ran, but some were too dumb to understand they had been beaten. But he wasn't too dumb, despite what others had always thought of him. Griml Jotun turned and ran.

Thorvald was also struck with fear. He realized he had pissed himself again, but he did not care. Loki had deserted him and now he was going to die. He saw Vidar's face in his mind. Vidar was smiling, like he had done in the tent when Thorvald had presented him to Griml. There had been none of the fear he had expected to see in the silent boy's face. Thorvald saw Griml turn and run. *Damn him! It was his fault.* He had wanted Thorvald to face his father. Thorvald only wanted them to lose; he wanted Ulf and Snorri to die. Then he would be the next jarl of Thorgilsstad. But now it was all lost. So, he lived up to his name and ran after Griml.

When most men gave in to their anger, they became clouded by it, unable to think straight. They fought blindly, hacking and stabbing at anything in their path, even their own friends and companions. But for Ulf it was different. When Ulf gave in to his anger, his fighting instincts took over. Fighting and war were in his blood because his ancestor was the bastard son of Tyr, the god of war. It was as natural to him as the skin he wore. The voices whispering in his ears were not the demons of his father. They were his ancestors fighting with him, driving him to move faster than those around him, warning him of attacks before they happened. At that moment, after recklessly charging at an army to avenge his fallen friend, he finally understood his father. His father had not abandoned him. His father had died protecting his friend like Ulf was now fighting for his friends and family. He dodged and twisted out of the way of swords, spears and axes, still roaring Vidar's name. He used the weapons of his family to kill his enemies. Ulf did not take joy in killing, but he did find joy in the fight. The sounds of swords clashing against shields, of men screaming and crying became the music he was dancing to, like the flames of a fire as they danced into the night. Ulf had embraced his blood and men were dying around him because of it.

A horn blew its echoing sound over the battlefield, silencing the symphony of war. Ulf, still trembling with battle rage, was gasping as he watched Griml's army run toward the trees like they were being chased by Odin's wolves, Geri and Freki. Around him, men cheered and hugged each other, too caught up in the euphoria of surviving to think about those who hadn't. But not Ulf. He turned and pushed his way through Snorri and his hirdmen.

"Ulf! What are you doing?" Snorri asked, his wide eyes shining bright through his bloody helmet.

"Vidar," Oddi said, understanding before the rest and then followed Ulf.

"Shit." Snorri's shoulders dropped, the elation of victory forgotten.

They found Vidar's body not far from where they were, lying in the blood-soaked mud. Ulf dropped to his knees, feeling the knot in his throat, but unable to summon the tears.

"Vidar," he groaned as he lifted his friend's head and held it to his chest. Snorri and his hirdmen removed their helmets, not sure of what else to do.

"Snorri, look." Brak Drumbr was pointing to Jarl Thorgils, who was also on his knees and clutching something to his chest.

"Shit," Snorri said again.

"Thorvald?" Asbjorn asked, wiping the sweat from his forehead and smearing it with blood.

Snorri shook his head, his face grim. "The coward ran." He took a deep breath and turned to Ulf. "Ulf?" But Ulf did not answer, he was too caught up in his grief.

"It's OK," Thorbjorn said. "We'll watch him, you go."

Snorri nodded his gratitude and walked to his father, now surrounded by Ragnar and Jarl Amund. When he got there, he saw his father was holding the sword he had given to Thorvald.

"I feel like the gods are laughing at us," Jarl Amund said as he saw Snorri.

Snorri looked up and saw the ravens fill the sky like stars in the night. "So do I," he responded. He looked at his father, who just stared at the sword in his hands with tears running down his face.

"Oddi?" Amund asked, glancing at the group of men surrounding Ulf.

"He's fine," Snorri responded. "Magni?"

Jarl Amund smiled, a strange sight under the circumstances. "He lives, although he is a little pale."

"His first battle," Snorri said and Amund nodded. Snorri looked at Ragnar standing over his jarl, his head bowed and lips pressed tight. "What happened?" Snorri asked him.

"I don't know," he said, his usually strong voice soft. "I walked into the tent to fetch Thorvald and the jarl's helmet. But as I left, something struck me from behind. I fell and that's the last thing I remember until Gunvald woke me."

"Thorvald hit you?" Amund asked in surprise.

"Must have done." Ragnar rubbed the back of his head. Snorri ground his teeth as he heard this.

"Snorri." Amund's voice made him look away from his father's champion to a group of men walking towards them. All around them, the men of Thorgils and Amund were watching them, distracted from their looting and searching for fallen friends. Snorri recognised them as the men of Eldrid's father, the ones he saw in Suðrikaupstefna. His hand went to the hilt of Tyr's Fury, but he saw they were unarmed.

"We wish to speak to your jarl," the leader of the group said. Snorri saw there was no blood on their armour.

"You can speak to me, I am the jarl's son, Snorri Thorgilsson." Snorri took a step forward. He felt Ragnar move behind him, putting himself between Thorgils and the new arrivals.

"My name is Aslaug Hjalmarson," the leader of the group responded with a nod.

"You are with Griml?" Amund asked.

Aslaug gave Jarl Amund a sideways glance. "No, we are men of Jarl Stigr. I think Snorri here will know who I speak of." Snorri nodded. "We came for his daughter, Eldrid."

"Why did you not fight with Griml. I thought he was your ally?" Snorri asked with a sneer.

Aslaug shrugged, "This was not our fight. You took Eldrid from Griml's camp, it was his responsibility to get her back."

Snorri nodded. "She's in my father's hall. You can bring two men with you and we'll take you to her."

Aslaug frowned as he watched the bloodied warrior before shrugging. "If you swear by Odin that neither me nor my men will be harmed."

"I swear by Odin," Snorri responded. "Ragnar–"

"I'll stay with your father," Ragnar said before Snorri could finish.

Snorri nodded and turned to Jarl Amund.

"I'll stay here. I'll bring the men back when they are done," Amund said.

"Thank you, I'll leave Oddi here as well." Amund smiled in response. Snorri turned to his hirdmen and signalled to them.

"Looks like we are leaving," Brak said.

Ulf looked up and was almost surprised to see the men around him.

"We'll get a horse for Vidar," Asbjorn offered and walked off.

They lifted Vidar's body onto the horse, which Thorbjorn led as they followed the injured men back to Thorgilsstad. Behind them, Ulf heard the ravens as they celebrated their feast. But over their calls, Ulf heard a different noise. He looked up and saw an eagle soaring above them, following them home.

They were met with muted cheers as they walked into Thorgilsstad. The women and children had heard of the victory, but Ingibjorg's grave face dampened the celebration.

"Mother," Snorri started. His mother held up a hand, stopping him from saying anything else.

"I know." She looked at her son. Snorri saw her red eyes and the dried tears on her cheeks.

"Did you know before or after?" he couldn't stop himself from asking.

Ingibjorg gave her son a sad smile. "It doesn't matter." She noticed the large warrior walking behind Snorri, seeing how he ran his eyes over their village. "You must be Aslaug Hjalmarson?"

"Aye, but how–" he looked to his two companions and saw they were as dumbfounded as he was.

"Eldrid is waiting for you in the hall. She will be happy to see you." Ingibjorg smiled at her guest. Aslaug nodded his gratitude. "But you will have to excuse us for our poor hospitality. There is something important which needs to be done."

Aslaug saw Ingibjorg look behind him and turned. He saw the short warrior leading a horse with the body of the boy Griml had killed on its back. He also saw the young warrior walking beside the horse, the one who had beaten his jarl in the holmgang.

"Snorri, please take Aslaug and his men to the hall. There is some ale for them."

"Yes, Mother." Snorri looked over his shoulder and saw what his mother was looking at. "This way," he said to Aslaug and led them to his father's hall.

Ingibjorg waited for Ulf to approach her. Around her the women of the village led the injured men away, asking them about husbands and sons.

"I'm sorry, Ulf."

Thorbjorn and the others decided to go to the hall, giving Ulf and Ingibjorg some privacy.

"You still think the gods are not punishing me?" Ulf asked her, his eyes strained with grief.

Ingibjorg looked at the body of Vidar draped over the horse. She was surprised at how clean he was. She thought of Hulda, and how she sat by the tree, the same grizzly smile on her throat. "I think there are many things we do not understand."

Ulf stared at her, then nodded. He didn't really expect a clear answer from her. "We have a funeral to prepare for."

"We do," Ingibjorg responded.

Ulf watched the flames as they consumed Vidar's body. His was one of many funeral pyres, as those who had fallen in the battle were honoured. The whole village had turned out to say farewell to friends and family. Unlike before, Ulf did not see the beauty in the flames. He looked to the starry sky and wondered if Odin was watching.

"Tomorrow they'll be going home," Snorri said. This time he and his hirdmen decided to stand with Ulf.

"Who?" Ulf asked, distracted from his thoughts.

"Eldrid."

Ulf looked to where she was standing with her father's men. He saw she was watching him, not the fire. Ulf also saw the hatred in her eyes. Hatred she felt towards him. "Good, she should be with her family."

"You'd think she'd be pleased. Because of us, she doesn't have to worry about that troll fucking her," Thorbjorn said, scratching at the cut on his arm.

"She blames me for her father, I know how she feels," Ulf answered, turning his attention back to the fire.

"How's your father?" Brak asked Snorri.

Snorri studied his father who was standing not far from them, Ingibjorg as always by his side. He saw the slumped shoulders and bowed head. His mother looked like she was in a trance, seeing everything, but also seeing nothing. "I don't know. I don't think I've ever seen him like this."

Ulf heard none of this as he closed his eyes and listened to the cracking of the fires.

He was standing in the bloody marsh, watching the troll run away. In his hand, Ulf held Ormstunga and behind him stood an army of men. He had reached the hill and they had fought the troll. To his side were the two cloaked figures. One with two ravens on his shoulders and another with a missing right hand. He couldn't see their faces but knew they were smiling. The cloaked figures stood aside and between them appeared another man. He was big and was dressed in a fine tunic and trousers, with leather boots. Ulf knew who it was straight away, even if he could not recognise his face. Vidar. Vidar smiled and then looked beyond him. Following his gaze, Ulf saw the troll running in the distance, now being followed by a fox with its tail between its legs. The message was clear.

His journey was not yet complete.

His vengeance not yet over.

Griml still lived.

THE END

GLOSSARY OF TERMS

Asgard: the home of the Norse Gods

Bóndi (pl. Bændr): a farmer, a husband

Brynja: a coat of chainmail worn by warriors

Drumbr: a byname meaning thick, fat or podgy

Einherjar: Odin's army of fallen warriors who live in Valhalla, they will fight for him during Ragnarök

Fafnir: legendary dragon that guards a great treasure

Fenrir: giant wolf and offspring of Loki

Gjallarhorn: the horn of Heimdall which he sounds to warn the gods of the coming of Ragnarök

Gleipnir: the magical chain forged by the dwarves of Svartalfheim and used to bind Fenrir

Godi: a chieftain, a priest

Gunwale: the top edge of the hull of a ship or boat

Heidrun: a goat in Valhalla which produces the mead the Einherjar drink

Hel: the underworld where most of the dead dwell, also the name of the ruler of Hel and offspring of Loki

Hirdmen: a retinue of household warriors

Holmgang: a duel between two men

Hrafnagud: Raven-god, a byname for Odin

Huginn and Muninn: Odin's ravens, they inform him of events in Midgard

Jarl: an earl, a Norse or Danish chief

Jerkin: a thick leather vest worn by warriors

Jól: a winter solstice festival

Jörmungandr: giant serpent that encircles the world's oceans while biting its own tall and offspring of Loki

Knörr: a cargo ship, shorter and wider with a deeper hull than snekkjas

Midgard: the world inhabited by humans

Mjöllnir: Thor's hammer

Niflheim: the world of primordial darkness, cold, mist, and ice

Norns: the three sisters who control the fate of men and women

Olgr: a hawk, a byname for Odin

Ormstunga: means serpent's tongue, from *orm* (serpent) and *stunga* (tongue)

Prow: the front end of a ship or boat

Ragi: a byname meaning craven or cowardly, from the old Norse *ragr*

Sax-knife: a large single-edged knife

Skald: a poet, a storyteller

Skjaldborg: a shield wall

Snekkja: a viking longship used for battle

Stern: the back end of a ship or boat

Suðrikaupstefna: Southern Market, from the words *suðr* (south) and *kaupstefna* (market)

Svartalfheim: the world inhabited by the dwarves

Tafl: a strategy board game

Thrall: a slave

Valhalla: Odin's hall where those who died in battle reside

Valknut: a symbol made of three interlocked triangles, also known as Odin's Knot. It is thought to represent the transition from life to death, Odin, and the power to bind and unbind

Valkyrie: Odin's female warriors, they choose who goes to Valhalla

Viss: wise

THE GODS

Æsir: the most prominent of the two tribes of gods

Odin: chieftain of the gods, also the god of war, poetry, wisdom and magic

Frigg: Odin's wife

Thor: god of thunder and fertility

Tyr: god of war, law and justice

Vidar: god of vengeance, also known as the silent god, will avenge Odin at Ragnarök

Vali: god of vengeance, avenged his brother Baldr's death

Baldr: son of Odin and Frigg, god of the summer sun and light

Loki: the trickster god

Heimdall: the ever-vigilant guardian of Asgard

Ran: mother of waves, those who die at sea reside in her hall

Vanir: the second tribe of gods

Njörd: god of wealth, fertility and the sea

Frey: god of ecological fertility, wealth and peace, son of Njörd

Freya: goddess of love, fertility

Made in the USA
Las Vegas, NV
29 November 2023

81703242R00193